PAI
OCEAN

THE
PAINTED
OCEAN

GABRIEL PACKARD

corsair

CORSAIR

First published in Great Britain in 2016 by Corsair

1 3 5 7 9 10 8 6 4 2

A CIP catalogue record for this book
is available from the British Library

ISBN: 978-1-4721-5113-1

Typeset in Sabon by SX Composing DTP, Rayleigh, Essex
Printed and bound in Great Britain by Clays Ltd, St Ives plc

Papers used by Corsair are from well-managed forests
and other responsible sources

MIX
Paper from
responsible sources
FSC® C104740

Corsair
An imprint of
Little, Brown Book Group
Carmelite House
50 Victoria Embankment
London EC4Y 0DZ

An Hachette UK Company
www.hachette.co.uk

www.littlebrown.co.uk

To Shruti and Sruthi,
to Lauren

and

to Peter
with much gratitude

Only the impossible can make me still.

— *A Small Place*, JAMAICA KINCAID

PART ONE
1991

CHAPTER ONE

When I was a little girl, my dad left me and my mum, and he never came back. And you're supposed to be gutted when that happens. But secretly I preferred it without him, cos it meant I had my mum completely to myself, without having to share her with anyone. And I sort of inherited all the affection she used to give to my dad – like he'd left it behind for me as a gift, to say sorry for deserting me.

And our relatives thought it was my mum's fault that my dad walked out, so they stopped talking to us. And we were the only Asian people in our town, and my mum couldn't speak any English, only Hindi and Punjabi and a bit of Urdu, so she couldn't really meet anyone – which was perfect, cos that meant I'd never have to worry about her going off and making friends and spending her time away from me. But just to make certain she'd always stay in the house, I kept her having a nice time here, by always being *extra* well behaved and, like, never complaining when she combed *amla* oil into my hair while we watched the telly, even though I hated how sticky the oil was, and it sometimes gave me a flaky rash behind my ears.

3

And it was this freezing night, in winter, and the grass on our lawn was sparkly cos of the frost. And no one had phoned us for like six whole weeks when the phone suddenly rang. And my mum turned off her sewing machine and started tidying up, really excited, and told me to play in my bedroom, to stop me listening in. So I sneaked off to listen on the upstairs line, holding down MUTE, which is sort of like a magic button that makes you invisible on the phone.

'*Hallo?*' went my mum.

'Your *chacha* mentioned a proposal from our community, the other day,' went my uncle, without even saying *hallo* back. 'He's from a good family. Lives in the most expensive district of Gurgaon, so he's not exactly serving up bread and water. Plus Gurgaon will put you out of the way of your *chachis*, so you won't have to deal with their bickering nonsense every day,' he went, speaking a mixture of Punjabi and Hindi. 'Now, he's willing to accept you. Never been married before, of course. But he doesn't want a wife with her own children. So you'll have to do something with Shruti.' And my uncle cleared his throat, like the next words were stuck inside it. 'They have homes where you can put unwanted children,' he went. '*Mushkil nahi hai, beta.* It's not that difficult.'

And I started crying, thinking about my mum dumping me in a children's home and disappearing. But no one could hear me, cos I was still holding down the mute button.

And my mum was like, 'I don't know. I'd need time to think about it, *Tayaji*.'

But my uncle kept on at her about how miserable she was

4

without my dad, and how she wasn't getting any younger, and she was dragging down the family's *izzat*, and this was her last chance, cos my uncle had called in all his favours and this was the only man who'd accept someone who'd been married before, but even *he* wouldn't wait much longer, my uncle said.

And my mum was like, '*Haanji*, but is there any way that he'd let Shruti come with me?'

'No, he was very clear about that,' went my uncle. 'But think of the life you can make for yourself, living in Gurgaon, plus an independent house in Delhi Defence Colony, right in B Block. And he's the only son in his family. Already manages his father's business. No girlfriends. No bad habits. Doesn't drink or smoke. So just say yes now – and I'll make the arrangement,' my uncle went. 'An opportunity like this won't come around again.'

'Let's just give it a little while and see if I start feeling any better, here,' went my mum.

But my uncle ignored her and kept telling her to just say yes.

'I'll think about it,' she went, getting a bit annoyed now.

'Well, in any case,' my uncle was like, 'it's been much too long. Why don't I come to England and visit you, and we can talk about it more?'

'Oh, *now* you want to visit?' went my mum. '*Now* you want to visit? You and the family all disown me for the past three months, raising Shruti on my own. And now you suddenly fall out of the sky and phone me up, and the first thing out of your mouth is *I've found someone who's willing to marry you.* No, *How are you?* No, *How's Shruti?*'

'You're my niece, and—'

5

'No, don't pretend that you miss me,' went my mum. 'You just want to get me married again. That's all you care about.'

'You don't talk to me like this,' went my uncle. '*Maine duniya dekhi hai*. I've seen the world. And I know what's good for you.'

'I told you that I'd think about it.'

'*You'll think about it*,' my uncle was like. 'What else is there to think about, you stupid girl?' And there was a rattling sound, and then the line went dead.

And my mum was like, '*Hallo* . . . ? *Hallo* . . . ?' and then she hung up.

And then there was silence coming out of the phone, and then that sad flat *oooooh* that means the other person's gone, and I just sat there for a bit, sort of letting it suck the sound out of my ears. And then the tone changed to that other note, a bit brighter but still sad, that means you've gotta dial a new number.

And I had to think of something to make my mum stay living here with me, instead of going off to India. So I was remembering through the stuff that she'd told my uncle on the phone. And the main thing was that she wanted to see if she'd *start feeling any better*. And if she did, then she'd stay. And if she didn't then she'd run off without me. So what I'd have to do was *make her* feel better, and then keep her like that, so she'd never leave.

So I went into the loo and splashed cold water onto my face, to wash away the feeling of crying out of my eyes and to make my brain clearer, to help me think up a decent plan. And then I walked downstairs, where my mum was clattering away on her sewing machine – making little girls' dresses that she got paid like 35p for each one – and sitting in front of the electric heater, which was just three glowing orange bars inside this rusty little cage – when she could've been off in India, with a new husband, and another big wedding, and all her family being kind to her again, and her *izzat* sorted out.

And she noticed me and turned off her sewing machine and sat me down next to her.

'Shruti, there's something I need to tell you,' she went. And she took my hands into her lap, and she gripped them hard, almost like she was trying to squeeze the words into me through my fingers, or like she thought I was gonna start floating away if she didn't hold onto me tight. 'Okay,' she went to herself, 'I'm just going to say this.' And she explained that she'd had a marriage proposal from a man in India, and she was thinking about it. But I wouldn't be able to come with her if she accepted, she said, so I'd have to go and live in a children's home. 'But this would be good for you,' she was like, 'because if I can marry him then I'll ask *Tayaji* to pay for you to attend a boarding school back here in England. And then you can get a good job and a nice husband. And you'll have a better life. Wouldn't you like that, *Shrutu*? Wouldn't that be better?'

'No,' I went. 'I just want to stay living here with you.'

'But this will be good for us,' she was like.

'It won't be good for me,' I went, burying my face in her arm, and hugging onto her tummy, to show her how sad I was, cos I was hoping that would make her change her mind. But she just went:

'If I had a well paid job here and I could support us, then I'd

7

stay with you. You know I would. But we're living in poverty,' she was like. 'I just can't give you a good life, the way things are.'

'I don't care about that,' I went. 'And when I grow up, *I* can get a job, and *I'll* look after us. And stop saying "good" all the time. Cos *none* of this stuff's gonna be good for me.'

But no matter what I said, she just kept telling me that I was too young to understand. So talking to her blatantly wasn't gonna stop her leaving – I'd have to, like, take some action, or whatever. And I'd have to do something pretty serious, to make her wanna stay here with me instead of going off to have a perfect new life in India. And I was only eleven so I couldn't get a job now or give her any money, or anything major like that, so I'd have to just do a million little things, instead, and hopefully they'd all add up to make her happy enough to wanna stay – which wasn't much of a plan, but I had to at least try something.

And first of all, I was thinking, I could clean the kitchen, just as a start. But I walked around it, and everything was spotless, even the pressure cooker, where she cooked the *dal* that dribbled everywhere when she dished up our dinner, at night: it looked like a little model of a house from the future, with smooth rounded walls and a glass ceiling and no doors.

So then I was thinking that maybe there was something I could do for her with speaking English, cos that was the one thing I could do that she couldn't. And I was the third best at reading in my class, on Red Level Five, plus I'd already started writing the note to the teacher, if I was poorly, to explain why I wasn't at school. And there was this pile of letters in our hallway that had come since my dad left, about three months ago. But my

8

mum had never even opened most of them, cos she couldn't read English, so what was the point.

So I sneaked off and brought the letters up to my bedroom, and I started opening them up, one by one, and trying to read them. And inside were all these bills off British Gas and British Telecom and the Electricity Board, and it looked like they were all gonna cut us off, but I couldn't see how to stop them. So this would be even better than I thought. Cos this was a chance to make my mum *super*-happy with me, by working out how to save us from this, like, disaster of the lights getting cut off and then surprising her with the good news. So I stuffed all the bills into my PE bag, ready to show my teacher the next day at school, to ask for help.

And it was so foggy, the next morning while I was walking in, that I could only see halfway down the road, and after that all the garden walls and the pavement and everything just faded into white.

And I showed all the bills to my teacher, at morning break. And she took me over to the corner where we have storytime and sat on her comfy chair and put a big storybook on her lap and spread the bills out on it. And she read them one by one, shaking her head slowly, and fidgeting with her necklace. And in the end, said she knew what a difficult time I was having at home and asked me if I wanted to live with another family who could look after me better, a foster family.

And I went, 'No, thank you,' but out with my words came all this crying, cos I was so frightened I'd get taken away from my mum. And the teacher lifted me onto her lap, so I was sitting on the storybook – like I was a giant picture popping out of the pages – and she wrapped me up in a big hug and was like, 'Oh, sweetheart, I know what you're trying to say. It's okay,' she went. 'It's okay.'

But she must've thought I was crying to tell her I was unhappy at home – which *wasn't true* – cos she sent this social worker round, after school, to trick my mum into saying she couldn't look after me properly. And we were all sitting there in my mum's living room, with the social worker filling in the spaces on this *Emergency Intervention Checklist* form she'd spread out on the coffee table. But luckily she couldn't speak any languages that my mum knew, so I had to translate, and I was trying to save us, by covering up all my mum's stupid answers, like when the social worker asked her what her biggest difficulty was, bringing me up on her own – my mum said, in Hindi, that the family's *izzat* was ruined cos my dad had left her. And blatantly that just made us look like weirdos, so I told the social worker my mum's biggest difficulty was *helping me with my homework*.

And then my mum started telling me to ask the social worker whether we'd have to pay any money to have me taken into a children's home. So I just ended up answering the questions myself, and blanking my mum, cos she *wanted* me to be taken away, it looked like. But after I began ignoring her, my mum started this stupid gentle wailing and rocking, and going, 'please, it's okay, please.' And that made it look like she couldn't even look after herself, let alone me. And all I could do was act ultra-normal – normal enough for me *and* my mum – so I sat up

10

straight and crossed my arms, like we had to do in assembly, to show that we were being good.

But then the social worker started all these trick questions, like she went, 'If there was an emergency, who'd phone the police or call an ambulance?'

'Me,' I was like. 'And I know how to use the phone, so we'd be fine.' And the social worker went:

'What if you cracked open your head and fainted? Who'd call an ambulance then?'

And I didn't have an answer. And the air in the room went dead. And I knew they were gonna take me away from my mum. And I started crying, but in a normal English way – just sitting there quietly sobbing, with tears dribbling down my cheeks – to show the social worker that at least *I* was normal, to show her that I'd been brought up well, to maybe change her mind about taking me away. But my crying made my mum start wailing and rocking even more, and tapping her bunched-up fingertips against her forehead and then her heart, like a stupid beggar off the streets. And she was too stupid to see that that kind of wailing might be normal in the village where she grew up in India, cos it's just what women do there when they're really upset, but over here it just made her look like someone with mental problems, and that's blatantly what this social worker was thinking.

And while me and my mum were sitting there, crying, the social worker was writing in this zip-up folder, about why they had to take me away, and basically saying that she was, like, the prince who'd come to set me free, and my mum was, like, the witch or the monster holding me prisoner. When really it was

11

the opposite – the *social worker* was the witch, coming to capture me. And I hated the way that everyone would believe whatever *she* wrote on her form, a million times more than anything me or my mum could ever say, and we were basically trapped inside whatever story the social worker wanted to tell about us.

And after she finished writing, she told me they were putting my mum on a watch list, for 'giving undue responsibility to a minor', whatever that meant, and they were putting my name on the county register of vulnerable children. And she said that they'd check up on us every four months and that my mum had to learn English, and if the situation didn't improve they'd take further action. And she zipped her folder shut and told me to explain everything to my mum, like translate it for her. But I didn't want Mum to freak out completely and make the social worker decide to take me away after all. So while the social worker was putting her coat on, I just told my mum that there was no problem and we were free. And my mum started doing that embarrassing Indian head shake from side to side and going, 'yes yes, thank you, thank you.' And I was telling her in Hindi to just keep quiet, cos she was making us look like weirdos again. But she wouldn't shut up. So I told her to cook something for us all, or it would be rude. And when she disappeared into the kitchen, I quickly showed the social worker to the front door, where it was almost dark outside, even though it was only five p.m., cos it gets dark so early in the winter, and there was this freezing drizzle swarming around the streetlamps.

And when I closed the door, my head felt like it was floating off and filled with poisonous gas swirled in with that laughing gas from a dentist, cos I was so relieved that the social worker didn't take me away, but I was dreading her coming back in four months, to check up on us like she said she would, and getting me then. And just opening the front door quickly had let all the warmth escape out of our living room. So I sat down on the carpet next to the electric heater, shivering, and trying to warm myself up on the metal flavoured heat.

And after that, I started noticing on the news these stories about families who'd had their children taken away by social workers just cos, like, the little boy told his teachers that his dad once shouted 'I'm going to kill you' at him during an argument, and it took years of the parents going through the courts before the social workers would bring the boy back home. And there was no way my mum would know how to get a lawyer and fight through the legal system to rescue me, like that boy's parents had done.

And there was this joke going round school that went, *What's the difference between a social worker and a Rottweiler? You might get your child back off a Rottweiler.* And I made my friend tell me that joke, over and over again, cos it gave me this horrible electrical fear that my brain sort of enjoyed feeling and hated feeling at the same time. And I kept asking my friend whether she thought that was true about social workers never giving the children back after they took them away, cos talking about that joke was the only way I could talk about Social Services without letting on what had happened to me at home. And blatantly my friend didn't have a clue about social workers, cos we were only

13

eleven, so in the end I forced her to ask her parents about it and report back to me. But they just told her she must never, ever talk to a social worker, and if she did, she'd end up in an orphanage. And everything was just secretly freaking me out more and more that I'd get taken away when that social worker came back in four months.

And obviously I learned that I couldn't trust my teacher, and I never showed her any more letters. (I'd just phone the help lines on the bills when I needed advice, and they taught me, like, how to start paying off the money we owed to British Gas, down the Post Office.) And when I had to write stories at school like 'What I did at the weekend', that just was another way for my teacher to spy on me, so I'd just invent stuff to make my mum sound normal, like I'd write that my mum taught me how to bake a sponge cake in the oven – stuff I remembered out of these *Simon and Elizabeth* books we learned to read from in infants.

And even though I was really good at protecting my mum, she used to get frightened and cry sometimes when I went off to school in the morning, cos she thought I was gonna get her into trouble with the social workers again. So I was always looking for ways to keep her calm and, like, contented. So I started sneaking into her bed every single night, and I'd cling onto her, like a baby koala, resting my head on her shoulder, and we'd sleep like that, which was super snuggly and warm, plus it was useful, cos if Mum started crying, I could make her feel better by hugging her extra tight. And sometimes I woke up in the morning with flowers printed on my cheek from where it was pressed against the stitching on her old *salwar kameez* she used to sleep in. And she told me that in her old village in India, waking up with flowers on your cheek like that means you get one wish. So I'd always wish that my mum would stay with me forever.

And when I was watching telly, one evening while Mum was cooking the dinner, I saw this advert for Indian films on Channel 4 at like three in the morning on Wednesday nights. So one by one, we started taping over all my dad's England vs India cricket videos with Late Night Bollywood, and my mum loved it, and each film made her start telling me millions of stories about her old village where she grew up, where her aunts would pour huge churns of milk into this saucepan the size of a bathtub and squeeze, like, thirty lemons in there to make it curdle into *paneer* cheese which they'd strain through a giant square of muslin-cloth, holding one corner each. And there was always the melted-butter smell of *ghee* on *fulka*, and the farmer smell of dung, and the puttering sound of the *tokka* cutter, outside, chopping up fodder for the cows. And the children used to run into the fields and meet by this old bamboo-and-straw scarecrow that was dressed in a turban and coat. And as soon as they got there, they'd say, Let's meet up again in ten minutes by the *kup* huts in the next field. Cos meeting up was a game in itself, and it made them feel grown up to have an appointment to keep. And she had a million stories like that, and I loved being able to make her happy by giving her someone to tell them to.

And every Wednesday night before bed, we'd look at each other scared for a second, just before we programmed the video to record the next Bollywood film, cos it felt sort of dangerous

15

like my dad was gonna tell us off for recording over his cricket matches (which was mental cos he didn't even live here, any more). And I'd usually have to talk my mum into it, by promising I'd tell my dad it was *my fault* we taped over his videos, if he ever came back. And my mum would get this excited look on her face, cos she was gonna wake up with a brand new film in the morning, which she loved, plus she probably got that naughty exciting feeling of breaking the rules. And I'd stick Sellotape over the little hole on the video cassette that stops you recording over important stuff, feeling horrible inside, cos my dad hardly left anything behind, apart from these videos, and we were wiping over them. But I had to do it anyway, for my mum. Cos we couldn't afford to buy blank tapes to record on.

And we'd watch the Bollywood film the next evening, with my mum squirming along to the music, next to me on the sofa. And sometimes I'd hide my head under her *duppatta* scarf-thing she wore round her shoulders, playing *luka-chuppi* peek-a-boo like I used to when I was little, cos I loved being able to feel like a baby again, around her, cos it felt so warm and safe.

And it was probably just time going past, and not the videos, but my mum started being happy again. And she was always singing Bollywood songs, plus she'd hum the jingles from the English adverts that we'd recorded mingled in with the films – like, *Now hands that do dishes can feel soft as your face, with mild green Fairy Liquid* – cos we'd watched those adverts so many times, we'd grown to love them, which sounds weird but it was true. And even when they stopped showing the adverts on the real telly, they never changed on the videos, which was something else I loved, cos it was like we had our own little secret space of history that never moved forward and never went away. And we'd have these long conversations about, like, how Amitabh Bachchan looks the most handsome when he's on a motorbike, like in *Shahenshah* or *Muqaddar Ka Sikandar* (and obviously in *Sholay*) cos he's blatantly doing his own stunts there, my mum reckoned, which shows how brave he really is.

And I was still worried about the social workers coming to take me away, or my mum secretly disappearing to get married in India and leaving me forever, or my dad coming back and going mental at me for taping over his cricket matches, or my uncle coming over to steal my mum away, cos the phone bills showed these long lists of international calls to him, while I was out at school. But even though I was worrying a lot of the time – at least my mum was happy, which was the main thing, cos hopefully now she'd stay.

And eventually we recorded over my dad's last tape. And in the background of the film, when we watched it the next evening, I felt like I could hear that spooky empty sound of people clapping from far away, like on the cricket matches we'd taped over. But I had to pretend to enjoy the film completely, cos I didn't wanna ruin it for my mum. And I knew that I was only imagining the clapping sound, anyway. But after we finished watching the film, I opened the front flap of the video cassette to see if I could see any of the cricket matches, left on the tape inside. And the tape was shiny and black and tight from the two wheels pulling it from opposite directions. And I could feel one of the wheels inside was heavier from the tape wrapped all around it, and the other one must have been empty. And obviously I couldn't see anything on the strip of tape showing in the front of the cassette – not the green and white of the cricket match and not the millions of different colours of the Bollywood film, just this black little reflection of my face.

CHAPTER TWO

And one evening, my mum's sewing machine started making this grinding noise that vibrated the living room floor and made it look like the little clay statues of Ganesha and Maa Sherawali were shivering, in our *mandir* shrine-thing on the bookshelf. And while me and Mum were turning the dials on the sewing machine, one at a time, looking for a way to make it quiet again, my mum went to me:

'Uncle Aadesh is coming to stay with us for a few weeks.'

And my heart fell through the floor, cos I knew what that meant: he'd work on her twenty-four hours a day, till she agreed to abandon me and marry this *khota* in India. Plus I hated my uncle anyway, cos he slapped me round the face once when I was five, at this wedding when I started giggling during the *saat phere*, while the couple was walking round the fire. (And really he was my *mum*'s uncle, not mine, but we both just called him Uncle Aadesh for some reason.) And my mum wouldn't listen when I told her to keep him away. And she had this little speech ready, saying this is good for us, and he took care of her when she was a little girl, and it's disrespectful to say no, and she didn't want to create another scene and add more *tadka* to the situation. 'If he's going to come, then let him come,' she was like. 'He's elder than me. So let's just do our duty.' And when I tried to argue back, she just pushed my hands away from the sewing machine and went, 'Sit back down, now. I need to get these dresses finished.'

And the sewing machine got louder and louder till it was completely drowning out the singing on the film we were watching. And after about an hour, the neighbours knocked on our door to complain. And they forced me to promise that we'd get the sewing machine mended the next day.

But when I got a repair man out of the Yellow Pages, he said that the 'central drive-spindle' was broken, and it would cost eighty-five pounds to mend it. And we couldn't afford that, in a million years. And my mum couldn't get any other job, cos she couldn't speak English, so she had to keep sewing.

And after a few more days, the neighbours couldn't stand the noise any more, so they called 999. And two policemen had a look around our living room and said that they'd report us to Social Services if we didn't get rid of the sewing machine cos it was 'child endangerment' to use 'industrial machinery' with me living there. So I promised them that we'd chuck it away, to stop them from grassing us up to the social workers. And after the police left, I just told my mum, in Punjabi, that we had to keep the noise down or the police would take her sewing machine away, so I could get her scared enough to actually do something about it but without freaking her out about Social Services.

So my mum bought these massive rolls of sponge, really cheap from the company she sewed for, and she nailed sheets of it onto the two living room walls that joined to the neighbours' houses, either side of us. And it sort of looked like yellow squashy wallpaper, or like one of those old-fashioned mental homes, where the walls are soft, to stop the nutter inside from bashing his own head against them on purpose. And my mum told me that the sheets of sponge would definitely soak up all the noise, even though blatantly she couldn't tell whether it worked or not, cos she could never go next door, to hear what it sounded like from the neighbours' side of the wall. So I begged her to only do needle-and-thread work, like the company sometimes gave her, cos that was silent. But my mum said there wasn't enough of that kind of work to make a living off, so she'd have to keep using the sewing machine, which was so loud it completely drowned out all the music in our films.

And it got closer and closer to the day that Social Services was supposed to come and check up on us – cos that social worker said they'd check up every four months. And if anything, my home had got worse since then, cos of the weird sheets of sponge covering the walls, plus my mum still hadn't learned any English, like the social worker said she had to, plus I'd promised the police that we'd chuck the sewing machine away, but we never did.

And the day the social worker was supposed to come back, I woke up in my mum's bed, and it all came down on me, all this cold dread about getting taken into a children's home that afternoon. And I clung onto my mum, so I could memorise what it felt like to be snuggling in bed with her – so I could bring those memories with me when I got taken away – like how she was glowing warm from being asleep, and I could squodge my fingers into the fat around her tummy and her sides, and her skin was almost like the colour of a brown pearl from where she washed her face with *gulab jal* rosewater every morning. And I felt this total loneliness, even though I was right next to my mum and my arms and legs were wrapped around her. And I wished she could help me – like maybe we could run away together to India before the social worker turned up – but I couldn't warn my mum *now*, cos she'd get angry that I'd been hiding it for so long.

And after school I walked home, just feeling all this fluttery panic flapping around inside my chest, sort of like a bat was trapped in there. And I got back to my house and clung onto my mum all evening, from the minute she opened the front door for me, cos I had to make the most out of this time, in case it turned out to be my last ever evening with her. And while she was cooking the dinner, I wrapped my arms around her from behind and joined my hands in front of her tummy. And I kept them there while she made the *tadka*, by heating up this ladle full of *ghee*, like watery gold, over the gas burner and then sprinkling in grains of cumin and *garam masala*, which was golden-brown like chopped-up tobacco, and chilli powder, which was this dusty red colour. And it all sizzled and spat over my hands a bit, as she sprinkled it in – which was good, cos that was sort of like burning those memories right onto my skin – and then she poured the whole lot over the yellowy-brown *dal* and made that sizzle too, and I breathed the steam into my lungs, cos that would mingle into my blood, and I could bring it with me to the children's home.

And I waited all evening, till it was time for bed. But the social

22

worker didn't come. And this was exactly four months after the first time she'd visited, so this had to be the right day.

And the next evening, there was still no sign of her. And nothing all that week. And as time went by, I got less and less scared that she'd come back, and my worrying slowly went off to the side of my brain and sort of stayed quiet, and that left me feeling all right again, cos my life at home went back to normal, pretty much, plus I loved it at my junior school, cos I had mates I could have a laugh with, and we'd play, like, piggy-in-the-middle and kiss-chase, and all that, at playtime, and I'd get invited to their birthday parties. And sometimes the naughty children called me Paki or Miss Pac Man, or they'd pretend to put on an invisible gas mask when I walked past – cos I was the only Asian girl in the school – and it made me feel horrible. But it was only once in a while, and the rest of the time I was having a laugh with my mates, so I could always handle it.

But when I was nearly twelve, I moved up to the comprehensive, and it suddenly got evil, cos I got put in a class with this group of hard kids from another junior school who I never knew before. And when the teachers weren't around, the hard kids would shout '*Paki-bashing!*' and then they'd punch me in the back of my head so hard that it made me dizzy with the pain, but the bruises were always hidden underneath my hair, so the teachers couldn't see anything. And the hard kids didn't care that I was a girl, they still beat me up. Plus they bullied anyone I tried to hang around with and called them '*Paki-lover*', so all my friends drifted away by the end of the first term, and I couldn't make any others. And these racist hard kids being so horrible sort of opened up the door for *anyone* to be horrible to me, even the weedy little sad losers from my old junior school who wouldn't have dared before.

And I couldn't tell the teachers about any of this, obviously, in case they got Social Services involved. Cos even though that social worker never came back to see us, like she said she would, I didn't want anyone reminding her that I even existed, cos I wanted her to just forget about me and Mum and leave us alone forever. Plus the hard kids said if I ever grassed on them they'd put bricks through our windows at home. And there was no way my mum could afford to get the windows mended, so we'd have to cover the smashed-in holes with, like, cardboard or something, and then the social workers would say that proved my mum wasn't looking after me properly, and they'd use that as an excuse to take me to a children's home.

So now that my school was so evil, the only nice time I had left was snuggling up with my mum on the sofa, in the evenings, and watching Amitabh Bachchan videos. And while we were watching them, she'd heat up some *amla* oil, in a tiny metal *kadai* over a little flame on the gas cooker, and she'd pinch in a few herbs, and then she'd sit on the sofa with me cross-legged at her feet, and she'd rub the oil into my scalp and then comb it through my hair with her fingers, and then she'd plait my hair into pigtails and tie them off with two hair bands, cos the *amla* oil made my hair darker and stronger and shinier, she reckoned. And I loved being the middle of absolutely everything for her. And I told her to be really gentle with my head (cos usually it

24

was bruised from the hard kids punching it, although I could never tell my mum that, cos she'd just worry). But I think she could see the bruises anyway, cos she'd mix up special types of herbs that soothed it or made it feel numb. And then after dinner and more films, I'd snuggle up with her every night in bed. And that was so lovely and snuggly and cosy, it would almost balance out the horribleness of the scum children at school, in the daytime.

And now, whenever I woke up with flowers printed on my cheek from the stitching on my mum's *salwar kameez*, I'd always use my wishes to wish that I could magically become white. Cos then all my problems would just disappear, and I could have normal friends, and boys would ask me out, and I could be invisible just like everyone else. But I felt guilty about wishing I was white, cos it was racist, I thought. Although I didn't know if it was possible to be racist if I was Asian myself. And it was all just a mess, really, in my head, all lonely and guilty and horrible.

And one time I came back from playing netball in PE, and I found my school uniform stuffed into three different toilet bowls, and the fabric was all wet and shiny-black, like a slug. So I had to wear my netball skirt and T-shirt for the rest of the day, even though it was November and freezing, and I had to lug my soggy clothes around in a bin liner that I begged off one of the cleaners.

And at afternoon registration, the hard kids went around telling everyone that I'd wet myself. And as soon as I opened my mouth to say what really happened, this boy called Gavin Lane shut me up by putting on a stupid Indian accent and shouting *'Bud-Bud Ding-Ding! Bud-Bud Ding-Ding!'* over the top of me, cos he reckoned that's how Indian people talk. And it made me realise that the hard kids would probably count it as grassing on them, if I told the truth, cos they were blatantly the people who'd flushed my uniform. So I decided to just keep quiet. And when I got into my English lesson, the girl I sat next to shuffled her chair to the other side of our two-person desk, cos she must have believed the hard kids saying that I'd wet myself. So I whispered to her:

'I didn't really wet myself. Someone just shoved my clothes into the toilets.'

'Oh, right,' she went. But she still kept to the other side of the desk, cos she didn't believe me. And I didn't even bother trying to convince her, cos there was nothing I could say – cos the hard kids were experts at making their lies stick to me so hard that I couldn't pull them off or climb out of them, so I had to just, sort of, wear them around like stupid clothes that weren't mine.

And halfway through the English lesson, an office runner came in and told me to report to the headmistress. And while I was walking out of the classroom, I passed Gavin, who was the worst one of the hard kids, and he looked up from the poem he was writing and put his finger to his lips, to tell me to keep my mouth shut. So I nodded my head to tell him that I would.

And I got to the headmistress's office, and she sat me down and went:

'Now, Shruti. People have different ways of saying things,

26

don't they? And often women are cut off from being able to use language, so they use their bodies instead of words.'

And I didn't really know what she was going on about. But I had to pretend that I did, cos I didn't wanna look stupid.

And she was like, 'Now what did you want to tell us by having this little accident today?'

And I hated the way that she'd blatantly heard the rumour that I wet myself, and she'd automatically believed it, without even asking me. But I couldn't tell the truth about Gavin and his mates flushing my uniform, cos I couldn't risk them bricking our windows. So I was just like:

'Nothing, really.'

'Shruti,' went the headmistress, 'you don't have to be embarrassed. Everybody communicates in their own way, especially when bad things are happening to them.'

So maybe she knew that I was getting bullied. And it would be amazing if she could make it stop. And I wasn't allowed to grass up the hard kids, but if the headmistress *guessed* that they were bullying me, I was thinking, then that would be all right – cos that wouldn't really be grassing on anyone. So I decided to see where she was going with this.

'Is this related to someone hurting you?' she was like.

'Yes,' I went.

'Has anyone in your family ever hurt you?' she went.

'Well, my uncle slapped me once, at this wedding when I was a little girl,' I was like. 'But that was ages ago.' And there was no way that me saying this could get him into trouble, I was thinking, cos it happened when I was, like, five.

'And what was his name?'

'Aadesh,' I went. 'And he's my mum's uncle, really, but we both just call him Uncle Aadesh, for some reason. I dunno why.'

'And is he still hurting you now?' went the headmistress.

'No,' I went, 'we haven't even seen him for, like, the last four years, cos he lives in India.' And I was waiting for her to ask me if anyone *else* was hurting me now, so I could tell her about the hard kids punching me all the time. But she was just like:

'Well, I'm very glad that you've told me this.' And she took off her glasses, folded them, and laid them on the desk. 'I'm going to file a warning report with Social Services, for your protection.'

'No,' I went, 'please don't do that. They'll blame my mum.'

'Shruti, it's purely as a precaution. And of course they won't blame your mother.'

'But it was nothing,' I went. 'Plus all my mates had their parents smack their bottom, when they were little. Are you gonna report them, as well?'

'I can't report people just on hearsay,' she went, chuckling my words away. And she took a sheet of paper out of her drawer and started writing on it. 'Jenny,' she went into this speaker-thing on her desk, 'could you come in here and take down a letter for me?'

'Please,' I went. 'Please don't tell the Social Services. Let's just talk about it here and not tell anyone else.'

But then the school secretary came in, with a notepad.

'Jenny, could you take down a letter for me?' went the headmistress, and then she went to me: 'Is there anything else you'd like to add? Or would you rather run along back to your lesson?'

'My lesson,' I went, cos I couldn't stand the embarrassment of

28

watching the school secretary hear about my uncle, cos I knew that she'd secretly think that *all* Asian men slap little girls, when blatantly *it was just one person doing it once.*

So I slinked off back to English, where Gavin came up to my desk and asked to borrow my ink eraser, and he picked it out of my pencil case, and he whispered:

'You kept your mouth shut, didn't you, Pac Man?' So I nodded my head. And he went, 'Good girl.' And with the white side of my ink eraser, he rubbed out two whole lines of the poem that I was writing for the lesson and then scribbled along those lines with my blue felt-tip pen. And you can't rub out felt-tips, and they'd banned Tipp-Ex from my school, so I'd have to keep Gavin's scribbling in the middle of my poem, with the teacher thinking that *I* did it, like I was some kind of baby scribbling over my own work. And all this angriness flared up inside my blood and started sort of rotting there, cos I knew there was nothing I could do to get him back.

And after he walked off, I drew an arrow to the bottom of the page and wrote those poem lines back in there, going:

The blossom looks like candyfloss all over the tree,
But the bluebird sitting next to it feels like a dead flower.

But then I rubbed out that last line with my ink eraser, cos the teacher might think the bluebird was me, and that was me trying to say I'm unhappy, cos of that 'feels like a dead flower' stuff. So I started trying to think of a line that rhymed with *flower* that I could put in there instead.

CHAPTER THREE

And one night I was heating up my mum's bed by keeping the covers over my nose and mouth and breathing warm air inside, while I lay there waiting for her to come in, cos I loved it when she'd climb into the bed and say, Oh, you've made it so toasty and warm in here. And I was sort of building a little nest inside myself, ready for her to put those nice words into, when suddenly I felt the pressure change in my ears – like when an aeroplane's going down – which meant the front door had opened and closed downstairs, cos that sort of squashes extra air inside the house. But I couldn't hear the clinking noise of Mum putting empty milk bottles on the doorstep, which was what normally made her open the front door so late. So I couldn't think what she was up to.

And then there was talking downstairs. And then my mum came in and said that everything was gonna be all right now, cos Uncle Aadesh had come to stay, and he'd be sleeping on the sofa and looking after us. And she told me that I had to get out of bed to say *Sat sri akal* to him. And my blood turned into this, like, electrified black dread, cos suddenly this was my last chance to save my mum from getting stolen away to India. And my plan was to pretend to be calm and to show my uncle that I was really polite and sweet, to make him proud of me, so that even if he did force my mum to leave England, he'd make sure that I went with her, cos blatantly I'd increase the family's *izzat* to the family and that would make my uncle look good. So we walked downstairs, with me in my pyjamas.

And there was my uncle, wearing a brown suit and poking at the sheets of sponge on the wall with a rolled-up newspaper. And with his other hand, he was holding our telephone to his ear.

'She's going to say yes within a few days,' he went into the phone, but looking right at my mum. 'Definitely no more than a week,' he went, speaking Punjabi. 'Of course I know for sure. So start getting some dates matched up for this month.' And then, while he was still listening to the phone, he shoo'd me out of the way of the telly, with his newspaper, lightly batting me with it – like he'd steer a bee out of a window – which didn't hurt. And I stood quietly off to the side, to show him how well behaved I was. But he wouldn't even look in my direction. He just kept on with his phone call, till eventually my mum told me to just go back upstairs, which I did straight away, to show that I respected my elders, but I don't think my uncle even noticed. And I climbed into bed in the dark, and I lay there, doing this weak whimpering crying and worrying about my uncle stealing my mum away.

And when my mum finally got under the covers with me, hours later, I asked her whether she was gonna disappear away to India. But she told me that she was too tired to talk, and if I kept nagging her she'd send me off to sleep on my own. So I kept quiet, cos I couldn't risk being kicked out of my mum's bed, especially

31

not tonight when I needed to snuggle up with her more than anything, to calm down all the frightening horrible thoughts that were swirling in and out of my head.

And Uncle Aadesh moving in was the worst thing that could have possibly happened. Cos obviously he was evil and trying to force my mum to go back to India and abandon me. But on top of that he was *always* around, all day and all evening. So, apart from when I was in bed with my mum at night, I couldn't have any nice time with her, cos my uncle was always watching us, and telling us off, and ordering us to make him *fulka*, only he didn't want us to use the *atta* out of the fridge, even though it was only from yesterday. He wanted us to make fresh *atta* at lunchtime, and then again at dinner. And he complained about my name, cos he said Shruti's a name for Gujarati girls and we're Punjabi. And he kept accusing my mum of ruining our family's *izzat* cos she'd 'allowed' my dad to leave her. And whatever my mum said back just made my uncle more angry, which is what he wanted, cos he enjoyed getting angry, just like normal people enjoy being happy, cos he loved making me and my mum scurry around trying to calm him down, cos that made him feel big and important.

So now the only safe place I had left was in bed with my mum at night. Cos it was the scum children being horrible to me at school, in the daytime, and then my uncle being horrible in the evenings and the weekends. And it was like that bed was a little island, with the sea gradually rising up all around it, cos the safeness was getting smaller and smaller each day, cos my uncle kept pressuring my mum to abandon me and marry that bloke in Gurgaon, and already my uncle had turned her from saying she'd think about it, to saying, *I'll probably be ready by the end of the month.*

And I kept begging my mum to make my uncle leave, before it was too late. But she'd always tell me that she could never do that, cos he was the eldest of the house, and he'd looked after her when she was a little girl, after her father had died. And she'd feed me these lies that my uncle had been telling her, like he might be leaving us soon anyway, cos he was thinking about buying this carpet shop down the High Street, with an 'investor', and then he'd move into the flat above it to get the business going and then sell it off at a profit – just total rubbish.

So I had to think up something on my own to get rid of my uncle, cos blatantly no one else was gonna help. And I had this idea that I could scare him into moving back to India by telling him that if he didn't leave our house, I'd get him put in prison for slapping me, at that wedding, when I was a little girl. Cos that must have been a crime. (And maybe I could make something out of the time he accidentally batted me with his newspaper, to move me away from the telly.) And blatantly I was never gonna really get him arrested, cos I didn't wanna ruin his life. I just wanted to threaten him, so he'd leave us alone.

So I decided to phone the police to start investigating how long he'd go to prison for, so that when I threatened him, I could say, *I've already asked the police, and they told me you'd get, like, five years.* Cos that would make him more scared.

So I waited till my mum and uncle were both out of the house, so they wouldn't hear me on the phone. And I dialled 999 and asked for the police. And the woman was like:

'Your name and phone number, please.'

'I just wanted to ask if something's a crime,' I went.

'I'll need to take your name and number first,' she was like, 'in case we get cut off.'

'Could I just quickly ask—'

'Okay,' she went, 'I've got Hadston-657-813,' reading out my phone number, and it sounded like she was typing into a computer, 'registered to a Mrs Parineeta Malhotra at 51 Smithfield Crescent.' So she must have been able to see my phone line, through her computer. And I just wanted to hang up, cos now they knew who *I* was, cos what other girl would be phoning from that house? But then I was thinking, maybe it was a crime dialling the police and then putting the phone down, and I could get done for it. So I had to say something. And I decided to make up a story and *then* hang up. But my mind went blank, and I was panicking, and all I could think of was the true reason I phoned, so I was like:

'I just wanted to ask if it's illegal if my uncle slapped me.' And I can hear how bad that sounds. So I try to take it back, cos I don't wanna get my uncle into trouble: 'He slapped me a long time ago, though, and it was only once,' I'm like. But now that I've said it, I'm thinking why would they care about something that happened years ago? And I don't want them to arrest me for *wasting police time* – cos I'm sure that I've heard that's a crime in itself – so I have to say something that *is* actually illegal: 'He batted me with a rolled-up newspaper, too,' I go. 'But only really lightly. It didn't hurt or anything.'

'Your uncle struck you with an object,' goes the woman, sort

34

of translating my words into crimes. And I can hear the plastic tapping sound of her typing. 'How old are you?'

'Twelve,' I go. 'But it didn't hurt.'

'Is your uncle still with you, now?' she goes, making her voice softer, now that she knows I'm just a girl, not a grown-up.

'No, he's out at the moment,' I'm like. 'You're not writing this down, are you?'

'All calls are automatically recorded,' she goes. 'Now, sweetheart, how often does your uncle hit you?'

'Never,' I go. 'I was just asking. And he never hit me with the newspaper, either. I just made that up. He's never done anything.'

'Sweetheart, you're not in trouble,' goes the woman. 'I just need to ask you a few questions, so we can get you to a safe place, if you're in danger,' she's like. 'Now, when did your uncle strike you with this object? Was it today?' And I can feel this trap closing around me, tighter and tighter with each word that I say. So I quietly put the phone back into its holster, dreading what I've done.

And I've gotta be so careful from now on, I'm thinking. And I should have phoned the police from a phone box and given them a fake name. And I'm hoping that this phone call won't make anything bad happen. But I'm pretty sure I'll be all right, cos I always have been before, like with that social worker coming round, and then the police telling us to get rid of the sewing machine, and then my headmistress saying she was gonna report my uncle to Social Services.

So I do some homework, to try to take my mind off everything. And I've gotta learn this French vocab list called *In the Café*.

And I'm thinking how wicked it would be if we could do lessons on Hindi instead of French, cos then I'd already know all the words – how to say them, anyway, even if I couldn't write them. And my mind's just starting to forget about my stupid phone call to 999, when I hear shoes scuffing up the front path, and there's a knock at the door. And I peek out of the living room window through the net curtains and see these two policemen at the doorstep in their black uniforms, plus this woman in normal clothes. And they must be coming to arrest my uncle. So I hide in the kitchen, hoping they'll just go away. But they keep knocking and knocking, and that woman calls through the letterbox, going, 'Shruti, we just need to make sure you haven't got a concussion,' she's like. 'You're not in trouble.'

And I dunno how they know my name, cos I never told them on the phone. But I suppose they must have it in their computer. And they keep knocking. And blatantly they aren't gonna leave. And the longer I let them stand out there, the more chance there'll be that my uncle will come home, and they'll arrest him.

And I did make the police go away last time, when they came round about the sewing machine noise, by promising them we'd get rid of it. So I think I can make these policemen leave as well. And I open the front door. And they're standing right on the patterns of the *rangoli* my mum chalked on the front path. Which twists up my insides a bit, with how much it would upset my mum. But I can't worry about that now. And I'm like:

'Everything's fine actually. So you can go, if you want.'

'We'll just come in for a moment, if that's okay,' goes the woman, who's wearing a long dark-green winter coat, not a police suit. And before I can say yes or no, she's walking past me and so are the two policemen, all the way into the living room. So I have to follow them in there. And the woman puts her hands on my cheeks and stares at my head for a bit.

'Could we get an ambulance?' she goes. So one of the policemen calls for an ambulance through this radio he's got buttoned to his shoulder. And the woman zips her folder open and pulls the lid off her fountain pen, which has got a pointy brass nib, like a flat metal claw. And I sit down next to her on the sofa, so that I can watch what she's writing about me. And for a second, I have this fantasy that they've come to tell me they're arresting Gavin and the scum children at school, for beating me up all the time. But then the woman starts talking:

'My name's Jackie Witford, and I'm the on-duty social worker,' she goes, flicking through the papers in her folder while she talks. 'I'm required to visit when a child's reported to be involved in a violent crime, just to check everything's all right in their home life.' And her voice isn't even interested in what she's saying, probably from years of saying the same thing over and over again to scum children like Gavin Lane and their scum parents who brought them up that way. And she's like, 'Who do you live with, here?'

'My mum and my uncle,' I go, being careful not to say anything she could use against me, cos she's dying to take me away to a children's home, and her eyes are snooping around the room, looking for evidence to say that my mum's a bad mother. And each time her eyes land on something, it almost lights up with how embarrassing it is, and how she'll take it as evidence against us, like the big sheets of sponge pinned to the wall – which have

37

started crumbling yellow dust onto the carpet – and the framed photo of my *nani*, with a dot in the middle of her forehead of red *sindoor* powder and grains of rice stuck onto the actual surface of the photograph, which is normal in India, but this social worker must think it's just dirt and she's taking it as evidence that my mum doesn't clean up properly. And the policemen are looking at the little blue plastic model of Shiva glued on top of my mum's sewing machine, or maybe they're just looking at the sewing machine itself and getting ready to arrest me for not throwing it away like I promised those other policemen I would. And I should have hidden everything before I opened the door. But I had no way of knowing they'd just barge in here.

'And where's Mum at the moment?' goes the social worker, which is a trick. 'And your uncle?'

'My uncle's gone for a meeting at the estate agent's. And my mum's up at Tesco's, doing the shopping,' I go, to show her that my mum looks after me properly.

'And when did they leave?' goes the social worker.

'My uncle's been out all day,' I'm like. 'And my mum left, like, two hours ago.'

And I can see the social worker writing down, *Two hours continuing absence*, on her form. And I realise that those two hours make it look like my mum's neglecting me, so I'm like:

'She stopped off to see her friend after shopping, I think.' But then I wish I hadn't said the words, *I think*, at the end, cos that makes it sound like I don't even know where my own mum is and I'm just guessing. So then I'm like, 'Actually, she's definitely at her friend's house.' But even that's no good. Cos now it sounds like my mum neglects me to just hang about with her mates. And the social worker writes down something I can't read, on her form. But whatever it is, it's gotta be something bad, cos she's blatantly only writing down the bad things.

'Two hours,' she goes, underlining where she wrote that on her form a minute ago. 'And has something happened to your face or your head?' she goes. 'It looks like someone's hit you.'

And maybe she can see where Gavin and his mates beat me up, cos she did call for an ambulance. So I can't say that there's nothing there – in case she can actually see some bruises, or whatever – cos it'll look like I'm lying. And I panic a bit, and I just make something up:

'I slipped over and smacked it on the floor,' I go.

'On the phone you said that your uncle hit you,' she's like, sliding a sheaf of papers out of her folder. And she flicks through them. And one of the pages, I notice, is a letter with my school's logo on the top, which is three little pine trees, lined up like the three lives you get in the corner of a computer game. And she keeps flicking through till she gets to this printed sheet with a police star at the top, and she reads from it. 'You said that he struck you with an object,' she's like. 'Is that true?'

'No,' I go. And my cheeks are burning, cos she knows that I'm lying. And I'm like, 'But this boy at my school called Gavin Lane beats me up, like, four times a week.'

But the social worker completely ignores that and goes, 'How long has your uncle been hitting you for?'

'He's never hit me,' I'm like.

'Well, you've already told the police operator and your

headmistress that he did.' And she looks at that letter from my school. 'You told your headmistress in November, last year.'

And she's got me. And I look to the two policemen, to see if they'll help. And one of them's staring at the sheets of sponge on the wall, and the other one gives me this sad, kind smile, to say, *Oh, poor you. Your uncle beats you up.*

'Does your uncle ever shout at you, or call you names?' goes the social worker.

'Not really, no,' I'm like.

'*Not really*,' she goes. 'So he does occasionally, then.' And she writes something on her form. 'Does he talk about honour and Izz-att?' she's like, only she says the word all wrong, like she's saying *howzzat!* – like the wicketkeeper shouts in a cricket match to let everyone know he's caught the batsman out.

'Um, I think all Asian families talk about *izzat*, pretty much,' I'm like, cos that is the truth. But the social worker doesn't ask me any other questions, so there's no space for me to explain that he doesn't talk about *izzat* in a bad way.

And then the social worker fills in another form, where it's a pink sheet, a yellow sheet, and a white sheet all sandwiched together, and she writes: *Female. 12 yrs old. South Asian. Suspected honour-related violence by uncle and possible neglect by mother. E.P.C.* And then she checks that her writing's gone through onto the yellow sheet underneath, and she tears it off and hands it to one of the policemen and tells him:

'I'm taking her into emergency protective custody, while we conduct a home safety assessment.'

'What?' I'm like. 'I was just telling you that everything's okay.'

'This isn't your fault, Shruti,' goes the woman.

'I never thought it was,' I'm like.

'We're just doing this to protect you,' she goes.

'I don't need protecting,' I'm like. 'My uncle's never done anything.'

'You'll be staying with a very nice foster family, just for a few nights while we make sure everything's all right here.'

'Everything *is* all right here,' I go. 'I've been telling you that.'

But she ignores me again. 'Let's call off the ambulance,' she goes to that same policeman. 'We'll swing by the clinic after we settle her into the foster home.' And the policeman cancels the ambulance through his radio. And the woman zips her folder shut.

'Can we just wait till my mum gets here?' I'm like. 'Cos she'll freak out if she comes home and I've gone.'

'No, there's no time for that,' goes the woman. 'We need to leave right now.'

'What if I say I'm not going?' I'm like.

'These policemen will put you in handcuffs, if need be,' she goes. 'But I'm sure it won't come to that.'

So I've got no choice. I follow her out of the house, crying my eyes out and trying to think of a way to get back home. Only it's impossible to think properly now that I'm crying, cos it's mushing up all my thoughts. And I get into the back of the social worker's car and sit next to this fixed-in baby seat called the Mothercare Turtle Shell, which is made of green plastic, with straps to stop babies falling out and smashing through the windscreen if there's a crash.

41

CHAPTER FOUR

And the social worker drives me to this married couple's house, and she rips the pink sheet off that three-page form and gives it to the husband, like she's a postman delivering a parcel.

And a week goes past, with me living with these foster parents. And no one bothers to tell me what's going on with my mum, till suddenly I get called out of History one morning, and a social worker drives me to this special room in the Radcombe Hospital, where the only furniture's these bright-coloured red and blue little plastic chairs for toddlers, and my mum's sitting on one of them, cos blatantly no one bothered to get her a real chair, cos they think she's just a stupid Asian woman who won't make a fuss, cos she can't speak English. And the social worker waits by the door watching us.

And my mum stands up and squashes me into a hug, taking in a huge breath like she's trying to drink me in through her lungs. And she kisses me all over my eyes and cheeks, and brushes a few stray hairs away from my face and then kisses me all over again. And this is the first time that anyone's hugged me in a week, and it's like my mum's warmness from her body and the clean soap-smell of her *salwar kameez* is filling me up, like warm water pouring into a bath.

And we sit down on the tiny chairs, with my mum holding onto both of my hands. And her cheeks have sunken in a bit, and her skin's dry and grey-looking, like she's hardly eaten since I got taken away, which is a good sign, cos that means she's been feeling sad, so hopefully she'll want me back, to make her feel happy again.

'I've missed you so much, *beta*,' she's like.

'So have you come to take me home now?' I go.

'I don't know,' she's like, fishing this folded sheet of paper out of her handbag. 'Social Services sent me this letter.' And the council's written it in Hindi for her. And she reads it to me. And the letter says that to get me living with her again, she'll have to sign a 'protection agreement' to promise that she'll kick my uncle out of the house and keep him away till after I turn eighteen.

And she folds up the letter. 'I could never sign that agreement,' she's like. 'I could never tell Aadesh to leave.'

'Why not?' I'm like. 'You hate Uncle Aadesh. He's horrible to you.'

'I just can't do that, *Shrutu*,' which is her little name for me. 'I could never do that to my own family.'

'*I'm* your own family. What about me?' I'm like. 'How can you do that to me?'

'You wouldn't understand,' she goes. 'It's a very different culture that Aadesh and I were raised in.'

'So you're giving me away, then. You're making me go and live

43

with this weird white couple where they make me do all their laundry and ignore me.'

And my mum's eyes flinch for a second, like she's been punched but she's trying to pretend it didn't hurt.

'This is the hardest thing I've ever done,' she goes.

'Well, don't do it then!' I'm like. 'Just sign that paper and let me come home!'

'I can't,' she goes. 'Please, *beta*. It's good for you.'

'Just sign the paper,' I'm like, talking as quietly as I can, even though I want to strangle her I'm so angry. 'Just sign the paper,' I go, 'and then let Uncle Aadesh come and secretly live with us again. And no one will ever know. And he was planning to move out soon, anyway, when he buys that carpet shop. So then we can meet up at *his* house.'

'I could never sign the paper,' she goes. 'You wouldn't understand.'

And I'm so angry I just want to hurt her so much that she'll change her mind and take me back, cos she'll feel so terrible. So I stand up, without even saying goodbye, and walk over to the social worker, and I'm like, 'I wanna go back to my foster home now.'

'Are you sure?' goes the social worker. 'You've got another two hours with your mum, if you want it. Plus lunch.'

'No, I just wanna leave,' I'm like.

And my mum must know what I'm saying, even though she can't speak English, but I don't care. I want her to, so it will hurt her and she'll take me back. And my mum comes over and goes, in Hindi:

44

'*Come on*, Shrutu. *Let's spend a bit more time together.*'

'*No, thanks*,' I go. And I'm stopping myself from crying. 'Can we go now, please?' I'm like, to the social worker.

'Okay, come with me,' she goes. And I'm holding in all my crying till we get outside. And I know what a risky thing it is that I'm doing here. Cos if this doesn't work, and doesn't make my mum come running after me, saying she'll sign the paper, it will make the social worker think that my mum's a terrible mother and that I don't even want to see her, so that will make it even harder for me to get back home.

And as I go through the doors, I look back at my mum.

'*Don't do this to me*, beta,' she goes, in Hindi. '*Don't do this. It's not my fault.*' And I just think, Fuck you. Of course this is your fault. And I get through the doors into the corridor and all this crying comes hacking out of me, it feels like, it's so sharp and jagged in my throat and my lungs. And I wish I could just go back and get a hug off my mum and tell her that I'm sorry. But I can't, cos I've already told the social worker that I wanna leave. So I won't be allowed to change my mind.

And while the social worker's driving me back to school, I stop crying enough to ask, 'What happens if I just go back home, without my mum signing the paper?'

'She'll be arrested for reckless endangerment of a minor,' goes the social worker, as she flicks on her indicator and then turns onto a roundabout. 'And you might be transferred to a foster home in a different part of the country, for your own safety,' she's like. 'I wouldn't recommend it.'

And there's this *click-chunk* sound of her secretly locking all the doors without even moving her hands off the steering wheel. So she must think I'm suddenly gonna jump out of the car, or something, into the traffic. And she must have a secret button somewhere, for emergencies, to stop people escaping.

CHAPTER FIVE

And I'm expecting that all the social workers and teachers are gonna be persuading my mum to just sign the paper so I can come straight home, cos that's blatantly the right thing for her to do. And each day, I'm waiting for my foster parents or headmistress to tell me she's done it. But no one tells me anything about anything.

And I don't wanna phone my mum, cos *she's* the one who should be phoning *me*. Plus I'm sort of scared that she'll go mental at me when we talk, after I was so rude to her at the hospital. So I ask my foster parents, and they tell me she still hasn't signed.

And then I have this idea that I could ask the police if they ever arrested my uncle for supposedly hitting me. Cos if he got put in prison, I'm thinking, I should be able to go home without my mum even having to sign, cos they can't say I'm in danger any more if my uncle's locked up inside a prison cell where he can't even touch me.

So I walk to the police station in the town centre after school the next day. And they make me wait for ages, and then this policeman comes out with a folder and takes me into a separate room, and he's like:

'The Crown Prosecution Service decided it wasn't in the public interest to prosecute your uncle, because you kept changing your story. So there's the lesson – shouldn't tell porkies, should you. It wastes everybody's time.'

'Well, if they don't believe my uncle hit me, I should be allowed to go home,' I'm like, 'cos they've admitted that he's not dangerous.'

'That's up to Social Services, love. I couldn't comment,' goes the policeman.

So I'm like: 'All right. Well, can *you* help me live with my mum again? Cos the social workers won't do anything.' And he's shaking his head, with the word *no* just inside his lips, waiting for me to finish talking so he can spit it out. 'I'll do anything,' I'm like. 'Honestly. I could talk to the judge, or whatever, to tell him what really happened. And I promise I won't change my story again.'

'Nah, it's too late for that,' he goes. 'They've already made their decision.'

'But no one even told me there was ever a court case,' I'm like. 'I had no way to know.'

And he closes his folder and stands up, to show me that he wants me to leave.

'Please,' I go. 'Is there anything you can do?'

'Sorry,' he's like, opening the door for me. 'Maybe try Social Services.'

'Well, could you have a word with them for me?' I'm like. 'Cos they won't listen if I talk.'

And he sighs.

'Please,' I'm like. 'I'm begging you.'

'Come with me, then,' he goes, 'I'll see what I can do.' And he takes me to the front desk and dials Social Services on the phone there, and he tells them that I'm a bit upset and asks them if they'll be extra nice to me. And then he puts me on the line with this woman social worker. And I ask her if there's any news about me going home. But she's like:

'No, I'm afraid, your mother still hasn't signed the protection agreement.' And I plead with the social worker to help me, and she's like, 'I've got to rush off to a case review right now. But I'm going to arrange for someone to meet with you at your school and give you as much help as you need.' And I'm pretty excited, cos *finally* someone's gonna actually help me out.

And a few days later I get a message to go to the school office at lunch break. And they send me to this room with two armchairs in it, where I sit down with this woman who asks me questions about my mum, so I answer them, so that she'll have all the info she needs to help me get back home. And eventually, I notice there's only five minutes left till the end of lunch break, and I haven't eaten anything yet. So I'm like:

'So what's the plan to get me home, then?'

And she puts her head to the side. 'You really do miss your mum, don't you, Shruti,' she goes, to dodge the question.

'Yes,' I'm like. 'But how can I get back home?'

'I'm a counsellor, Shruti,' she goes. 'These sessions are designed to help you deal with your feelings.'

'But can you actually *help* me?' I'm like.

'Yes,' she goes. 'I can help you deal with your emotions and cope with this new situation.'

'But the only reason I'm feeling these emotions is cos I can't get home,' I'm like. 'I need someone to help me get back with my mum, and then these feelings will go away on their own.'

But she just goes on about how it's important to stay emotionally healthy and have someone to support you and blah, blah, blah. Cos basically her job is to trick you into feeling better about being screwed over. When I don't want to feel better about it – cos that'll make me stop trying to solve the problem of how to get home. So I never go back to see that counsellor again. Cos it's basically a trick. Anyone can see that.

And I can't believe how I'm getting screwed over, here, and no one even cares. Literally no one. And I remember when I first got to this foster home, I imagined this office full of social workers, somewhere, filling in forms and phoning people up, and doing everything they could possibly think of, to get me living with my mum again. But that's blatantly not happening. All they did was ask my mum to sign the protection agreement, and when she said no, they just gave up. So I've gotta do something for myself.

And all I can think of now is to phone my mum, on my own, and try to persuade her to sign. And blatantly, *she* should be the one who's phoning *me*, cos she's the mother – which is why I didn't just phone her in the first place – but I haven't got time to wait for her, cos all the time I'm living with these foster parents, it'll be much easier for my mum to abandon me forever and marry that bloke in India, cos she won't even have to worry about finding a new home for me. So I've gotta get back with her as quick as possible.

So I force myself to pick up the phone, that evening, through this sort of cloud of fear that she'll say no, and hatred that she's being so evil and stupid. And I dial her number, and she asks me if I'm eating properly. And she says how much she misses me and how she's devastated without me there. But that's a load of rubbish, cos when I beg her to sign the form, she still says she could never do that and that it's a collective decision taken by the family, taken by elders, and she doesn't have a say in it, but in the long run it's good for both of us. Plus she reckons the police will use that form against my uncle to get him put in prison, if she signs it – and she won't listen when I tell her what the police said about the courts not wanting to prosecute him.

And while she's explaining all her stupid evil reasons and reassuring me how much she still loves me, I just sit down on the stairs, crying and holding down the mute button, cos I don't want her to hear what a sad wreck I am, cos then she'll never want me back.

CHAPTER SIX

And at school things go back to normal, and it even starts feeling normal living with my foster parents – which is terrifying, really. Cos I'm literally the only person in the world who cares that this freakish, horrible thing's happening to me. Everyone else has just accepted it. And I spend a lot of time choked up with this dried-out worrying that I'll never see my mum again, which is good cos it keeps me desperately looking for any possible way to get back home.

Like in our form room one morning the teacher tells us all that a new girl's joining our class. So I've gotta make friends with her, I'm thinking, the minute she gets here, before she finds out that nobody likes me. Cos that might make my mum want me back – me having at least one friend again and being happier and more fun to have around. Plus it would be nice, just for myself, to have someone I can hang about with at break time.

And the teacher asks for a volunteer to show the new girl around, so I put up my hand straight away.

'What are you gonna show her?' goes Gavin Lane. 'How to

be a dirty Paki loser?' And he rocks back on his chair, as everyone laughs.

'That's enough,' goes the teacher, who never tells the hard kids off for the racist stuff they say, she just tells them to stop. 'Okay, does anyone else want to volunteer?' she's like, cos she's embarrassed to have the new girl being shown around by me. But no one else puts their hand up. So she has to let me do it.

And in my lessons for the rest of the day, I secretly work on a list of all the places I need to show the new girl, starting with the most important, like this bench opposite the school secretary's window where it's pretty much safe from getting beaten up, cos the ladies in the office are always looking at you. And then I go home and write up the list in this special glitter pen that writes in sparkly blue – like a little river on the paper – that I won in a poem competition at the start of the year and I've been saving it for a special occasion. And I keep re-writing the list till there's no crossings-out, which uses up nearly the whole glitter pen, but it's so worth it. Cos this is the first thing I'm gonna show the new girl, so it's gotta be perfect, to make her like me. And I'm so excited that I'm gonna have this new best friend in the morning. And the next day I wear all my best clothes, even vest and knickers and socks, cos I read in this magazine called *Cosmopolitan* down the newsagents that wearing nice underwear makes you more confident.

And I'm waiting in registration, the next day. And the new girl walks in and she's Asian! And I feel like I'm turning into ice cream and flowers, cos this is the best thing that could have possibly happened. Cos now I'm not the only Asian girl in the school any more. Plus this means she's *gotta* be friends with me. And we can talk about how horrible it is getting bullied all the time. And our mums can be friends with each other, and talk in Hindi, which my mum will absolutely love. And *I'll* be the one who set it all up, and my mum will be so grateful that she'll let me live with her again.

And I slide my list of places out of my bag and hold it under the desk, ready to show the new girl, who looks ultra-cool, with these swipes of almost golden blusher along her cheekbones, to make them look sharp and modern, like a model. And she's completely relaxed, looking around the room like she's sizing us all up to see whether we're good enough for her.

And the teacher's like, 'Can we have some quiet, please?' But everyone's still talking. 'I said *quiet please*,' she goes. 'Thank you. Right: this is Meena Saigal, who'll be joining our form. So please could you all make her feel welcome. Okay, Meena, if you could go and sit next to Shruti.'

'That's right, Miss,' goes Gavin. 'Keep the Pakis together, so we can keep an eye on them, yeah?' And everybody laughs.

'That's enough!' goes the teacher. 'Don't mind them, Meena. Just have a seat.'

And Meena pauses like she can't believe what she's just seen.

'So you don't punish students for being racist, then?' Meena goes. 'You just ask them to stop?'

'Well,' goes the teacher, 'it's more a matter of—'

'Cos I'm not telling you how to teach, or nothing,' Meena's like. 'But at my old school, a teacher got sacked for allowing hate crimes in his classroom.' And I dunno where she got the word *hate crimes* from, but it makes the teacher's body go all stiff and worried. And the teacher's like:

'Well, it's not exactly—'

'Maybe you just sit down, yeah,' goes Meena, 'and we'll pretend it never happened.'

'Right,' goes the teacher. 'Well, I wasn't going to sit down, actually, so . . .'

'Suit yourself,' Meena's like. 'Stand up, then. I don't care.'

And the teacher stays standing up and leans over the desk as she calls the register, looking really uncomfortable, cos she always normally sits down to do that. And somehow we can all tell that Meena's won. And I've never seen anything like that: a pupil controlling the teacher, and the teacher just letting her do it. Cos usually the teacher would tell the pupil off or send her to the headmistress. And this feels sort of dangerous, like there's no one in charge any more. Or maybe Meena's in charge now. But whatever's going on, this is brilliant, cos Meena's gonna be my best friend, so hopefully she'll be able to put the social workers in their place, like that, as well, and get me back home.

And Meena walks over to me. And my heart's going like a hamster in a wheel. And I'm trying to remember the words that I practised to say hello to her. But my mind's gone empty. And Meena drops her bag on the desk next to mine.

'You all right, mate?' she goes, giving me a little wink. 'Look after my bag, yeah?' And she walks straight over to the back corner, where the hard kids sit. And she walks right up to Gavin Lane, which is suicide, cos he's the most racist person in our class, plus he's the third hardest boy in Year Seven. And I'm thinking she must want to tell him off for being such a racist prick. And then when he slags her off, she'll come back to me and we can start being friends.

'Where's the weed connection?' Meena goes to Gavin, quietly so the teacher can't hear.

'Talk to me at lunchtime,' he's like.

'Can't wait till then, mate,' goes Meena. 'Can you sort me out, or should I ask Nick Burrell?' Who's the hardest boy in our year, and apparently he's won fights against actual grown-ups, even though he's only in Year Seven. And I dunno how Meena knows about him, if this is her first day at our school. And honestly I dunno how on earth Meena knows all about drugs as well. Cos we're only twelve and I didn't think anyone our age was even drinking, let alone doing *that*. 'Nick's a good bloke, actually,' goes Meena. 'I'll just ask him instead. Don't worry about it.' And Meena looks at Gavin's mates with a little shrug, like she's saying, I suppose Gavin isn't as hard as he thinks he is.

'No, don't ask Burrell,' goes Gavin. 'He's a twat. I'll sort you out. What do you want? A 'teenth?'

And Meena laughs in his face. 'A 'teenth?' she's like. 'Where are we? Fucking playschool, or something? Get me an eighth. And no home-grown shit, or leaves. And it's cash on delivery,' she goes. 'And that's not cos I don't trust you, mate. But you know how it is with a new supplier.'

'Yeah, totally,' goes Gavin. 'Totally.'

'Sorted,' goes Meena. 'And this is mates' rates, obviously. So no marking it up.'

'Yeah, yeah,' goes Gavin.

And Meena has a sneaky look round the classroom. And in the other back corner, it's the pretty girls like Donna and Melanie, and that lot, giving Meena evils. And without even thinking about it, Meena walks up to them.

'Listen to this,' she goes, and she gathers them around her and Meena whispers to them for like five minutes, till everyone in the whole class is staring at them. And then they all crack up, laughing. And Meena goes, 'There's more, listen to this,' and she goes back to whispering. And all the hard kids are shouting stuff like, 'It's a mothers' meeting' and 'She's chatting up your bird, Gav!'

And when they finally break apart, the girls are all shaking their heads like they can't believe whatever Meena's just told them.

'Anyways,' she goes, 'I better get back to my chair.'

'Don't sit next to *her*,' goes Jo Radcliffe, who's the prettiest girl in the class. 'Just sit over here.'

'Is there room?' goes Meena.

'Course there is,' Jo's like.

And Meena asks Jo's mates: 'Is that all right with everyone?'

'Yeah, whatever,' goes Jo's mate Natasha. 'Don't worry about it.' So Meena takes the chair from next to me – even though *I'm* supposed to be the official person showing her round – and she sits chatting with the pretty girls for the rest of registration and flirting with Gavin and his mates.

So I slide the list of places I was gonna show Meena back into my bag, which feels like a police siren telling everyone how pathetic I am, cos I couldn't even make a friend when the teacher, like, assigned me one. And I'd always thought that everyone hated me cos I'm Asian, but that's blatantly not true now. Cos this Meena girl's Asian, too, and she can get the coolest people in the class to be friends with her straight away. And everyone's staring at me and thinking exactly the same thing – that it's not cos I'm Asian, it's cos I'm a total loser. And it's crushing me down, that I've got nobody. And this was my only chance to at least have one friend. But I blew it.

And then the bell goes for the end of registration. And Meena's walking out with her new mates, and she grabs her bag off the desk next to mine. And she leans in so close to me that her lips are touching my ear. 'I've gotta ignore you, for now,' she whispers. 'But I'll take care of you, mate. Don't worry.' And she pats me on the shoulder. And she's gone.

And the next day, we're coming out of Geography, and this boy I don't even know from another class walks past me in the corridor and goes, 'All right, Miss Pac Man!' And I just try to ignore him, like normal. But out of nowhere, Gavin grabs this boy's collar and goes, 'Watch your mouth, you little twat.' And he points the boy's face so he's looking at me. 'Now say sorry,' goes Gavin. So the boy goes, 'Sorry' to me. And Gavin pushes him away, by the back of his neck, so the boy has to stagger forward with giant steps to stop himself from falling over.

And that happens a few more times, with people calling me Paki, or whatever, and then getting beaten up by Gavin or his mates from around the school. And by the end of the week, no one says anything to me. And I'm completely protected, which is amazing. Cos it's like my own little police force. But even so, if I could, I'd swap that protection for just being friends with Meena. Cos she's so unbelievably cool. And I always overhear her telling these amazing stories about, like, getting two boys to each steal a car to impress her, or blagging her way into the audience on *Top of the Pops*, even though you're supposed to be sixteen to get in, and I actually see her on the telly that week, in the *Top of the Pops* crowd.

And I think she might be able to get me back home, cos she's so good at controlling people, even grown-ups. But it's impossible to find her on her own, to ask her. Cos she's always surrounded by Gavin and his mates and the pretty girls from all around the school, even the Year Tens. And even when she goes to the loo, she takes two girls along, like bodyguards.

CHAPTER SEVEN

And about three weeks later, my mum phones me up at the foster home.

'*Beta*, I have some news,' she's like.

'So what,' I go, to show her that I'm still angry about how she's been treating me, but I can't be too rude, cos I don't want her to hang up. And my mum pretends she can't tell how annoyed I am, and she asks me about school, and what kind of food they're giving me at the foster home, and she tells me that my uncle managed to buy that carpet shop down the High Street. And I just say 'fine' to whatever she says, so the conversation runs out. And there's a pause. And then my mum's like:

'The wedding's fallen through. So I won't be marrying that man in Gurgaon any more.'

And my heart jumps over the moon, cos finally this is the Happily-Ever-After I've been waiting for.

'So Uncle Aadesh can leave now,' I'm like, 'and I can come home again?'

'Not exactly,' goes my mum. 'Aadesh was thinking it would be a good idea if I moved back to Punjab, anyway.'

'We'd go there together, you mean, so we could live with each other?'

'No, it would be on my own,' my mum's like. 'He wants me to have a fresh start.'

'But you could have a fresh start with me, though,' I'm like. 'And then no one could arrest us.'

'No, this is all planned out,' goes my mum. 'Your uncle's going to stay in England for a while, to keep an eye on you while he renovates the carpet shop. And I'll be leaving next month, on the fifteenth,' she's like. 'He's already bought my plane ticket.'

'Next month?' I'm like. 'How am I ever gonna see you if you move to India?'

'We'll sort out the details once I get there,' she goes. 'But maybe you could visit in a year or two. Or sooner.'

'How, though?' I'm like. 'How am I even gonna keep in touch with you? They haven't even got phones there.'

And from the background, my uncle's like:

'Come on, now. That's enough.'

'I've got to go now, sweetie,' my mum's like.

'Don't go,' I'm like, with tears bleeding out through my words. 'Please don't go yet. I want to just say something else.'

'What is it, *beta*? Did you need something?' and then there's a scuffling sound, and then I hear my mum talking with her mouth away from the phone: 'I just need two more minutes, Aadesh.'

'No, come on,' goes my uncle, from the background. 'Let's go.' And there's the little rattle of the phone being fitted back into its holster, and then the line goes dead.

61

CHAPTER EIGHT

And I keep phoning my mum, but she won't change her mind, no matter what I say. And she won't even tell me what her address is gonna be in India, or the phone number. So if I let her move there, she could easily just melt away forever, and I might never find her again. So I desperately need to stop her from leaving. But blatantly she won't listen to anything I say, and I can't ask my teachers or my foster parents for help, cos they'll just grass up my mum to the social workers. And I've got no friends I can tell, so I have to keep all my fear and worry cramped up in this secret, heavy space inside me. And keeping it trapped away like that feels like it's, sort of, making all the fear start to panic and thrash around inside my chest, while I'm laying in bed at night, like it's desperate to get out.

And eventually there's just one week till my mum leaves, and all I can think of is to beg Meena to help me. Cos she's amazing at making people do things for her. So maybe she could persuade my mum not to leave or persuade her to bring me with her to India. So I write Meena a note and sneak it into her schoolbag, in the changing rooms in PE. And my note goes:

Hi Meena!

I know you don't like me. But I'm absolutely begging you – please can I talk to you about something really important tomorrow lunchtime!!! And I promise I'll never tell anyone we met up!!!

Luv, Shruti

PS – I'll wait for you by the teachers car park. Hope you come!!!

So as soon as the lunch bell goes that day, I leg it out of English and run all the way to the meeting place. And I wait and wait. And I need the loo, but I can't leave even for one minute in case Meena turns up while I'm gone and I miss my chance. And just before the end of lunch break, she comes round the edge of the fir trees that separate off the car park, where I'm standing.

'All right, mate?' she's like, and she lights up a fag, even though a teacher could easily catch her and probably get her suspended for that. And while I'm trying to find the right way to start it all off, she just comes out and asks:

'Is this about that foster home you live in?'

'I'm not in a foster home,' I'm like, trying to laugh it off, even though that makes no sense, cos the foster home is pretty much what this is all about.

'Well, blatantly you are, cos everyone knows it,' she goes. 'So why don't you just tell me what's going on, and stop wasting time?'

And I'm not ready for her to start having a go at me, and it makes me start crying. So she gives me a hug and calms me down, and gets me to explain about how my mum's gonna move

63

to India in six days, cos my uncle told her to, so basically I need Meena to stop my mum from leaving.

'We're gonna have a word with these people,' goes Meena, which sounds like she might be quoting a line from a film. But before I can ask her what she means, the bell goes for the end of lunch break, so she stamps out her cigarette and chews up some gum and then rubs it over her fingers, I suppose to cover over the smell of the smoke. 'Tell your foster parents that you're staying at my house tomorrow night,' she's like.

And she starts walking off across the playground, which is emptying out now, cos everyone's heading to afternoon registration. So I run to catch up with her. And I've got this electricity flowing all over my skin, with the excitement and fear about what Meena's got planned. 'Are you gonna get some of your mates to scare them?' I go, running to keep up with her, cos she walks so fast.

'Better than that,' she's like.

'Cos my mum flies away, like, really soon, so there isn't much time.'

'Don't you worry about that, mate,' she goes, still walking at full speed. 'Just meet me at home time, by the Texaco. And if you're not there, I ain't waiting.'

'I'll be there,' I'm like, but she's already walking off, across the playground, cos she doesn't wanna be seen coming into the classroom next to me. And above her, the sky's just one white sheet of cloud, so the sun looks cold trying to shine through, even though it still burns into my eyes when I look at it.

CHAPTER NINE

So after school the next day, I walk with Meena back to her house, which is literally three times as big as mine, and it's got this new car in the front that looks like it's sinking into the gravel of the driveway and with those tiny little rubber feelers on its tyres. And maybe Meena can get her family to help my mum with money, to persuade her to stay, cos they're blatantly minted. And Meena's mum's in the kitchen drinking a glass of wine and wearing these fashionable skintight jeans and a halter-neck top. And she kisses Meena on the cheek, and they talk to each other like friends about the new clothes down Monsoon and Top Shop. And this could be the ultimate solution to my whole life, I'm thinking, cos Meena can get me back home, and then she's gonna become friends with me, and then her mum can teach me how to become stylish and popular, like she's done for Meena.

And we eat dinner and then me and Meena watch telly in her bedroom, while she reads these brochures for acting schools in Los Angeles. And it gets later and later. And I eventually build up enough courage to go:

'It's nine o'clock, Meena. So if we're gonna talk to my mum, we've really gotta leave soon.'

'Just wait a bit longer,' Meena's like, lounging back on her bed. And she flicks through the channels on her remote control for a second and lands on an old episode of *Only Fools and Horses*, as if that's supposed to keep me happy, and then she goes back to her acting school brochures, leaving my insides stinging with anger at her for being so rude as to leave me hanging without even bothering to tell me what the plan is or to properly even reassure me, like I'm just a charity case who doesn't even deserve an explanation and should be grateful for whatever crumbs she throws at me. And what makes it worse is that I'm not allowed to show her that I'm angry, cos she is my only chance, so I can't afford to annoy her and risk her calling off the plan, whatever it might be.

And it gets to midnight, and it's blatantly too late to do anything, now. And my heart feels like it's drying up, cos I had such high hopes that Meena would actually help me. But she's just wasted my time. So now I've only got five days left till my mum leaves and no plan and absolutely no one to help. And maybe Meena's friends with me now, which is better than nothing. But the disappointment's still crushing me. And at half past midnight, Meena's mum knocks on the door.

'You girls all right in here?' she goes.

'Yeah,' Meena's like, 'we're just watching telly.'

'Night then,' goes her mum. 'Lovely to meet you, Shruti.'

'Good night,' I go. 'Thanks for letting me stay.'

And we hear her mum's bedroom door shutting.

'Right,' goes Meena. 'We're gonna sort out your uncle, tonight.' And she hands me a rucksack that weighs a ton, and I unzip the top, and there's a couple of two-litre Sprite bottles in there. And Meena's like, 'Put that on.' So I lug it onto my back. And she puts on another rucksack herself. And she sets the video to record the TV programmes playing on BBC1, and we sneak downstairs, which is completely dark now, apart from these nightlights plugged into the wall, giving off little glows, like magical flowers, or something, out of a children's book. And we get two mountain bikes from the side of the house and walk them out to the road. And I'm like:

'What exactly are we gonna do to my uncle?'

'Burn his fucking house down,' goes Meena.

'What?' I'm like.

And Meena laughs at me. 'We're going to a party, all right?' she goes, climbing onto the saddle of her bike. 'Does that make you happy?'

'Sort of,' I go, although I still can't tell what's actually going on. But Meena's already pedalling off down the road, so I have to just ride after her, with the freezing invisible night-time wind stinging my cheeks and my fingers.

CHAPTER TEN

So it's one a.m. now, and we ride these bikes through the town. And the sky's black, and there's a thin moon, like a clipped-off fingernail. And the only people we see on the streets are one bloke walking his dog and then a group of kevs drinking Diamond White on the benches in the town centre. And we turn onto the High Street and stop in front of that carpet shop my uncle kept saying he was gonna buy. And the shop windows are dark, and so is the flat upstairs. And there's a sign in the front saying, UNDER NEW MANAGEMENT.

'Did my uncle really buy this shop?' I ask Meena. 'I thought my mum was just making that up.'

'Jesus Christ,' Meena's like. 'Don't you know anything?'

'Does he live here, as well?' I'm like, hoping the answer's no, cos I don't wanna see him, cos he'll go mental at me.

'Obviously, he lives here,' goes Meena, leaning her bike up against the shop window. 'How can you not know that? He's your uncle.'

And I have this unbelievable pang of regret, cos if I'd only waited till now, and not phoned the police, then my uncle would have just moved out, like he said he was going to, and I'd have got to spend all my time with my mum again. But it's too late now. And anyway, he'd still have sent my mum back to India, so it wouldn't have really helped me in the long run.

And my rucksack's slicing into my shoulder bones and making my back ache, cos it's so heavy. So I take it off and rest it on the ground. And I lean my bike next to Meena's.

'Right,' goes Meena. 'Tell me if you see anyone coming.' And she pulls on a pair of gloves and gets out a fat black marker pen, and then she crouches down and writes in big letters on the pavement in front of the shop: FUCK OFF PAKI SCUM! GO HOME! So I suppose she's trying to scare my uncle away. And I feel so evil for letting Meena call him a Paki, cos that's what horrible people have always called me and my mum.

And Meena passes me one of the Sprite bottles from my rucksack, unscrews the lid, and guides my hands so I'm pouring it through the letterbox and into the shop. And she shows me how to squeeze the bottle to stop it glugging, so the liquid squirts out with this quiet *whishing* sound. And then she squirts another bottle through, herself. And I'm thinking, Oh, I was right, we're just trying to scare off my uncle, by pouring Sprite onto his carpets and doing graffiti on the pavement. But I doubt this'll make him run away, if he's just spent all his money on buying this shop. And all this disappointment drains through me again, cos this is the best Meena could come up with, and it blatantly isn't gonna stop my mum from leaving.

And the Sprite smells weird, sort of like petrol. And I think I know what's really going on here. But I can't let myself believe it. But just in case, I practise what I'll tell the police, if they catch us, which is that I thought it was just Sprite, to ruin the carpets.

And then we pour in the third and fourth bottles through the letterbox as well, so that's eight litres in there now, and it absolutely stinks like a petrol station. And then Meena packs the empty bottles back into the rucksacks. And she gets out a rag, and I try to make myself believe that it's just to wipe our hands on. But then she gets a cigarette lighter out of her trouser pocket. And I suddenly can't pretend to myself any more. And I grab her hand with the lighter in, and I whisper:

'Meena, please don't do this.'

'Too late, mate,' she goes. 'We're already doing it.'

'Let's just leave the petrol to ruin the carpets,' I'm like. 'I don't wanna start a fire.'

And Meena's like, 'If you don't do this, what are you gonna do?'

And I've got no other plan.

'What are you gonna do?' she says again. 'Come on. Tell me.'

'How is this even gonna help, though?' I'm like.

'Jesus,' she goes. 'Would you rather lie in bed and cry and do nothing? Or at least try to get your life back?'

'At least try, I suppose,' I'm like, cos I have to say that, cos otherwise Meena will get angry that I'm so ungrateful after she's putting herself in so much danger to help me. But honestly I'd rather do nothing than do this.

'Right then,' goes Meena. And she tugs at her gloves so they're tight over her hands. And then she pokes the rag almost all the way through the letterbox, leaving just one corner sticking out. And she tries the lighter a few times, but it doesn't work. And

70

I'm praying that it's broken. But then on the fourth time, it lights this yellow flame with a tiny blue cone in the centre, and she touches it to the corner of the rag, so flames creep over it, and then she lifts up the flap of the letterbox and lets the burning rag drop inside. And there's a *whoosh* sound as the petrol catches fire, and the glass at the bottom of the door lights up orange, from the flames behind it, and then it cracks.

'Run,' whispers Meena.

And we grab the bikes and cycle back towards her house, as fast as we possibly can, with the cold air stinging my eyes and making them water. And I'm feeling this weird rush, thinking about how I'm hopefully gonna live with my mum again. But underneath that, I've got this terrible black worry about starting the fire, and I'm praying someone will call the fire engines before the actual flames get to my uncle or do any real damage to the shop.

And when we get back to Meena's place, we change into our pyjamas, and Meena puts the Sprite bottles and rucksacks and her gloves into a bin liner which she leaves out for the dustmen to take away in the morning, she says. And she shoves all the clothes we were wearing into the washer-dryer in the kitchen and sets it to do a full cycle while we're asleep. And then we watch the snooker and news that Meena taped off the telly while we were out. And then we go to bed, top to tail. And I try to feel happy, cos I could be living back with my mum tomorrow. But I keep having these dark thoughts clotting up my blood and my lungs, worrying about what I might have done to my uncle and what will happen if we get caught by the police. And I dunno

71

how exactly this fire's gonna make my mum cancel going to India, but I don't let myself think about the details, cos Meena must have thought this through, cos she wouldn't have done such an unbelievably risky thing if she wasn't sure it was gonna get results.

And the next morning, while we're walking to school together, I ask Meena what we should do if we get caught.

'We ain't getting caught,' she goes, sparking up a cigarette with that same lighter she started the fire with. 'My mate's cousin's done this like three different times. The police will just say it's a hate crime and fit someone up for it.'

'But what about—'

'You know who the people who get caught are?' she goes. 'The ones who keep worrying about it and asking questions. Me and you are the only people who know what happened. And we're keeping our mouths shut. So stop being a baby.'

'Can we just go to the shop, though, to see if my uncle's still alive?'

'That's a good idea,' goes Meena. 'And why don't we go to the police station and write our confessions, while we're at it?'

So I just let it drop. Although I can't stop thinking about it. And as we keep walking to school, it grows bigger and bigger inside me, blowing up like a balloon, and I just need to talk with someone, to let the air out. But Meena's the only person I can tell, and she's not interested. So I hold it in and just try to focus on real things instead, to take my mind off it, like this bloke in a suit, in front of us, walking his dog before he goes to work. And the dog's straining its neck against the lead so hard that its front legs lift off the ground. And it looks like the dog's virtually strangling itself. Although I suppose it must have a super strong neck, otherwise it wouldn't pull against its lead like that.

CHAPTER ELEVEN

And everyone thinks it's just a normal day at school. But inside me, it's like a magic jungle, with all these amazing monsters and horrible monsters fighting each other. And all day I'm watching the door, waiting for an office runner from the headmistress to come and tell me I should go to my mum's house tonight, instead of the foster home. But it never happens. And after school I ask my foster parents if there's anything they were supposed to tell me, but they say no. And I can't push it, cos I don't wanna look suspicious, cos I'm not supposed to know about the fire. And nothing happens all evening, so I have to just go to bed, gutted.

And the next morning at school, Meena tells me to meet her by the staff car park, at morning break. And when I get there, she shows me a copy of the local paper, and the front page goes:

BLAZE INJURES LOCAL BUSINESSMAN

And there's a big photo of my uncle's shop with sheets of wood nailed over the windows and smoke stains screaming up the walls. And the writing goes:

> A fire, which police are treating as arson, swept through Imperial Carpets on the High Street, at approximately 1:40 a.m. on Wednesday, causing burns and respiratory problems to the owner Aadesh Verma, 67, who lives in the flat above. Police also found racist graffiti on the pavement in front of the building.
>
> 'We believe this fire was started deliberately, possibly as a racially motivated attack,' said Inspector Mike Rabbins, of the Hadston Police Central Investigation Unit, 'and we are appealing to anyone who may have seen suspicious activity in the early hours of Wednesday morning to come forward.'
>
> According to Inspector Rabbins, the blaze was started by an accelerant, probably petrol or diesel, being poured through the letterbox and then ignited.
>
> The shop's owner, Mr Verma, is being treated at Radcombe General Hospital, where his condition is said to be stable. He had taken ownership of the shop, with a business partner, just three weeks prior to this incident.
>
> 'I am very sad about what has happened,' said Mr Verma. 'But I will not be defeated by this fire. It will only make me stronger.'

'This isn't gonna help me,' I'm like. 'It's just making him stronger.'

'That's bullshit,' goes Meena. 'Does he sound stronger to you, lying in hospital on life support?'

'What happens if the police arrest us?' I'm like.

'Then you'll keep your mouth shut,' goes Meena. 'And if you

start yapping, then *you'll* be the one who gets put away, cos you've got a motive.'

'I already said I won't grass us up,' I'm like.

'Well, keep it that way,' goes Meena, and she looks behind me to where a bunch of her mates are walking over to us. And she casually stuffs the newspaper into her schoolbag and starts chatting with them. And I desperately wanna ask her how all this is supposed to stop my mum from leaving for India, cos I feel like this is the time when Meena should be explaining everything to me. But Meena just keeps chatting with her mates till the bell goes for the end of break time, and then she walks to her next lesson with them. And then I can't find her alone for the rest of the day, and she won't come and have a quiet word with me, when I ask her to. So I'm left on my own again, trying to work out what to do next, cos my mum's leaving in three days.

So after school I phone my mum's house about fifteen times in a row, but she never picks up. So I walk over there, cos I've gotta find out whether she's still leaving or not. And there's a string of mango leaves hanging over the front door like a row of pointy teeth, from *Diwali* a couple of weeks ago. And the last leaf's caught in the side of the doorframe.

And everything inside me's telling me to just leave now, cos then I won't get crushed by hearing that my mum's still going to India. But this little corner of my mind can still think properly, and it knows that I've gotta find out what's going on, even if it's bad, so I can try to stop my mum from leaving, if she's still planning to.

So I ring the doorbell. And while I'm waiting for my mum, on the front path, I make sure I'm not standing on the *rangoli* she's drawn there – which is this sort of multi-coloured pattern – cos I've gotta do every tiny thing possible to make my mum like me, so she'll hopefully listen when I beg her not to leave.

And my mum turns up, all wobbly behind the ripply glass of the front door, which she keeps closed while she talks:

'You'll have to go away, *beta*,' she's like. 'Your uncle doesn't think I should see you.'

'Are you still moving to India on Saturday?' I go.

'Oh, *Shrutu*,' she's like, 'don't make this any harder on me.'

And I start crying, cos what she said means yes. 'Can you show me the plane ticket?' I go. Cos if I can grab it off her and rip it up, I'm thinking, then she could never afford another one.

'*Shrutu*, I can't—'

'Please,' I'm like. 'Just show it to me for two seconds, and then I promise I'll leave.'

And she hesitates. And then she disappears. And a minute later she taps on the living-room window, where she's wiping tears off her cheeks with one hand, and with the other she's holding up the ticket, which says her name and LONDON HEATHROW–INDIRA GANDHI INT'L DELHI, and the date's for three days away, and it's all written in letters made out of tiny black dots. And obviously I can't grab it away from her, cos she's behind the glass. But I'm trying to look for the flight number, so I could maybe go to the airport and stand in the doorway of the plane to block her from getting on. Or maybe I could even beg the plane driver not to fly anywhere. But before I can even find what airline it is, she takes the ticket away, and she pulls the curtains closed, so I can't see her any more.

77

And I keep shouting, '*Mum!*' And I'm crying, which is making my words all blurry. But she turns the telly on loud, to block out my voice. And I knock on the window, but then the neighbours start staring at me from inside their houses. So I have to stop, cos it's too embarrassing that they know that my own mum won't even talk to me. So I shout, 'All right then, Mum— Yeah, I know— Ha ha, yeah that's right— I'll see you later.' To make it look like we're just finishing up a conversation. And then I slink off through the estate, hating myself, cos I dunno why I've given up so easily on something so important, for the most stupid possible reason of being embarrassed by my mum's neighbours. But that's what I've done.

CHAPTER TWELVE

'This is fucking bullshit,' goes Meena, when I tell her the next day about what happened at my mum's house. 'We're going over there after school.'

'No, please. Let's not go over there,' I'm like. Cos I don't want Meena to, like, attack my mum, or anything. 'Maybe we could just write her a letter.'

'Well, I'm going,' Meena's like, 'and you can come with me or not. I honestly don't care.'

'Oh, please, Meena.'

'That's the last word, mate,' she goes.

So I have to go with her, to try to keep her under control. And we meet after school, and we're walking down my mum's road. And I just need a few minutes to get my head together, before we talk to my mum, but Meena's already walking up the front path, and she steps around the *rangoli* and rings the doorbell, so I have to follow her. And my mum opens the front door.

'Shruti's got something she wants to talk to you about,' goes Meena, in Hindi.

And my mum looks at me. And I wasn't ready for that. I

thought Meena was gonna do the talking. So I'm scrabbling around, going:

'Well, I mean . . . I don't exactly . . .'

'Oh, for God's sake,' goes Meena. '*She wants to know, are you still moving to India?*'

'*No, not exactly,*' goes my mum. '*Things have changed.*'

And Meena gives me this smug look, to say, I did that for you.

'*So are you going to sign that form, now,*' goes Meena, '*so Shruti can live here again?*'

And my mum's like, '*It's complicated.*' And she looks over her shoulder, at the stairs behind her. '*Do you think you could come back tomorrow? It's not really a good time now.*'

'*No, we ain't going anywhere,*' goes Meena, '*so start being an adult and give your daughter a straight answer for once.*'

And I see this pair of men's shoes stepping down the stairs, behind my mum, and I start crying. And Meena's like, 'What's up, babes?'

And obviously, it's my uncle. And he walks down the stairs and stands in the doorway. And he's got white bandages wrapped around his left arm, from the wrist to the elbow, and there are big raw wounds over his right cheek and his neck, and his trousers look puffed up, so maybe there's bandages wrapped around his legs too.

'*You're not welcome here, any more,*' he goes to me. '*Calling the police and telling them lies about me. And making people want to destroy my shop. Go on. Get away.*'

'*Are you gonna say sorry to her?*' Meena's like, and my uncle starts talking:

80

'I've got nothing to say. She's brought so many problems to this—'

'You shut your fucking mouth, you piece of shit,' goes Meena. 'I was talking to Shruti's mum.'

'Is this what your parents have taught you?' goes my uncle to Meena. 'Is this how they brought you up – to talk to your elders like this?'

'I said shut it, you fucking child molester,' goes Meena, 'or I'm gonna knock on every door in this road and tell them what you do to little girls. And I'm gonna say that's the reason Shruti got taken away in the first place. And we'll see what happens to you then, shall we? We'll see if it's more than just your face that gets burnt off. All right, big boy? That all make sense, does it?'

'You don't even know the meaning of these words, you stupid girl,' goes my uncle. And he looks at my mum. 'Look at the company your daughter is in. This wonderful English culture.'

'Yes,' goes Meena, butting in again. 'It is pretty good living here, actually, cos people don't have to take orders from stupid old gits like you, just cos you're the oldest man in the house. So why don't you just piss off, now, and leave us alone. All right?'

And my uncle goes to my mum: 'You stay here and enjoy yourself with these gutter-pigs. I'm going to lie down.' And he starts limping up the stairs.

'That's right,' shouts Meena, in English, so everyone in the road can hear. 'Go on, you child molesting *gaandu*. Run away from me. And the longer you take, the longer I'm going to spend telling everyone on this street that you're a dirty child molester. Go on. Up the stairs.'

And he limps away, muttering, '*Always bringing some* tamasha *to our lives. They don't even let us live.*'

'*Anyway,*' goes Meena to my mum, talking in a mixture of Hindi and Punjabi again, '*I think there's something you wanted to say to Shruti.*'

'*It's a difficult situation, dear,*' goes my mum, '*you wouldn't—*'

'*Oh, I understand perfectly, dear, and so does Shruti. And I hope you understand that you're a spineless idiot for giving up your own daughter, just because your uncle's telling you to.*'

'*Like I was trying to say,*' my mum's like, '*it's difficult—*'

'*All right,*' goes Meena, '*we've heard enough.*' And then she switches back to English. 'Come on, babes,' she goes to me, 'we're out of here.' And she leads me away.

But my mum comes catching up to us, down the road. So me and Meena stop walking, to hear what she's gonna say.

'*Look,*' my mum's like, '*he'll just be staying with me for a few more months, till he recovers and he can get the carpet shop up and running again,*' she goes. '*He's sunk so much money into that place, he can't just walk away. But when the business is going again and he leaves my house, I promise I'll sign the paper.*'

And Meena chips in: '*Would you prefer him to just leave you alone, right now, so you can live with Shruti again, without having to ask his permission?*'

'*Yes, of course,*' goes my mum.

'*Well, my dad's a lawyer,*' Meena's like, '*and he could get a restraining order to make Aadesh leave and never come back. Or if you wanna do it another way, I've got mates who could* just beat him up and make him leave this evening. But either way, he's gone, if you want it.'

'Well . . .' goes my mum.

'Do you want Shruti back, or not?' goes Meena.

'It's more complicated than that,' my mum's like.

'Well, you've got to make a choice between keeping Aadesh happy or being a real mum to Shruti,' goes Meena. 'Cos you can't have both. And the only reason you're squirming now. No, don't walk off. You stand right here. You ain't going nowhere till I've told it to you straight, cos blatantly no one else will,' Meena's like, going into this Punjabi slang. 'Do you want Shruti living with you again, or not? Cos she'll forgive you in a heartbeat. You won't get no trouble from her. And you won't get any trouble from Aadesh. Cos when people like him accidentally fall down the stairs, the police know that it's just an accident, and they don't investigate it too hard, if you know what I mean,' goes Meena. 'So just say the word, and Shruti will be living with you again in no time. Do you want it?'

'Ah,' goes my mum, looking anywhere but at Meena. 'It's just so complicated.'

'No, it isn't. It's one question. One simple question. Do you want Shruti back? Yes or no? Cos if you do, we'll make it happen. And my dad's a lawyer, so we can do the whole thing without roughing anyone up.'

'Well,' goes my mum, 'can I think about it?'

'Nope,' Meena's like. 'You've had the whole six months since Shruti got taken away to think about this. Do you want her back, yes or no?'

'Well . . .'

'Yes or fucking no, you fucking idiot? Stop all this "well" and "it's complicated" nonsense. Yes or no?'

And my mum looks at the pavement, like a little girl getting told off, even though she's an adult and Meena's only thirteen. And I dunno how Meena learned to tell off grown-ups like that.

'All right,' goes Meena. 'Let's make this simpler, shall we? If you don't say yes, that means you're saying, no. And we can all get on with our lives. And you can go back to being a puppet and a doormat, and supporting this man who's breaking up your family, which apparently is what you want,' Meena's like. 'So what's your answer? Is it, yes you want Shruti back? Or is it, no?'

And a bus drives past and puts us in shadow for a second.

'No,' goes my mum quietly. 'It's no.'

'All right then, well, at least we know where we stand. And Shruti can stop getting her hopes up that you're gonna be a real mum for her. And may God forgive you for what you're doing.'

'I'm sorry,' my mum's like. 'I'm very sorry.'

'No, you're not,' goes Meena. 'If you were sorry then you'd find a way to get Shruti living with you again.' Then to me, Meena goes: 'Do you want to have a word with her before we leave?'

So I'm like, 'Yeah.'

And Meena walks down the road a bit, and has a cigarette, to leave us alone.

'You know how hard this is, don't you, sweetie,' goes my mum, 'and how complicated?'

'Yeah. But will you ever sign that paper?' I'm like.

'Of course,' she goes. 'Of course I will. Your friend doesn't know what she's talking about.'

'But when, though? Cos it's already been six months.'

And my mum's like, 'It'll be soon. I promise.'

'Like, before Christmas?'

'Yes, definitely before Christmas,' goes my mum.

'Do you really promise, though? Cos my foster parents are going on holiday that week, and they said I might have to stay in a children's home, while they're away.'

'I promise, by Christmas,' my mum's like. 'I absolutely swear.'

'But how are you gonna get my uncle to agree to it?'

'Oh, I've got some ideas,' she goes. 'I know how to handle him.' And she glances over my shoulder and suddenly looks scared to death. And I turn around, and it's my uncle limping towards us. 'I've got to get back,' she's like. And she hands me a copy of her front door key and gives me a quick, hard hug, like she wants to make up for how short it is by squeezing me extra tight. And then she hurries off to my uncle, who grabs her by the wrist and starts walking her back to the house.

And Meena comes over. And I tell her what my mum said, as we walk off. And Meena's like, 'This is gonna be hard for you to hear, but it's important that someone tells you the truth about this,' she goes. 'I don't think your mum's ever gonna take you back.'

And I burst out sobbing.

'You probably don't believe me, do you?' goes Meena.

'I believe you, in my head,' I'm like, between sobs. 'But the rest of me believes my mum.'

'Come here, you muppet,' goes Meena and she gives me a big hug, just standing there on the pavement. And another bus goes past, in the other direction. 'What's the matter with you?' she's like. And I'm laughing, a bit, through my tears. Although I dunno why, cos it feels like if Meena wasn't holding me up, my skeleton would fall apart, and I'd just crumble down into a pile on the floor.

CHAPTER THIRTEEN

And after that, every time I phone my mum's house, my uncle answers and then hangs up as soon as he hears my voice. And it feels like I'm getting kicked in the stomach, each time. So I stop phoning. And my uncle keeps this CLOSED UNTIL FURTHER NOTICE sign on the wooden boards covering his shop's windows, so he's blatantly not moving out of my mum's place any time soon. And the only good thing that happens over the next few weeks is that Meena starts being sort of friends with me, and asking me how I'm doing, every couple of days.

And it gets to a fortnight before Christmas, and my foster parents are getting excited about their week in Spain, and they remind me that I might have to stay in a children's home while they're away. But I don't care, cos my mum promised that she'd sign the paper by Christmas, and even if she doesn't, I've got her door key, so I'm going to visit her on Christmas Day. And I've saved up £4.35 from my pocket money, and I buy this silver necklace from Oxfam, with a little silver hummingbird dangling off it, as a Christmas present for my mum. And the ladies in the shop give me a little velvet pouch to keep it in.

And that evening, while everyone's watching telly at my foster home, I dial my mum's number, to find out what her plan is for getting me back and how she wants me to use that front door key. And the line's ringing, and I'm hoping that my uncle will have started letting my mum answer the phone again by now, cos it's been weeks since I last tried to call.

But it's my uncle who picks up. 'Parmindar has disowned you,' he goes, when he hears my voice. 'You're not her daughter any more, and she's not your mother. And we've signed the official papers at the County Registrar's Office. So don't phone here again, and don't bring any of your wretched little friends to the doorstep – or I'll call the police on you.' And he hangs up.

And I feel like I'm collapsing. And I'm such an idiot for believing that my mum would have taken me back in the first place or even wanted to see me. And I never hassle Meena, outside of school, cos I don't want to be a pain. But I've gotta talk to her, this time, even though it's the Christmas holidays. So I phone her house.

'Hello?' goes some bloke's voice, and there's booming music and people shouting and laughing in the background.

'Can I talk to Meena, please?' I'm like.

'Yeah, hang on a second,' he goes. '*Meena!* . . . *Meena, you dopey cow*, it's the phone for you.' And then there's a sort of scuffling sound while he's passing the phone over.

'Hello?' goes Meena.

'Meena, I really, really need to see you. Can I come over?'

'Stay where you are, mate,' she goes. 'I'll take the call upstairs, all right?'

And then she comes back on the phone with quiet in the background. And I tell her what my uncle said about my mum disowning me.

'I know this'll be rough to hear,' goes Meena. 'But your mum doesn't even phone you. So I don't think she wants you back.'

And I start crying and I'm like, 'Do you think she has really disowned me, though, legally?'

'That doesn't even matter,' goes Meena. 'Even if she signed something, she could always undo it. It's what she *wants* that's important. Not the legal stuff. And she doesn't want you.'

And I start crying my eyes out.

'Oh, I didn't mean that, babes,' goes Meena. 'She *does* want you. But she's getting manipulated by your uncle. And she doesn't know how to stand up for herself.'

'What would you do, if you were in my shoes?' I'm like.

'To be honest, mate, if it was me,' she goes, 'I'd probably, I dunno, like, kill your uncle and then do the time in young offenders'. Cos I'm only thirteen now, so I'd be out by the time I was, like, seventeen, and then I'd be living with my mum again. And everyone's criminal record gets wiped at eighteen. So I'd be laughing, really. But I could handle myself in a young offenders' prison, and you'd get eaten alive. So I dunno what I'd do if I was you. I suppose I'd probably—'

'We're moving on to the club, Meena. You coming?' goes this bloke's voice from the background.

'All right, I've gotta go, mate,' goes Meena. 'But I'll see you back at school, yeah?' Which is her way of telling me to leave her alone for the rest of the holidays.

So I go up to my room and lie in bed, in this sort of numb trance. And I wait till everyone's gone to sleep, and then I pocket my mum's door key and pick out the two longest knives from the kitchen drawer – one jagged bread knife and one long smooth meat knife – and I shove them into a plastic Tesco's bag. And I quietly sneak out of the back door. And while I walk off down the road, I let that numb feeling hover all around my brain, so I don't have to think about what I'm actually doing here. And I wind the bag tight around the knives, to stop them from clinking against each other.

CHAPTER FOURTEEN

And I walk all the way from my foster home to my mum's house, which takes about forty minutes. And when I get there, her lights are still on, even though it's ten past midnight. And I sneak up to the window and look through the net curtains. And my mum walks in from the kitchen and brings a mug of warm milk to my uncle, who's reading a newspaper and ignoring the news on the TV. And I was expecting to see him, like, shouting at her. But this is worse, cos it's so normal my mum could easily carry on like this forever and never want him to leave.

So I walk around the estate, to waste time till they go to bed. And at quarter past one, I go back, and their windows are all dark. So I slide the front door key into the lock, and it turns. And I slip quietly inside and close the door behind me. And I stand there for a minute, listening to the darkness, in case any noises come out of it. But it's silent. So I think everyone's asleep now. And first of all I go into my mum's bedroom. And through the dark, there's a rustle from the bed, and my uncle's voice goes:

'Get back to your own room. I'm trying to sleep in here.'

And my blood turns into ice. And I back out and close the

door. And straight away I realise that I haven't got the guts to do anything with the knives. I honestly dunno what I was even thinking, bringing them along. All I really want to do is spend a bit of time with my mum. And I suppose she must be sleeping in my old bedroom now. So I open that door, and through the dark, I can make out the rectangles of my old posters on the walls, of Take That and Jason Donovan, which came folded inside magazines. And that shows that my mum wants me back, I'm thinking, cos if she definitely thought I'd never live here again she'd have taken them all down by now. And the air smells like face cream. And I go over to the bed. And it's my mum lying there, with her hair spread out over the pillow, and I think she's wearing her old *salwar kameez* with the *hakoba* stitching of flowers around the collar, although it's difficult to tell, cos the room's so dark.

And I put down my bag and slip off my coat and shoes, and I climb into bed with her, like I always used to. And she's laying on her back, breathing minty breath at me. And I nuzzle into her shoulder. And with my fingertips, I'm trying to feel what kind of pattern the stitching is around her collar, like I'm a blind person reading braille.

'*Shrutu?*' she whispers, really sleepy.

'Yeah,' I go. 'It's me.' And I'm waiting to hear what she's gonna say.

'I told you we'd be all right, didn't I?' she goes. And I dunno exactly what she means. But I don't wanna ruin the moment. So I just go:

'Yeah, we're all right now.' And I feel my cheek to try to tell whether there's any flowers, or anything, printed there yet, but obviously it's much too soon for anything to have happened.

And this could be amazing, I'm thinking while we lie there, cos I could sneak in here every single night, after my uncle's gone to sleep, and snuggle with my mum for hours on end and then leave before my uncle wakes up. And sometimes me and Mum could sneak out to a twenty-four-hour McDonald's, or something, and we could have a whole secret life with each other, in the middle of the night, and no one would ever know, apart from us.

And my mum's breathing gets really slow and heavy, so I know she's asleep again. And I lay there till the sky goes from black to inky blue, through the gap in the curtains, and I'm drifting in and out of this light sleep, when I notice the smell of sandalwood incense, and I hear this murmuring singing coming through the wall, which must be my uncle, so I've gotta get out of here, pronto, cos he chants the *gayatri mantra* a hundred and eight times, after he wakes up, but I dunno how long he's been going for. So he might be near the end already and about to come out of his room, which would trap me in here.

So I climb straight out of bed and put my shoes and coat back on and pick up the plastic bag with the knives inside. And I sneak out of my mum's room and down the stairs and out of the front door. And it's really fresh and cold outside, and the grass is crispy and white with frost, and the sky's deep blue, but it's about to get bright. And I walk all the way home, feeling amazing, cos I've got this brand new secret life now, every night, like a magical garden that only I know about.

And I sneak back into my foster home and put those knives

back into the kitchen drawer and climb back into my own bed, and I've got this warm feeling all over me. And I'm trying to think how I can start sleeping during the daytime, so I won't get too tired being awake all night. Plus maybe I can buy a bike, so that I can get over to my mum's house quicker and spend more time with her and less time walking. And maybe Meena will let me borrow one of her bikes seeing as she's got two. And sod Meena, actually. Cos she said that my mum didn't want me back and there was nothing I could do to spend time with her again. But I found a way, all by myself.

And I decide that I'll wait till Christmas Day to visit my mum next, cos I want a special occasion for us to plan out this new secret life with each other. And the best time would have been *Diwali* – cos my mum doesn't really care about Christmas, cos they never had it where she grew up – but we've already missed that. And Christmas will still be good cos it's only two weeks away and I might be staying at a children's home then, so that will make my mum feel extra guilty, so she'll have to be really kind to me and agree to see me whenever I want, at nighttime.

And even though it's six-thirty in the morning, now, and I've barely slept all night, I'm trying to stay awake so I can keep thinking all these lovely plans that are, like, blooming in my head like flowers. And that reminds me that I forgot to check whether I got any patterns printed on my cheek from my mum's *salwar-kameez*, and I wanna get up and look in the mirror. But it's so late and I'm so tired that my mind just slips away from me, and I drift off to sleep.

CHAPTER FIFTEEN

And my foster parents keep warning me that there's always a shortage of beds over Christmas, so I'll probably have to go into an actual children's home while they're on their holiday in Spain, which they never invited me to. But I don't care, cos even if they offered me a million pounds to come to Spain with them, I'd still say no, cos I'm gonna be with my real mum instead. Plus if I get sent to a children's home, it'll be even easier to sneak off to my mum's house without anyone noticing.

And in the end, on Christmas Eve, my foster mum drives me to the Hadston children's home. And it's this horrible old building from like a hundred years ago, off the main road, with fields and some woods opposite.

And at lights-out, I get under the covers, still fully dressed and wearing my school shoes, ready to run away. And there's rain lashing all over the windows, and it's pitch black and cold outside. And I'm laying there, waiting for everyone to fall asleep so I can sneak away. But the girls in my bedroom are all fired up and chatting like mental, probably cos it's Christmas. And it gets to two a.m., and they're still chatting. And I can't wait any longer, or it'll be too late to walk to my mum's house. So I think, sod this. And I get up, and I'm like, 'I'm just going to the loo.' And one of the girls shouts:

'The new girl's escaping!'

And I freeze. But no one comes. And the other girls in the room just laugh at me, so they were only messing around, not trying to grass me up. And I go downstairs and creep into the canteen which is totally dark now, except for this glowing sign that says EMERGENCY EXIT. And I go over there and feel around for the long bar of the fire door. And I push on it, and the door swings open, and freezing rain flies into my face, like a handful of gravel, and this deafening alarm goes off. So I just start legging it down the driveway. And the rain's so hard it's already soaking my jumper and my trousers, cos I stupidly didn't think to put on my coat, but I can't turn back now. And then I'm out on the road. And the rain's lashing down, so after about ten minutes of legging it along the pavement, I'm literally soaked to the skin – even my knickers and vest are soaked – which makes it feel like the coldness has sort of painted itself right onto my skeleton, it's so freezing. And my teeth are chattering, and I'm getting this killer stitch in my ribs, and my ankle bones are splintered from running in my school shoes, with no padding in the soles.

But finally I get to the edge of the estate where my mum lives. And I keep running, cos the quicker I get to my mum's house, the more time I'll have with her before my uncle wakes up and I have to leave. And I get to her street, exhausted, and my throat's frozen and my leg muscles are drained out of energy and filled up with achy tiredness. And the air's still black and rainy, and the sky's covered over with dark rain clouds. And my feet squelch each time I take a step. And I tread carefully around the *rangoli* on my mum's front path, walking on the mud of the lawn instead, cos I can't afford any more bad luck. And then I stand on the doorstep and reach into my pocket, and that little velvet purse is completely soaked, but that doesn't matter cos the necklace and the door key inside it are both made of metal, so the water can't ruin them.

And I let myself in and stand inside the hall. And all I can hear through the dark is the ticking sound of water dripping off my clothes. And my face is so numb from the cold that I can't even feel the droplets rolling down my forehead, until they drip into my eyes and make me blink. And there's no way I can snuggle up in bed with my mum, all soaking wet like this. So I creep upstairs to the airing cupboard – where the boiler tank's bubbling away all nice and warm, although on my hands it's just prickly heat – and I take out a towel and dry my hair, and I then pat down my clothes, to soak up as much water as I can. And then over my jumper I wrap another towel around my chest, like after a shower, so I won't get my mum's bed too wet. And my shoes are still squelching as I walk down the landing.

And I sneak inside my old bedroom where my mum's asleep. And I quietly take off my shoes, which have got gritty mud on the soles from when I walked over the lawn just now to keep from stepping on the *rangoli*. And the room smells like sandalwood incense, like my uncle burns, which is good, cos that should cover over the mud smell. Plus my mum's breathing sounds gravelly and deeper than normal, so I think she's got a cold, which should stop her from being able to smell the mud properly and getting angry about me treading it into the house. And I place my shoes neatly on the middle of the rug, so they'll be easy to find when I leave, and I reach underneath the towel wrapped around me and pull the velvet pouch out of my jeans pocket, and I climb into bed next to my mum. And the rain's thrashing against the window, almost like someone's throwing handfuls of tiny stones against it. But my mum still hasn't woken up.

'Mum,' I whisper. 'It's me.'

And through the darkness of the bedroom I focus on her face, which is much older than it was two weeks ago and all deformed, with her cheeks all dark and fat, and her hair's been cut short, and her skin's leathery and wrinkled. And my blood stops flowing. And I'm such an idiot. Cos it's my uncle that I've climbed into bed with, obviously. They must have swapped bedrooms. So I climb carefully out of the bed, holding my breath, to stay as quiet as possible. And I pull the duvet up, so it's covering him, and he snorts and turns over, but he doesn't wake up. And I creep out of the room and close the door behind me.

And I walk down the landing, till I'm standing in front of my mum's actual bedroom. And I wrap the towel tight round my chest, on top of my soaking wet jumper and jeans. And just as I close my fingers around the doorknob, I realise that I've left my shoes next to my uncle's bed. And I've gotta get them, cos when my uncle wakes up and finds my shoes on the floor, he'll know something dodgy's going on. Plus I'll need them for when I walk back to the children's home.

So I creep back to my old bedroom. And I slowly open the door, and standing there looking right at me, is my uncle. He's wearing his white *kurta* pyjamas and holding a lit match to a little cone of incense on the dresser. And he freezes for a second, staring at me, like his eyes can't swallow what they're looking at. So I dart out of there and start legging it down the stairs, with my uncle chasing after. And as I get to the bottom of the stairs, the towel wrapped around me falls down around my ankles and trips me up, so I fall forward onto the floor of the hallway. And my uncle's limping down the stairs as fast as he can. So I scramble to my feet and kick the towel away from me, just as my uncle's getting to the bottom of the stairs. And I'm fumbling with the latch of the front door, but before I can open it my uncle grabs me in a bear hug. And he drags me back towards the stairs and pushes the front door closed with his foot.

'Mum!' I shout. 'Mum! Come and help me!'

'How dare you step into this house!' goes my uncle. 'How did you get in here?'

'The door was open.'

'Lies,' he goes. 'You stole the spare key. I've seen it's missing. So hand it over, or I'll search you and find it myself.'

So I give him the key, to stop his skanky hands from groping all over me. And I'm such an idiot for not making a copy of it.

And my uncle's like, 'Now, get out.' And he opens the front door.

'Please,' I go, 'can I just give my mum a Christmas present? That's the only reason I came here. I swear.'

'What Christmas present?' he's like. 'We don't celebrate Christmas.'

'It's just something that me and Mum do,' I'm like. 'Please. Can I just give it to her, and then I promise I'll leave?'

'Show me, and I'll decide,' he goes.

So I pull the necklace out of its little velvet pouch. And I let the silver hummingbird pendant fall so it stretches the chain out into a straight string, to show my uncle how pretty it is, so he'll want my mum to have it. And my uncle takes it out of my hand. And he calmly puts his foot through the loop of the silver chain and pulls it, till it snaps. And then he takes the toolbox out of the cupboard in the hall, and he picks out the pliers with sharp edges near the hinge, and he snips the long nose and the wings off the hummingbird. And then he clips its body in half, and he then snips the chain into tiny little pieces. So it's all just silver dust on the doormat.

'Now get out, and don't show your face again,' he goes, and he puts the toolbox back into the cupboard.

And my blood's boiling up from being so angry, and I can't think properly, and I look around the hall for something to smash my uncle in the jaw with, cos that's all I wanna do right now. And leaning in the corner by the door, there's a cheap little pound shop umbrella, but that's too light, and a wooden walking stick, but the hallway's too cramped to get a proper swing with that. And anyway, I've gotta focus on what's important here, which is to talk to my mum. Cos this is my only chance, cos my uncle blocks me from talking with her on the phone and seeing her normally, and now that I've lost the door key I can't even visit her at night. So I hold down my anger, and I'm like: 'Can I please just see my mum for one minute? And then I promise I'll leave.'

'Okay, fine,' goes my uncle. 'You wait outside, and she'll come to see you.'

And he opens the front door and shoos me out and shuts the door behind me. And it's getting light outside now, and the rain's stopped, although I'm still soaked from before. And I'm standing there, wearing my socks and no shoes on the wet concrete path, which is freezing the bones in my feet. And after a while, I knock on the door, but no one answers. So I keep knocking and ringing the doorbell, for about five minutes non-stop, till the door suddenly opens with my uncle behind it.

'Go away!' he screams in my face. 'Go away before I stab your bloody head with a knife!' And he's shouting so loud that his throat goes raspy.

'I'm just asking to see her for two minutes, and then I'll go.'

'You cannot see her for *one second*!' he's like. And he pushes me so I stagger and trip over backwards, and the back of my head smashes on the concrete path. And I'm lying there on the floor, with my head stunned and throbbing in pain. And I can see that my uncle's mental in his eyes.

'You've ruined my life, you witch!' he screams, standing over me. 'You told the police that I beat you, when I didn't. And word got around, and thugs burnt down my shop. And then you brought your wretched little friend over here, screaming to the neighbours with lies that I'm a molester. And after that, three men dragged me out of this house and beat me so badly that I've lost most of the vision in my left eye. And all you care about is forcing your mother to sign that paper to get me put in prison. And you wonder why we don't want you here! Everything you do brings *tamasha*. Just keep away. I'll give you one minute, and then I'm calling the police.'

And my uncle walks back indoors.

And my whole body's shivering from being soaked, and it's so cold laying there on the concrete path that I'm losing the feeling in my legs and my hands. And my head's dizzy from smacking the concrete, but I manage to get to my feet.

And I feel the back of my head with my fingers, but I can't see any blood when I look at them under a streetlamp – which is sort of a shame, cos if there was some blood there, then maybe I could grass up my uncle to the police. But I can't, cos there's no proof.

And I walk off down the road, with no shoes, and my socks are completely soaked and filthy, and the weight of the water's making them stretch and keep slipping down my feet. And I do feel terrible, hearing about my uncle getting beaten up and starting to go blind. Especially cos it might have been Meena's friends who battered him, for all I know. But still, he's ruined my life, just as much as I've ruined his. And all I was asking for was two minutes to see my mum. And there's no reason for him to stop me. And I go round and pick a load of stones out of people's flowerbeds, big stones about the size of cricket balls. And I put one in each of my pockets, and I hold two more in my hands.

And I get back to my mum's front garden. And I'm just pulling my hand back to lob the first stone at the living room window, when someone pounces on me and pins my arms to my sides like a straightjacket. And it's my uncle. 'I knew you'd come back, you little witch. And I'm calling the police,' he goes. 'I've got you red handed.'

And he clamps both of my wrists inside one of his rough, hard hands, which are really strong from working on a farm all his life. And he marches me inside the living room and calls 999. And he sits me on the sofa, holding my wrists and telling me how I'm never going to see my mum ever again, after this.

And all I can do is sit there crying and getting angrier and angrier and wishing I'd stabbed him to death with those knives, when I had the chance. And after about ten minutes, two policemen come to the door.

'She broke into our house with a stolen key,' my uncle tells them, 'so we made her leave. And now we caught her trying to smash our windows with these stones.'

'Oh, dear,' goes one of the policemen to me. 'This isn't how you should be spending Christmas, is it?'

'Get this fucking man off me!' I go, struggling to pull my wrists out of my uncle's grip. 'He just smashed my head open on the pavement.'

And my uncle lets go of my wrists on purpose, waits for me to land a few punches on his shoulders and arms, and then he finds my wrists again and grips them even tighter. 'She gets very violent,' he goes, and he gives the policemen this *see what I mean* look.

'And what's your name, sweetheart?' goes the policeman.

'I said just fuck off!' and I struggle to lash out at my uncle again, but he clamps my arms against my sides. And it's so evil what my uncle's doing to me – winding me up till I'm furious to make me look like an animal, in front of the police.

'Her name is Shruti Malhotra,' goes my uncle. 'She's run away from her foster family.'

And the policeman says my name into his radio. And the radio says back that I'm missing from the children's home in Radcombe. And then he's like:

All right, sweetheart. We're gonna take you back home.'

'I don't fucking live there, you fucking idiot! You fucking piece-of-shit idiot!' I go. And I wish I could turn into a chainsaw and slice everyone's faces off. And I'm thrashing around inside my uncle's arms, which are tight around me, like an evil hug.

'Okay, love,' the policeman's going. 'You're going to have to calm down, or we'll have to put the handcuffs on you.'

But that just makes me even more angry. And I try to bite my uncle's arm, but I can't reach it with my mouth. So then I flick my head backwards to try to head-butt his face with the back of my skull. But I can't connect with him. And I'm crying hysterically.

'Why can't I just move back in here?' I'm going. '*He's* the one's that beat me up. He's the one that just threw me on the floor and beat me up. Why don't you take *him* away?'

And the two policemen handcuff my wrists, and stuff me into the back seat of their police car. And I'm looking to see whether my mum's at the bedroom window. Cos if she'd just wave, that would at least show that she wants to see me. But she's not there. It's just my uncle standing at the front door, as the police car drives away.

And the police drive me back to the children's home. And the manager there puts my clothes into the tumble dryer while I have a shower, and then he lets me go to this private bedroom, where it's just me. And I sleep there all day. And they let me stay in that room for the rest of the week, only coming downstairs for meals. And then I go back to my foster family.

CHAPTER SIXTEEN

And two years go past, living with those white foster parents while my normal life with my mum drifts further and further off, like it's on a boat sailing slowly away from me. And I try to keep up my Indian languages, by talking to myself in Hindi before I go to sleep. But when I start forgetting normal words – like *flowerpot* or *empty* – I have to stop doing it, cos it just reminds me of how much of myself is disappearing. And thinking about it every single night, like that, makes me feel like I'm *rotting* away, but when I keep it out of my mind it feels like I'm only *fading* away, which is easier to live with.

And my uncle won't let my mum have anything to do with me. So the only time I come anywhere near her is, like, randomly once in a while seeing my uncle walking her through the High Street. And this one time I see her wearing her orange-and-yellow sari with a white cardigan over the top, and I see him whispering to her, *Don't look at the girl. Don't make eye contact* and then my mum doing that Indian side-to-side head shake and then glancing over at me quickly, to see where *not* to look, and then walking on, with three heavy bags of shopping in each hand, while my uncle limps along next to her, leaning on his walking stick, like she's a beast and he's the handler, ready to beat her with his stick, if she starts wandering off.

And seeing her makes all these feelings start burning into me. And the main one is sort of like love but turned inside out, like I can't get to the love part, but it's right there, just underneath the surface. And all mushed in with that is, like, the same old embarrassment from everyone on the pavement staring at my mum's sari. And I'm glad it's chilly and she's wearing the cardigan, which hides the rolls of flab around her ribs that show through the gaps in the sari fabric, which is the most embarrassing thing about her. And all that embarrassment has still got, like, a plus side and a minus side joined inside of it, like a battery or a magnet. Cos half of me wants to stand next to her, to be loyal and to protect her from the white people staring at her, but at the same time I wanna keep my distance and pretend she's nothing to do with me, so people don't think I'm strange like she is.

And then on top of that, I'm ashamed that everyone knows I've been put into foster care and everyone thinks that my mum's a bad mother. And there's nowhere to hide from it, cos even the people who didn't know to start with can work it out, cos why else would I be living with a white couple? And I hate the way that my family's always, like, on display cos we're Asian, so everyone can keep track of us.

And I walk back from the High Street, shaken up and upset, but I don't mention anything to my foster parents when I get home, cos they can never be bothered to understand the little details of my life. And they are kind to me, which is something. But I can always see the edges of their kindness, like if the council stopped paying them or if I became super-naughty, they'd just give me up – not like real parents who'd keep me, no matter what. Plus I hate hearing them talk about my real mum – even when they're, like, trying to comfort me, or whatever – cos if they say they're sorry that she won't take me back, then they're ignoring how hard it is on her and what a different culture it is that's putting pressure on her to act like that. But if they say sympathetic stuff like my mum's not fully to blame, I hate that too. Cos at the end of the day, it *is* still my mum's fault for letting me slip into foster care and not catching me out of it. And I feel like a sort of soldier, guarding this line that separates exactly how much blame my mum should get, on one side, and how much she should be forgiven, on the other. And the line's all twisty and intricate, like a river on a map, and I can't stand anyone even coming near it in a conversation. Apart from Meena. Cos she's sort of earned the right to talk about my mum and my uncle, I suppose cos she's Asian, so she understands much more about it, plus she's proved that she's willing to actually *help* me try to get back with my mum – she's not just snooping around, looking for gossip and throwing in her opinions for fun and to feel superior, like everyone else.

And it's weird, but I even hate people slagging off my uncle – even though he's ruined my life – cos no one hates him *in the right way*. They think he's just a monster, like, a frankenstein or whatever, who looks pretty much like a human but hasn't got a proper brain or a heart, so he's got no feelings and that's why he's ripped my mum away from me, they reckon. When really, my uncle's got proper reasons for everything he's done – even though I don't agree with them – cos my mum is like a daughter to him, cos he raised her from the age of four, when her own father died, and in India marriage is important in a way that people don't understand here, and letting your niece or daughter stay unmarried is almost like a bloke in England letting his daughter sleep on the streets – well, not quite that bad, but it's still pretty terrible, and basically it just makes you look scummy and makes everyone you know think you're a bad person and that you don't care about your family. But I can't explain that to my foster parents or teachers or other white people, cos they just think I'm *justifying* what my uncle's done and saying it's okay, when I'm not – I'm just *explaining* that different countries have different ideas about what's good and what's evil, which everyone here *pretends* they understand but really they think that brown people's ideas of good and evil are primitive compared to white people's. So I always just try to avoid talking about it or even coming near it in a conversation with anyone except Meena, cos everyone else just bullies me into agreeing that my family are bad but I mustn't let it get me down because I'm better off without them and there are people here to support and love me. Total lies, that people force me to agree to in these stupid little pep talks, to make themselves feel like they've helped me, without actually giving me anything except words.

CHAPTER SEVENTEEN

And on my fifteenth birthday, my foster parents take me to Pizza Hut. And while we're waiting for our food, my foster dad's like:

'There's something we wanted to talk to you about.'

And I'm gearing up for him to tell me that they're kicking me out of their house.

'We really love having you at our home, Shruti,' he's like, 'and we'd like to adopt you. If that's something you'd want.'

'No, I'd better not,' I go.

'Oh,' goes my foster dad. 'Well, we were rather hoping you'd say yes. And it would mean you'd legally be part of our family, even after you turn eighteen.'

'It's nothing against you,' I'm like. 'But I just prefer things the way they are.' And blatantly the real reason I turn them down is that if they adopted me, my mum could never have me back. But I can't tell them that, obviously, cos if you tell people the real reasons for stuff, they just use that to manipulate you. And even though I literally haven't talked to my mum for two years, I've gotta keep my options open, in case she changes her mind and decides she wants me back.

'Well, it's completely your decision, Shruti,' goes my foster dad. 'We respect that.'

And then a few months later, this new foster child called Rebecca gets placed with us. And at Christmas my foster parents tell everyone that they're adopting her. And I'm gutted. Cos even though I didn't want them to adopt me, I didn't want them to adopt anyone else.

And then just after my seventeenth birthday, I phone my mum's house, cos I haven't seen her in the High Street for like six months. And some woman picks up the phone, and I'm like:

'Um, can I talk to Parineeta Malhotra, please?'

'No, I think you've got the wrong number,' goes the woman.

So I try again, making absolutely sure that I dial my mum's phone number without any mistakes. But the same woman answers.

'Is this 51 Smithfield Crescent?' I'm like, cos that's my mum's address. And already, my insides have turned dark and hollowed out, cos I know what's coming.

'Yes, but no one named . . .' and she can't remember my mum's name. 'No one named that lives here.' And then she calls out to someone: 'Michael! What was the name of the people who lived here before us? Can you remember?'

'It was an old Indian chap and his niece,' goes the man from the background. 'They were moving back to India, I think.'

And then the woman goes to me:

'I think the person you're looking for's moved away. Sorry about that.'

'That's all right,' I'm like. And after I get off the phone, I feel like I've been run over by a car, and I have to sit down on the stairs. And the news isn't even sinking in. It feels like it's sort of hovering around inside the room, blocking out the light and draining me away, like when you keep a plant in the cupboard, and it turns that sick yellowy colour from getting no sun. And I instantly know it's true that my mum's moved to India. And there's blatantly no point in going to Social Services, cos they're not gonna help me now that my mum's moved to the other side of the world, if they wouldn't even do anything when she still lived in the same town. Plus I know that all the social workers and my foster parents will just think to themselves, *Oh, we always knew that Asians are evil and heartless and they don't care about their daughters, and now we've got the ultimate proof.* So I decide never to tell anyone about this, except Meena.

And I go up to my bedroom and try to calm down. And I lean out of my window and take a few deep breaths of cold air from outside, to clear my brain. And then I check myself in the mirror and practise smiling and looking normal. And after I've got my head together a bit, I walk downstairs and find my foster dad who's re-potting seedlings in the garden shed, and I'm like:

'Would you still wanna adopt me, do you reckon, if I said I wanted it?'

'Oh, I don't think we could at this stage,' he's like, pressing down the compost around a little green stalk in a flowerpot. 'We've just adopted Rebecca. And you're almost eighteen now.'

'Totally,' I go. 'I was just asking hypothetically.'

'Oh, right,' he's like.

'Yeah, it was just hypothetical,' I go, and I pretend to laugh it off. But really I'm completely gutted. Cos that was my last chance to have parents, cos you can't get adopted after you're eighteen.

'This is something we should probably talk about, though,' goes my foster dad, 'just so we're all on the same page, in terms of expectations.' And he sits me down on this tatty blue deckchair. And he takes off his gardening gloves, and lays them on the table, next to the trays of seedlings. And he explains that after I go off to university it'll be time for me to begin my adult life, so I'll need to find my own accommodation over Christmas and the summers, and everything. And I pretend that I knew that all along, when really I was secretly hoping I'd be able to keep coming back here and staying with my foster family forever.

So now I'm almost completely on my own. My real family's already gone. My foster family'll be gone soon. And the only person I've got left is Meena. So I've gotta stick with her no matter what, cos she's the only person who looks out for me and would help me in an emergency, and she's not gonna cut me off, like my foster family's about to. And we're still pretty good friends, cos she talks with me every few days to ask how I'm doing. But we're coming up to the end of school now, so I've gotta make sure we keep the friendship going when we go off to uni.

And we get our predicted grades for A-levels, and mine are two B's and an A – which is just what I need, cos that's much better than Meena's, so I'll be able to get into any university that she can. And I secretly apply to all six places the same as her on my UCAS form, only I apply for Chemistry, and Meena puts all this weird stuff like Theatrical Arts with Gender Studies. And I don't tell Meena that I'm applying to the same unis as her, to stop her from telling me not to, or secretly changing where she's applying. And I could blatantly get into much better places, but I don't care, cos sticking with Meena is more important.

And we get our A-level results in the summer, and Meena decides to go to Brighton & Hove Guildhall College. So I secretly accept my place there too, without telling Meena, even though the list in *The Times* says it's one of the bottom five universities in Britain. But Meena wants to go there cos its theatre programme has a year in industry that places its students with the BBC and Channel 4, and whatever. And I secretly phone up the college and find out which halls Meena's gonna be living in, and I sign up to live in the same ones. And Meena should absolutely love me when she finally finds all this out, cos I'm proving how much I care about our friendship, by going to a dump like Brighton & Hove Guildhall – when I could have easily got into, like, Durham or UCL – just so we can stay friends with each other.

CHAPTER EIGHTEEN

But when we start uni, Meena's never around, cos she instantly makes friends not just with people in our college, but at Brighton Uni and Sussex Uni as well, plus she's got all these mates in London she goes off to hang about with. And I'm completely left behind. And Freshers' Week is all right, cos people invite me out, and there's loads of parties that anyone can go to, and I'm thinking that maybe I can make other friends and not even need Meena. But by week three, everyone's in these little friendship groups. And somehow I didn't get into one. So I'm always on my own, listening through my bedroom door, while everyone else is getting ready to go clubbing in Brighton. And I keep texting Meena and leaving her voicemails and writing on her notice board. But I can never even get her to text me back, let alone meet up.

So I've gotta think of a plan to build up our friendship again. And I'm pretty sure that if I could just get more popular then she'd want to hang around with me, cos then I could introduce her to new friends and invite her to parties, and whatever. So I go along to this university South Asian Society bowling trip, cos the people there have *gotta* like me, cos that's the whole point of it – Asian students go there to make friends with other Asian students. And I turn up at the bowling alley and find the group, over by the desk where you swap your normal shoes for those red-and-blue bowling shoes with smooth soles.

And there's about twenty Asian students there. And this is the first big South Asian Society event of the term, so a lot of them are still getting to know each other. And while we're waiting for our lanes, I go and stand with this group of girls who are chatting as they're lacing up their bowling shoes. And as they talk, they keep finding out that, like, their cousins know each other, or their dads have said they can't date anyone at university. And each time they hit on something they've got in common they get excited and go, *Oh, my God, me too!* and then they name as many different details as they can, to rack up extra things that are the same about their lives, like they're scoring bonus points in a quiz show. And I keep completely quiet, cos no one's said anything that's the same as me, yet. But I'm trying to build up enough courage to just come out and ask if any of them ever got bullied at school, so I can break into the conversation – when this bloke Akshay who's standing with another little group of people goes, so loud that everyone can hear him, 'Oh, my God. My mum's phoning me again!' And he sends the call to voicemail, and then he shows around his MISSED CALLS screen, which says MUM (23 CALLS). 'This is just so embarrassing,' he goes, putting on this girl's voice, which sounds stupid. But everyone already loves him, so he can get away with it. And then he starts up this massive conversation, with everyone from all the different little groups chipping in about how much their family phones them now they're at uni, and how embarrassing it is, and how much they hate it. When blatantly they *love* it. Cos if they were really embarrassed they'd keep quiet, just like I'm doing. And they're all so excited and happy that they've all got so much in common, right now. But I feel like I'm standing out in the car park, and it's just my face here, fake smiling and nodding, and pretending that I'm just like them, when blatantly I'm not, cos they all grew up in these massive normal Asian families surrounded by aunts and cousins and trips to India, and weddings, and people smothering them with love and cooking and rules, while I was growing up in a white foster family, who got paid by the council to have me and who've only phoned me once since I left them, even though I've written them six long letters and two postcards from Brighton.

And I was secretly hoping that when I finally got to spend time with a load of Asian people my own age, I'd just fit right in, and the girls would be friends with me and the boys would ask me out. And that was one of the things I'd always looked forward to about university. But actually, now that I'm here, it just makes me worry that I might never find anyone else, apart from Meena, who really gets what it was like for me growing up.

And we go over to our lanes, and the boys in each group type in our names, which come up one at a time on the computer screens over our heads, to show whose turn it is. And while I'm waiting for my first turn, this girl asks me where I'm from, so I tell her Hadston, in Wiltshire, and she's like:

'Oh, do you know Meena Saigal?'

'Yeah, totally,' I'm like, 'we're best mates.' And finally I'm one of those people who's found something in common with another student they just met. And it does give me a little buzz, uncovering this secret little link between us. And maybe I was wrong about not fitting in here, I'm thinking. Cos this girl wants to be friends with me. 'How do you know Meena?' I'm like.

'I met her a few days ago, at this party for the Theatre Society,' goes the girl.

And right then my name comes onto the screen, to tell everyone that it's my turn. So I throw my first ball down the lane and knock over a few pins. And while I'm waiting for the underground conveyer belt thing to bring my ball back, the computer screen shows a diagram of the seven pins I've got left and an arrow showing exactly where my second ball needs to hit, to smash them all down in one go. And the girl's like:

'What do you think about Meena going to live in America?'

'What?' I'm like. 'Who told you that?'

'She was showing everyone at the party her plane ticket,' the girl's like.

'When's she leaving?' I ask her.

'I can't remember,' goes the girl. 'But she said she's swapping to a uni in, like, California, or something, to start her degree again, over there.'

And the conveyer belt spits out my ball back into the rack. But I can't concentrate, cos of what that girl told me about Meena, so when I throw my second ball it rolls into the gutter and doesn't even touch a single pin. And I keep asking the girl if she can remember any more details about Meena leaving for America.

And the first couple of times she says she's sorry she can't, but she'll let me know if she remembers anything else. And then I ask her a few more times, throughout the evening. And eventually, she goes:

'Look, just stop bothering me, all right?' really loud, so everyone stares. And then Akshay chips in:

'Yeah. Take a hint, stalker!'

And everyone laughs at me. So I wait till the conversation moves on, and then I say that I'm going to the toilets, but really I sneak out of the bowling alley, cos I'm so embarrassed. And I walk to the town centre and wait for the shuttle bus, which only runs once an hour, in the evenings, but there's no other way back to the campus, apart from a taxi, which I can't afford, cos I've only got student loans and this Foster Child's Higher Education Allowance to last me all year, including paying for somewhere to live over Christmas and the summer holidays. And there's no family I can ask for money, like everyone else can.

And I get back to our halls at about eleven p.m., and I wait and wait by Meena's door till she finally gets home at twenty past four in the morning, wearing this sparkly mini dress. And I ask if I can have a word, so she's like, 'Course you can, mate. Come on in.' And while she's unbuckling the tiny straps on her heels, I ask her about America. And she tells me that she's leaving in January, to transfer to The Performing Arts Institute of Los Angeles to complete her degree over there. And a thousand people audition each year for thirty places in the acting programme, she says, cos they've got such good connections in the Hollywood studios. And this university holds 'satellite auditions' in London, which is what Meena did, and she just found out she was offered a place. And she's gonna stay living in LA, even in the holidays, so she'll be available for acting jobs and auditions.

'How much is all this gonna cost?' I'm like.

'The tuition's twenty-eight grand,' she goes, wiping a little cotton pad over her forehead, and then looking at the grey-and-brown smear on there, for a second, and then throwing it into the bin. 'Plus rent and food, and all that, and it'll probably come to, like, forty thousand dollars a year.'

So I'm screwed. Cos there's no way I could ever afford that. So I can't follow her out to America. So I've gotta do something drastic, to keep from losing her forever.

'Listen, mate,' goes Meena, starting up her laptop while she finishes wiping off her make-up, 'I've got an essay due in like four hours, so I'm gonna have to kick you out. But we should catch up soon, yeah?'

So I spend the next few days thinking about how I can keep from letting Meena disappear. And by the end of the week I have this idea that we could go on this amazing holiday-of-a-lifetime, over the Christmas break, to bring us close together again, so that when she leaves for America, she'll remember us as being amazing friends like we were at school – not virtually strangers, like we are now. And then we can be friends for life, and I can visit her in America. Or maybe during the holiday I could even persuade her not to leave England, at all. And this is my last chance. Cos I blatantly can't get close to her during term-time, the way things are going. And if she leaves like we are now, then this is all she'll remember – that we weren't that close – and she'll make loads of new American friends and forget all about me, and that'll be that. I'll have absolutely no one.

So I do all this research about different holidays. And the best one in the whole world is this working holiday in New Zealand, where you see all these glaciers and go scuba diving and ride quad bikes, and then you earn back all the money you spent, from this job they find you, and you might even make a profit.

And I'm looking for Meena for a whole week, to tell her about it. And eventually I bump into her at seven o'clock one morning, while I'm just walking to the showers before my first lecture and she's coming home from a night out. And I follow her back to her room, in my dressing gown, telling her all about how amazing this New Zealand trip's gonna be.

'It sounds wicked, mate,' she's like, 'but I'm honestly so wasted I can't think about it.'

'But we'll have to book it up soon,' I'm like, 'cos it takes four weeks for them to arrange your work placement, if you want to get the best one, which is working in a bar, cos that's the most fun plus you make the most money.'

'Right,' she goes, unlocking her bedroom door. 'I don't think I can afford it, though, really.'

'But you *make* money while you're there,' I'm like. 'Remember? Plus *I'll* pay for everything up front, and you can just pay me back out of your wages you earn in New Zealand.' And I follow her inside her bedroom.

'Ah, mate, I am so wasted,' she goes, and she struggles out of her leather coat and throws it onto a chair, where it slides down onto the floor.

'Just say yes, just let me book it up, and I promise it'll be the most wicked thing in the whole world,' I'm like. 'And it's completely free. Cos you earn back all your money working in a bar.'

'All right, then,' she goes, 'why not,' flopping down onto her bed. And she stretches out and closes her eyes, still wearing all her clothes.

'Are you a hundred per cent sure?' I'm like. 'Cos if you are, I'll book it up today.'

'Yes,' she goes, grabbing the edge of her duvet and wrapping it over herself. 'Yes, that's fine.'

So I switch off her light, so she can go to sleep. And I walk straight to the computer room, still in my dressing gown, and I load up NewZealandWorkingAdventures.com and start booking two places for me and Meena. And I type in all our details and my debit card number, which I've got memorised, for the full £4,348 for both of us, leaving at the start of exam week – cos first years don't have exams. And I get to the final screen where it goes:

Legal Notice: If you fail to arrive in person at your work placement in Auckland, New Zealand, by 9 December 1998, your work placement will be cancelled and your fee(s) will not be refunded. It is strongly advised that you arrange to arrive at least three days prior to this date, to allow for travel delays.

[I agree to the terms: Confirm Booking]   [Reject Booking]

And that's pretty frightening. Cos if Meena backs out at the last minute, and we don't get there in time, then I'll lose all that money forever. And that £4,348 is nearly everything I've got in the whole world.

But then I'm thinking, this could actually help me, cos it will mean Meena *won't be able* to back out at the last minute, cos she'd never make me lose all my money like that. And I feel guilty, cos it would be sort of manipulative to trap her like this, cos she was half-asleep when she agreed to come on the holiday. But before I can think about it too hard, I find myself clicking the CONFIRM BOOKING button. And then I print out the confirmation page. So it's done now.

And I get into the shower and shampoo my hair. And then I rub in a load of conditioner and leave it all white and bubbly over my head and neck, like one of those wigs a judge wears, while I wash my arms and legs, and everything. And I'm feeling guilty about forcing Meena to come on this trip. But all I'm really doing is making her *keep her word*, cos she did agree to it. Plus *Meena* blatantly doesn't mind doing mental things, when she thinks there's no other choice, like starting that fire at my uncle's shop. So she can't really have a go at me for doing something drastic. And the fire was much worse than this, cos this isn't hurting anyone – I'm just giving Meena this wicked holiday-of-a-lifetime for free. But even so, I wish I'd taken a few days to think this through, before I'd made the decision, cos now I've gotta just go with it, no matter what. So I try to stop thinking about it. And I let the water wash over me, and rinse out most of the conditioner, but I leave a little bit in, to give my hair that deep shiny-black colour.

And after my morning lectures I ride the shuttle bus into

Brighton, which is about forty minutes away from the campus, and I go into STA Travel. And I tell the woman that I want two plane tickets to New Zealand, but only if they're completely non-refundable and won't let me change the dates, and if I miss the flight I'll lose all my money. And she looks at me like I'm mental. But this is the only way I can stop Meena from backing out – by making it so that I'll lose absolutely everything if we don't get on that plane.

And the woman searches for ages, and then she calls over the assistant manager, who asks me why on earth I'd want that kind of booking. But I just say there's complicated reasons related to my family. And then the assistant manager and the woman search for about twenty minutes, and eventually they find me these seats on a British Airways plane, but the tickets are available through a code share with this Saudi Arabian airline, which has a completely non-refundable ticket policy and doesn't allow any date changes once you've paid.

'So if we miss the flight, I'll lose all my money, right?' I'm like.

'Yes,' goes the woman. 'But are you absolutely sure you want do this? Because I can get you on exactly the same flight with flexible dates, for the exact same price.'

'I'm absolutely sure,' I'm like.

'Okay,' she goes, shaking her head at me, as she types on her computer. 'But don't say I didn't warn you.'

But I don't care what she thinks. And it's none of her business anyway. And I give her my debit card to buy two of those non-refundable tickets, for me and Meena, on a flight that gets us into New Zealand at six a.m. on the ninth of December, which is the last day we can arrive at the work placement. And those plane tickets wipe out virtually all my savings and my student loans, and it leaves me just enough money to pay for my meals for the rest of this term, plus a few hundred to pay for a suitcase and the coach ride to the airport.

And the travel woman gets up to print out our tickets, while I stay sitting there at her desk, looking up at the huge world map stencilled on the wall, till she comes back with a blue cardboard wallet that says YOUR TRAVEL DOCUMENTS on it. And she hands my debit card back to me, and I look at the numbers and my name, raised in little silver letters in the plastic. And I turn the card over to look at the hologram – on the back – of the little silver dove with its wings spread out. And I tilt the card from side to side, to make the dove's wings beat up and down, like it's trapped inside the plastic, ready to flap its way out.

CHAPTER NINETEEN

And a few weeks go past. And I'm, like, ninety-five per cent sure that Meena's gonna flake out completely and never come on this trip. Cos whenever I email her about the plans, she won't write back. And I can't find her around campus any more, cos she's apparently started living with her boyfriend now, and she's stopped going to lectures. And I wish I'd never even booked this stupid trip, to be honest, but it's too late for that, cos it's all non-refundable. And all I can do is at least *try* to get Meena to come along, and I make all the preparations for her, on the million-to-one chance that she will come through at the last minute. Cos everything I've already spent on our flights and agency fees is gone forever, whether she comes or not. And I'm trying to keep my hopes down and remember that I can still earn back at least part of the money, by going to Auckland on my own, I'm thinking, and working in that bar, without her, on the work placement. Plus that'd, sort of, show Meena that I don't even need her any more, and I can make my own friends and get on with my life. And that would be something. Although obviously, I still desperately want her to come with me, if I can possibly get her to, even though it's a massive long shot.

And first of all, I need to get Meena a student work visa, to let her work in Auckland, if she does somehow decide to come. So I sneak into her room, by telling the warden that I'm Meena Saigal and that I forgot my keys. And he unlocks it for me. And I search around till I find Meena's passport in there – in her desk drawer – which is a bit creased and worn out, and the passport photo's from when she was thirteen, and Meena's already got her student visa for America, stuck in the back pages. And I bring both our passports to the New Zealand Embassy in London and get us both working visas for the Auckland trip.

And I'm saving up magazine pages with travel advice on them like why to order the vegetarian meal on your flight, and, like, the best way to bring your dog in the 'hold' of a plane, by giving him a block of ice in the water bowl in his little cage, apparently, so it'll melt slowly and give him cold water to drink throughout the flight, and it won't all slosh out onto the floor in one go, if the plane goes over a bump, like normal water would. And I'm just texting Meena, every now and then, to casually mention the dates of the flights, to remind her that the trip's getting closer, but without putting too much pressure on her, cos that'd drive her away completely, I think.

And on the day we're supposed to leave, it's my absolute last chance to get Meena to come. And obviously, I can't find her anywhere. So I try texting her, saying that I'm sorry for sneaking this trip on her, without asking properly, and I know that she's not coming to Auckland, and that's fine, but I just wanted to say goodbye to her, in person, and thanks for everything she's done for me, cos I dunno when we'll see each other again, after she leaves for California. And I'm expecting no response, like normal.

But amazingly, Meena texts back and says that I can meet her at this hotel, near Kensington in London, to say goodbye, if I want, plus her boyfriend wants to meet me. And I suppose that does sort of make sense. Cos we might literally never see each other again, otherwise, if Meena really is leaving the country for good, like she says she is. So I sneak into Meena's bedroom again in the halls, like last time, by pretending that I'm her, and getting the warden to unlock her door for me. And then I load up my suitcase with a ton of Meena's best clothes and shoes – or really the best stuff I actually can find in there, cos her really nice stuff like her Jimmy Choos and whatever's already gone, and I think she's already taken it over to her boyfriend's house. And I make sure that I only grab the stuff of Meena's that would fit me and that I'd like to borrow in Auckland – like her Gucci pumps with the creamy leather soles – plus I grab some of Meena's make-up, as well, which she'd probably want, if she decides to come.

And I lock all Meena's stuff that I grabbed, inside my suitcase, along with her passport and visas and plane tickets (plus my own clothes). And if she flakes out completely, like she's basically planning to, then I can just give her all this stuff back, at the hotel, and I'll explain why I brought it. And, to be honest, I might not even ask her, if it's clear that she'll just say no – I might just post everything back to her, instead, from a Post Office, on the way to Heathrow, or something, to save myself from even more aggravation. But either way, I'll have all her stuff together, in one place, so I won't forget to give her anything. And I'm keeping my own passport and tickets separate, in my carry-on bag, so I won't mix them up with Meena's by mistake. And I rush off.

And I'm pulling my suitcase along this path through the campus rugby pitches, towards the bus stop, with all these slices of mud with little bullet holes in them, off the rugby blokes' boots, melting into the puddles, which I'm trying to keep the suitcase away from, to stop any muddy water soaking into Meena's clothes through the suitcase fabric.

And I get the bus to Brighton, and then the train to London, and then a tube to this hotel, where Meena said to meet her. And it all takes much longer than I thought it would. So I'm already running late by the time I get there. And I knock on the door of this hotel room. And I'm trying to rub the mud splashes off the suitcase, from the rugby path, cos I've gotta make a good impression on Meena. Although really, I'm trying to not feel *anything* about her and especially not hope, cos it's only gonna get knocked down more, the more good feelings I have.

And Meena answers the door, and gives me a massive hug, and tells me how much she's gonna miss me, which feels like a mixture of this warmth, from her affection, mingled in with the coldness of wishing I wasn't letting myself get dragged into this, like, disappointment again. And then this much older bloke, about forty-eight, I think, takes my coat and my carry-on bag, and hangs them up in the hotel room cupboard for me. And he turns out to be Meena's boyfriend, and his name's Steve. And I think he's minted, and he's not bad looking for someone that old, I suppose, a bit like Colin Firth, or whatever, but much shorter, so I suppose I can see why Meena's into him, although *I'd* never go out with anyone like that, in a million years.

And it's obvious, from the word go, that Meena's *not* gonna come on this trip, cos she's talking about her plans to spend Christmas with this Steve bloke. And she'll be going around for the next few weeks, she reckons, saying proper goodbyes to all her friends and cousins, and whatever, before she leaves England for good, which is why she wanted to see me today. And she won't be going back to campus till just before her own trip, in the middle of January, she tells me, just to clear out her room, cos 'transfer students' don't have to start till later, apparently, in America. And she still hasn't told our university that she's dropping out yet, cos she's already paid for her room for the whole year, and she doesn't want them to make her leave early.

So she wasn't planning to say goodbye to *me*, then, I'm thinking – if I hadn't texted her this afternoon – which is a pretty ugly thing to hear. Although I don't want to ruin the moment, so I don't say anything, and I have to just swallow that rejection and leave it, like, empty, down at the bottom of my stomach and my throat.

And I'll just post all Meena's stuff back to her, from a Post Office, I think, which was basically my plan B, anyway.

And I look at the time on my mobile, and I haven't got long till I'm supposed to check in for my flight, so I tell Meena and Steve that I should be leaving. But they persuade me to stay a bit longer, and Steve gets us all to drink these strong gin and tonics, from this bottle of Tanqueray they've got. And it gets me pretty hammered, actually. Cos I haven't really eaten anything today. And I try to leave again, but then Meena starts telling Steve about

130

the situation with my family. And Steve offers to get the head of his company's 'asset location department' to track down my mum for me, in India, which would be amazing, actually, cos I can't even find out what her new name is, let alone where she lives, cos I think she's re-married.

But then it starts getting, like, really scummy and weird in here. Cos then Steve starts trying to talk me into staying the night at this hotel, and he'll get me a free plane ticket to Auckland tomorrow morning, he reckons, on business class with his air miles. And Meena's trying to persuade me to stay, too, so we can all 'say goodbye properly' and 'really catch up'. And it seems pretty dodgy, wanting me to stay the night with them – especially as this Steve bloke's much older and sort of sleazy in the way he talks to me. And I'm pretty hammered, from these gin and tonics, which is also pretty suspicious – cos why are they getting me to drink so much? And I wonder if this was part of their plan, all along, to sort of trick me into staying here, for some weird, like, sexual stuff, or whatever. So then I tell them that I've really gotta leave now, to catch my plane, cos my tickets are non-refundable. And I am actually running really late. So I hurry over to the door, and Steve pulls my coat out of the cupboard and quickly helps me on with it, and I grab my suitcase – while they're talking about this dinner they're planning to go to – and I rush downstairs.

And Meena's gonna have to do something pretty huge if she ever wants to be friends with me again, after this. Cos I wish that I'd never even gone into that hotel, it was so humiliating – like the way that she's just ignored me for months on end, so rudely, and then she clicks her fingers, and expects me to come

131

running over to her – miles out of my way – and have her weird, older boyfriend hit on me in some random hotel room and make me late to check in for my flight. And I hate the way that I didn't even *try* to persuade Meena to come to New Zealand with me. And I'm not twelve any more, and I can't keep pinning all my hopes on someone forever, if they keep on disappointing me, again and again, even if they are friendly to my face – and even if they have been nice to me in the past.

But maybe it's just me, I'm thinking. Or maybe it's at least *partly* me. Cos really a big part of this is my fault – that Meena isn't coming on this trip – cos I did spring it on her when she was wasted and half-asleep. And I'm the one who made sure that everything was non-refundable, on purpose, to try to corner Meena into coming. So maybe I shouldn't be blaming everything on her. And I suppose it is possible that her boyfriend was actually gonna get me on business class tomorrow with his air miles, and track down my mum, just to be nice, but I couldn't even see it, cos I'm overly suspicious. And when they invited me to stay the night, maybe they'd have booked me my own room and wouldn't've tried something dodgy in theirs. But anyway. It's done now. And I've gotta just move on with my life and try to make the best of this time in New Zealand.

CHAPTER TWENTY

And I have to get a cab all the way to Heathrow cos I'm so late. And I'm still a bit wasted, off that gin. And I arrive with only ninety minutes to spare till *the plane takes off*, which is cutting it a bit fine. Although I have still got thirty minutes till the check-in closes, so I should be all right. And I join the end of the queue. And I see everyone else with their passports and tickets ready in their hands, so I start looking for mine. And my heart freezes. Cos I realise that I've left my carry-on bag – *with my passport inside* – in that hotel room, where Steve put it away for me, in the cupboard. But he never brought my bag out again, when he gave my coat back. So my passport's still in there, on the other side of London. And that was a thirty-five minute cab ride away. So I won't have time to go back to that hotel to collect it, and then get back here in time to catch my flight.

And I need some serious help with this. And there's a massive long queue at the airline's information desk and only one person serving customers. And I haven't got time to wait. So I walk off and phone the airline's customer service number instead on my mobile. And I explain that I've had a massive emergency and ask if there's any possible way I can change to a later flight this evening. But they look up my booking and say the same thing they always tell me, each time I've phoned them – that there's absolutely no way to change these flights, not even to a later one tonight, cos of the code share restrictions from that Saudi airline that I booked the tickets through. And when I absolutely beg them, they say the most they can do, in a genuine emergency, is let me check in forty-five minutes before take-off, but then it'd be up to me to reach the boarding gate on time, and the plane won't wait if I miss it.

But I'm pretty sure that I will be able to get to the gate in under forty-five minutes, if I run all the way. And that'd still give Meena time to bring my passport to me from that hotel. So I phone her. But she doesn't pick up. So then I text her, asking if she'll bring my bag to me, and I'll pay for the taxi. But she just texts back saying that she's really sorry, but she's at dinner with Steve now, in a different part of London, so she doesn't think that she'd get here on time, even if she left right away. So I text her again, begging her to please just get my passport, and bring it, cos I'll lose everything if she doesn't – and she can at least *try*, I'm like, even if she might not make it in time. But now she won't even text me back.

And I'm racking my brains for any possible way around this. Like just showing up at the hotel and pretending that I'm Meena – cos I have still got her passport in my suitcase, which I could show the hotel as ID. But I haven't got time to try that, now. But *then* I'm thinking that maybe I can try *flying* on Meena's passport and pretending to be her, just to get over to New Zealand. And then once I arrive, I'll tell the British Embassy over there that it was all a mistake, and I must've grabbed Meena's passport by accident, instead of my own, and I never looked at the tickets that closely, I'll say. And then I'll ask them for a new passport, in my own name.

And that seems completely mental, when I first think of it. Cos it's illegal, obviously. But the more I'm thinking, the more it seems like it might actually be worth a shot. Cos the worst that could happen really is that someone here, at security, will say, Oh, this isn't your passport. And then I'll pretend to be surprised and go, Oh, I must've accidentally picked up my friend's one, who was supposed to be coming on this trip, but she dropped out at the last minute. And then the airline people can look up both our names on the computers and see that we're booked on seats next to each other. And that'll be pretty good evidence that this was just an honest mistake, which it sort of was. And then the worst that'll happen, hopefully, is that they won't let me get on the plane, and they'll send me home – so basically, I'll be no worse off than I am now. Plus Meena's passport is from 1993, when she was only thirteen, so whoever's checking the passports here will hopefully just assume that I'm what the girl in the photo grew up to look like, in the past five years, now that I'm an adult. Plus the warden at the halls believed that I was Meena, twice, so we can't look *completely* different from each other.

So basically, I don't think there's *too* much risk in trying this. But if I don't, then it's a hundred per cent certain that I'm gonna lose everything that I've spent on this trip, and I won't be able to earn any of it back by working at that bar in Auckland, so I won't even be able to pay for my accommodation at uni next term. Plus I'll be gutted that I didn't at least have an amazing holiday by myself and at least get *something* out of all the money I've spent. So I'm gonna just roll the dice, here, and give it a try.

CHAPTER TWENTY-ONE

And first of all, I'm thinking, I could change into some of Meena's clothes out of my suitcase and put on a bit of her make-up too – to maybe look a bit more like her. So I wheel the suitcase over to the girls' loos, and I walk into a disabled cubicle. And I lay the suitcase on its back and open up the lid and look at all of Meena's designer shoes and her clothes folded in there. And I think about how much this must all be worth. And it's easily two grand. And I'm keeping all of it – as compensation for Meena leaving me in the lurch like this – no matter what happens with all the passport stuff.

And I change into Meena's Gucci pumps, and a pair of her Monsoon jeans that've got pockets for my wallet, and this Dolce & Gabbana cardigan. And then I rush over to the sinks and quickly put on some of Meena's blusher and mascara and lipstick. And that's all I've got time for, cos the check-in's about to close, and I don't wanna put any extra attention on myself by asking for a special late check-in. So I grab the suitcase and start legging it through the airport.

And I rush over to the check-in desks. And I'm practising

Meena's name and birthday and everything, which I know really well, anyway, but: Meena Saigal, Meena Saigal, Meena Saigal. And I go over to this airline bloke, who's walking around the queue for checking in, and I tell him that I'm trying to catch flight sixty-four to New Zealand. And he guides me straight to the front – to this middle-aged woman's check-in desk – and he's like:

'Any chance we can squeeze this young lady onto flight sixty-four?'

'We'll see what we can do,' she goes. 'Could I see your passport and tickets, please?'

So I hand over Meena's passport and visa and ticket.

'You're Meena Saigal. Is that right?' goes the woman, typing into her computer.

And I'm sure this is a trap, where I'm going to say yes and then they're going to arrest me. And I'm bricking it now. But I've gotta pretend to be calm. And I lift my suitcase onto these scales, by the side of the woman's desk. And she has a quick look at the passport and types into her computer, wraps a barcode around the suitcase handle, and prints out two cardboard boarding passes, which she hands me, along with the passport.

'Boarding begins in twenty minutes,' she goes, 'so you should go straight to gate thirty-five.'

So I hurry off, before she can change her mind. And I get to passport control and hand over Meena's passport to the bloke at the desk, with Meena's boarding passes tucked into the photo page, to make it more convincing. And he just has a quick glance at it and then hands it back to me. And then I go through the x-ray machines, without any trouble. And then I leg it down this massive long tunnel walkway-thing, looking out of the big windows at the runway covered in rows of lights, to show the planes where to drive. And the planes' tails are lit up, with the different airline logos, like a giant red kangaroo, or an angry silver eagle.

And I get to gate thirty-five and get on the plane, and I'm sitting in the window seat – that I booked for Meena – which is what the magazines recommended for long-haul flights, so you can rest your head against the window and sleep when it's getting late. And I'm sitting there, reading the in-flight magazine and the flight-safety card. And I'm thinking that it'd probably be best to wait till the very end of my trip before I ask the British Embassy for a replacement passport in my own name. Cos if they don't believe me, that this was an honest mistake, then they might arrest me or deport me. And if that happens, then I want to have had my entire holiday already, before they punish me, and I want to have earned back as much money as I possibly can. And I'm not entirely sure whether that is actually the best way to go, to be honest. But I've got a whole, like, twenty-six-hour flight to keep thinking this through properly and get my plan straight for how I'm gonna handle all this.

And while I'm still thinking about it, the captain comes on the radio and tells us that in LA the weather's eighty-nine degrees and sunny and in Auckland it's seventy-eight. And we drive onto the runway and gradually start speeding along it.

And as the plane takes off, I get pushed slightly back into my chair, from the force. And out of my little oblong window, with its rounded corners like an old TV, I can see we're driving up into the sky, and we're climbing and climbing, and I can see the giant speckled smudge of white lights that must be London, sort of painted there on the blackness of the planet. And then a layer of grey cloud rushes over us, as we drive up through it. And then it's just black everywhere I look, apart from the big round moon reflected on the tops of the clouds. And the plane tilts sideways and turns a corner, which must be the driver following his, like, invisible road through the air.

And I can feel all these layers underneath me, starting with the creamy leather soles of Meena's shoes on my feet, with the word GUCCI sunk into them in neat little brown letters. And they're resting on the next layer, which is the carpet, with this row of lights stitched into it, that the flight safety card says are supposed to start shining if there's an emergency and light up the path we can follow to lead us out of the doors to escape. And underneath that, they keep the dogs in little cages in a room, waiting for their blocks of ice to start melting so they can have a drink. And then under that, there's another layer filled with suitcases. And then right at the bottom, it's the compartment where the aeroplane wheels are folded up, like the way birds tuck their legs into their tummies, while they're flapping around, or gliding, like I saw on these white swans once with their long necks and their orange beaks and their dark eyes, flying right the way along the Hadston River, and turning exactly where the river turned, like the water was a motorway someone had laid down there, that only those swans knew about, just following each little curve of the riverbanks and keeping in line with each other, till I couldn't see them any more, and I was just looking at the invisible twisty line they'd flown along, through the massive rivery sky.

PART TWO
1999

CHAPTER ONE

It's four days before the end of my holiday in New Zealand. And I'm asleep in bed when I get a call on my mobile, and the clock says 6:23 a.m. and the screen says MEENA SAIGAL, which is the first time I've heard from her since that hotel in London, weeks ago.

'All right, mate?' goes Meena's voice, when I pick up. 'You're never gonna believe this, but we're getting a free holiday in India.'

'What are you talking about?' I'm like, cos she's mental if she thinks I'm going on holiday with her again.

'I phoned up British Airways,' she's like, 'and I got them to change "my" tickets for a round trip to India. Plus I got "you" a free stopover in New Delhi on your way home.'

'You can't change the dates on those tickets,' I go.

'Yeah, well, maybe you couldn't do it, but I'm already in India, so . . .'

'Well, whatever,' I'm like. 'I'm not going.'

'Look, mate, I've already changed your flights,' she goes, 'so you sort of have to now.'

'No, I don't,' I'm like. 'I'll just change them back.'

'Come on, mate,' goes Meena. 'I'm really sorry about what happened in London. And just think about how wicked it'll be to see India and get back to our roots and everything.'

'I don't care,' I'm like. 'I'm not going anywhere with you.'

'All right,' goes Meena. 'Well, I'm gonna ask you nicely one more time, and then I'm gonna make you.'

'You can't make me do anything,' I'm like.

'Whose passport are you planning to use, then, when you come home?'

And she's got me.

'Whose passport?' she's like.

'That doesn't matter,' I go. 'I'll just tell the British Embassy that I lost mine, and they'll give me a new one in my own name.'

'No, you won't,' she goes. 'Cos they'll check with immigration and see that no one flew into New Zealand with your real passport, so you must've come in on a stolen one, which you did. And *then* you filled in the government forms, at Auckland Airport, with *my* details, and signed on with that work agency as me, cos I phoned up and checked. And that's immigration fraud. So you'll end up with a criminal record for the rest of your life. And the punishment's up to seven years in prison. And that'll be it. Seven years, mate. And if you thought that children's home was bad—'

'I'll just tell them it was a mistake.'

'They don't care about that,' she's like. 'Whatever you do and whatever you say, if you don't come to India, you're fucked. And I'll make sure of that. Cos I'll phone the police in New Zealand to come and arrest you, plus I'll phone the police at LAX and

146

Heathrow, in case you slip through the net,' she's like. 'Or you can just meet me in India.'

And I can't believe this is happening, here. She's got me.

'Okay,' goes Meena. 'I'll take that as a yes. So write this down: British Airways flight 104 from Auckland Airport, leaving this morning at—'

'Leaving this morning?'

'Yes, leaving this morning.'

'I've still got another four days in New Zealand,' I'm like. 'I've got stuff planned out. I'm going scuba diving on Tuesday.'

'Not any more, you ain't,' she goes. 'Now write this down. BA flight 104, leaving Auckland at 11:55 a.m., for New Delhi,' she's like. 'And before you leave for the airport, swing by the Indian Consular Services Office in Auckland and pick up a tourist visa. And tell them you need to visit a dying relative in New Delhi, so your flight's booked this morning, and they'll give you a visa on the spot,' she's like. 'Your plane ticket's waiting for you at the BA check-in desk. And I'll be there to meet you at flight arrivals in India. And the accommodation and everything's taken care of. My treat. And it's gonna be wicked, mate. Just like the old days.'

And I dunno what I'm gonna do exactly. But I've gotta at least write it down, to give me the option of meeting up with her.

'Right, I'll see you there,' she goes. 'And if you're not on that flight, you're going to prison. So you might as well do it. Plus you're getting an extra free holiday. So . . .'

'Bloody hell, Meena. I dunno why I was ever friends with you.'

'Ha ha, you know you love me,' she goes. 'See you tonight.

Oh, and I've got a mega surprise for you, when we get there. Your flipping head's gonna explode when you see who it is.'

'Who?' I'm like. 'Is it my mum?'

But Meena's already hung up.

And I stay laying in bed for a while, trying to think how I can get out of this. But I don't think I can. Cos I can't risk getting a criminal record. Plus, whatever happens, Meena won't keep me there for more than about a week, cos she's gotta fly to California to start uni. So really, it's just, like, seven more days with Meena, and then I'll never have to see her again for the rest of my life. Or maybe she really is sorry, and this is her way of trying to make it up to me before she leaves, which would be all right. Plus it is possible that she's gonna bring me to see my mum, which would be the best thing that could possibly happen in the entire world. Cos I can't even find out where my mum lives since she moved to India, cos I don't even know what her new name is. And I phoned up the few people I could find numbers for in my family and they wouldn't even tell me what state she was living in. But maybe Meena's found a way to track her down, like through Steve's contacts, or something.

So first of all, I phone British Airways to confirm that my flights have actually been changed, which they have. And then I pack all my clothes into my suitcase and wheel it to the bank and withdraw the 5,800 New Zealand dollars I've saved up, which is about two thousand quid, cos I did every single overtime shift I could possibly get, and I was really careful about saving up. And I shove this big wad of hundred-dollar bills into my pocket. And I get the bank woman to look up the address of this Indian

148

Consular Services Office, and I take a taxi there and get the tourist visa, which is printed on a green square of cardboard they staple into Meena's passport. And then I phone up the manager at the bar where I've been working and tell him that I've gotta leave New Zealand right away cos of a family emergency. And then I catch the bus to the airport, with my stomach swirling around with worrying about the million ways that Meena could screw me over, mixed in with these bright white swirls of hope that she might actually wanna be proper friends again or that she might have found my mum.

CHAPTER TWO

And the minute my plane's wheels lift off from the runway, it suddenly hits me that Meena might have grassed me up to the police in India, to get me arrested over there, which would have the worst prisons in the world, to get maximum revenge on me for nicking her passport and clothes. And that would explain why she only phoned me a few hours before the flight – so I wouldn't have time to think it through. But I'm trapped on the plane now, so there's nothing I can do about it.

And I get out in New Delhi, and I queue up to have my passport checked. And I'm bricking it and remembering that film about the American woman who got put in prison somewhere in Asia, where the minimum sentence is like twenty-five years, and with like ten people in each cell, where the lights stay on all night and you have to sleep on the concrete floor, and you wake up with, like, a fat brown beetle crawling over your lips. And the only people who do all right are the ones whose family come to visit them all the time to bring them cigarettes to bribe the guards with. But blatantly no one would come and visit me, and I'd be totally and completely alone.

150

And right as I get to the front of the passport queue, I suddenly realise that the workers checking passports here are gonna be the *best in the world* at spotting the difference between two Indian girls, cos everyone here's Indian. So they're gonna see straight away that I'm *not* the person in the passport photo, and the game will be up, even if Meena never even grassed on me. But before I can think of a plan, the bloke at the desk starts waving me over. So I step up and hand him Meena's passport. And he looks at the photo page and scrunches up his eyes. So I go:

'I was just on holiday in New Zealand,' and I reach over and turn the little stiff passport pages back to the one with the New Zealand stamp, which is a red triangle with a date in the middle, to show him that I've been using this passport all over the world. 'And there's a pretty cool stamp from Los Angeles,' I go, turning the next page. But he slaps my hand away.

'Okay, okay,' he's like, and he stamps my passport and tears off half of the green visa stapled in there and hands the passport back to me, and then he looks over my shoulder and waves the next person up to his desk.

So I stroll off, feeling pretty chuffed with myself for dodging the bullet there. And I get to the arrivals hall and look along the line of people waiting by the metal railing. And Meena's not there. And all the air drains out of my heart, like a balloon. And I knew this would happen, that I wouldn't get to see my mum. And probably Meena was never even in India in the first place, cos her call did come through from her mobile, so she probably never even left England. And either she was just playing a total trick on me, sending me to a random country for no reason. Or she had this big idea of us going to India but then couldn't be bothered to follow through and come to meet me. And I try phoning her on my mobile, but it won't let me make any calls, and the screen just says NO NETWORK.

And I stand in front of the railing, so Meena can find me if she turns up late, and I stare all around this massive arrivals hall. And along one wall there are people sleeping on strips of cardboard, even though it's the afternoon. And blokes in monkeycaps and chunky sweaters are swarming around the businessmen coming from the flight, pestering them for something.

And I feel so completely alone. Cos everyone else getting off my plane's got a big family waiting to meet them, or at least a driver holding up a name placard, but I've got no one and nowhere to go. And I watch this teenage boy walk up to his family, where there's a mum, dad, brothers, cousins, grandmother, little children, and a driver in a uniform. And the mum hugs him, puts a garland of orange flowers around his neck and a *laddu* sweet into his mouth. And then the rest of his family clamours around him, and one by one he touches their feet, and then taps his own forehead, and then hugs them.

And I wish Meena was here, even though she's been such a bad friend to me, cos then at least I wouldn't be the only person with no one to meet them. And people keep pushing past me. So I walk on, but as slowly as I can, cos I don't really wanna get right into the arrivals hall, cos then I'll have to decide what I'm gonna do next.

So I step out of the flow of people, and stand against the wall.

And really when I take a minute to think about it, this is okay. Cos now I've done what Meena asked me to, and *she's* the one who didn't turn up. So I'm free now. And I can just get the next flight home to England, either by asking British Airways to change the date on my ticket, or if they won't, then I can just buy a new one with the cash in my pocket. And then Meena can never screw me over again, cos I won't be abroad on a stolen passport.

So I start looking for a British Airways desk, when this bloke comes up and grabs my arm.

'Madam want taxi,' he goes. '*Acha* price. Good price.' And he reaches out and grabs the handle of my suitcase.

'Fuck off!' I go. Cos I'm like that now. I don't take rubbish from anyone. Although I didn't wanna be quite that rude. And a few people walking past stare at me. And the taxi driver's stunned for a second. But then he starts up again.

'Taxi, taxi. This way,' he goes. 'I'll give you best deal, full deal. Taj Mahal, Red Fort, hotel tour.' And he's still gripping my suitcase handle. So I hold onto it with both of my hands and wrench it away from him. And while I'm walking off I feel this hand on my shoulder, and a woman's voice goes:

'Taxi, taxi. Come with me.'

So I don't even turn around. I just start walking faster, towards the toilets. Cos taxi drivers aren't gonna follow me in there.

'Taxi for the slapper rude-girl,' goes the voice. And I turn around, and it's Meena standing there. And she's got blonde highlights streaked through her hair, actual pale yellow blonde highlights, which I didn't think was even possible for

153

Asian black hair, cos it usually just turns orange when you bleach it. And she's got a choker made of little white shells around her neck, and a silver nose ring, and brown leather flip-flops. So she's apparently turned into some kind of beach hippy, in the last two months.

'Oh, my God,' she goes. 'You are hilarious!'

'Jesus, Meena,' I'm like. 'I didn't think you were coming.'

'I loved the way you told that taxi driver to fuck off. That was classic,' she's like.

'Yeah, well, I don't take rubbish from anyone any more.'

'Ooh,' goes Meena, 'I'd better watch you then,' blatantly taking the piss. But I don't care, cos I really do stand up for myself now.

'Listen, mate,' I go. 'Can I just get the next plane back to England? Cos I really don't wanna be here.'

'What do you mean?' she's like. 'You've only just got here. What's the point of coming all the way to India and not even having a look round?'

'Where are we even going, though?' I ask her.

'That's more like it,' goes Meena. 'Come with me.'

And she gets us a taxi to the railway station and leads me to this train, where we've got our own little compartment, with narrow little bunk beds to the left and right, covered in these greyish-blue vinyl mattresses. And in front, there are two windows, with a fold-up table screwed to the wall between them, and a mirror above it, and a fan in a cage near the ceiling. And the walls are this laminated cream colour, with cold air drifting in through two metal vents.

And I slide my suitcase underneath the bottom bunk on the left.

'Why haven't you got any luggage?' I go.

And Meena doesn't know what to say. And she thinks for a second. 'Cos my clothes are in your suitcase,' she's like.

And I'm gutted, cos I've been thinking of these clothes like they were mine. But now Meena's gonna make me give them back to her. And I feel this disappointment drying me out, cos I'm backing down already, and I've only been with her for like an hour and a half. So I've gotta make sure I still stand up to her in other ways.

And we sit on the train till nighttime, and at 8:15 p.m. the train finally starts moving. And after rattling along for a while, we leave the city and it gets pitch black outside. And this train worker delivers us each a soft parcel wrapped in brown paper, with this address printed on it: MK Dry-cleaning Company. Shop No. 14, F-Block Market, Ashok Vihar, Phase-I, New Delhi-110087, but Meena won't let us open the parcels yet, cos she says it's part of the surprise. And that turns the address into a clue. And I'm trying to work out what it means, that we've got parcels from a dry cleaner's. And I'm guessing they're clothes that we have to wear this evening, at whatever place Meena's bringing us to, and maybe it's a beautiful sari with mirror-work and *Parsi*-work embroidery to make me look special for when I meet my mum again after so long.

'Can you give me a clue about where we're going?' I'm like.

'All right,' Meena goes. 'Basically it's gonna be wicked. And you don't have to pay for anything. And you're gonna meet someone you never thought you'd see again.'

'Okay,' I'm like. And I can't nag her for details, cos I don't want the surprise to get ruined. And I'm trying to stop myself from hoping that she's taking me to see my mum. But I can't stop the excitement brimming over inside of me, like a bottle of champagne that's been shaken up and it's about to be opened and come bursting out all over the place. Cos really, who else can it be apart from my mum? So I just sit back on my bunk bed, and focus on the tiny lights and fires right out in the distance of the big black spaces that we're travelling through.

CHAPTER THREE

And a train worker brings us two aluminium trays covered in silver foil, which we peel back to show compartments with different food in each one, like yellow *dal*, and *aloo*-and-greenpeas curry, and rice, and lime pickle. And we each get a little plastic cup of curds and two *rotis* wrapped in foil, and one plastic spoon and one napkin. And for dessert, in a little compartment on the tray, we get *gulab jamun*, which is condensed milk deep fried with sugar-syrup – all foods my mum used to cook, and I remember her talking about riding the trains around India when she was a little girl.

And if we really are travelling to meet my mum now, I can tell her all about the things I've learned on this train ride to show her that I haven't turned completely English since she left, which will give me more in common with her and bring us closer together.

And me and Meena finish our dinner, and the train worker collects our trays. And then a bloke comes round selling 'cold drink', and another comes round selling ice creams, so Meena buys us each a Thums Up Cola, a Limca and a Gold Spot orange drink, and then she buys me a Kwality Choco Bar and herself a Mango Bar.

'Open the suitcase, mate,' she goes, while we're eating them. 'I've gotta get something to sleep in.'

'Sleep in?' I go. 'How long's this train ride gonna be?'

'Just, like, three days.'

'Three days!' I'm like. 'What's the point of that? We're only in India for a week. Why are we spending three days on a train? Or six days round trip? We'll have to turn round as soon as we get there. We should have flown. We should have just flown straight there and met at the nearest airport.'

'Honestly, mate, I can understand why you'd think that,' goes Meena, 'but when we get to this place, everything will make absolute sense. I promise you. Plus this train journey's part of the whole experience. Cos I thought this would give us a chance to, like, talk and become friends again. Unless you don't wanna be friends any more,' she's like. 'I suppose, I could understand that.'

'No, I definitely still wanna be friends,' I go.

'Well, that was part of the surprise,' she's like. 'And so's this long train journey. Cos this is A/C two-tier, with seat numbers in the high twenties, so the tickets cost three hundred quid each, cos this is the best cabin there is. Plus there's a massive surprise waiting for you when we get there.'

And her eyes are wide open and looking right into mine. And her face is kind of nervous, like she's got this ninety per cent smile, but she's waiting for me to say okay, before it can become one hundred per cent. So I nod my head and her face relaxes into a full smile. And either she's the world's best liar, or she is telling the truth. And above the window, this quick little rattling sound comes from this fan in its little cage, as the train goes over a bump in the tracks.

And then I remember that Meena wanted to look in the suitcase, so I unlock it, and she starts rummaging around, messing up my packing system. And I can't stand it. So I get in front of her and pull out a skinny-rib green New Zealand T-shirt I bought as a souvenir. And Meena yanks the price tag out of the collar and puts it on.

And then she tears open her brown paper parcel that the train bloke brought earlier, and she pulls out fresh sheets and a blanket and pillow, and I do the same, and we make up our beds. And I'm gutted obviously, cos Meena made it sound like there was gonna be something important inside those parcels. And we both get washed at the toilets at the end of our carriage. And then we take it in turns going to the loo, which is literally just a hole in the middle of the floor, with the dark ground rushing past beneath it.

And back in our compartment, Meena gets into the top bunk on the left. So I change into another T-shirt and get into the bottom bunk on the right. And the weather's getting hotter and, like, steamier, the further we travel, and it feels like we're driving into a jungle and like the dangers and the excitement are mixing together and I'm breathing them in. And Meena turns on the fan, whose blades go whizzing round in their little cage, and blur together into one ghosty circle.

And I usually read a book before I go to sleep, but I haven't got one with me here, so I pick up the brown paper wrapping

159

that the sheets were packed inside, cos it's got these *Clothing Care Tips* printed on it, so I glance through them, just cos I like the feeling of words brushing over my mind, cos it calms me down before bed. And the first tip says: *1. Do not try to clean stain with water. This can produce rings that are harder to remove than the original stain.* And they're all like that – basically a trick to make you take your clothes to the dry cleaner's, instead of washing them yourself, so the dry cleaner will make more money. But I still like the feeling of the words brushing over my mind and the knowledge that some Indian blokes in their little shop in Delhi were out there, scrubbing away, washing and ironing and folding these bedclothes just for me.

CHAPTER FOUR

And the train journey's like this magical ride through the stories my mum told me when I was a little girl, cos each time we stop at a station, people come up to our window and sell us things my mum used to tell me about, like this really old man sells us tea in clay cups (but that only happens once; usually it's in plastic cups), and other people sell us hot *pakodas*, which are plantains deep fried in gram-flour batter and wrapped in newspaper banana leaves; and bracelets made of wooden beads. And some people climb onto the train and walk down the corridor, and sell their stuff door to door, and Meena buys one of absolutely everything that comes our way, plus she pays this little boy to clean our floor with a dry rag, and she buys a string of white jasmine flowers from a lady who measures them against the length from her fingertips to her elbow, and then Meena weaves it into my ponytail, which makes our cabin smell like a garden.

And the train starts to get dirty by the end of the second day, and there's old tissues and sticky spilled tea on the floor of the corridor, and the ends of the carriage near the toilets start to smell, which must be why it's good that our compartment is in the high twenties right in the middle, away from the toilets.

And on the third day, we pull into a station whose sign's written in this squiggly language that looks like *jalebi* sweets, those little bright orange pretzel things. And a man comes to our window and sells us each a cup of warm yellow water, with cumin in it to help with digestion. All stuff I already know from my mum's stories. And it's like riding this train has magically changed those stories from half-made-up – which is how they used to feel – to completely real.

And a beggar comes right up to our window and points towards his mouth with all his fingers, like he's hungry. So I look around, to see if there's any food in our cabin. But there's nothing. So I'm like, in Hindi:

'I'm sorry. We haven't got any food.'

And he starts trying to talk to me in another language.

'Do you know where we are?' I ask him, in Hindi and then in Punjabi. 'Where in India?'

But he doesn't seem to understand. He just keeps chattering on in another language, and touching his bunched-up fingertips to his heart and then his lips. And then the train starts pulling out of the station, and the man gets left behind.

And in two more stations, the train guard tells us this is our stop. So we cram all our stuff into the suitcase, including all the new bracelets and carved elephants and other knick-knacks that Meena bought, and we rush off the train before it starts driving again. And we're at this village station, with one small building with a sloping pot-tile roof, a small waiting room with wooden benches and one ticket worker inside an office. And in front of the building, there's a road with jungle on the other side. There's no taxis or auto-rickshaws. And Meena pulls out a sheet of paper with handwritten notes on it, and she leads us down the road to a bus stop, like a small shed, whose back walls are plastered with overlapping movie posters. And next to it there's a tiny shop, which is basically just a wooden crate on stilts, serving tea and rows of bright pink and green and yellow coconut pastries, and a washing line with newspapers clipped onto it with plastic clothes pegs. And the shopkeeper's sitting inside, and he's got a wire connected to a lamp post nearby to power a fan and a black-and-white TV showing cricket. So we have a cup of tea and a pastry to kill time. And eventually the bus pulls up, and it's already packed full, with someone in every seat and people standing all the way along the aisle, but the driver lets us cram ourselves on anyway, with the suitcase. And Meena tells the driver where we want to go, reading off her sheet of paper. And the first four rows of seats are all women, and one of them's tying the stems of jasmine flowers together.

And the road's surrounded by all these dark green leafy trees everywhere and bunches of green coconuts in some of them. And we can glimpse these little rivers through the jungle. And I see a monkey!

'Look at that, Meena!' I'm like. 'It's a monkey.'

'Yeah, I know,' she goes. And her face is proud and happy, I think cos she's glad that I'm enjoying this place she brought me to. And after a while of driving, a rainstorm suddenly starts up, and a couple of people try to shut their windows, but they're all jammed open, so people just turn their faces away from the rain blowing in. And the rain stops after about five minutes anyway.

And eventually the road starts running parallel to a wide river, and the bus driver tells Meena that we're at the stop she asked for. So we get off the bus. And along the riverbank there's little houses, and next to each one there's little wooden boats tied up, in the river, each painted with two bright colours, and there's bamboo poles stuck into the ground, with fishing nets hanging up on them to dry.

And Meena's leading us along the dirt edge of the river, past the houses, to where it's just a row of little boats roped to wooden poles sticking out of the water, and with men working on them or squatting down on the riverbank. And the men have got thick curly black hair, like I've never seen on Indian people, and it's glistening with some kind of gel. And they're all wearing white shirts and white sort of wrap-around skirts. And a few of them are eating bowls of this delicious smelling coconut and pork stew, dipping what look like crepes into it.

And a few men are sorting fish into baskets, with a different colour of fish in each one, like pink, or grey, or white. And Meena's reading from her sheet of paper and leading me along the row of boats, looking at the numbers written in white paint on the back of each one, till she gets to this boat, about ten times bigger than all the others, with 59987 painted on it. It's about as big as a minibus, and it's made of wood. And there are old car tyres chained around its sides, to protect it when it bumps against the riverbanks. And it's tied up to five bamboo poles and to some

164

wooden stakes all hammered into the earth of the riverbank where we're standing. And it's bobbing slowly on the water.

And Meena yanks on this piece of string that leads to a makeshift bell hanging on the deck of the boat, made of a rusty spoon inside a small oil can. And Meena clangs it a few times. And a Chinese-looking bloke comes out of the little square room-thing on the top of the boat and says something in Chinese, I suppose to his mates inside the room, and two more of them come out. And I think they might all be in the same family, cos there's an older one, who could be the granddad, and then a middle-aged one, who's like the father, and then a teenage boy, who's probably his son.

And Meena shouts:

'I'm Meena. You're supposed to be taking us on your boat.'

And the father one goes:

'*Mee-noah, ma?*'

And Meena's like, 'Yes, Meena,' and she points at herself.

'Oh, oh, oh, oh,' the father goes, nodding his head. And the young Chinese bloke, the son, who's only about thirteen, jumps onto the river bank, where me and Meena are standing, and he picks up my suitcase by the handle and swings it over to the father standing on the boat who carries it on his shoulder down some steps and puts it away, while the granddad and the boy line up a wide plank from the side of the boat to the real ground where me and Meena are. And local men are crowding around, most of them with thick curly hair, and some of them are wearing crazy bright green or yellow fishnet vests, and calling out to me and Meena in a local language we can't understand, and pointing out the Chinese blokes on our boat and making jokes about them.

And Meena turns to face me. And she's literally panting, although we haven't been running or anything. And her face is sparkling from sweat. And she's got this weird scared smile on her face. And she grabs me by both shoulders.

'Right,' she goes. 'We're gonna do this thing. We're actually gonna do it!' But she's blatantly just hyping herself up, like someone trying to make herself jump off a diving board. 'This is gonna be so amazing, Shruti. I can't believe we're actually doing this!'

And the Chinese dad's started the engine on the boat, so it's growling and the plank's vibrating.

And Meena holds onto my hand and leads me over the plank and onto the boat. And the boy unties the ropes around the bamboo poles and the wooden stakes, and then he runs up the plank, pulls it into the boat, and we start cruising along this inky black river, which is lined on both sides with coconut trees, stooping right over the water, and for long stretches the trees from each side meet above us, to make a sort of leafy tunnel that we're sailing through. And on the banks, I see goats and cows just wandering around in what I think are people's gardens, and roosters and chickens.

And eventually this backwater opens out into the sea, and I start panicking a bit, cos I still don't know where we're heading, but before I can even think about asking them to let me off, the boat speeds up so fast that after twenty minutes we can't see any land at all – just water in every direction, and the sun's getting low in the sky, and its reflection looks sort of like gold coins sprinkling into the waves.

And me and Meena stand at the front of the boat, holding onto these metal railings, with the sea spraying up at us each time the pointy front of the boat hits a wave. And the sun's drying the salt onto our skin, cos I can taste it when I lick my lips. And Meena keeps thinking something and shaking her head.

'Meena, please can you tell me where we're going, now?' I'm like, cos this isn't exciting any more. I'm actually getting worried.

And Meena's mouth tries to make a few words, while she's shaking her head. 'It's just the most incredible, amazing thing in the whole world.'

'Can you be a bit more specific?' I go.

'All right,' she's like. 'Imagine becoming a millionaire and having all your dreams come true for the rest of your life,' she goes. 'It's like that.'

'Wow,' I go. And I dunno what she's going on about, but I'm praying that she's taking me to see my mum. And Meena grabs me with one arm around my waist, and pulls me towards her.

'We're doing it!' she shouts into the wind. 'We're actually doing it!'

And I have to hang onto the railings twice as tight, cos I'm holding on for Meena, now, as well. And the boat's going so fast that it feels like it's skipping over the tops of the waves, like it's literally flying like a rocket, and waves are just reaching up, every now and then, trying to grab on, but they're just skimming off the wooden planks of the bottom.

CHAPTER FIVE

And after about an hour it's getting boring, cos it's just massive miles of dark blue water all around us, with these huge dirty-coloured patches, far off in the distance, that might be, like, coral reefs or swarms of fish, or something, but they've always disappeared by the time we get to them. And I'm knackered and thirsty from standing in the sun for so long. And now the wind's picking up, so my hair's flying all over my face and into my eyes.

'Have they got any drinks on here?' I ask Meena. And I have to shout, cos the wind's blowing right into our ears.

'What?' goes Meena.

'*Drinks*,' I'm like. And I pretend to drink a can of Coke, to show her what I mean.

And she heads towards the big window where they're driving the boat. So I follow her, crouching down while I walk, to stop the wind from pushing me into the sea.

And the three Chinese blokes are all sitting there, out of the weather, in their little cabin. And the dad's sitting in a metal driving seat bolted to the floor, with one of his hands on the steering wheel. And behind him, the granddad and the son are sitting at a plastic table playing a game with these fat white Chinese dominoes.

And Meena pretends to drink a Coke and goes, *'Drink?'* to them all.

And the granddad slaps the teenager's leg with the back of his hand and says something in Chinese and points to this crate of brown glass bottles. So the teenager opens one of them and holds it out to Meena who smells it and pulls her face away, with her nose wrinkled up.

'No,' she goes. 'Water.' And she does a waves-on-the-ocean move with her hand. *'Water.'*

And the granddad and teenager playing dominoes start cackling, on their plastic chairs, and saying dirty things about me and Meena in Chinese. And the old one jiggles his knees up and down, and he pats his left thigh like he wants Meena to sit on it. And then he reaches out and grabs her by the wrist and tries to pull her towards him.

But Meena yanks her arm free. And I hurry off to the pointed front of the boat, which is the furthest away we can get. And I'm expecting Meena to follow me. But she doesn't. She just stands there telling off the granddad and the boy, while the middle-aged one ignores it all and faces forward steering the boat and looking at his little radar screen every now and then.

And then Meena comes over to me, and she's like:

'Where the fuck did you disappear to, right when I needed some backup?'

'I thought we were both gonna run away.'

'Run where, you fucking idiot?' she's like. 'We're on a boat. There's nowhere to run,' she goes. 'We've gotta show them that we stand up for ourselves.'

'Well, I didn't know that, did I,' I'm like. 'I didn't know you were gonna bring us in danger, where we'd have to be watching our backs all the time.'

'You're useless,' Meena's like. 'You're so weak and useless, it's pathetic.'

And she leaves me feeling like dirt for a while, trying to think of something to say. And then when she's satisfied she's made me squirm for long enough she's like:

'Come on, then, you loser. I think they're bringing out some food for us.'

So I follow her back to the cabin, feeling worse than ever, cos now I know for sure that Meena hasn't changed one single bit, and that she's still just as horrible as she ever was, and she doesn't want to have a new kind of friendship where we're both kind to each other, and I can trust her to look out for me. And I was an idiot for ever believing that anything would be different.

And when we get back to the cabin, there's this green plastic cool box on the floor. And the middle-aged bloke driving the boat says something in Chinese to the teenager and the old man, who carefully pick up this wooden board they were playing dominoes on and take it through the little door that leads to the downstairs room, and the middle-aged bloke waves us towards the table and chairs.

So me and Meena sit down. And I open up the cool box, which isn't cold inside, and it's got this dank mouldy smell. And there's four warm bottles of Gold Spot in there and a few hard *naan* breads and peeled boiled eggs, and some chocolate bars melted into one big lump – all of it just loose in the cool box, not wrapped up or anything. So me and Meena make an egg sandwich each, and they taste of the dank musty smell of the plastic cool box, with a tinge of chocolate on everything. And after each bite, I try to wash away the taste with a swig of Gold Spot, which is basically just fizzy orange squash. And then we each scoop out a few fingerfuls of chocolate for dessert, which pretty much gets rid of the taste.

And the sun's starting to set down near the horizon, massive and the colour of a peach, and it's making this sort of orangey-red road on the sea. But we're not heading towards that road. We're swerving further and further off to the left.

CHAPTER SIX

And after the sun goes down, it gets completely dark on the boat apart from the green radar screen shining on the driver, up front. And me and Meena are sitting at the table behind him.

'Ask him how long it's gonna be till we get there,' I go to Meena.

So she walks up to him and points to her watch. '*How long?*' she goes.

And the driver spreads out his hand and points to each finger, in turn, and then he does it again.

'I think he's saying ten hours,' goes Meena.

'So I'm gonna miss the start of uni, then?' I go.

'What difference does it make if you're a few weeks late?' she's like.

'A few *weeks?*' I'm like. 'What are you talking about a few weeks? I never agreed to that. I'll have to repeat my whole first year.'

'Would you calm down?' goes Meena. 'You're ruining this experience for me.'

'What about me?' I'm like. 'What about *my* experience? You're ruining my life.'

'I have honestly never met anyone as dramatic as you,' Meena's like. 'Why can't you just enjoy the positive aspects of this situation?'

'You shut your stupid mouth about positive aspects of this situation,' I'm like. 'There's no positive aspects. You tricked me into coming out here. And we're not even going to meet my mum, are we?'

'If you don't stop shouting,' she's like, 'I won't tell you how to get back in time for uni.'

So I pretend to be cool, even though my blood's on fire. 'How can I get back in time for uni, then?'

'Just wait till we get to there – to this place where we're going. And if you don't like it, you can just stay on the boat and come straight home.'

'With you?' I'm like.

'Er, no,' she goes. 'I'm not cutting my trip short just cos you can't hack it.'

'Meena, you've gotta come with me.'

'I'm not talking about this any more,' she goes. 'And if you start wingeing again – if you say one more word about it – I'll tell them not to drive you home. Do you understand?'

'Yes,' I go, cos I have to.

'Good,' she's like. 'Now, I'm gonna get a jumper.' And she knocks on the little door behind us. And the old Chinese bloke answers it, letting out a waft of alcohol and screechy Chinese music from the downstairs room. And Meena squeezes past him

173

and climbs down the little staircase inside. And I follow after her. And the downstairs room's really dim with just two weak light bulbs burning on the ceiling. And the air's cloudy with cigarette smoke. And there's a triple bunk bed, with twisted-up grey blankets that look like they've literally never been washed.

And the old granddad's clearly pretty lashed, cos he can't even line up the flame of his lighter with the end of his fag. So the boy has to light it for him. And then the granddad suddenly grabs me round the waist and pushes his hips right in next to mine and starts swaying me from side to side, in time with the screechy music, holding his cigarette between his lips.

'Get off me!' I go, and I try to push him away, but he just grips me tighter. And he's probably sixty, but his hands and arms are strong, like he's been working hard all his life, and I can see the scrawny muscles over his arms and shoulders cos he's wearing a sleeveless vest. And I can't get free. And then he grabs my boob, really hard, pinching it with all his fingers, like he's trying to hurt me, not even like it's turning him on.

'Meena!' I go. 'Help me!'

So Meena comes straight over, plucks the cigarette out of the bloke's mouth and stubs it out on his bare shoulder.

And he yelps and springs off me, shouting a question at Meena, over and over again. And the boy tries to calm him down. But the granddad shoves him away and walks right up to Meena and keeps shouting at her and pushing her shoulder. And she just shouts back at him and keeps knocking his hand away. And I wanna split them up, but there's blatantly nothing I can do, cos the granddad's too strong for me.

So I run up the little staircase and point out what's happening, to the bloke driving the boat, cos he's the person in charge, and hopefully he'll calm everyone down. And he pulls back this handle next to the steering wheel, and the boat stops moving. And then he walks down the steps and stands in between Meena and the old man, who starts explaining his side of the story in Chinese and pointing to his shoulder, where Meena burnt him. And the boy's joining in, and they're both trying to explain things at the same time to the middle-aged one, who tells them both to shut up, and they do. And then he lets the old man tell his story first.

And then, while the teenage boy's telling his version, the middle-aged bloke lights a cigarette for himself, and I can see the flame from his Zippo bend as he sucks it in. And then he hands the lit cigarette to the old man and quickly grabs Meena in a bear hug. And the old man's walking towards her with the cigarette, which he's gonna stub out onto Meena's skin, as revenge.

And there's nothing I can do to overpower them. And Meena's thrashing around, but she can't get out. And then I remember my 5,800 New Zealand dollars, which might be more than these blokes earn in a whole year. And it's just sitting there in my pocket, and I could just pay them off with some of that, and I'm sure they'd stop. But then I'm thinking, Why should I? Cos Meena's screwed me over so much. And this is the only money I've got in the whole world, and it's just enough to scrape by on for the next year at uni. So I can't start giving it away. Plus, if I show these blokes that I've got a wad of cash, they'll keep making me give them more and more money, till it's all gone.

So I stuff my hand into my pocket and grip the wad of banknotes and leave it there, while the old man stubs his cigarette right into Meena's shoulder. And Meena does this scream that makes my blood feel like it's separating, like sour milk. And then they let her go. And the boy's laughing and jiggling around, really excited. And the old one's looking really smug at Meena. And the middle-aged one seems like he's a mixture of bored and disappointed at us all, like we're children that he's sick of having to look after. And he takes the other two blokes out of the room and shuts the door behind them. And I slide the bolt across to lock it into the doorframe, to lock them out, and I rattle the handle. And it feels like it's locked tight.

And Meena's doing a painful grin and cupping her hand over her shoulder. And then she uncovers it to have a look at the little round burn mark, and I can see it's raw and dark red, and a tiny bit crispy on the surface like burnt meat. And she sits down on the bottom bunk bed. And a piece of me – and I feel horrible even thinking this – but a piece of me feels like Meena got what was coming to her. Like that cigarette burn is her punishment for all the horrible things she's ever done to me. But then I feel so evil for even thinking that, I wanna just give Meena my whole 5,800 dollars, and tell her how absolutely sorry I am, and beg her to forgive me and let her take anything she wants from me. But I can't do that, obviously, cos I need that money to pay for uni.

And I've gotta say something, but I dunno what.

'Jesus Christ,' goes Meena. 'Stop staring at me like that. It's just a cigarette burn.'

'Sorry,' I'm like. 'I just dunno what to do.'

'Why don't you look for a first-aid kit?' she's like.

'I've got some first aid stuff in my suitcase,' I go. And it's a relief to be doing something useful to make Meena feel better. And I look inside these big cupboards at the back of the room, one by one, till I find our suitcase in there. And I unzip it and take out my toiletries bag. And I drip some orangey-brown Dettol onto a ball of cotton wool and dab it onto Meena's burn to disinfect it, and then I stick a plaster over the top of the burn. And I give Meena two paracetamol. And I take out some sweatshirts, to keep us warm. And I give Meena the black one, in case her shoulder bleeds on it, so it won't show the blood. And I ask if she wants to lie down, but she doesn't.

'Do you mind if I go to sleep?' I'm like.

'Yeah, do what you want,' she's like. 'It's fine.'

So I put on my sweatshirt and pull the hood over my eyes, to block out the light. And I kick off my sandals and lie down on the middle bunk, just over Meena's head so I'll be close if she needs anything. And the bunk's made of a big piece of canvas stitched onto two long poles that run along the long edges. And it smells of mud and sweat. And I close my eyes, and the guilt about letting Meena get burnt feels like evil beetles eating away my insides.

CHAPTER SEVEN

And I wake up and there's tubes of dusty light shining in through these circle-shaped windows in the wall. And the engine's stopped, so nothing's vibrating like it usually is. Everything's still. And the boat's bobbing gently up and down. And I can hear footsteps on the wooden floor, above me. And there's an English man shouting. I suppose he's another tourist. And then there's shouting in Chinese.

'No way. I'm not going to pay, after you burnt her arm with a cigarette,' the English bloke's saying. And I think I know his voice.

And there's shouting back in Chinese.

And I can hear Meena going, 'That man held me down, and that other one burnt me.'

More shouting in Chinese.

So I get out of the bunk bed, put my sandals on and go up the steps into the little room on top of the boat. And we're right next to a real island, with this thick forest of palm trees, and blue sea all around, and a white sandy beach, off to the side, and this rocky ledge that the boat's at, tied to a tree trunk.

And the three Chinese blokes are standing on the back of the boat, facing away from me. And there's Meena, holding our suitcase. And next to her – I cannot fucking believe this, but it doesn't surprise me at all – it's Meena's boyfriend, Steve, from that hotel.

He's wearing combat shorts with his shirt off, and his muscles are pretty buffed, and he's got a shiny brown tan. And he looks a bit like an American film star getting old, with this neat short beard and crow's feet around his eyes, and his hair's got some sandy-brown highlights now, probably from the sun. And I'm sort of glad to have him here, now that there's some sort of argument about money. Cos if it was just me and Meena versus the three Chinese blokes, we'd definitely lose. And *I'd* be the one who'd end up having to pay out of my New Zealand dollars. But now that Steve's here, he should be able to stand up for us.

And Steve goes:

'You get on the island, Meena, and I'll sort this out.'

So Meena steps onto the wide plank resting between the boat and this rocky ledge thing we're tied to. But the middle-aged Chinese bloke grabs her by both wrists and pulls her behind the other two blokes, shouting:

'You give dollar! You give dollar! Then you get woman!'

So he can speak English when he wants to, then. And no one's seen me yet, cos they're so focused on each other and I'm hidden inside the boat's little driving room, watching them through the back window.

And Steve picks up my suitcase by the top handle and lobs it onto the rocky ledge thing on the island, where it skids along on its back and comes to a stop. Then he pulls some banknotes out of his pocket and counts out ten of them. And the middle-aged Chinese bloke comes over, still holding Meena by one wrist. And with his other hand he takes the money from Steve and then lets Meena go. And Steve's like:

'Go onto the island now, Meena. I need to discuss something with these gentlemen.'

And he waits for her to walk over the plank onto the island. And then he walks right up to the middle-aged Chinese bloke, pulls out a gun – I think from his pocket – sticks it under the bloke's chin and shoots him through the face. And the bloke's mouth opens up and he slumps down onto the floor. And then the old bloke and the teenage boy sprint towards me, along the right side of the boat to get away from Steve. So I duck round to the left side, to stay hidden. And the boy scampers up onto the roof of the driving room. And Steve catches up to the old bloke, next to the steering wheel and smashes him in the mouth with the handle of the gun, so the bloke falls onto the floor. And then Steve points the gun at his face, and he's about to shoot him. But just before the bang, the boy on the roof rams a heavy plank of wood down onto Steve's head, which makes Steve stagger forward just as he fires the bullet, and his face looks dizzy. And then the boy slams the plank down again, but this time he misses Steve's head and smashes it into his shoulder. And before the boy can hit him a third time, Steve stumbles to the front of the boat, out of reach. Then he turns and shoots the boy, who grabs at his hip, and blood starts soaking his shorts and dripping from between his fingers. And Steve fires more bullets, but the boy's already leaping down onto the back of the boat, where Steve can't see him. And the boy grabs this fat sword thing and quickly chops through the rope tying the boat to the island. Then he disappears down this hatch in the floor and closes it after himself.

And Steve comes round the side, sees me, and puts his finger to his lips to tell me to stay quiet. And he pulls this little rack out of the handle of the gun. But it's empty, and I suppose there's meant to be bullets in there. '*Shit*,' goes Steve under his breath. And he pats down his pockets and goes '*Shit*' again.

And then he cocks the gun, like an American cop in a movie, and he opens the little door behind the plastic table and chairs, and disappears into the room under the floor. And I notice the little round windows down by my feet, showing the boy downstairs. So he might have been looking up here and might've seen that Steve's got no bullets left. And I crouch down so I can get a good look through the windows.

And the boy's standing there holding the sword-thing in front of him. And Steve's pointing the gun at the boy's head. And he's only about thirteen, and he's scared to death. And Steve's waving him to throw the sword on the ground. And he does it straight away, like he's relieved to have someone to tell him what to do. And then Steve walks up to the boy, keeping the gun pointed at his face, and smashes him in the jaw with the gun handle, so the boy falls against the wall. And Steve smashes him in the face over and over again, with the gun, till the boy's going unconscious on the floor. And then Steve lifts the boy's chin so his neck's exposed and slices across it with the long sword-knife thing. And I have to turn away, cos it's so horrific I can't stand looking. And then Steve comes back up to the deck, holding that fat sword thing, which is dirty now. And I'm crying.

'That should take care of it,' goes Steve, pretending to play it cool, even though his voice is trembling now, and he looks like he's about to cry himself and like he's in shock. And he throws the sword thing onto the deck. And he tries to calm himself down with a few deep breaths. And the boat's drifted, like, ten metres away from the island now.

'Okay,' Steve's like, wiping away some tears. 'Okay, well, at least we—'

But he gets smashed forward by another fat plank of wood getting rammed into his back. And it knocks him staggering to the very edge of the boat, and then another blow pushes him right over the side, and he splashes down into the water. And I look up, and it's the old bloke standing on the roof of the driving cabin, holding the plank. And there's blood over the side of his neck, which must be where Steve shot him. And he clambers down and grabs my wrist and drags me over to the steering wheel. And he presses a button that starts up the engines. So I've gotta decide whether I wanna get stuck on the island with Steve, after what he just did, or stuck with this pervy old Chinese bloke on the boat.

And we start chugging away from the dock. And if I don't jump right now, it'll be too far to swim back, so I'll have to stay on the boat with this Chinese bloke, who'll do God knows what to me. He could keep me locked up here for my whole life, if he wanted to.

And he's grabbing my wrist really tight. So I look around for some kind of weapon. But there isn't anything. So I just push my fingers right into the open wound on his neck, which feels like slimy hard strands of spaghetti, which must be his veins, and he literally shrieks. And he grabs his neck and lets go of me. So I run to the edge of the boat and dive off.

CHAPTER EIGHT

And I come up for air and start to breathe in, but a wave forces a massive gulp of disgusting seawater into my mouth, which I accidentally swallow so it sloshes down into my empty stomach, like drinking cold, watery puke. And I push my hair out of my eyes, while I'm treading water in the freezing sea, so I can see the island. And I only got my 50-metres swimming badge at school, which was two lengths. And this island looks at least six lengths away.

So I pull off my sweatshirt, which is weighing me down, and I start swimming towards the island, as hard as I can. But after about fifteen minutes, I'm still no closer. It must be the water pushing me away. And I remember this thing in *Cosmo* about beach safety on holidays. And it said if you get stuck in a current – which this must be – you're supposed to swim sideways along the beach, to go around the current, and then you can swim back to dry land.

So I swim parallel to the island, trying to head towards it, every so often, but the current's still stopping me getting any nearer. And my arms and legs are getting tired, which is making my face get lower in the sea, which makes me keep swallowing more saltwater. And that makes me feel disgusting, and I think it's draining even more energy out of me. And there's a few massive rocks sticking out of the water, up in front. And they're further out from the island than I am now. But at least it'll be somewhere to rest.

So I swim away from the island and over to the first rock. But it's so high and steep I can't even bring my elbows up on it, like you do on the side of a swimming pool. I can only cling onto the side and keep kicking my legs to stay afloat. And all the blood's drained out of my muscles, and I'm getting even colder now that I've stopped swimming forward. And this is what kills you in the water. The cold. I read about it. So I push off the rock with my legs and try to swim towards the island again, but the water pushes me back, and I can't get anywhere. So I cling back onto the big rock. And I've gotta come up with a plan. Cos I'm gonna die of cold if I just stay here. And my feet are numb. And I try to reach down to warm them up with my hand, but when I let go of the rock the waves start carrying me away. And I have to struggle through the water with all my strength to get back and cling on again.

And now I can't feel my feet at all, and my ankles and calves are going numb. So I work my way in a full circle around the rock, to look for somewhere I could climb up, to get out of the cold and have a proper rest. But it's too smooth and steep all the way round to climb up it. And the numbness is spreading up to my knees now. And I can't scrunch up my toes at all. And I bring one foot up to the surface of the water and it looks sort of purpley blue and slightly swollen. And if my legs go numb like that, I won't even be able to swim anywhere, or even stay afloat here.

So I swim around the rock one more time, looking out to see whether there are any other rocks I could swim to, lower rocks that I could climb onto and have a rest. And there are a few sticking out of the water that I can see when I get round the other side. And I can't tell whether I'd be able to climb on top of them or not. And they look even further away from the island. But I've gotta at least try. Cos if I stay here, I'm gonna freeze to death or drown when my legs give out. So I start swimming, and the current's pushing me further and further away from the island. But I keep swimming as hard as I can. And after maybe twenty minutes, I reach another rock, only just sticking out of the water, and sort of wedge-shaped like a door stop. So I pull myself onto it with my hands and elbows and sit on the highest bit, like a mermaid, with the waves washing over my feet.

And I poke each foot with my finger, but I can't feel anything down there at all. And I hope it's not that thing where your blood actually freezes and the nerves permanently die of, like, frostbite, or whatever. And I'm lifting one foot at a time up and rubbing it in both of my hands, trying to get the feeling back. And I just sit there, resting, so I can hopefully get enough energy to have another try for the island.

But after a while, I notice that the rock's getting smaller and smaller, which must mean the tide's coming in. And pretty soon the whole rock's covered in water. So I stand up on the highest point of the rock, with the waves washing over my feet. And then the water's up to my ankles, and it's only gonna keep getting higher.

And there's another rock, even further from the island, but at least it's still sticking out of the water, so I'll be able to have another rest on there. So I turn and face that way and I dive off, but when I hit the water I smash down on something hard. It's like I've just dived onto concrete. And the cold makes this stinging, aching pain stick to the bones in my elbows and wrists and knees and shins. And I'm on this sort of flat ground of rock, under the surface of the water. And I stand up on the rock bed. And the water only comes up as high as my waist, and my knees are completely gashed and so are my arms, with pinkish-red flesh showing, and the skin's white and ragged around the edges of the wounds. So I hobble towards the island, wading through the sea. But the water gets deeper and deeper, till it's up around my neck. And then the ground disappears completely. And there's probably about one swimming pool length left to the island, but no more rocks are sticking up. So I start swimming in that direction and hope for the best. And my legs are numb up to my knees, and my muscles feel like lead.

And after about thirty minutes of slow swimming, I've got no more energy left. I can't keep going like this. So I swap to backstroke, cos that way I can just take deep breaths to stay afloat. And I'm looking down, every now and then. And the water's really clear with white on the bottom, probably sand. And a little way over, the bottom of the sea turns black, which might be more of that rock-bed thing that I'll be able to walk on. So I float on my back and kick through the water. And after

187

another, like, fifteen minutes, I try to stand on the rock, cos it looks really close to my feet. But I sink under and come up spluttering with my belly full of saltwater again. But I think my toe touched the rock, when I was under there. So I swim a bit more. And when I try the next time, I can walk on the rock on tip toes. And as I walk, the rock gets higher and eventually the water's only waist deep. And I'm gonna make it to the land.

And when I'm almost there, and the water's only knee-deep, I get this weird feeling like there's burning tiger-stripes all over my feet and legs. And there's this flesh-coloured blob sliming all around my feet, with long hair floating off it. I think it must be a jellyfish, stinging the fuck out of me, but I can't feel it properly cos I'm so numb. And it's so disgusting and slimy it makes my whole body feel like it's being licked by the most disgusting filthy old men in the world. And I freak out and scream and kick my foot out of the water, which makes the long hair of the jellyfish flick up at my face and then my eyes start screaming in pain. Cos I must have flicked the jellyfish stingers right into them. And my lips are burning and stinging, and so's my whole face. And I can't keep my eyes open at all. So I walk as fast as I can in what I hope's the direction of the island. And the water gets lower and lower, and out of nowhere I smash into a sort of rocky ledge. And when I feel around, the ledge thing's about as high as my chest. So I climb onto it, roll onto my side and lay there in the recovery position they taught us in swimming lessons, with my eyes on fire, like someone's poured acid into them, and the skin all over my face and neck feeling like it's been burnt off by chemicals. And as my legs start warming up in the sun, the stinging gets stronger and stronger, until it feels like they're laying in acid. And I puke up a whole belly-full of pure seawater.

And I try to open my eyes again, but when I do, it's like witches are rubbing fire into them. So I scrunch them tight shut. And I can hear the waves hitting the rocky ledge that I'm on top of. And the pain all over my body's throbbing and screaming in time to the rhythm of the waves, and each time one smashes against the rocks, it's like someone's ripping rows of fishhooks through my flesh, like ploughing a field.

And I puke again, with nothing left to come out, so my stomach's sort of turning itself inside out, and twisting and ripping itself up inside me. And I feel like I want to go to sleep more than anything in the world, but the pain won't let me. And it keeps getting stronger and stronger, and throbbing in time to my pulse and in time to the waves, so I try to make my pulse start beating at exactly the same time as the rhythm of the sea, so that I'll only get one throb of screaming pain every second, instead of two. And I think I've done it, although maybe it's just my imagination. And I'm lying on my side, in case I pass out, so I won't choke on my own vomit.

And I try to open my eyes again but they scream with pain and I can only see a blur. So I shut them again straight away. And my head feels fuzzy, and I start drifting in and out of sleep.

CHAPTER NINE

I wake up and everything sounds different. There's these hooting birds and these birds that sound like evil laughing. And I try to open my eyes again. And they don't sting now, but I can't see anything. And I hold my hand in front of my face and wave it from side to side, and I can't see it. And my brain's scrambling and panicking around, trying to work out what's going on. And I can't feel any sun on my skin. So I think it's night time now. But even in the middle of the night, I should be able to still see my hand, just really dark. So I dunno what's going on. And I won't let myself think that I've actually gone blind.

And I scream out, 'Meena!' as loud as I possibly can. 'Steve!' And then I listen for any sound that might be them. And I do it a few more times, but there's nothing. Just this massive empty island all around.

And I could be miles away from where Meena and Steve are, and my eyes don't work any more, so I can't even look for them. So even if I was passing right next to their tent, or whatever, I wouldn't be able to see it. And my whole body feels like it wants to just stop living, like my heart can't be bothered to beat any more, it's all so hopeless.

And I'm trying to think up a plan, which is hard cos I'm panicking now and my mind's just spinning its wheels at top speed and going nowhere. And it's dehydration that kills you first. And my mouth's completely dry, and I feel that deep thirst, like all the cells in my body are shrivelled up like dusty dried peas. And there's pain digging into my skull, from where my brain's dehydrating. Which isn't surprising after I drank all that seawater and puked so much. So I listen again, to see if I can hear any rivers or waterfalls. But there's nothing, apart from the sea, which is no good cos it's saltwater, which would only dehydrate me more. And I shout out again for Meena or Steve. But nothing.

So I think about what blind people do in England, to get around. They have a white stick. So I get on my hands and knees to feel for a branch I can use. And when my shin touches the ground it stings like a bastard. And I sit down again and feel it, and it's all sticky and there's a massive gouge taken out of it, probably from diving onto that rock-bed thing. And there's all this grit and dirt in it, and slimy strings from the jellyfish still on there that sting my hands when I touch them. So I start trying to wipe the dirt out of it, but it stings so much when I touch it, I decide to wait till I can find some fresh water to wash it with, or at least some clean leaves I can use.

So I get to my feet and start walking. And I lost my sandals ages ago, probably as soon as I jumped off the boat. And when I walk now, it feels like I'm walking on knives. But I've just gotta deal with it, cos who knows if anyone will ever find me if I just sit here.

So I'm walking slowly, feeling in front of me with each foot before I put my weight on it. And I head away from the sound of the sea, in case I fall in. And my foot comes down on something that feels like a long stick. So I bend down and grab it but it's fixed to the floor, so it must be a root.

And I keep walking slowly away from the sound of the waves, patting the ground with each foot before I put it down, with my arms stretched out in front of me like a frankenstein to keep me from walking into a cliff, or whatever. And eventually I find a tree trunk in front of me, and I reach around it, and it feels all hairy. And I feel all the way down, and there's these big rubbery branches sprouting out of its base. So I grab onto one of the thinnest ones, which is about as thick as three fingers. And I wrench it and wrench it, and I can hear these fibres snapping, and after about five more pulls it comes loose. And there's a massive wide rubbery leaf on the end. So I tear away the leafy part, till it's just the branch. And I try it out, sweeping it around in front of me like blind people do in England with their white sticks. And it works quite well. And I can feel when there's a tree coming up in front of me, or a big root on the floor, so I can step over it. And soon I can walk around pretty quickly. Although I still don't know where I'm going.

And I'm walking for probably an hour or two, and I still haven't found any water, just lots more of those hairy trees with the big rubbery leaves. And my shin's got a gouge of pain killing me more and more, and I think I can feel things crawling and wriggling around inside the wound, although that might just be my imagination. But whatever, cos I could still get an infection if I don't clean it, and I doubt there's a hospital here, if it's just a tourist island. And that's how people used to die in the olden days, from basic infections.

So I feel around for another one of those rubbery trees, and when I find one I rest my stick on the ground, roll up my trouser leg, and touch the wound with my fingertips. And it's slightly scabbed over now, it feels like. But I've gotta do this, I've gotta keep this wound clean. So I dig my fingernails into the scabs and peel them off. And I scrape out all the dirt and stones that I can feel. And it shoots waves of pain right through my blood and into my brain. So I have to force myself to keep going. And I tear off a patch of leaf and use that to wipe out as much of the grit as I can. And then I press another patch of leaf onto the open wound, and I'm hoping the leaf might have some kind of natural disinfectant in it. Or maybe even a natural anaesthetic that might kick in later. But the leaf falls off as soon as I stand up, and I can't make it stay. And I think I'd probably have been better off just leaving the wound to scab over and letting my immune system try to fight off the grit and germs and whatever. But it's done now. So I've gotta just deal with it.

And I pat around on the floor and pick up my feeling stick, and I'm off again. And I'm so thirsty now, it's like my blood's turned to dust. And I'm trying my best to walk in a straight line, but it's impossible to tell whether I am or not, cos I can't hear the sea any more, and that was the only way I could tell what direction I was going – when the sea was getting quieter, then I knew I was walking away from it.

And after a bit I find myself kicking through all these round stones as I walk, about the size of cricket balls. And I bend down and pick one up, and it's got this waxy skin, and it smells like leaves but slightly sweet. And maybe it's a type of mango or something. So I try to peel it with my fingernails, but the skin's too tough. So I feel around for a tree root, and I smash the fruit-thing open on there. And inside, it's bitter and leafy smelling, but at least it feels slightly juicy, like the inside of an apple. So I might be able to suck some water out of it, even if it doesn't taste nice. And this is the first watery thing I've found in probably six hours of looking, so I've gotta at least try. And I have a bite, and straight away I spit it out, cos it tastes like shampoo mixed with unripe pear. It's sick. And I spit on the ground to get the taste out of my mouth, which wastes even more water out of my body. And I throw the fruit away and keep on walking. And my head's aching like there's a clamp tightening around it. And after a few more minutes my stomach feels like it's stapled together. And I'm cramping up. And after a few steps more I suddenly puke out just stomach acid. And my stomach's so empty, it has to screw itself up and wring itself out, like a flannel, just to get enough juice to flush out that horrible fruit thing.

And I keep walking, feeling my way with the stick, like an insect with one head-feeler. And the air's getting much hotter, so I'm pretty sure it must be morning again now, which means another night's gone past. And I make a note in my head that it's been two days since I last ate or drank anything, which was that egg sandwich and fizzy orange squash on the boat, Gold Spot, or whatever. And then I went to bed, after that meal, and then the next day is when I jumped off the boat, when I was lying sick for at least a day and night, I think, and I clearly didn't eat or drink anything then. And then, after that, I spent the next day wandering around here, with no food. And so if this is the morning again, that means I've had two days without food or drink. And I think I read that humans can only live for three days without water, cos it's always three things that kill you – three *minutes* without air, three *weeks* without food, or three *days* without water. But that's in normal conditions. And I'm already dehydrated from puking and drinking mouthfuls of the sea, plus I'm ill, plus I've been hot and sweating from the temperature here, and I think I might have a fever as well. So if it's already been two days since my last drink that means I might only have one day left.

And I sit down on the floor, to feel if there might be any berries or puddles or anything – anything I might be able to get water from, that I might have been missing just feeling with my feet and the stick. And it's all mossy and cool down here, and I just wanna lie down and rest my face against the moss to cool off and go to sleep. And on films that always means you've a killer disease, if you wanna sleep – and if you actually do go to sleep, your brain will shut down and you'll die, so on films your friends always make you sing or dance to stop you from nodding off. But there's no one here to stop me. And the ground's so cool and soft and springy, and I'm so tired. And I try to think of some scary things to keep me awake, like what a horrible life I'm gonna have now that I'm blind and that I might die if I go to sleep. But the air's so warm and still, it's like a blanket around me. And the sounds from the trees are like a pattern on the blanket – the squawk of the birds is like star shapes, and this rattling clicking sound is like stripes made out of wooden glitter. And I put my stick down and lay out on the floor, with the cool, soft moss on my cheek, and I just drift away.

CHAPTER TEN

And I wake up and my mouth feels like it's just eaten a bucket of sawdust that's had salt sprinkled over it. And my tongue's like a papery snake skin in a museum. And all I can think about is water. A cool, iced glass of water, poured out in a kitchen in England on a rainy, grey afternoon. And the water will be crystal clear, with frosty condensation covering the outside of the glass that'll show my finger marks like transparent tiny windows. And I'll feel it, fresh and cool down my throat as I drink it, and it'll spread out through my veins and carry this fresh wetness through my whole body, right the way out to my fingertips and toes. And this is just driving me mental, thinking about it. So I try to stop.

And I open my eyes, and I still can't see. But my brain won't even worry about the fact that I'm completely blind and my life's ruined. All I can think about is how thirsty I am. And I feel my face, and it's boiling hot and coated in a layer of sweat that's draining even more water out of me. And all my clothes are soaked in sweat. And it feels like the heat's coming from inside me, not from the sun.

And I've gotta find water. So I sit up and pat the ground till I find my stick. And my leg's aching with this low, deep stinging pain, like someone's slowly going over the actual bone with a sheet of hot sandpaper, and gradually grinding all the nerves out. And the wound feels sticky, but it's crusty in some places. So I suppose it's scabbing over, which means it's healing. So I'm just gonna leave it like that and I hope that I got all the germs out when I cleaned it before, and I'm not gonna touch it again, cos I can't afford to bleed any more and waste any more water out of my body.

And I stand up, but my knees and legs are so shaky that I stagger around and then I literally fall over. And I lie there for a minute, panting. And I try to stand up again, but I can't even get past kneeling up this time, I'm so weak and trembly.

So there's nothing else for it. I start crawling on all-fours. And I shout again, and listen, just in case there's anyone around, cos now it's morning again, I think. But it's quiet apart from the squawking sound from birds above me and these lightweight hissing-rattling sounds that I think are insects. So I'm crawling along the floor, and now that I'm down here, the moss feels so cool under my hands and knees I feel like just eating it, like a horse. Cos there's gotta be at least some water inside it. But that would just make me sick again. So I keep crawling.

And after about half an hour, the soft mossy ground fades away into hard stone, with sharp cracks and splits in it that kill my knees. And sometimes there's bony tree roots that dig into my kneecaps so painfully that when I get to a patch like that, with lots of roots, I have to drag myself along on my side.

And I realise that I should look for some sharp stones, to help

198

me open pieces of fruit, if I can find any. So as I'm crawling along over the rocky ground, I feel around and pick up a pointy stone about as big as my hand and stuff it into my pocket.

And I keep crawling. And after a while the air starts to smell like garlic. So I'm thinking that as long as it's an edible plant, I've gotta be able to get at least some water out of it. And the garlic smells strongest from over my left shoulder, so I turn and crawl in that direction until my hands walk onto this patch of long thin leaves sticking up, like giant grass. And I dip my face down into it, and it smells just like fresh garlic. And I tear off one of the long thin leaves, but it's covered in this crusty stuff, which I lick with just the tip of my tongue, and it tastes chalky and bitter. It's probably some kind of mould or maybe bird droppings, or something. But whatever it is, I don't think I should eat it, cos it might be poisonous or make me sick again. And I feel around all over the patch of garlic, but it's all covered in that crusty stuff. And it's not even real garlic, anyway, cos real garlic is like a little fat ball, not leaves. So this is probably just a trick. So I just leave it alone.

And I feel myself getting even weaker, and my whole body's burning up and it's covered in sweat. And now my arms are getting shaky as I crawl along, and there's this burning pain in the middle of my chest. And the pain turns into cramps, like someone's stuck a big fork into my insides and is twisting them round like spaghetti. So I lay down on my side and curl up and hug my knees into my chest, to try to squeeze the pain away. And my whole body's damp with sweat, which is draining more and more water out of my blood. And I just keep getting hotter and hotter, and all I wanna do is sleep, but I can't cos I've gotta find water. Cos this is day three with nothing to drink. But I feel like I've been awake for ten years, and I've gotta sleep now. So I just lay down right where I am. And I'm so tired, I can't even be bothered to get into a comfortable position, I just close my eyes and sleep.

CHAPTER ELEVEN

And I'm drifting in and out of sleep, so it's impossible to keep track of time, or even how many days are going past. But I think it's four days since I drank anything, cos I think I remember three night times of cooler air. And I dunno where my body's finding the water, but my clothes and hair are still drenched in sweat. I suppose my body's draining it out of my eyeballs and my liver and the last few places that are still wet inside me.

And I've gotta keep looking for water. So I force myself to get up on all-fours again, when I can get a bit of energy together, and keep crawling. Cos there's gotta be something to drink around here somewhere, or some fruit trees or coconut trees. And I keep crawling and crawling, for hours, with nothing. Until, in the distance, I can hear a sort of shushing sound. So I stop moving. And I listen hard. And underneath the sound of those squawking birds, it's a shushing, rushing sound, from far away, which might be a river. So I crawl in that direction. And I'm trying not to get my hopes up. Cos even if it is water, it might be seawater, which I can't drink. But it's impossible not to get excited about it. And I can't stop thinking about having a massive delicious long drink of cool fresh water out of this sparkling clear stream and the cool water trickling down my throat and into my stomach.

So I'm crawling towards the shushing sound. And the hard rocky ground's getting warmer underneath my hands and knees, and the sun's baking down on my back stronger and fiercer, so I suppose I'm coming out of the trees and into open ground. And soon the rock's so boiling hot from the sun, it's burning my hands and my knees through my combat trousers. And I try to force myself to keep going, cos I can hear the water now, with these splashing gurgling sounds as well as the shush of the stream. But the ground's literally burning my skin, like a hot saucepan. So I have to turn back the way I came.

And my hands and knees and toes are scalded from that boiling rock. So I have to go right back into the jungle where the rock's cooler, and I blow on them to soothe them a bit. And I've gotta find something to make into, like, gloves and knee protectors to shield them from the burning hot rock floor, so I can crawl over it to reach that river.

So I roll up the legs of my trousers, so there's a fat roll around each knee. Then I take off my shirt, so I'm just wearing my tank top underneath, and I wind the arms of the shirt round my hands, to use as pads. And I crawl back over the rocky floor towards the sound of the river, not letting my feet touch the ground at all, and just balancing on the points of my knees and my hands wrapped in the fabric of my shirt. And I crawl over the rock as quickly as I can towards the sound of the water. And it's getting louder and clearer. And I can start to even hear individual splashes. It sounds like the water's splashing down into a pool, like it's a little waterfall. And the sun's blazing hot. And I've never felt it full on like this, cos I've been in the shade the whole time, in the jungle. And it's beating down on me, heating up my hair. And the pads of fabric under my hands and knees are starting to get hot as well. But I keep crawling.

And then my head smacks into a solid wall of stone. And I stop. And feel out in front of me, but the wall thing's too hot to touch properly, cos it must have been in the blazing sun all day. And I just pat it quickly a few times, so I can feel it but not leaving my hand there long enough to get burnt. And the rockwall goes up higher than I can reach from kneeling down. But the sound of the water's crystal clear, and it sounds like it's just above me. So I crawl along the bottom of the wall for a while, hoping it'll get lower, so I can reach the water. But it stays just as high all the way along. And I can't stand up, cos my legs are still shaky and weak, and I can't risk losing my balance here and falling over where I could crack my head open on the stone. So I unwind the shirt from around my hands and whip it up the stone wall thing.

And I whip the shirt up there a few times. And it's not catching. But on about the sixth or seventh time, the cuff comes back wet! So it must have dipped in the water. And I hold it to my forehead, to cool me down. Cos heat's blasting all over me from the sun. And it's bliss as the water trickles down over my face and neck. And when it gets to my lips it tastes salty, but I tell myself that's just from the sweat of my forehead.

And I flick the shirt again, as high as I can. And it comes back, after a few times, with half the arm soaked. And – this is pretty skanky, but I don't care, cos I'm gonna die otherwise – I put the wet sleeve in my mouth and I suck the water out. But it's fucking saltwater! I can't believe it. It's only gonna dehydrate me more.

And it's breaking my heart in half. But I might as well wash my hands and face, and cool off, even if I can't drink it. So I kneel up again. And my head feels like it's collapsing from the sun baking down on it and the fever inside it. And I keep whipping my shirtsleeve up there. And now that the sleeve's wet, it's easier to direct, cos the end bit's heavier. And I can feel when it dips in the water, cos it sort of sticks for a second. And I wring out the wet sleeve over my hands. Then I do it twice more and wring it out over my arms. And then I whip it up there again and squeeze it out over my face. But when I feel the water on my lips, it doesn't taste as salty as it did the first time. So I whip it up there again and wring a bit more water into my mouth. And it definitely isn't the thick salty taste of seawater. This is just normal water with a bit of salt in it, and for some reason, it's less salty than last time.

So I keep whipping the shirt up there, and then wringing out the sleeve and dabbing my tongue on it. And after doing that about fifteen more times, it's fresh water! And I suck in a whole mouthful of it. And, oh my God, it tastes amazing. And I can literally feel it trickling down my throat and into my stomach, just like I imagined it. And even though it's warm – I don't care. It's delicious. So I suck it dry. Flick it up there. Suck it dry. And I do that probably about five times in a row.

And I'm trying to think why it's turned from saltwater into

fresh water. And for a minute I really do wonder whether this is some kind of magic river that becomes fresh water if you want it badly enough. But then I think harder, and I realise that I was wearing this shirt in the sea. So I suppose the fabric of the shirt got salty then, which made this water taste salty. But now I've rinsed it clean, so the water tastes fresh.

And when I've drunk as much as I can, I feel like I've gotta go to sleep again. So I force myself to have about three more mouthfuls of water. And then I wring out the shirt over my trousers and tank top to cool me off. And I wrap the shirt round my hands again and crawl back to the shady floor of the jungle, where I lay down on my side, and scrunch up my damp shirt for a pillow and fall straight to sleep.

CHAPTER TWELVE

And I wake up with something wet brushing over my cheek. I think it's a wet leaf or something, so I reach up and I feel the furry face of some kind of animal. So I fucking freak out and scream my head off. And the animal does this evil screeching hissing growl, like *whhhkkkkhhh*. And I scramble to my feet, and my legs are shaky and weak, like one of those baby cows who's just been born. And I stand up against a tree. And I've gotta get away. So I start stumbling towards the sound of the water, as fast as I can, with my hands out in front of me, to let me hold onto each tree as I come to it. And all the fear's given me energy. And when I get onto the rock floor where the trees stop, the rock's still scalding hot, but I can sense that animal coming after me. So I run out onto the scalding hot rock, but I only let each foot touch the ground for a second, so it never gets a chance to properly burn me. And I follow the sound of the water, with my arms out in front, till I reach the stone wall. And while I'm hopping from foot to foot, I feel up to the top of the wall, which is only just higher than the top of my head. So I jump up and grip this flat ledge at the top with my elbows. And I shuffle up till it's right under my armpits and then – it takes a few tries – but I swing one of my feet up. And then I roll over, so I'm lying on top of the ledge, and I roll over one more time, and I fall completely into this pool of water, which is warm like a bath and flowing gently over me. And the bottom's covered in smooth rounded pebbles. And there's a rushing, splashing sound a little way off, which I think is a waterfall.

And it's so relaxing and safe in here. And I lean my head to the side and have a drink of the water, which is crystal clean and warm. And then I rest my head back and feel the water flowing over me and washing the dirt and salt off my body and out of my clothes, and carrying it away. And I slide down so that just my face is sticking up above the surface of the stream. And I comb my fingers through the knots in my hair and pull out bits of twigs and leaves and mud. And the water carries it away from me. And I just lay there in the river for probably two hours. And it must be nighttime, cos it's getting cooler, and the air's getting still and thicker.

And now that I've found water, I'm not gonna die. Not of dehydration, anyway. But what about food, I'm thinking? Cos I can't live off water forever. So I've gotta keep moving forward to find something to eat, or I'll starve to death. And I decide that the best plan is to follow this river, cos that way I'll always be able to have a drink from it, plus hopefully I'll find some fish swimming around that I can catch, or some fruit trees growing on the banks or some people living near the river who can help me.

So I get to my feet and I start walking against the flow of the water, cos the other way will just lead back to the sea, which is the last place I wanna go. And the water's about knee deep. But after about twenty steps, the river's filled with all these massive boulders and water spraying in my face and this loud gushing splashing from behind them. And I can't start climbing over boulders, now that I'm blind, cos it's too dangerous. And I can't get round either side of them, cos it's a steep drop on the left, back to the rocky floor where I came from, and a steep wall of rock on my right. So this must be a little ledge near the bottom of a mountain or something. So my only option is to climb back down onto the rock floor and try to walk along keeping near to this river.

So I drink as much water as I possibly can, and then I lower myself down onto the big wide rock floor, where I came from. But I forgot how scalding hot it is on my feet, especially now that they're all soft from basically having had a long bath in that river. So I hop from foot to foot and then I start leaping over the ground, heading for the shady trees. But I'm running and running, and I can't find them. And my feet are getting more and more burnt. So I decide to try to climb back into the river, to just cool them off. But now I can't hear the water any more. And I'm feeling dizzy. And I have to keep running, or my feet are going to burn, but they're scalding anyway. And I've got no idea what direction I came from. And I feel myself getting lightheaded.

And I wake up and I'm lying on the floor. And my head hurts like crazy. And my skin's glowing in scalding pain like sunburn. So I stand up again. But I feel like my brain's dissolved, I'm so dizzy. And I feel myself falling over, and I know it's going to smash my skull, but it's sort of happening in slow motion, and as I fall, I can feel myself about to pass out, which just feels like a relief.

CHAPTER THIRTEEN

I wake up, and I'm in some sort of bed. And I open my eyes. But I still can't see.

'Hello?' I'm like. But no one says anything back.

And it's quiet and closed-in feeling, so I'm indoors, I think. And I think I'm still on the island, cos the air's warm and humid. And I'm guessing this is a hospital. Although it must be in a village, or something, cos it sounds like there's chickens clucking outside, and a sheep or something, like, bleating, and then it's Steve and Meena's voices talking to each other, in the distance. And I'm about to call out to them. But I stop myself. Cos once they know I'm awake, they'll just start lying to me about what's going on. But if I pretend I'm still unconscious, then I can secretly listen in to them talking the truth. So I try to hear what they're saying, but I can't make out any words, cos they're too far away. So I keep my eyes shut and just wait, hoping they'll come closer to me and keep talking. But instead, their voices just drift away and disappear.

And I wait for hours and hours, and finally I hear footsteps coming into the room.

'All right, mate?' goes Meena's voice. And the mattress tilts and creaks as she sits down on the edge of the bed. And I pretend to be asleep.

And I feel her fingers rubbing something wet and warm and salty onto my lips. It must be soup. And then she takes her hand away, and there's a teeny *plip* sound, which must be her dipping her fingers into a soup bowl. And then she slides them inside my mouth, so I get the salty, meaty soup taste. I suppose she's been feeding me like this to keep me alive but to stop me choking on real food, while I've been unconscious. And she keeps dipping her fingers in the soup and sliding them into my mouth, which is watering like mental, cos this is the first food I've tasted in probably, like, five days. And she gradually slides her fingers further and further along my tongue, until they're going almost to the back of my throat.

And she does that for about ten minutes. And when she's finished she lets out a big sigh. And I hear a metal bowl clinking down on a stone or tile floor.

'Right then,' goes Meena. 'Let's see if Steve's been a naughty boy, shall we.' And she pulls down the sheet that's covering me, and I realise that I'm not wearing any clothes at all. And she lifts my ankles apart so my legs are spread out, like a Y. And I can feel her eyes burning into my, like, private parts.

'Good boy,' she goes, putting my legs together and pulling the sheet up. 'Good boy, Steven.'

And I dunno what she thinks she's seen down there. But blatantly she thinks she can tell something important from just looking at me. And I suppose it's good that Meena checked, cos

I wouldn't know what to look for. And then I hear her pick up the metal bowl from the floor, and her footsteps go out of the room.

And I wait around all day, and I feel the air get cooler and damper, so I know it's evening. And Meena comes back and dips more soup into my mouth with her fingers. And then I wait around bored out of my mind for another few hours. And I'm just thinking that Meena and Steve have probably gone to bed for the night, when I hear voices outside.

'—okay, so I'll reinforce the chicken coops tomorrow,' Steve's going. 'We can't afford any more escapes.'

'And let's start eating the eggs again,' Meena's like, as they walk into the room.

'That's not an option,' goes Steve. 'We have to hatch them all.'

'Nothing's hatched, though,' goes Meena. 'We might as well just boil them.'

'Are you questioning me?'

'No,' Meena's like.

'Because that's what it sounds like,' goes Steve.

'Honestly, I wasn't questioning you,' goes Meena.

And she waits, but Steve doesn't say anything. And there's the sound of her kissing him.

'Are you angry, babe?' goes Meena. 'Baa-aabe. Babe, come here. Don't be angry.'

'Remember what happened to Amanda,' goes Steve.

'No, don't talk about her,' Meena's pleading. 'I promise I won't question you again. I promise.'

'Get ready,' goes Steve in this moody voice.

And then I feel the sheet being pulled back and the mattress suddenly slopes down next to me, with the weight of someone getting into the bed and then shuffling over till they're touching me, with these smooth soft legs, so it must be Meena. And then the bed creaks as someone else gets in, which must be Steve. And it's good that I'm pretending to be unconscious still, cos this will let me know what on earth they've been doing to me while I've been passed out.

And I feel Meena turn away from me. I think she's wrapping her arms and legs around Steve.

'I was thinking, babe,' she goes, 'that maybe we should change the gold into American dollars. Cos then it'll be easier to spend, if we get in trouble.'

'That's the worst possible thing we could do, you fucking imbecile,' goes Steve. 'We've been through this: dollars are constantly losing their value, whereas gold tracks inflation.'

'But you can't spend gold in a shop, can you.'

'Meena, are you questioning me?'

'No, I'm—'

'Are you questioning me?' Steve's like.

'No,' goes Meena.

'Good,' Steve's like.

And then I hear the little suction sound of Meena kissing Steve, and after a little while the sheets are being pulled around, so they must be starting to, like, mess about over there. And then I feel this sort of fast shaking, like someone scratching themselves really quickly, but I know it isn't that, it's something dirty. And I wanna keep pretending to be unconscious, but I can't. Cos this is making me feel like I'm actually gonna be sick, and my whole body's telling me to get away from this, to stop me from having to, like, witness them having sex with each other. So I try to say something, to make them stop. But my throat's so dry it just comes out as a croak. So I swallow and try again.

'What's going on?' I go.

And Meena screams and her body jerks like she's had an electric shock.

'Jesus Christ,' goes Steve.

And Meena's panting, like she's just done a ten-mile race.

'You're not planning to die, then, I take it,' goes Steve, to me.

'Not really,' I'm like.

'That's the spirit,' he goes. 'How are you feeling?'

'Pretty weak,' I'm like. 'But all right.'

'Good,' he's like, 'because everybody here works. So you'd better build up your strength.'

'Where are we?' I'm like.

'In the Garden of Eden,' he goes.

'Yeah. But, like, where exactly, on a map?' I ask him.

'You don't need to know.'

'Are we still on the island, though?' I'm like.

'Bloody hell,' goes Steve, 'you really are clueless, aren't you. Yes, we're still on the island.'

'It's amazing here,' Meena chips in. 'There's like nine different beaches.'

'But what's actually going on?' I go. 'Is it a sort of holiday camp, or something?'

And they both start laughing in my face, which makes me feel like an idiot. I've gotta stop saying stupid stuff, so they'll stop doing that.

'No, I own this island,' goes Steve. 'We live here.'

'During your holidays?' I'm like.

'No, I bought it,' Steve's like. 'And we're living here forever.'

'And when's the next boat coming?' I'm like.

'There aren't any boats,' goes Steve. 'Those Filipino gentlemen were the only people who knew we were here. And we had to shoot them in self-defence – remember that, Meena? How they were trying to kill us?'

'Yeah,' goes Meena, 'they'd have killed us if we didn't do something.'

'Well, anyway. They're dead now, so no one else is coming.'

'So how can I get off the island?' I'm like.

'Swim,' goes Steve.

And I laugh, to try to turn that into a joke. 'Seriously, though,' I'm like. 'When can I go home?'

'You can't,' goes Steve. 'We haven't got a boat. No one's coming to see us. And no one knows we're here.'

'So it's just you, me and Meena?' I'm like.

'Yup,' goes Steve.

'So what the fuck am I doing here, then?' I'm like. 'Whose idea was that?'

'You won't swear in my presence,' goes Steve. 'Do you understand?'

'What?' I go.

'Say your question again, but without swearing.'

'You just swore,' I'm like. 'You just said "bloody".'

'I'm in charge here,' goes Steve. 'Now rephrase your question without the swearing.'

And I suppose it's worth changing the way I talk, just this once, to get the information.

'What am I doing here, then?' I go. 'Whose idea was that?'

'Meena's,' goes Steve. 'She thought it would be nice to have a friend to keep her company.'

And my mind's scrabbling around, looking for some words to even begin to say what an evil, evil person Meena is, ruining my entire life, so she can have a mate to hang about with. But it's like my mind can't even grab onto anything, it's like trying to run up a hill covered in loose stones that won't let you get any kind of grip at all, it's such a bizarre thing that's happening to me. And before I can get myself to speak, Meena starts talking:

'You're gonna love it, here,' she goes. 'Plus you can do my work for me, so I can spend more time at the beach.' And then she laughs it off. 'Nah, mate. I'm only joking.'

'No way,' I go, with my blood boiling. 'I ain't doing nothing.'

'*I'm not doing anything*,' goes Steve. 'Say it like that.'

'What is he talking about?' I go, to Meena.

'He just likes it when we speak correctly,' Meena's like. 'He doesn't want his children growing up talking like commoners.'

'What children?' I go. 'I thought it was just us.'

'Obviously there's no children yet,' Meena's like, 'but—'

'All right, I get it,' I go, cutting her off, cos I don't want to have this conversation, which is basically gonna lead them into explaining how Steve's gonna start sleeping with me. And I know that they expect me to start freaking out that they're

215

holding me prisoner, or whatever. But to be honest, I don't fully believe anything they're saying. Cos they've both lied to me in the past and tricked me. And I can't believe they've kidnapped me onto a desert island for the rest of my life. That's just gotta be another lie.

And the conversation goes quiet. And I think we're going to sleep. And I realise I haven't told them yet that I've gone blind. But there's no way to fit it into the conversation now. It would just sound weird if I just came out and said it.

And then I feel Meena moving away from me and climbing on top of Steve. And the bed starts rocking. And Steve's breathing really hard, with a bit of voice bleeding through each time he exhales. And Meena's doing the same thing, but with a higher voice. So I cough really loud, to let them know I'm still awake, so they'll stop. But the bed keeps rocking. So I shuffle to the edge and let my feet fall onto the floor. And I try to stand up, but my legs collapse under me, and I fall onto the ground. So I drag myself over the floor and work my way along the wall until I feel a doorway. And I drag myself out of the room and onto a dirt floor, outdoors. And I'm getting covered in dry mud, but at least I don't have to listen to Meena and Steve any more. But then straight away, I hear light footsteps and Meena's voice is like:

'Steve says that you've gotta come back.'

'Have you, like, finished?' I ask her.

'Obviously not,' goes Meena. 'How long do you think it takes, you muppet?'

'Well, why does he want me to come back, then?' I go. 'That's disgusting.'

216

'Oh, just do it, mate,' goes Meena. 'It's only one night. And he'll force you to come back, anyway, if you say no. Plus he'll punish you.'

'For God's sake,' I'm like. 'Gimme a hand, then.'

And Meena lifts me under my armpits and helps me stand up with the tiny bit of muscle I've got left in my legs. And she brushes some dirt off me and says how slim I look and how it's gonna be amazing living on this island and how I'm her best friend in the world.

And she walks me back and helps me to lay down in the bed. And she pulls the sheet over me.

And then there's a bit of fumbling around, and they start doing whatever again. And I thought I'd feel completely disgusted having to listen to them and feel the bed rocking and the smell of skin and sweat. But I just feel lonely. I feel like there's no one here for a million miles in any direction. And there's a massive deep hole dug out inside me, like a massive deep well where they get coal out of, and I'm lost at the bottom of it.

CHAPTER FOURTEEN

And I wake up the next day. And I can hear that Meena and Steve are gone, cos it's completely quiet in the room. And I wrap my left hand around my right arm, and it's so thin I can touch the rough texture of the bones through my skin. And I just lie there, feeling my muscles and flesh rotting away.

And I keep hearing that cock-a-doodle-doo sound, from outside, like chickens do in cartoons. And I open my eyes and everything's completely black, except there's something bright out of the corner of my eye. So I turn my head, and there's a blurry bright oblong, which must be the door. It's like a sudden jolt of happiness. Cos now I can see a tiny bit instead of nothing. And outside, this *chip-chip-chip* sound starts, like someone chopping at a tree trunk.

And there must be some way to escape off this island. Maybe I could build a raft in secret, or something. And the best thing I can do is get the maximum information out of Steve and Meena, cos that'll help me think up a plan to escape. Plus I've gotta get strong again so I can properly explore and look for a hidden boat or a mobile phone or a gun or anything that'll help. So I dangle one of my legs over the edge of the bed and put a bit of weight on it, with my foot on the floor, doing a sort of press-up with my leg. Cos I'm not strong enough to stand or walk. And I do seven of those, till my leg muscles are tired. And then I wriggle over to the other side of the bed and do seven with my other leg. And I might as well make my arms stronger as well. So I roll onto my stomach and try to do a normal press-up. And even though I can't even lift myself up off the bed, just pushing makes the muscles work, and after three tries my arms are knackered. And then I do one sit-up and my stomach muscles are done in. And my whole body aches, which means it's getting stronger.

And I shout for Meena, hoping I can talk some info out of her. But she doesn't come. So I just lie around, drifting into these deep sleeps that I can feel are healing my muscles and my heart and my blood, and whatever.

And I think it's lunchtime when Meena finally comes in.

'All right, mate?' she goes, in her fake friendly voice. 'How are you doing?'

And I can see a blurry dark smudge where she is.

'I think I need the loo,' I'm like.

'Come on, then,' she's like, and she helps me sit on the edge of the bed. 'You'll have to use this,' she goes, and she puts a plastic washing-up bowl into my hands. 'I'll be back in a few hours to give you dinner,' she's like, and she starts to walk out of the room.

'Is there any lunch?' I go. Cos even though I'm not hungry, I need the food to help me get stronger.

'You slept through lunch, so there won't be any food till

dinnertime,' she goes. 'I gave you soup while you were sleeping, though.'

'Please,' I go. 'Just bring me anything. Coconuts or whatever.'

'I'll see what I can do,' she's like, and she's just a dark shadow moving over the blackness of the room as she leaves.

And I wriggle to the edge of the bed and grip the big plastic washing-up bowl between my feet and wee into it. Then I lay back down and wait till Meena comes back with a plate of food which I start eating with my fingers, and it's cold, boiled cubes of this stringy potato-type vegetable. And Meena's leaving again.

'What's it like outside?' I go, cos even if I can't get out, I wanna start collecting information.

'It's like a holiday,' she goes.

'But what does it look like?' I ask her.

'I just told you,' she goes, getting pissed off. 'It's like living on holiday. Is there something wrong with your ears?' So I just let it go, cos she'll only keep getting nastier.

And I try another way to get info. 'What are you and Steve doing today?'

'Crops. The goats. The chickens,' she goes. 'Fishing. Work on the buildings. You know, like, normal stuff.'

'What kind of buildings are there?' I ask her.

'Everything,' she's like.

'Like houses or shops, or like what are we talking about?' I go.

'Are you trying to undermine me?' she goes.

'No, of course not,' I tell her.

'You better not be,' she's like, with this hard voice, trying to sound like Steve. 'Or that'll be the last food you ever get.'

'I'm just asking a question.'

'Whatever,' she goes. And her shadow moves into the bright doorway, and then she's gone. But I don't care, cos I've got my plan to focus on now, which is to get strong, and explore the island, and get as much info as possible out of Meena and Steve, and then find a way to escape. And I finish all the cubes of that stringy potato-stuff, even though it tastes grim and I'm not hungry, cos I need all the extra energy I can get. And I'm glad I did those exercises, cos now I feel the tissues inside my muscles breaking down and building up more powerful, underneath my skin, like a really slow, really weak version of the Incredible Hulk.

CHAPTER FIFTEEN

And I do my exercises each day. And Meena brings me food. And they give me a T-shirt and shorts to wear. And at night Steve sleeps in the middle of the bed, between me and Meena, and they have sex twice – but Steve never touches me – and then we all fall asleep.

And after a week my eyes are back to normal, and I'm strong enough to walk around the bed, as many times as I want, although I haven't been outside yet, cos I don't want Meena and Steve to know how strong I am, cos this way I might be able to escape while they're not expecting it. And I can't see much from the doorway, cos there's a tall wooden fence in front of the door, woven out of sticks, but I've peeked round the side of it a few times, and there's an open square of land there, with a long chicken cage on the right, and on the left there's a brick building – maybe another bedroom, like this one – with an open stone fireplace next to it. And opposite me, on the fourth side of the square it's just jungle.

And our room's got old scuffed lino tiles on the floor, which are torn up near the door, showing the concrete underneath. And the roof's made of these neat rows of branches of long spiky leaves, held up by this frame of wooden planks. And the walls are made of big grey bricks, and not painted, and there's dried cement oozing out between them, like jam in a Victoria sponge cake. And there's the big bed that we all sleep in. But there's no other furniture, except for a wooden crate turned on its side with five porno mags inside, which are all full of disgusting pictures, of like two women doing it with one bloke. And the words are in a language I don't know. But I keep flicking through them, cos I'm bored out of my mind all day, and there's nothing else to do.

'Enjoying yourself?' goes Steve, while I'm looking through them one afternoon. I didn't hear him come in.

'No, I was just looking for something to read,' I'm like, and I can feel my face getting hot. 'I wasn't . . .' but I stop myself, because whatever I say, it'd have to be about sex. And he leaves me hanging and squirming for about a minute trying to think of an excuse, cos he doesn't believe I was just bored. 'Can I have a look around the island?' I'm like, to change the subject. 'I'm pretty strong now.'

'All right, then,' Steve goes. 'I'll show you the basics.' So I follow him out of the room, and I'm slightly gutted, cos that was supposed to be a secret, how strong I am now. But most of all I'm excited, with my blood pumping extra fast in my neck, cos this is my first chance to properly look for ways to escape. And we walk around the woven wooden fence in front of the door. And I'm out in real sunlight for the first time for ages. It feels like honey on my skin. And the sunlight pinches the backs of my eyeballs. And the ground's browny-orange mud, which is so hard and hot, it burns my feet, so I have to walk on shadows, where it's cool.

And it's jungle all around, except for the little square courtyard I'd seen before. And the big chicken cage on the right side is almost empty, except for one chicken lying on the floor, while two others peck at him. And behind me, there's the little shack where we sleep, with no windows and made of grey concrete blocks, and that roof made of rows of palm tree branches laid over a wooden frame, which I suppose stops the shack getting too hot in the sun. And on the left side of the square there's another concrete shack, just the same as the one we sleep in, except it's got a metal door with a fat metal bar locked over it. 'Who lives in there?' I'm like.

'That's a store room,' goes Steve. 'No one lives there.' And in front of it, there's a brick fireplace and a concrete water-well – big enough for a person to fall down – with a white plastic bucket covered in dirty scratches, on a long chain.

'Can we have a look inside the store room?' I'm like. Cos there might be, like, guns in there, to help me escape, or keys to a boat.

'No,' goes Steve, in his way of talking that tells you no one's allowed to argue with him. 'Let's go and visit Meena.'

And we walk along this path through the jungle till we come out in a little clearing, with two dirty white goats in a metal cage that looks like an actual prison cell for humans, the bars are so thick, and it's just about as tall as I am. And just seeing it makes my stomach lurch, for some reason, like I'm standing on a rooftop and looking over the edge.

'Meena's down here, working on the crops,' goes Steve. And

I follow him down another path, off to the left of the clearing, and we come out in an open patch about twice as big as the penalty box on a football pitch, made of this sandy-looking mud, with jungle around it on all four sides.

'This is our crop field,' he goes.

'This?' I go, looking around, and seeing a few tiny shoots, here and there, all dried up and brown, and then the rest of the field's just dried mud covered in, like, a massive spider web of long cracks. 'This isn't gonna feed anyone, mate,' I'm like, and I hear how rude that sounds, so then I say: 'But I suppose the plants just haven't come up yet.'

'This isn't food, you stupid fucking imbecile,' goes Steve. 'What kind of shit-brained stupid comment is that?' he's like, shouting right into my face, with his whole body getting angry. And I'm scared he's gonna batter me. But he just walks off along the side of the field, so I have to follow after him, to try to calm him down.

'I'm sorry, I didn't realise,' I'm like. 'I thought it was food, when you said crops.'

'We're harvesting the strong plants that survive, and next year we'll plant their seeds, you stupid girl, and after a few years we'll have a strain that's suited to this island,' he's like, still walking away from me at full speed and talking in this cold, hard voice, and I have to jog to keep up with him. And he has this way of making me feel like I've done something terrible, even though I haven't. And it fills me with dread. And I know that I shouldn't be giving in to it and acting scared of him, cos that'll only give him more power over me. But I can't stop myself, cos I truly am

225

scared of what he might do, or what he might do if I don't at least *act* scared like he wants me to.

And he stops suddenly and has a look round the field with his hand making a shade over his eyes. 'This is a decades-long project we're embarking on, here,' he's like. 'Everything's done for the long-term.'

And I wish I could lock him inside that goat cage and torture him till he tells me how to get off the island. But I'd have to lock Meena inside it as well, otherwise she'd just let him straight out. But this is all just whatever, cos I'm blatantly never gonna do that.

And Steve's looking over at the jungle, round the edges of this field. And eventually he sees what he's looking for, and then he walks off without me, so I have to run to catch up with him again, and I follow him around the edge of the field, and eventually I can see Meena laying on her back on the mossy jungle floor, just next to where the field ends, with one hand under her head, like a pillow, and one hand on her tummy.

'I've got a surprise for you,' goes Steve.

And Meena's got her eyes closed, and she doesn't even bother to open them.

'Is it a packet of twenty Bensons and a lighter?' she's like.

'Better than that,' Steve's like. And then he turns to me, and nods, like he's saying it's my turn.

'All right, Meena?' I go.

And she opens one of her eyes and sees me. 'All right, mate. How you feeling?' she goes. 'You're back on your feet then.'

'Yeah, I'm pretty strong now,' I go.

'Come and sit down here,' goes Meena, sitting up and crossing her legs. And I can sense this is something her and Steve have planned out. And me and Steve both sit down next to her, so we're in a sort of circle, like a children's party game. And Meena sits there watching Steve, and waiting for him to start talking.

'Now, I'm in charge here, obviously,' he's like, 'but even so, there are some principles that we all subscribe to.'

And Meena's half listening in, like she's heard this a million times before, and she's picking at the little round blisters where her fingers join the palm of her hand. But I've gotta focus on what Steve's saying, cos they're acting like it's important, so I have to play along.

'And I don't know if you've ever seen the statute books in England . . . ?' he goes.

'No,' I'm like.

'Well, they're virtually incomprehensible unless you have a law degree. And even then, there are so many laws, it's impossible to know them all. So we've done away with all that. And our laws – well, mine and Meena's, and yours if you choose to subscribe – can be summarised in just one word: love.'

'Okay,' I'm like.

'It's as simple as that,' goes Steve. 'So, for example, no matter what kind of disagreements we may have: at the end of each day, we'll always end in a state of love. And any rudimentary rules we might have can always be changed, if it's done in a loving way.'

And I can't really argue with that, although I'm sure it's some kind of trick.

'And remember when Meena defended you against that

Filipino sailor, while you were sailing over here? That was love,' goes Steve. 'It's pretty basic, really. So would you like to join our community and subscribe to our principles?'

'Yeah, I suppose so.'

'Is that a yes or a no?'

'A yes,' I go. And I suppose it is sort of exciting to be starting our own country, with our own rules and everything.

'Do you wholeheartedly agree with the principle of love, as a guiding force? Because I don't want anyone who isn't fully committed. So if you aren't sure, now's the time to say so.'

'No, I'm wholeheartedly saying yes.'

'Good. We'll have a dinner to celebrate, this evening,' goes Steve, standing up and brushing off the back of his shorts. 'I'll try to catch some butterfish, or a rainbow fish. What do you feel like?'

And I've never heard of either of them. So I go, 'Butterfish,' cos that sounds tastiest.

'Wise choice,' he goes, and he gives me a little wink. 'All right,' he's like, 'I'm going fishing. I'll leave you ladies alone.'

'Can I come with you?' I go, cos I wanna see as much of the island as possible, to keep looking for ways to escape. 'I could help you catch the fish.'

'No. It's dangerous there,' he's like. 'Why don't you stay here and have a rest?'

'I don't need a rest,' I go. 'I'm fine.'

'Are you questioning me?' he goes, with his voice suddenly getting sharp and hard, like the edge of a knife. 'Because that doesn't sound like love, to me.'

228

'No, I'm not questioning you. I was just—'

'Good,' he goes.

'Tell him you're sorry,' Meena whispers to me.

'What?'

'Just say it,' she goes. 'Trust me.'

'I'm sorry,' I go.

'Right,' he's like. 'We'll make an exception, as this is your first day. But you'd better buck your ideas up, if you want to be part of the community here. Because you're either in, or you're out. And if you're out . . .' he goes, leaving his words hanging in the air. 'Meena, would you like to explain what will happen?'

'Not really,' goes Meena.

'Well, it's not a very high quality of life, Shruti,' goes Steve. 'Let's put it that way.'

'Sorry,' I go, again, cos that's what they want me to say, even though I dunno what I'm supposed to have done wrong. And they want me to be scared, although I'm not. And we watch Steve walk off, along the edge of the field, and then disappear along the little path that leads to the goat cage.

'Right,' goes Meena, as she stands up, 'I've gotta get back to work.'

'So how did you and Steve end up coming here?' I ask, just to get her talking.

'Really, mate, I've gotta get to work,' she's like. 'There's so much to get done.'

'Well, I could come round with you, while we chat.'

'No,' she goes. 'Steve doesn't like us talking about that kind of thing.' And she walks over to this big metal plough with handlebars on the front and these curved metal sword things on the bottom. And Meena pushes it through the ground in long rows, across the field, and it churns up the mud. And it's no wonder nothing grows here, cos it would be almost like trying to grow plants on the beach, the mud's so sandy.

So I stretch out on the mossy ground, by the side of the field, and the sun's all ripply and warm on my skin, through the shade of the leaf patterns, and I close my eyes. And I'm actually pretty tired, now that I'm lying down. So maybe I'm not as recovered as I thought I was. And I drift off to sleep.

CHAPTER SIXTEEN

And I wake up, and the sun's really low in the sky, and the sky's streaky pink and grey. And the air's a little bit moist. And my mouth's completely dried out. I was probably sleeping with it open. And I look around and Meena's nowhere. That plough she was pushing is upside down at the edge of the field. So I walk back down the path to the goat cage, where I find Meena sitting on a stool, outside the cage, brushing this goat's fur, really quick over and over again. And the goat's got a dog collar round its neck, attached to a chain, which Meena's got pinned under the leg of her stool, to stop it running away. And the goat's just standing there chewing, and puts its head down and has a mouthful of leaves from a pile on the floor.

'All right?' I go.

And Meena jumps. 'Bloody hell,' she goes. 'Don't sneak up on me like that.'

'Sorry,' I go. 'What's going on?'

'I've just gotta brush her coat, for the wool.'

'For like jumpers and stuff?' I go.

'Yeah,' Meena's like.

'Can you knit, then?'

'No,' she goes, 'but Steve's got a book on it, somewhere, so I'm gonna learn.'

'I never thought I'd see you knitting a jumper,' I'm like.

'Well, I never thought I'd be living on a desert island, so . . . You never know what's gonna happen, in life, do you?'

'Nope,' I'm like.

And it looks like she's dying to tell me something. Like the words are crawling all over her face and making her lips twitch.

'Is there something you wanted to say?' I go.

'Course not,' she goes, and turns back to brushing. 'I'm nearly finished here. Then we'll go back to the garden.' And she's pulling clumps of goat hair out of the spikes of the brush and stuffing them into a cloth bag. And then she leads the goat back inside the cage, takes its collar off, and snaps a padlock shut on the door. And she picks up a plastic bucket of milk. And she leads the way back to the garden, like she called it, which is basically the sleeping room, and the store room and chicken cage.

And when we get back, the air looks purple, I suppose from the pink light from the sunset mixing with the dark blue of the rest of the sky. And there's a big bonfire going in the corner, with a ring of stones around it. And Steve's standing next to another fire in the stone fireplace next to the store room, with orange glowing bits of coal smouldering down at the bottom, with a saucepan of water bubbling over it on a brick shelf.

'This bark burns up a treat,' Steve goes, holding out a few sheets of what looks like curling-up cardboard. 'It's almost like birch,' and he feeds a piece of it into the bonfire, which spits and sparks. 'It's just what we've been looking for.'

'Nice one,' goes Meena, and she puts down her bucket of milk, and puts her hand around his waist and kisses him on the neck.

'Don't say *nice one*,' he goes, pulling his head away from her. 'It's common.'

'Sorry, babe,' Meena goes. And she places the bucket of milk and the bag of wool on this shelf built into the side of the store room, without even thinking about it, like she's done it a million times before – like this is normal life, even though it's a freak show. And I feel like I've gotta remind myself that this isn't the slightest bit normal, to keep myself sane and to keep myself from getting completely sucked into Steve's version of reality, even while I'm pretending to believe in it.

And Steve picks up a long stick and pokes at the bonfire, which sparks and sputters. 'Why don't you girls get ready?' he's like. 'I just started slow roasting the butterfish in the oven,' which I suppose must be this little metal door above the fireplace. 'It'll take a while to cook.'

'Come with me,' Meena's like. So I follow her back along the path towards the goat cage. And I dunno what 'getting ready' means, here. And I'm wondering why I never heard them eating dinner every night, when I was sleeping so close to the fireplace.

'Do you need to go to the loo?' Meena asks me.

'Yeah, I do, actually,' I'm like.

'Number ones or number twos?' she goes.

'Meena!' I'm like.

'I'm only asking cos we have to go in different places depending on what it is.'

'Number ones,' I go.

'Come this way, then,' she's like. And we walk down a new path, into the trees of the jungle, which is almost completely black now that it's evening. And to start with we both crouch down and wee next to each other in the jungle.

'Right,' she's like. 'I'll show you where to go, if you need to do a poo. Cos we've gotta keep it a long way from the well.'

And she takes me all through the jungle for about fifteen minutes, till I can hear the waves of the sea. And by the time we get there, I realise I'm actually dying to go number twos. And Meena points out this stone ledge, hanging over the sea.

'What do you use for toilet paper?' I go.

And she grabs a branch on this bush and shakes it, so the leaves rustle. 'These leaves have got these sort of absorbent hairs on them.'

'I think I've gotta go,' I'm like, picking five big leaves off the bush.

'I'll be over here,' she's like, and disappears into the trees.

So I squat over the ledge. And when I'm finished she's comes back without me having to call for her, so she must have been, like, watching, which is sort of disgusting, although she acts so normal about it, it doesn't feel weird. And she's like:

'Now pick one of these other leaves and scrunch it up in your hands, and it's like a disinfectant,' she goes. 'Smell that.'

And it does smell sort of chemically. So I rub one of them between my hands. And I'm looking out at the sea, which is black, and the sky's navy blue over the top of it, with sprinkles of stars. And I look back at the jungle where we came from, and it's pitch black now, behind the leafy shadows, like looking down into a black hole. And I have this awful feeling that something bad's gonna happen when we get back to the garden. And at the same time, I'm feeling this weird closeness with Meena, like I can trust her. Maybe because we just did such a private thing together, of going to the loo, or maybe it's just cos I'm so alone out here, and she's the only other halfway safe person around.

'Meena,' I'm like. 'Is there any way off this island? Seriously.'

'Not any more,' she goes. 'We did have those Filipino blokes in the boat going back and forth, to buy us stuff, but then Steve shot them all. So no one even knows we're here now.'

'But that granddad bloke was still alive,' I'm like. 'He was still alive when I jumped off the boat.'

'He was losing blood from a massive wound to his neck,' she goes. 'And there's no way he'd survive the journey. It's like twelve hundred miles to the mainland. You saw how long it took us to get here.'

'Meena,' I'm like, and I dunno where this comes from, but I just have to say it now. 'I've never had sex before.'

'Oh, babe,' she goes, putting her arm around my shoulders. 'You're so cute.'

'What's really going on, Meena? Why did you bring me to this island?'

'I can't tell you, exactly, cos Steve wanted— well, *we* wanted it to be a surprise. But just think of it this way: if it's gonna be your first time, you want it to be a special memory that you can

235

always look back on, don't you? Not a horrible nightmare where you're fighting someone off even though it's gonna happen anyway.'

And I'm crying, now. And I can feel the tears dripping off my cheeks.

'But he might not even want to,' Meena's like, trying to backpedal. 'I shouldn't have said anything. I just wanted to help you out, if it does go that way.'

'Yeah,' I go through all my crying. And even though Meena's screwing me over, I've still gotta be nice to her, cos if I lose her as a friend I've got absolutely no one.

'Come on,' goes Meena, giving me a big hug, which makes me feel like I'm this fake, filthy object, not even a person, cos she's so blatantly using me. And I hate myself for not even trying to fight it. 'Let's have something to eat,' she goes, 'and this will all blow over.' And I follow her through the jungle, holding onto her shoulder, cos she knows the path and I can't even see it.

CHAPTER SEVENTEEN

And we arrive back at the garden. And a gust of wind whips the bonfire flames out towards my ankles, like a dog on a chain, as I walk past. And Steve's set up this big, like, throne carved out of a tree trunk, where I suppose he's gonna sit, which is ridiculous, but I'm not allowed to say anything. And then next to it, there's a table and two chairs coated in white paint that's peeling away, showing the rusty metal they're made of underneath.

'I'll get the vegetables on,' goes Meena, like she's playing someone's mum off the telly. 'You have a seat and wait for the feast.'

'The feast?' I'm like, with a little laugh. 'Do you mean dinner?'

'Don't mock our traditions,' goes Steve.

'Sorry, I was just—'

'Well, now you know. So show some respect,' he's like.

'Sorry,' I go, although I dunno how you can have traditions if you've only lived somewhere for, like, a few weeks. And I sit at the table and put my hands in my lap, like they used to make us do at primary school, to show we were ready for dinner.

237

And Meena goes to the shelves built in to the side of the store room, and pulls two fat hairy root things out of a wooden box and then rests them on the table in front of me and starts sawing one of them into slices, using this wire with wooden handles at each end.

'What are you doing?' I go.

'Getting the potatoes ready.'

'That's not a potato,' I go.

'*Ste-eve*,' Meena's like, like a little girl calling for her dad.

'Don't worry,' I go. 'They're potatoes.' Cos there's no point having an argument I can't win. And really, it doesn't matter what I say, as long as I still know they're not potatoes in my head – as long as *I* still know what's real and what's Steve's fantasy, and I keep them separate.

And Meena goes to the well and lowers the plastic bucket down there on its chain, hand over hand, and I'm waiting to hear a splash, but instead there's just the dry, echoey sound of plastic on sand, and she jerks the chain a few times. But it's the same sound.

'Steve,' she's like. 'I think we might have to roast the potatoes.'

'Good,' he goes. 'I love roast.'

And I can tell they're sort of embarrassed cos their well's run out of water. And I feel like I have to be loud and nice, to soak up some of their embarrassment. So I'm like, 'Roast potatoes are my favourite, too, actually.'

'Bring the slices over here,' goes Steve. And he opens the little door of the oven above the fireplace, which lets out a waft of rotten fish. And Steve uses a wad of leaves like an oven glove to

238

pull out this flat metal pan, and Meena drops the slices of 'potato' into it. And Steve shuts the pan back into the oven.

'Let's start off with some mango, shall we?' Steve goes.

So Meena reaches into another wooden box on the shelves and pulls out three little apple-things, which look nothing like mangos, and she hands them out. And I bite into my one, which is hard and powdery and bitter, like an unripe pear. And I want to spit it out, but I can't cos Steve will say that I'm disrespecting his traditions. So I smile and go, 'Mmmm. Do all the mangos taste like that, on this island?'

'Obviously,' goes Steve. 'This is what all mangos taste like, everywhere.'

And I just try to divide my mind into two separate compartments – one half for what I know is real, like the fact that these are not mangos, and the other half for the rubbish I have to pretend to believe, to stop Steve from shouting at me.

'How long until you get that half-acre ploughed?' Steve's like.

'A few days,' goes Meena. 'And I was thinking, babe, maybe we should eat those last two chickens, cos they can't breed now, can they?'

'Dish up the food, Meena, please,' goes Steve, ignoring what she said.

'I think the potatoes might need a bit longer,' goes Meena. And Steve just gives her a hard look. 'Sorry, babe. I'll serve it up,' Meena's like.

And I'm gutted that there isn't even any sarcasm in her voice – like there would be if she got forced to apologise to a teacher – cos that would at least have told me that she thinks Steve's rules are stupid and that she, like, secretly hates him a little bit. But she's completely respectful, so that leaves me on my own with hating him.

And Meena places three metal dinner plates on the table, where I'm sitting, and she opens the oven with the stick, and pulls a few thick rubbery-looking leaves off a bush.

'Get the leaves *before* you open the oven,' goes Steve. 'You're letting the heat out.'

'Sorry, babe,' goes Meena.

And she brings the metal tray out of the oven, using the leaves to protect her hands. And I'm expecting to see three giant sizzling fish in there, covered in butter and herbs and everything, cos Steve kept talking about butterfish. But there's just one small flat fish about the size of a hand, and the top of it is black and crispy, and it's still got its head on, with an evil little beak for a mouth, and there's white creamy stuff oozing out of its eye. And around it, there are the slices of those 'potatoes' that Meena cut up. But they've only been in there for, like, five minutes, so they blatantly can't be cooked. And there's a black bubbly coating dried over the bottom of the pan.

'Now, Shruti,' goes Steve, 'this might not look like much. But this is a feast, in the traditional sense of the word, like a traditional meal,' he's like. 'This was the first meal that I had when I arrived here, same for Meena, and now you're back on your feet, we want it to be the same for you.'

And I'm staring at his face to try to work out if he's telling the truth, or it's just an excuse for such rubbish food. And his skin's shiny and dark from his suntan, and his eyes are sparkling, and the firelight's making his skin flicker brown and orange. I can't tell if he's lying or not. But I don't think it even matters any more. Cos Steve weaves truth and lies together to make up this whole twisted reality of his own, to trap me in, like a spider web as big as this island. So it's really not a choice between truth or lies – it's a choice between Steve's version of reality and my version of reality. But I'm sure I can keep them both separate in my head.

And Meena's dishing up the food with a flat wooden spoon, trying to cut the fish into three pieces. But the spoon's blunt, so it's mashing the fish, cos she has to press so hard to grind through its backbone. And eventually she grinds it into three bits. And then she goes to dish up the head, but she has to chase it all round the pan with the spoon, cos she can't scoop it up. And eventually she traps it in the corner, with a load of potato slices. And I'm praying that isn't my bit, cos the head's gotta be the most disgusting part of the fish, and there can't be much meat on there. But luckily she puts it on her own plate. Then she goes to dish up the middle of the fish – like the stomach – which is the best bit cos it's got most meat. But she gives that to Steve. And then she gives me the tail. And I really wanna ask why there aren't any knives around. But I sense that I'm not supposed to be asking questions, and that I'm just supposed to be being respectful and pretending everything's delicious and enjoyable. And then Meena dishes up the potato slices, giving half of them to Steve, and the rest to herself and me. And she scrapes around in the pan, and chips up some of the burnt-on sauce and sprinkles it onto our plates.

'There we go,' she's like. And she leans over and gives Steve a kiss, like they're my mum and dad.

'All right, then,' goes Steve. 'Let's dive in, shall we?'

And the tail's mostly scales and bones. Plus it's got little hairs all over it from the hairy potato thing. But I'm not allowed to complain, cos that'll, like, offend their traditions, or whatever. Even though that's rubbish, cos I could turn around and say, Well, it's my tradition that I don't eat disgusting food. But they'd shout me into the ground and punish me for even saying anything, cos they've got the power to make their traditions more important than mine, so I keep quiet. Plus I've gotta keep Steve sweet, cos he's being so nice to me, and I don't want him to stop, cos if I can just get through tonight without him forcing himself on me, I'm thinking, then I might set a precedent, or whatever, and over time that will just become normal, and I can avoid him forever. And the best way to keep him sweet is to pretend his version of reality is true.

And Steve goes and pokes the fire with a stick, sending orange sparks squirting through the darkness, like mini fireworks for elves.

And Meena goes to me:

'We're gonna do the stories next.'

And *fuck*, it feels like someone's stabbed a spear into my arm. And I can smell burning. And Steve's burnt me with that stick he was poking the fire with, which is glowing red at the end like a cigarette. And Meena pushes her chin down onto her shoulder, and she waits while Steve burns her arm as well, which makes her screw up her face in pain, but she keeps completely quiet.

'This is to commemorate the love that Meena showed you, Shruti, when she saved you from the Filipino sailors and they

242

burnt her arm,' goes Steve. 'Tell Meena that you love her for saving your life.'

'I love you, Meena, for saving my life,' I go, because I don't want him to burn me again.

'Can we have the stories now?' goes Meena, either to save me from what Steve was gonna say next, or cos she genuinely likes stories – maybe cos there's nothing else to do on this island.

'All right,' goes Steve, in this annoyed voice. 'Let's make it quick, though. And then we'll go to bed, and we'll have the next part of the traditions.'

So I've gotta try to make this last as long as I possibly can, to keep Steve from going to bed until super late, so he'll be exhausted and sleepy, and he won't wanna do anything to me.

'Meena, why don't you start us off?' goes Steve.

'Okay,' goes Meena. 'Well, me and Shruti used to live in this evil world where everyone was evil and no one loved each other,' goes Meena, like she had this memorised. 'And everyone hated me and Shruti cos we were Asian, and cos we were women, and poor and young. And then we moved here, and now we all love each other.'

'And what else?' goes Steve. 'What about the journey here?'

'When we were coming here,' goes Meena, staring into the corners of her eyes and stretching out the words to give herself time to think. And her eyes are round and glassy, like horse's eyes, and they look like they'd feel like cold wet marbles, if I licked them, and her forehead and cheeks are shiny.

'When we were coming here,' Meena goes, 'we got stuck on a boat with these evil men.' And she doesn't mention it was her and Steve's fault we were even on that boat. And she tells the story of how that old drunk Chinese bloke was grabbing me in a pervy way. But Meena exaggerates everything, saying he was trying to tie me up with a dog's lead. And she says she pulled the cigarette out of the Chinese bloke's mouth, and stubbed it out on his arm, which is true. But then she says that he started trying to stab us with a sword, and she kept dodging out the way and protecting me. And all she had to defend us with was love, she reckons, and that's why we survived.

And this stuff's easy to keep separate in my head – these massive blatant lies. It's the little twisted details that are difficult, like calling that hairy root thing a 'potato', which I've started to do in my mind, cos there's no other word for it and everyone else is using that word.

'Very good, Meena,' goes Steve. 'Now, it's time for bed.'

'What about Shruti's story?' goes Meena. 'We're all supposed to tell one.'

Steve gives her an evil look and then goes:

'Would you like to tell a story, Shruti? You don't have to.'

'Yeah, I would actually,' I'm like. And I'm gonna tell a story that will literally last for ten hours, so Steve will get so tired he won't wanna do anything to me. 'When I was a little girl,' I go, cos I decide to start right at the beginning, to make it last longer. 'When I was a little girl, my dad left us and he never came back,' I'm like. And I tell the whole story of when I was a little girl and my dad left us and I got taken into that foster home, right up to the point when it comes time to fly to New Zealand, and I have to find Meena at that hotel, and Steve's there. And then I manage to get to the airport, and I go to New Zealand. And then Meena makes me meet her in India and makes me get on that boat. And now here I am. But that's all I can think of, and I'm staring at the silhouette of that dried-up well, trying to think of something else to say.

And Meena and Steve are sitting there. And the fire's died right down. But that's as much as I can think of to talk about, cos that's the longest story I know, cos that's my whole entire life. And there are no clocks anywhere, so I dunno how long it took exactly. And Meena's resting her forehead on her hands, like she's bored out of her mind or drifting off to sleep, cos she already knows pretty much everything I talked about, cos she was there while it was happening. And I'm hunting all round my brain for more things to say, but I can't find anything.

And Steve's like: 'You know, I've never told Meena this,' and Meena lifts her head up, 'but I used to have a daughter.' And Steve walks over to the fireplace and pushes this big fat burning log with his foot so it rolls over coated in soft flames like fur on an animal and it gives out this soft whistling popping sound for a second.

'What happened to her?' I'm like, although I can tell there's something not right about what he's saying.

'She died of leukemia,' goes Steve. 'And I've always found there's been a gap in my life ever since.'

And immediately I know that I've made a terrible mistake by telling them my whole life story. And I'm certain this daughter thing is a trick to manipulate me, and I know where this is going.

'It's funny how events pan out, though,' Steve's like, 'because in a way, we've formed our own little family here.'

And now I'm supposed to feel like he's the dad that I never had, and he'll pretend that I'm replacing his daughter who died. And it's so blatantly fake, but I'm not allowed to say that.

'Can we go to bed, babe?' goes Meena. 'Cos seriously, I'm knackered.'

'All right,' goes Steve. 'You two do the washing up, and I'll make this fire safe.'

And I'm trembling and short of breath, thinking about what's gonna happen to me tonight. And me and Meena collect the plates and spoons and baking tray off the table, and I follow her behind the big brick store room. And Meena kneels down in this sandy patch of ground and starts rubbing sand from the floor onto the baking dish.

'What are you doing?' I'm like.

'It gets them clean, but it saves water,' she goes. 'Cos the well's running dry.'

'Great,' I go.

And she finishes rubbing sand over the plates and the spoons, one by one, and then she stores them back on the shelves. And I think about running away and hiding in the jungle, but I'm too weak to survive out there. Plus they'd just find me like they did before. And even if they didn't – what am I gonna do: hide there for, like, sixty years, or whatever, till I die of old age?

And me and Meena go into the bedroom shack and Meena takes off all her clothes and gets into bed. And I get in next to her, still wearing my shorts and T-shirt.

246

'I'd take my clothes off, if I was you, mate,' goes Meena. 'Honestly. Cos he'll just cut them off with a pair of scissors if he sees you like that, and then you'll have to mend them yourself, on top of all your other work. And then you'll look like crap, in weird stitched-up clothes, cos you can't even sew properly.'

'God,' I'm like. And I wriggle out of my clothes and leave them folded on the floor.

'Is there any possible way I can get out of this?' I ask her.

'Not really,' goes Meena. 'But like I say, it's gonna happen anyway, so you might as well just enjoy it. Just pretend he's your boyfriend.'

'You can't pretend something like that, you idiot.'

'Well, just have a horrible time,' goes Meena. 'I don't care.'

'Yeah, well, I've still got some ideas of how to get out of this, so . . .'

'Right,' goes Meena. 'Good luck with that.'

And we just lie there, and my body's literally shaking, cos I'm so frightened, and my teeth are chattering. And we're listening for any kinds of sounds from outside, and eventually we hear footsteps coming closer. And then Steve comes in and makes small talk with Meena, while he's unbuttoning his shirt and kicking off his shoes, about how the crops aren't doing well, and he's gonna expand the planting area. 'But that was a great dinner this evening, wasn't it,' he goes.

'Yeah,' goes Meena. 'And Shruti's story was good.'

'She's had a truly remarkable life,' goes Steve, climbing into bed next to me. So I shuffle away from him and squeeze as close to Meena as I can.

247

'Okay, then,' goes Steve. 'Now that you're fully part of our family here—'

'Wait,' I go. 'Wait, before you say anything else,' I'm like, 'when we were talking in the field today, you said that we have to end every day with love.'

'Exactly,' goes Steve. 'You pledged that this is what you want to do – to end every day in love. In making love.'

'No, but that's not the same thing,' I'm like.

'Yes it is,' goes Steve. 'Isn't it, Meena?'

'Yeah, basically,' she's like.

'It isn't,' I go, as he starts putting his hands all over me and I'm trying to push them away. 'Plus you said that we can change the rules if we do it with love. So I wanna change the rules.'

'That's absolutely fine,' goes Steve. 'But we need to be in a state of love, which we're about to start right now, if you'd just stop being difficult.'

'So basically, "love" to you means "fucked",' I'm like. 'You have to agree to be fucked, to talk about changing the rules.'

'This is my island,' he goes. 'And they're my rules. And you've agreed to them.'

'But I never even wanted to be here,' I'm like. 'And I can't leave. It's not fair.'

'All right, I'm getting bored of this,' he goes. And he grabs my wrists and forces them up above my head and pins them down on the pillow, so he's holding both of my hands in one of his. And then he forces himself on me, which is like having all the happiness I've ever felt in my entire life ripped out of me, even out of my past, and replaced with these filthy, dirty, used, dark feelings that don't even have a name, they're so disgusting and unwanted and evil. And these dark feelings slither up inside me, like however internal bleeding must feel.

And while Steve's still in the middle of raping me, he goes to Meena, who's just lying there next to us, 'What are you crying about? You signed up for this.'

And I look to the side and Meena's legitimately crying and wiping her tears away with her palms. 'I know,' she goes, choking on her words. 'It's fine. I'm fine with this. I'm just a bit jealous. But it's fine.'

'Bloody hell,' goes Steve. And he keeps forcing himself on me. And I turn away, so I don't have to look at either of them. And at one point, I even try doing what Meena said: pretending that he's my boyfriend and that I want this, but I can't even make myself believe that for one single second. And what makes this even worse is that this isn't just a one-off evil event – it's me crossing over into this dark, horrible new life, where this is gonna happen again and again, every single night until I die or until Steve dies.

And eventually a big sigh forces itself out of Steve's mouth, and he flops down on top of me, trapping my face under his sweaty chest, which is getting bigger and smaller, really quick from where he's panting, like a sea creature who can't breathe properly on land. And my head's trapped under his sweaty chest-hair, and I'm facing the wall in the opposite direction to Meena. And I feel someone squeeze my hand twice. And first of all I think it's Steve giving me some kind of signal, like he's telling me he's gonna go two more times, or something. But then the hand just strokes my arm, and the fingers are thin and soft, so it must be Meena. And what the fuck does she think she's doing – comforting me, or something? She thinks I'm too stupid to see that what Steve just did to me is totally and completely her fault. So I screw my hand up into a fist, and shake her off me. And she takes her hand away. And this is the only tiny thing I can control in my entire life. Rejecting Meena's small crumb of kindness that she threw to me. That's how pathetic my life is – that the only thing I can control is something that makes my life worse and isolates me from the only person who can ever offer me anything like friendship for the rest of my life. And I feel like I'm falling and falling into this black pit inside myself.

And Steve's lying right on top of me, crushing my chest, so that each time I breathe in I have to lift his whole bodyweight with my rib muscles and my lungs and whatever. And it's hurting me, but I sort of like it, cos the pain's blotting out some of the despair that's soaking into my bones like ink into a sponge. So I start trying to bring down more physical pain on myself, to try to blot out more of the despair by letting all the air drain out of my lungs, hoping that I can deflate them enough for Steve's weight to snap my ribs, and then I won't be able to think about anything except that pain. Cos right now all I can think about is how dirty and horrible Steve's made me feel. Not just from the sex, but the way he did it, telling all those lies about the rules of the island and how we do everything with love, just so he could use that against me, and how he told that lie about how he used to have a daughter who died, to make me feel like this was gonna be my new family, but then he couldn't even be bothered to keep the lie up. And the way he was rude to Meena, right in the middle of forcing himself on me. It was all just like he was wiping dirt off his shoes.

And I'm such an idiot for saving my first time for someone special. I should have just done it with that Russian bloke I met the first night in New Zealand who tried to get me to come back to his youth hostel. I should have just done it with anyone.

And it seems like when Steve had been doing it with Meena on other nights, it took much longer than it took him with me. So maybe he was quick cos he was trying to be 'nice' to me, for my first time. Or maybe he finished quick cos he wasn't enjoying it, and he wanted to get it over with. Or maybe he was loving it, and he was quick cos he got too excited. And I realise that my brain's trying to get a handle on what's just happened by trying to understand it from different angles, like it's a spider crawling all over a rotting body of an animal, but it can't understand it or get inside it. And that doesn't even make sense I don't think, but I can't be bothered to make sense, cos I'm just languishing in this rotting, dying, filthy, slick body that I happen to be lying inside, it feels like.

And Steve climbs off and this wet slime slides out of me, down there. And then I can't believe this, but Steve climbs onto Meena. Straight onto her.

'You ready for a real woman?' she goes, the fucking bitch.

'Why?' goes Steve. 'Do you know where I can find one?'

'You're such an arsehole,' she giggles, and they start kissing and then having sex. So at least he's not going to force himself on me again this evening, cos he only ever has sex twice in a night.

So I turn away from them and lay on my side. And in the centre of this black despair, I've got this empty floating feeling, sort of like an airship that's been cut loose and it's drifting around. Cos before, I had all these things I needed to do, like trying to keep Steve away and escape from this island before it was too late. But now, there's no way to stop Steve, and there's no way to escape. And it's like all the ropes tying me to the ground have been slashed.

And these random thoughts are eating their way through me – like insects, or something, eating through a rotting slab of steak – like I'm thinking that it's not the physical actions of rape that are the worst thing. Cos if I had a boyfriend and he did exactly the same sex things to me, I'd probably be all right with it, like Meena said. It's the fact that it makes you feel like total shit, like someone's using you in every single way and doing this really private, special, intimate thing with you in the same way that they'd wipe dog shit off their shoes. And they're stealing your sense of safety from you and ruining your sense of intimacy forever and risking giving you diseases and making you pregnant – but *they're actually enjoying it.* They're not even sorry. And the more you hate it, the more it probably turns them on.

And my whole body's shaking, I suppose from the shock of what just happened. And there's nothing I can do, and no one I can tell. And I know I shouldn't say this, but I keep thinking that at least with a girl who's raped in a park in England, she can go to her mum and her friends and they'll all be really nice to her. And it's just one night for her, and then it's over, and she can start trying to move on with her life. And the police might catch the bloke who did it, so she can get revenge on him. But there's no one here to comfort me. And no one to catch Steve. And no one that even thinks what he's done to me was wrong. Plus for me this isn't just a one-off horrible event – this is crossing over into a new dark life where this will happen every day and everyone will think it's completely normal.

And I'm trying to think of a way out of it, but I can't think properly, cos my brain and my body feel like a sponge soaking up more and more horrible inky poison, except a sponge gets full eventually, but I keep sucking up more and more of it, and it's making me heavier and more saturated with despair.

CHAPTER EIGHTEEN

And in the morning, Meena wakes me up and tells me I've gotta come and work in the field with her.

'I'm still pretty weak,' I'm like. 'Plus I'm feeling horrible from what Steve did to me last night.'

'You shut your fucking mouth, all right,' Meena's like. 'You shut up about my boyfriend.'

'Don't get angry at me.'

'I will get angry at you, you little slut,' goes Meena. 'Cos it's one thing for you to sleep with him, and something else for you to start slagging him off. So shut it. All right?' And she throws my clothes at me, so they wrap themselves around my face. 'You'd better be dressed by the time I come back, or I'll get Steve to beat the living shit out of you. Understand, do you? You fucking whore.' And she walks out of the shack, leaving me to get dressed. And then she comes back and I go with her along the path towards the crop field.

'We wanted to keep this quiet till after the celebration,' Meena's like, 'but we've only got two weeks' worth of food left, and nothing's growing.'

254

'What about all the goats and the chickens and the fish?' I ask her, and I'm on edge, worried about her going mental at me again. And I'm desperate to talk about what Steve did to me. Cos the whole thing's this massive swirling blackness inside me making me wanna start crying, and I need to hear someone agree that Steve is an evil horrible person. But blatantly I won't be able to get that from Meena.

'The goats and the chickens are dying off from diseases, for your information, you stupid idiot,' Meena's like. 'And there's hardly any fish out there, which is why no fishing boats come near here. I honestly never realised how fucking stupid you really are. But I suppose you never really know a person till you live with them, do you?'

'But we had fish last night,' I'm like, and I start sobbing. I can't stop myself. 'Steve could just,' I sob, 'catch more.'

'That's the first fish he's caught in a week,' Meena's like, completely cold, but smirking about the fact I'm crying, cos this is what she wants. 'And he's been out fishing every single day.'

'What about the potatoes and mangos, and whatever?' I'm like, through my tears, which make me look stupid, like I'm crying about the food. I don't even know why I'm saying any of this.

'Steve bought them off the sailors,' Meena's like. 'They don't grow here.'

'So are we gonna starve?'

'No, we've just gotta get the wheat to grow before the stores run out.'

'In two weeks?' I'm like, still sobbing, but trying to get into the argument, to take my mind off how wretched I feel.

'Stuff grows quickly here, cos it's so hot,' goes Meena.

And I can't keep this up. I need to stop talking with her. Cos this is just driving the despair and sadness deeper and deeper inside me. And on the outside, it feels like I've got this large delicate wound that I need someone to help me put a bandage over and protect, to help it to heal – not start ripping into it with their dirty fingernails, and calling me a slut like Meena did. So I've gotta keep it completely hidden from her.

And I keep following Meena along the path, and I let my crying dry up. And we come to the field, which isn't even mud. It looks more like sand, like you'd get at the back of the beach. And there's no way that anything's growing in there, ever, let alone in two weeks when our food's gonna run out. And a quarter of the field's got a crusty white powder over the surface.

'What's that white stuff?' I go.

'That's where we tried to water it with seawater. But the salt just killed everything.'

'Steve should have brought coconut trees instead of wheat,' I'm like.

'Yeah, well. It's done now. So we've gotta make the best of it.'

And I'm like: 'So Steve sits around fishing all day, does he?'

'No, he doesn't "sit around",' goes Meena. 'Fishing actually takes more skill than working in the fields.' Which sounds like a total lie to me. But I can't prove it, cos I've never done either of those things. 'Right, we've gotta get this done,' goes Meena. 'I'm ploughing, and you're planting.' And she hands me a plastic bag filled with tiny brown seeds, plus a big woven sack filled with stinky clusters of slick black animal droppings, like clusters of sticky marbles, I think from the goats.

'What's this?'

'Fertiliser,' Meena goes. 'You've gotta go along in the ploughed bit, and take a little ball of fertiliser, like this, and then you put a seed on the end of your finger, like this, and poke it inside the fertiliser, and then plant it in the ground,' she goes, bending down and burrowing it into the sandy soil and then patting the ground over it. 'These are the last seeds left, so we've gotta make sure every one of them grows.'

'And what if this doesn't work?' I ask.

'Then we'll die,' she goes. 'That's the general plan.'

'Glad we've got that cleared up, then,' I go. And Meena doesn't lay into me. So maybe I can finally stand up to her, now. Cos really, there's nothing she can do against me. Cos things can't get any worse. I'm already trapped here. And Steve's already forced himself on me.

'What if I say no?' I'm like. 'There's nothing you can do, is there?'

'There's a lot of things I could do, actually, mate. But just to give you an idea, we can lock you in that cage where the goats live. And if you don't believe we'd do that, we already have. Cos there used to be a girl called Amanda here, and we did it to her.'

'There used to be another girl here?' I'm like. 'Where is she now?'

'Don't you worry about that, mate,' goes Meena. 'You just worry about planting those seeds, so we don't starve to death.'

And I keep asking her about this Amanda girl, but Meena completely clams up and won't tell me anything else. She's just like:

'Start in this corner of the field and plant them in lines, one hand span apart. And bury them all nice and deep,' she goes. 'I've already started ploughing it, so it'll be churned up for you.'

So I take a little marble-sized ball of fertiliser, poke a seed in, and burrow it into the ground with my fingers, which is easy cos the ground's so sandy and soft from where it's been ploughed up. And after planting ten seeds, my back's killing me, from bending over. So I get down onto my hands and knees instead.

And Meena ploughs up more of the field, but she has to keep stopping each time she gets to a big stone to dig it out – using a little trowel she keeps tied to the plough handles – and then she heaves it out of the ground and then carries it to the edge of the field and dumps it in the trees, unless it's too big to carry, in which case she rolls it over there.

And my hands get totally dried out from the sandy dry soil. And the sun comes up higher and burns down on me and makes my hair so hot I can't even touch it. And I'm wondering how we have haircuts on this island. I suppose they've got a pair of scissors somewhere. And how does Steve keep his beard so short, I'm wondering? Has he got clippers, or a razor or something? And it must have taken me at least an hour and a half to do the first row, and there's probably hundreds of rows in total. So this is gonna take days. Maybe even weeks.

And after probably a few hours, Meena puts the plough down and walks over to me. 'I'm gonna bring lunch for us both,' she's like. 'You keep going.'

'I've gotta wash my hands,' I go, holding them up, all crusted over with dried goat poo and sand and a few seeds that have stuck to it all.

'Well, go where we went to the loo last night. And you can use those disinfectant leaves.'

'Right,' I'm like. And I follow the path there, going past the goat cage, where Meena reckons they locked some girl inside to punish her, which makes my stomach lurch just thinking about it. And I go to the loo, crouching over the stone ledge, into the sea, and I wash my hands.

And when I get back to the field, Meena's there with two wheat-cake things and one small piece of dried fish and a small tin with one pineapple ring in it. So I put the fish between the two wheat cakes, to make a sort of sandwich, but Meena slaps my hand away.

'Hey!' she goes. 'That's for both of us.'

'Oh, come on,' I'm like. 'That's not even enough food for *one* person.'

'It's all we can spare,' she goes. 'And this is the last of the dried fish, and the last of the pineapple. And we've only got ten more of these wheat cakes.'

'We should start looking around the island for food,' I'm like. 'There's gotta be fruit we could pick, or birds or monkeys or something we could shoot.'

'We haven't got any bullets left,' she goes. 'Plus we've already looked everywhere and there's no edible plants. That's why no one ever settled on this island.'

'This is stupid,' I go, tearing the fish in half and putting my half on one of the wheat cakes. 'We'll starve to death if we keep going like this. Aren't you worried?'

'Course I am,' she goes, which makes me feel slightly less alone, cos at least she has got some real thoughts left in her head that aren't just lies to protect Steve. And she nibbles on her wheat cake and then changes her mind. 'You have this,' she goes, holding it out to me. 'I'm not hungry.'

'Don't be stupid, Meena. You eat it.'

'Yeah, I suppose you're right,' she goes. And we both finish our lunch and have half the pineapple ring each, and then we drink half the syrup each, from the tin. And Meena's got this big metal bottle of water, and we each drink half of that. And then Meena goes off to refill the bottle.

And we work all day like that, even though all the time we're working, we're wasting time that we could be spending out in the jungle making traps to catch monkeys, or doing something faster than planting wheat. Cos I'm sure wheat takes much longer than two weeks to grow from seeds, even if the weather is really hot.

And my back's killing me. And my mouth's dried out. And my hands and knees are raw from crawling along the sandy mud all day in the boiling sun. And the sun's starting to go down, now, and I've only done six and a half rows of planting seeds. And Meena's probably done about three rows of ploughing, cos there are so many stones. And Meena tells me she's gonna tend to the goats and the chickens, but I should keep working. And when she comes back, she brings me that metal bottle quarter-filled with goat's milk, which is warm and sweet and nutty-tasting, but there's only about three gulps and then it's gone. And I'm so starving hungry it feels like I'm hollow. And I can't wait till dinner. Cos hopefully Steve will have caught another fish, and we've at least got a few wheat cakes. And any food tastes delicious when you're starving.

And I plant another half a row of seeds and then Meena says we can finish. So I bring the bag of seeds and the sack of manure with me. And I walk back with Meena to the garden. 'We'll wait to see what Steve caught, and then we'll make dinner,' she goes. 'Do you wanna have a bath?'

'Definitely,' I'm like, remembering that beautiful warm stream I found when I was blind. 'That would be amazing.'

And she leads me back down the path through the jungle, and I'm looking forward to rinsing out my clothes and my hair, and soaking in a warm bath again. And Meena pushes the branches to the side, and there's a little turning off to the right which I hadn't noticed before.

'We've gotta be quick,' goes Meena, as she starts leading me along this dark path through the trees. 'If Steve thinks we're slacking off, he won't let us have any dinner.'

'Well, let's just skip the bath, then,' I'm like, 'cos I can't risk not eating tonight.'

But Meena ignores me and keeps walking. So I end up following her, telling myself that I'll force her to be quick, so we don't miss out on the food.

And she leads me down to these rock pools, by the sea. And she strips down to her underwear and lays in one of the pools, with the water only coming halfway up her. 'Come on,' she goes. 'It's lovely in here.'

So I strip down to my underwear as well and walk down there. And the rocks themselves are warm under my feet, but the water inside the pools is freezing seawater. And when I lie down in one, next to Meena, it's so cold I can't enjoy it at all or relax, and ridges of stone are digging into my back. And while I'm lying there, this big wave comes out of nowhere and smashes on the rocks, spraying freezing cold water over us, which makes me gasp in shock.

'Bloody hell, Meena,' I go. 'This isn't a bath. This is horrible.'

'Well, this is the best we've got. So we've gotta make the most of it.'

'When I was lost, out there,' I'm like, 'I found this deep stone pool next to a waterfall, as warm as a real bath, and the water was so fresh you could drink it.'

'Right,' she goes. 'When you were blind.'

'I swear that's true,' I'm like.

'I've been all over the island, mate,' goes Meena, 'and I've never seen nothing like that.'

'Well, whatever,' I'm like. 'Cos this is the crappest bath in the world. And I'm getting out.'

And as I stand up, another massive wave smashes on the side of the rock pools and slaps right over my legs. 'Huuuhhh,' I'm like, cos it's so freezing. And I tread back onto the main part of the land. 'What do we use for towels?'

'Nothing, you just dry off in the sun.'

'The sun's gone down, though,' I'm like.

'Well, dry off in the moon then,' goes Meena. The stupid bitch.

'We should be getting back, if Steve might cut off dinner,' I'm like.

'I am trying to relax here,' goes Meena. 'Could you stop ruining the atmosphere, please?'

'Meena, I'm so starving, I can't risk missing dinner tonight.'

'Just give me fifteen more minutes, and I'll come. Maybe half an hour.'

And I didn't have any breakfast, and lunch was that tiny wheat cake with a bit of dry fish and half a pineapple ring. And this dinner is all I've been thinking about all afternoon.

'We've gotta go back,' I'm like. 'What do I have to do to get you moving?'

'Ha ha!' she goes. 'Look, it's just like the good old days!'

'Fuck you,' I'm like.

'There you go,' she's like. 'It's just like your trip to New Zealand.' And she puts both hands on her stomach. 'Am I showing much?'

'Showing what?'

'Showing that I'm pregnant,' she goes. 'That's one of the reasons I came here. So the baby would be with his dad.'

And there's a good chance that she's just making this up. But if she really is pregnant, and if her baby's a boy, I'm thinking, I could marry him when he grows up. Cos there's no one else for me to marry on this island. Which is a bizarre thought, but it does sort of make some kind of sense, I think.

'Come on, then. Give us a hand,' goes Meena, reaching up towards me. So I step back into the rock pools, grip her hands and pull her up. And now all of a sudden, she starts acting like a pregnant woman off the telly, with one hand on her lower back and the other on her belly, and going *ooh* each time she moves. And we get dressed. And our clothes are sticking to us, with see-through wet splotches on them. And that bath was such a waste of time, cos we put our disgusting work clothes back on that make us stink again.

And when we get back to the garden, Steve's sitting on his stupid big wooden throne carved out of a tree trunk, next to the rusty metal table.

'Sit down,' he goes. 'Both of you.'

And I wanna tell him it was Meena's idea to have a bath, but I don't think we're allowed to talk. So I sit down at the table without saying anything, and so does Meena.

'We're in serious trouble,' goes Steve. 'I don't know if it's the tides, or overfishing, or the mating season, or what, but I didn't catch a single fish today. Nothing. Not even a small one to use as bait. Our first half-acre hasn't germinated at all. And the second half-acre with the manure is taking too long to plant,' he's like. 'This evening, I opened our last crate of food – which we were saving for absolute emergencies like this – and it's completely rotten and infested with maggots. So the long and the short of it is this: we've got one more meal's worth of food left, which we'll eat now, and that's it. So we're going to work all through the night. I'll keep fishing by moonlight, and you two will keep up the field work.'

'Can we look for food in the jungle?' I go.

'I'm sorry, that sounded like you were trying to change the rules.'

'No, I'm just saying—'

'Changes in the rules have to be suggested with love.'

And that word *love* makes my blood separate out from itself, like milk that's gone rancid, cos of what it means here.

'I'm not suggesting a change, but—'

'Well, that's all right then,' goes Steve, cutting me off. 'Meena, get the last of the food ready.' And Meena gets up and starts clattering around in the shelves built into the store room. 'This is going to be our last meal until the crops come up,' Steve goes. 'Until then, we'll have to live on the goats' milk.'

'What about eggs from the chickens?' I go.

'We can't touch them,' Steve's like. 'We're trying to hatch every single egg that comes along.'

'What about killing a chicken?' I go.

'Never. We have to keep the maximum potential for an egg to hatch.'

'Are we growing any vegetables?'

'No, our only seeds are the wheat in that bag you're planting from. The Filipino sailors were due to bring a selection of vegetable seeds and fruit tree saplings, but they couldn't get them in time. And they won't be coming back, now.'

'And what happens if the wheat doesn't come up?' I'm like.

'Then we'll die,' goes Steve, like Meena did. Which isn't the answer I was expecting. But I suppose at least he's honest. 'Now there's a good moon coming out tonight,' he's like. 'A harvest moon, I think it's called in the business. So we'll be able to see well enough to keep going through the night.'

And the one good thing about working all night, I'm thinking, is that he won't be able to force himself on me again. That's something, at least.

And Meena comes over to the table with ten wheat cakes, each about as big as a pack of cards, and two small bits of dried fish, and two tin cans: one with runner beans in it, and one with bean sprouts like you get at the Chinese restaurant, except soggy and brown.

And Meena lays out three metal plates and Steve helps himself to about half of the food. And then Meena divides the rest evenly between herself and me. And we all eat without talking. And Steve sips some juice out of the runner bean can.

'Do you want this, Meena?' he goes.

And she shakes her head. So he just empties the juice out on the floor, from both tins, without asking me if I wanted it. Which I didn't. But they should have asked me. And these little scraps of food just make me more hungry, it feels like, cos it's like eating quarter of a meal when I was expecting a whole one.

And we go out to the field, through the twilight, and the moon's out in the corner of the sky, and the sun's gone down, but it's spreading light up, from below the horizon. And there's streaky clouds, in purple and pinky-orange. And it's getting chilly.

'You can take it from here,' goes Steve. 'I'll try my luck with the fish.'

'Right,' Meena goes to me. 'We're gonna keep going like before, till we've got the whole field planted.'

So I find the last little mound of earth where I planted a seed. And I keep planting, along that row. And after a bit, I listen out for the scraping sound of Meena's plough slicing through the soil. But I can't hear anything. So I stand up, and I can see the dark outline of the plough standing still in the field. And it's suddenly really spooky, cos I thought Meena was here, but actually I'm alone.

'Meena!' I call out.

'What?' comes back her voice.

'Why aren't you working?'

'I am having a baby. I can't do this kind of work any more.'

'That's not fair,' I go, walking towards where her voice is coming from, cos I still can't see her, cos it's almost dark now. 'You were fine, like two hours ago.'

'I was *not* fine, for your information. I was feeling terrible.'

'So was I,' I'm like.

'But I was feeling terrible cos of the baby. And that's something you wouldn't understand cos you're not actually an expectant mother. So I'd appreciate it if you stop denigrating my feelings.'

'I'm just trying—'

'Well, stop, all right?' she's like. 'Just stop. Cos this stress is extremely damaging for the baby's health. And if you don't cut it out, right now, I'm gonna tell Steve. And this is his baby as well, so I really don't think you wanna go there. Just get back to work.'

So I slink back to the field, plotting a way that I can kill Meena in her sleep, for being such an absolute bitch to me. And I keep planting right through the night, until the sky turns deep blacky-blue, which means it's just about to get light for the morning. And some birds are tweeting and squawking in the treetops. And I think we should be trying to catch these birds for their meat, and maybe we could keep them in the chicken cages and breed them and eat their eggs. And I decide that I'll try to capture one on my own, and maybe I could become the bird catching expert, and then I could do that all day, instead of planting the field, which is blatantly the worst job on this island, cos it literally covers you in poo every day.

And eventually I've planted rows of seeds right up to the point where Meena left the plough. And from there on, the soil's all packed down hard, and I can't burrow my hand into it, to plant the seeds. And I'm not sure if I'm supposed to plough the rest of the field myself or I'm supposed to stop there and wait. And I don't want Steve to get angry with me, for doing the wrong thing. So I walk to where Meena's sleeping under the trees.

'Meena,' I'm like, shaking her shoulder. And she wakes up, groggily, screwing up her face and wriggling her head, like she's burrowing out of sleep like a mole.

'What's up, babes?' she goes.

'I've planted right up to the plough. Should I wait, or plough the rest myself?'

'No, plough the rest of it,' she goes. 'And then plant the rest of the field.' And she goes back to sleep.

And I'm such an idiot, I realise now, cos I should've kept my mouth shut. Cos then I could have gone to sleep myself and said I thought I was supposed to do that. But now I've gotta keep working.

But even though I'm dead tired, it is sort of satisfying trying to plant this entire field pretty much all on my own. And I copy what Meena was doing with the plough. And I grip the two handles, which are like big bicycle handlebars, and I try to push it forward to make the blades on the bottom churn through the mud. But it won't budge. So I yank it backwards, so there's a little bit of ploughed earth in front so I can get a sort of run up to the packed-down area. And that works, and I start cutting through the earth. But it's such hard work, cos I've gotta keep my arms curled right up with my elbows bent and my shoulders lifted, to keep this heavy plough off the ground. Plus I've gotta push it forward through the earth, which is packed down hard, and that takes a lot of strength. And after two minutes of this, my arms are knackered. And my hands are raw. So I put down the plough, and I shake my arms, like we used to do for the warm up in PE.

And then I plough again for another couple of minutes till I hit something hard and I can't move the plough at all. And the air's bright and clean now, with the first proper sunlight of the day just below the horizon, waiting to rise up. And in front of the plough blades there's a big stone, about as big as a football, but flat. So I pull the plough back a bit, and I kneel down in front of the plough, and start digging the stone out with the little wooden trowel strung onto the handles of the plough, which Meena was using to dig out stones while she was ploughing. And I dig a little moat all the way round the stone, deeper and deeper till I can get my hands right underneath it, and it's about as big as – as a baby, I suppose.

And as I pull it out, I'm thinking about how everything will change when Meena's baby comes. And how that baby's gonna get treated better than me. And it'll go: Steve at the top, then Meena, then the baby, and me at the bottom, getting treated the worst. And probably when the baby becomes a child, they'll let him order me around as well.

But I try not to think about that now, cos it makes my future look like a black cliff that I have to fall off the edge of. And instead I focus on getting this ploughing finished, so I can go to sleep, even though I'm blatantly not gonna get this whole field finished anytime in the next week. So I hook both of my hands underneath the big stone, and I pull it out of the hole. And it's too heavy to carry, so I roll it across the field, to the edge where the trees are, and I leave it there and keep on ploughing. And I'm so tired now, I just wanna go to sleep. And I try closing my eyes while I'm pushing the plough, but my brain starts shutting down when I do that. So I force myself to keep them open, cos I don't wanna pass out and crack my face on the metal bars. And I keep going for as long as I can, but I feel my brain shutting down, as I'm ploughing. And finally, I just think, Sod this: I've gotta get some sleep.

So I leave the plough where it is and walk into the trees by the side of the field – the opposite side to where Meena's sleeping – and I curl up with my hand under my head as a pillow and fall straight into this deep, warm sleep that hugs me into itself.

CHAPTER NINETEEN

'Why have you stopped working?' Steve's shouting, to wake me up, and he's kicking the soles of my feet. 'This is unacceptable. The rest of us worked all night, and you're slacking off. Get back to work,' he's like. 'This is strike two. One more strike, and we'll put you in the cage.' And he starts to walk off, while my brain's still trying to wake up properly, even though my body's strung up with electric-feeling fear and sadness. And Steve calls over his shoulder, 'Meena, make sure she doesn't do that again.'

And Meena's standing there, like his evil little sidekick. And she tells me to plough the rest of the field. And I stand up, and my spine hurts just from holding up the weight of my own body, cos of all that planting and ploughing I did yesterday. And my muscles ache so much it's painful to even walk. And my brain's shot, cos I must have only got about two hours' sleep.

And Meena's watching me try to pick up the plough and not even being able to lift it, cos my hands are so raw with red puffy blisters where my fingers join my hands, that the skin will rub off to uncover the raw flesh underneath if I do any more ploughing. And I'm hoping Meena and Steve will give me some time off, cos

I legitimately can't pick up the plough. And when I was ill before, they did let me just lie in bed all day.

'Why aren't you ploughing?' Meena shouts over.

'I can't even lift it,' I'm like. 'My hands are done in. My whole body's killing me.'

'Well, just use the little trowel to loosen up the earth and plant by hand,' she shouts.

And I'm gutted. Cos I can still do that. So I get down on my hands and knees. And it takes me about two hours to plant the row that I ploughed last night. And then when I reach where the plough's sitting, I take the little trowel off its string and get back down on my hands and knees and start digging into the hard, packed-down unploughed ground with the trowel. And I have to stab it into the soil three or four times to loosen a little patch up. And then I pick out a seed and reach into the sack for a ball of manure. And yesterday the manure was soft and moist, like Plasticine, but now it's dried hard, so I have to dig my fingernails right in, to claw off a piece. And that forces tiny splinters of straw from the manure underneath my nails, which stings like crazy. And then I can't poke the seed into the manure with my finger, cos it just starts crumbling apart. So I have to wrap the crumbled pieces around the seed instead and pack them all into the hole in the ground. And this all takes much longer than yesterday. And there's easily another two weeks of planting, at this rate, to finish the field.

And I'm getting lonely out here. Cos when Meena was working with me, at least there was, like, camaraderie. So I wave to Meena, who's sitting with her back against a tree. And she sees me, but she can't even be bothered to lift up her hand to wave back. So I don't bother again, cos it only makes me feel lonelier to get shot down like that. And I finish my second row of seeds for today.

And I realise that the germs from the manure could infect my blisters, cos it's animal droppings. And there's no hospitals here, and I could die from an infection, like people did in the olden days. So I put down the trowel and the bags and walk to Meena, to ask to wash my hands. And she's reading porno magazines. 'What on earth are you reading?' I go. 'That's disgusting.'

'This is all there is,' she's like. 'We ain't got no books, or nothing.'

'So I can never read, like, *Tess of the D'Urbervilles* and The *Wizard of Oz*, and all that?'

'You never wanted to read those books, in the first place, you muppet. What are you talking about?'

'I wanted to read them *one day*,' I go. 'When I'm old, or whatever.'

'You're such a freak,' she's like, and she starts turning the pages of the porno mag, through this photo shoot in a garden of apple trees, where three girls are all over this one bloke. And it hits me – that I'm never gonna read any famous books, or see all the famous films, or visit America or the pyramids, or even meet any people except for Meena and Steve, and any children they have. And maybe Steve might make me pregnant. And actually if I had a baby, that could stop my life being a pure nightmare. Cos my own child would always be on my side, no matter what happened, and then I'd always have someone who'd love me. But actually, what if they took the baby away, and trained it to hate me and order me around? Or what if they made my baby a servant, like me, and turned us into a race of servants, doing work for Meena's children? Plus, if I had a baby with Steve I'd be tied to him for the rest of my life, even if I could escape this island. Plus it would make it harder to escape, bringing a baby with me. But whatever. I gotta try not to think about any of this, cos it'll only make me feel worse. And I've gotta just look after myself and stay healthy, so I can escape if an opportunity ever comes up. So I'm like:

'Can I wash my hands, cos I've got blisters and they might get infected?'

'All right,' Meena goes. 'You keep working, and I'll go and get you some of those leaves.' And I go back to planting, and Meena brings me some of those disinfectant leaves plus the metal bottle filled with water. And I drink the whole thing. And I scrunch up the leaves and rub them over my hands.

And I keep planting, all day. And by the time the air starts to go that purpley-pink twilight, I'm so worn out I can hardly hold my head up, even crawling along on all-fours. And there's still weeks of planting left to do, at this speed, cos I keep getting slower and slower as I get more worn out.

'Come over here,' Steve shouts at me. He's standing next to Meena, though I didn't see him turn up. So I put down my trowel and go over. And he's brought a bucket half full of milk, and three metal cups. And I sit down with them, leaning against a tree. And Steve dips us each a cup of milk, which is warm, so it must be completely fresh, straight out of the goats' udders, and it's so sweet and nutty and creamy, it's delicious. And there's

274

enough milk for three cups each. And it's so good to just have something in my stomach. And I look at my arms, and already they're getting thin, like they were when I first woke up from being blind. And it feels so good to be just sitting down and resting, and with other people.

'Did you catch any fish today?' I'm like.

'Not even a bite,' goes Steve. 'Remember when you first got here, Meena, and I'd have twenty fish before lunchtime, and then we'd have a barbecue and I'd help you in the field?'

'Yeah, and all different kinds. Like that little shark. Remember that little shark?'

'I'm embarrassed, really, Shruti, that you had to find us like this,' goes Steve. 'But if this wheat comes up, and the fish start biting again, we can get back on track.'

'It's not your fault,' I tell him, cos he wants me to.

'All right, then,' goes Steve. 'That was dinner. We're all going to keep working all night, again, until the entire acre's planted. It's in solidarity with you, Shruti, just so you know that you're not alone.'

'Could I do the fishing for a bit? And you do the field?' I go. 'Cos honestly, my whole body feels like it's dying here.' And I show him my palms.

'No, that won't work,' he's like. 'Fishing's highly skilled, and I've had decades of experience,' he goes. 'You stay with the fieldwork. And once you've planted it, we'll all sleep.'

And he stands up and brushes off his shorts. 'Meena, can you put away the bucket and the cups?' And he walks to the end of the field, and disappears onto the path. And Meena's like:

'You'd better get back to work,' she goes. 'Then we can all get to sleep properly.'

'Fuck you,' I'm like. 'You shut your fucking mouth. Don't tell me what to do, just sitting around here on your arse doing nothing and telling me what to do, you lazy bitch.'

'Oh, dear,' she goes. 'You're gonna pay for that. You better be working hard by the time I get back here with Steve, or you're gonna be in some serious shit.'

'Don't tell Steve,' I'm like. 'Please. I'm so tired I dunno what I'm saying. I just snapped. I'm really sorry.'

'Too bad,' goes Meena.

'Please, I'm begging you, Meena. Don't tell Steve.'

'All right,' she goes. 'But you never talk to me like that ever again. You got that?'

'Totally,' I'm like. 'I'll never do that again. I swear.'

'Good,' she goes, and she takes the bucket and the cups away. And I go back out to the field and keep planting, feeling stupid for losing control like that. Although, really, Meena and Steve have done things a million times worse to me. But they've got the power to punish me, and I've got no power at all, so I've still gotta watch my step, even though it's not fair.

And after a while Meena comes back with a blanket wrapped round her shoulders. And I keep planting. And there's just a tiny bit of light left, the air's dark purple, I hear these footsteps coming towards me over the field, but from the opposite direction to Meena, which is a bit weird, but I suppose she just went for a walk around the field and she's coming from the other direction.

'Meena?' I'm like.

'No, it's Steve.'

And my heart sinks, cos I bet Meena's told him that I shouted at her just now, and he's come to tell me off. And the trees have turned dark against the sky, since last time I looked, and they're looming up all around the field in one solid black scribbly wall, like they turned black and surrounded me when I wasn't looking.

'I just wanted to say thank you for doing such a great job, out here,' goes Steve, and he squats down next to me. And I keep planting, stabbing the trowel into the ground, to loosen it, in case this is a trick to make me stop working so he can punish me. And I claw out a little ball of fertiliser and force a wheat seed into it with my finger – even though it's so dry it splits apart when I force it in there – so Steve can see I'm still following his rules for planting the wheat.

'I think there's something we've forgotten, this evening,' he goes, and he leans over and starts kissing me.

'Please,' I go. 'Please. I know you're gonna make me do everything else. But can we not kiss?'

And he hesitates for a minute. And then he doesn't say anything. He just starts pulling down my shorts and my knickers and he moves me round so that I'm kneeling on my hands and knees, facing away from him. And then he starts having sex with me backwards, so he's kneeling up behind me. And I start crying, I just feel so horrible already, and my whole body hurts, and I'm so tired, and it's actually really painful what he's doing, which feels like it's opening up this black hole in my heart and scraping all the pain from all over my body down into it, and it's gouging the walls of my heart as it falls down and down. And I remember how the physical pain last time helped drown out the sadness. So on purpose, I rub the blisters off my palms, so the raw sticky red flesh is torn and stinging on my hands so hard I can feel the pain throbbing out from behind my eyeballs. But this time, it doesn't help at all. It just merges in with the sadness and the black despair and makes it even worse.

And Steve grabs a handful of my hair and yanks my head right back, ripping a load of hair out at the roots. 'Say, *Thank you, master,*' he goes, while he's forcing himself into me. 'And keep repeating it until I say you can stop.'

So I say, *Thank you, master. Thank you, master,* over and over again. And I try to say it as fake as I can, to show that I don't mean it. But Steve doesn't care, cos if he did, he'd make me say it differently. He just keeps forcing himself on me till eventually he finishes, panting like he's just completed his evening jog around the block. And then he stands up, buttons his shorts and just walks off, without even saying a single word. And I try to get back to planting, but I'm crying so hard I can't do anything. So I just have a little break, while I'm crying.

And when my crying dies down a bit, I can hear this sort of animal noise or bird noise. And I realise that it's Steve doing it with Meena, over at the other side of the field. And I'm trying to hear whether he's making her say, *Thank you, master,* as well. But I don't think he is. She's not saying any real words. And it's impossible to see them through the darkness, cos it's completely black down in the trees, where they are.

And I just sit on the ground, and then I lie down and curl up on my side, feeling like absolute shit. And for as long as I can hear Meena, that means no one's gonna come over here and I'm safe. And then when Meena stops, I get back on my hands and knees, and I start planting again. But I can't stop myself feeling worse and worse, and it literally feels like I'm falling and falling into a hole, and the deeper it gets, the worse I feel, and the more I know I'll never come out of it. And I've gotta get away from here. I don't even care if anyone sees me. And I'm thinking that I might kill myself, maybe stab the trowel into my wrist until I bleed to death, cos that can't feel any worse than this, and if Steve catches me and puts me in the cage, I don't even care. Cos he's basically made me into a slave already. And I bet Steve isn't fishing all night. I bet he's just going to sleep, like Meena is, while I'm working, out here. And they've probably got loads of nice food, which they secretly eat without me. And that's probably why Meena offered me her wheat cake and fish, yesterday lunchtime. Cos she'd never give me her own food, if we'd genuinely run out. She's much too selfish for that.

And sod this. And I dunno what I'm gonna do, exactly, and I don't really care. I've just gotta get away from here and have some proper sleep. I've gotta be a person again. Even if it is just for a few hours till they catch me and punish me. A real person. Instead of a slave or an animal. And I don't bother to check whether anyone's looking. I just stand up and walk off the field in the opposite direction from where Meena's voice came from.

And I just walk and walk for probably three hours. Wading through these ferns that come up as high as my waist and sometimes smashing my shins into logs, cos it's so dark I can't see much in the jungle here, apart from different shades of black. And I keep walking till I can hear the sea. And then I lay down on the floor, which is covered in moss, and I go to sleep.

CHAPTER TWENTY

And I wake up with water drizzling all over me. And the air's still the bluey-black dark of the middle of the night. And I'm so tired I wanna keep sleeping, but I can't cos these big raindrops keep falling into my ear and on my eyelids, and my clothes are getting soaked. So I get up, feeling like my brain's been flattened out by a rolling pin, it's so tired. And I'm thinking, What on earth am I doing, trying to run away and live on my own on the island? It's just stupid. Cos Steve's gonna find me and punish me. And it's gonna be much harder to ever escape again, cos he'll always be on the lookout after this, and I'm wasting my advantage of surprise, or whatever. Maybe I should just sneak back, I'm thinking, and probably no one will ever know that I left, and I wouldn't even get into trouble. Cos really, what am I gonna do? Hide in the jungle for the next sixty years, till I die? Steve will hunt me straight down, cos I don't even know how big or small this island is, and Steve knows every inch of this place. And the more I think about it – although I hate the idea of going back to live like a slave again – the more I realise I haven't got any choice, cos I'll just get caught. And Steve said I was already on my last chance, before he'd lock me in that goat cage. And I think about that girl Amanda who they locked up like that. And I wonder what ever happened to her. Cos either she escaped or she died, or they killed her. Cos she's blatantly not here now.

And I've gotta just go back to the field before anyone notices I've gone. So I try to walk back the way I came. But everything looks the same, in every direction, cos it's the middle of the night, and just darkness and shadows of trees and ferns all around me. So there's no way to even tell if I'm going the right way. And I'm so screwed. And the rain's getting harder, which means the crops will probably start springing up soon, so my job will get much easier, if I can just get back.

And I start to panic. And I start running. But then I stop again, cos it's pointless, cos if I'm going in the wrong direction, running will only take me *away* from the field quicker. I've gotta calm down and think of a plan. But I can't. My chest's all fluttery, and my blood's pumping around my face really fast and hot. And I dunno what to do. And I'm so screwed now.

'Help me! I'm lost!' I shout out as loud as I can. And I listen. But there's nothing. And my body's still killing me. It's like every single one of my muscles has turned stiff and raw, and every time I bend or move, they crack pain into my bloodstream. So I try standing completely still, but that just makes the pain worse in my hands which are raw and bleeding. And the rainstorm's getting harder – it's pelting down on me with fat hard raindrops.

And if I was gonna escape, I should have planned it all out in advance, and got lots of sleep, and stored up food, and learned my way around the island and where the good hiding places are and found out where Steve does his fishing. This is so stupid, the way I've done it.

So I try to think of a way I could get back to the crop field or the garden. But I can't think of anything, except to keep walking and walking and hope I find it through good luck, before they notice I've run away. And then I have the idea that I can look for food, while I'm out here. Cos at least if they catch me, I can say, Look, I got lost, but I found this wicked apple tree, or whatever, so we don't have to starve to death any more. And maybe I can find more of that plant that smells like garlic, like I found when I was blind. Maybe I could dig up a load of it and bring it back and plant it in the field. But I can't smell any now. And I'm thinking it'll probably be brighter if I can get out from under these trees, cos I'll probably get more moonlight, and it'll be easier to find food or see something I recognise to help me get back home. So I just pick a random direction, and start walking. But I walk and walk for at least an hour, it feels like, and I'm still in thick jungle, completely lost.

So I just sit down on this big fallen-over tree and wait for it to get light, cos it should be easier to find my way home then. So I sit there. And I tear off a big rubbery leaf from a bush and roll it into a giant ice cream cone shape and hold that up, to collect water, and every so often, when it gets full, I tip it into my mouth and have a drink, or empty it on my hands, to soothe the burning raw pain.

And eventually it gets light. And the only thing I can really do is pick a direction and start walking. But it's just more and more forest, with trees that all look the same. And I can't find anything that looks like food. I hear some birds, but I can't see them. And I'm so absolutely knackered, I keep finding myself looking for somewhere dry and hidden where I can sleep. And after a while I find another tree that's fallen over, with thick rubbery leaves overlapping each other like roof tiles. And the ground's pretty dry underneath it. So I curl up under there, and I'm still so tired, it doesn't take long for me to fall asleep again.

CHAPTER TWENTY-ONE

I wake up to someone kicking me quite hard in the back. And I try to look behind me to see who it is, but my hair rips out at the roots when I try to lift my head, so it must be pinned to the ground.

'Gotcha!' goes Steve's voice, with this evil glee.

'I just went for a sleep, and I got lost,' I'm like.

'I don't give a shit,' he's like. 'You're going in the cage.'

'I won't try it again, I promise.'

'Well, your promises don't really mean that much, do they?' goes Steve. 'You promised you'd keep working until the field was planted.'

'I was so tired I couldn't—'

'Shut it,' he goes. And he grabs me by the hair – I suppose he was standing on my hair before, to pin it to the ground – and he ties a cloth bag over my head and twists one of my arms tight behind my back and marches me through the trees.

And after a long walk, I hear the goats making their *meh-heh-heh-heh* noise, and my blood's turning icy, cos I know what's coming next. And he rattles something metal against the bars of the cage, probably a padlock. But then we keep walking. And he pulls the cloth bag off my head, and we're back in the field.

'Back to work,' he goes. 'Keep your promises. And stop letting down the community.' And he lets go of my wrist. 'Next time you go anywhere outside of this field without permission, we're cutting off one of your toes. Then one of your feet. Then one of your legs. And so on, until you learn your lesson. Do you understand?'

'Yes,' I go, although I don't understand whether I'm gonna have to go into the cage or not. But the way he talks tells me that I'm not allowed to ask any questions.

And he blows a shiny metal whistle three times, right in my ear, which makes my hearing go fuzzy. 'Any time you hear this whistle,' he goes, 'you have to run over to me or Meena, whoever's supervising you at the time. Do you understand?'

'Yes,' I go.

'One blast means we're in the field. Two means the goat cage. Three means the garden. And if you don't come immediately, you'll be punished. Got it?'

'Yes,' I'm like.

'Good,' goes Steve. 'Get back to work.' And he turns his back on me and walks off.

So I go back to planting wheat seeds in the field, which is covered in pools of muddy water from the rainstorm. And it gets mud all over my legs and all up my arms, as I crawl along on my hands and knees. And the bag of seeds is all soaked from the rain, which might have ruined them. But I'm blatantly not gonna tell anyone about that, cos they'll only blame me.

And the one good thing about the rain is that it does make the ground softer, cos now I can just poke the trowel in once, rock it around a bit to open up a hole and then drop the seed in and pat the earth back into place. Plus the rain's soaked through the sack, which makes the manure stickier, so I can poke the seed neatly into it with my finger, without it crumbling. And while I'm working, I hear one blast on the whistle, so I quickly stand up and look around the field. And I run stiffly towards Meena near the path that leads to the goats. And I'm doing a sort of crippled jog, cos my arms and legs are cramped from being hunched over on the floor, and my muscles still ache.

'Here's a glass of milk,' she goes, handing me a metal cup. And she looks me up and down, like I'm a filthy homeless woman.

'It was raining,' I go, 'so I got all muddy.'

And she just sniffs out a smug little laugh, like she's saying, *Whatever, you skanky pig.*

And I drink the milk. And I can't give her any lip, cos I've gotta be extra good so she won't grass me up to Steve, and hopefully he'll forget about putting me in the cage.

'What's gonna happen when I finish work today?' I'm like.

'You're going in the cage, I think. But I'll have to check with Steve.'

And my heart sinks and withers. 'For how long?'

'Don't you worry about that,' goes Meena. 'You just get back to work.' And her voice is so completely cold. You'd never know we'd ever been friends with each other.

And I go back out to the field. And my only hope now is that if I can finish planting the entire thing, then Steve will let me off going in the cage, cos I've done such a good job. So I work like crazy, as fast as I possibly can. And after about six or seven hours of work I've finished a quarter of the field, which is a pretty impressive achievement in itself. And I wanna have a sleep, but I can't now, cos I have to be ready in case Meena or Steve blows that stupid whistle. I can never relax ever again, cos of that thing. So instead, I walk around the field. And there's a few tiny green sprouts, here and there, sticking up though the massive patch of filthy mud. But then I hear two blasts on the whistle, so I jog over to the goat cage, and Steve and Meena are standing there with the cage door open. And Steve's like:

'You can either walk inside on your own, or I can force you to go in.'

'Can't we just let her off?' goes Meena. 'She did plant, like, quarter of that field on her own.'

'Meena, go back to the garden,' Steve's like. 'And Shruti, get in the cage, now.'

And I don't move, cos I'm waiting to see if Meena will stand up for me again. But she gives me a little shrug, to say, Sorry that's all I can do. And she stands there watching.

'All right, then,' Steve goes to me. 'We'll do it the hard way.'

'No, no, no. I'm going, I'm going,' I'm like, and I walk inside the cage. And the ceiling's low. And the two goats are dirty white, and they've both got thin wispy beards and pointy little hoofs that *clip* on the metal floor of the cage when they walk. And their wiry fur brushes against my legs. And the cage has metal bars all around me, and thick slabs of metal for the roof and the floor. And on the floor, there's a few branches with the leaves all chewed off, and apart from that, it's just bare metal, with clusters of black goat droppings, and a pool of greeny-yellow urine in one corner. Meena's already disappeared off down the path.

'How long do I have to stay in here?' I'm like.

'Just until we start work tomorrow morning,' goes Steve. 'And then at the end of each working day.'

'For how long, though?'

'Don't you worry about that,' goes Steve, using the same evil phrase as Meena. 'You just worry about doing a good job in the field and coming quickly when you hear the whistle, and being a good little girl. All right?'

'Yes,' I go, cos I have to.

And he closes the door of the cage and slides the bolt over and then clips the padlock closed and then rattles it, to make sure it's locked. And the rattling metal noise makes the goats go *Meh-heh-heh-heh.*

'Goodnight,' I go to Steve, cos I still want him to still think of me as a human and not an animal. But he doesn't even look at me when I talk. He just jingles the keys in the pocket of his cargo shorts and walks off back to the garden.

And it's twilight now, and at least I'm totally exhausted, so hopefully I'll be able to get to sleep quickly. That's the best thing I can do. Just sleep, so I won't even know where I am. So I pick up the few stripped-off branches from the floor, and bunch them together like a sort of broom, and sweep the pool of urine out through the bars of the cage. And I sweep away most of the piles of droppings. But a few piles, which must be the freshest ones, smear on the floor when I try to sweep them. So I scrape away as much as I can with the branches, and then I store those branches just outside the bars of the cage, cos I'll need them again next time I need to sweep up. And I lie down at the end of the cage nearest the door – cos that's the opposite end to where the pool of urine was. And curl my hands up under my head, and the muscles in my fingers are throbbing in pain, and the skin's so raw that it's like they're on fire. And my body's covered in mud, which is drying tight over my skin and cracking, like I'm growing scales like a reptile. But I'm so tired, I don't even care any more. I just go to sleep.

But I get woken up by loud clanging on the bars. And it's still twilight, so I can't have been asleep long. Unless I've been asleep for a whole twenty-four hours. And it's Steve. And immediately I realise what he's come back for. And he forces himself on me and makes me say all this horrible stuff about how much I'm enjoying it, as he pushes my face into the bars of the cage. And this time, I'm trying to take my mind off it by thinking about how I wish I could murder him, by smashing a heavy stone down on his face, again and again, until I've crushed the bones of his skull into sharp broken triangles that slice down and embed themselves into his brain and slice into his windpipe. But that wouldn't even make me feel better. What I really want is someone to just be nice to me. And I dunno why Steve's doing this. It's not the sex. Cos if he just wanted sex, Meena would give him as much as he wanted. And I dunno why he came straight out and raped me straight away. Cos he could have at least *started out* trying to be nice. And maybe I might have gone along with it, after a while, if I knew that there was no one else, and if he was extra nice to me, and if we had, like, a sort of wedding or something first. But he didn't even try that, which doesn't make sense. Cos why make someone suffer like that, if you wanna keep having sex with them? But that *is* the reason, I think, although I don't actually understand it: making me suffer is what he enjoys. And he was probably gonna put me in this cage at some point no matter what I did, cos he enjoys making me suffer so much.

And when he finishes, he's like:

'Say, "Thank you, master. I enjoyed that very much."'

But I'm crying so much it deforms all the words that come out of my mouth. And he keeps shouting at me to tell him I enjoyed it. And I keep trying, but I can't get any words out properly. And eventually he gives up and leaves me in the cage and locks me in. And there's nothing I can say or do apart from hold the bars, crying and waiting for him to leave.

CHAPTER TWENTY-TWO

And I wake up the next morning to the clang of metal throbbing in my brain, and it's Meena slamming a metal bucket against the bars of the cage as hard as she can. And there's a stabbing pain in my leg, which I think was one of the goats treading on it with its sharp little hoof.

'Couldn't you have just tapped me on the shoulder and said, It's time to wake up?' I ask her.

'We have to do this to scare the goats,' she goes, in this cold voice. 'It gets the milk flowing if they're scared.'

And they tell so many lies, her and Steve, I can't even be bothered to work out whether that's true or not. Cos who cares, really? Plus, even if it is true, she could have woken me up nicely and then clanged the bars of the cage afterwards. And then I remember that it's not a world of truth versus lies, it's a matter of Steve's reality, which Meena lives inside, versus my reality, which I've got no chance of preserving, cos Steve's reality's blatantly crushing mine to dust.

And Meena unlocks the padlock, and slides the bolt across, and opens the door. 'Come out then, you fucking whore,' she goes.

'What are you having a go at me for?'

'Because you're a fucking whore who can't stop seducing my boyfriend, cos you just can't control yourself.'

'What?' I'm like. 'You think I want that to happen? He's raping me, Meena.'

'Well, that's not what he told me.'

'Why would I want him to keep having sex with me, when I hate him doing that and I hate his guts?'

'You shut your fucking mouth, you whore, all right. That's the father of my child you're talking about.'

And there's blatantly nothing I can say to change her mind. And just when I think things literally couldn't get any worse, now Meena apparently hates me all the time, as well. And the more Steve forces himself on me, the more she's gonna hate me. And Steve's blatantly turning her against me, on purpose.

And I look down at myself, and my clothes are absolutely filthy. I do look literally like an actual homeless person now, who lives on the streets. Cos my legs are covered in old mud, and there's mud and leaves in my hair, which is so oily and greasy and dirty my head itches all the time. And my T-shirt's crusted and stiff where muddy water has dried into the fabric. And there's this disgusting sharp acidic smell, coming off the side of my T-shirt, and it smells like old wee. And I'm thinking, maybe I wet myself in the night, but then I look down at the floor of the cage, and there's a pool of yellowy-green urine which the goats must have done, right where I was sleeping, and it must have soaked onto my clothes.

'What are you waiting for?' goes Meena. 'Get out, you whore. I've gotta milk the goats.'

293

And my mouth starts watering when I think of the goats' milk, all creamy and warm and nutty and sweet. So I walk out of the cage, and my body aches. And Meena buckles collars round the goats' necks, with chains on them. And she brings the first one out of the cage. And traps the end of its chain under the leg of a wooden stool, lines up the metal bucket underneath its udders and sits down and starts milking. And there's nowhere for me to sit. So I just sit on the floor, with my back against a tree. And it's so soft and cool down there, compared to the hard metal floor of the cage, I stretch out and lie down on my back, and I let my muscles relax on the cool mossy earth on the forest floor. And I can hear the goat's milk squirting against the side of the metal bucket, with this zinging sound. And it's so relaxing there, with the heat of the day just starting to pick up, I drift off to sleep again.

'You're such an animal,' goes Meena. 'Get up off the ground.'

'I'm tired,' I go. 'I'm just relaxing.'

'Look at you,' she's like. 'You look like a filthy pig.'

'Well, let me have some clean clothes then.'

'We're not wasting clean clothes on you – you'd just get them filthy and ruined.'

'Well, don't call me dirty then, if you won't let me get clean.'

'I didn't call you dirty. I called you a filthy animal. Which is exactly what you are.'

'*You're* the animals,' I go, 'you and Steve are the animals, cos you just do whatever's best for you, without caring for anyone else. It's like you can't even control yourselves—'

'No, it isn't—'

'Yes, it is,' I go. 'Every bit of power you have, you've used to screw me over, as much as you possibly can. And if the two of you felt like it, you'd probably kill me, only it wouldn't suit you, cos then you couldn't keep me as your slave any more, and you'd have to plant the field yourselves, which you can't be bothered to do. But it's not because you care about my life, or care about me as a person, that you don't kill me. It's because you can get more benefit from me alive than dead. But that's all I'm worth to you. What you can exploit out of me. You're the filthy animals, mate. Not me.'

'Look at yourself, though. Look at the state of yourself, lying on the floor like a pig.'

'I'm lying on the floor cos I'm exhausted from working hard, and cos there's nowhere else I can lie. There's nothing dirty about that. That's what anyone would do in my situation. What you and Steve are doing, though – that's dirty, mate. That's the dirtiest thing I've ever seen. Cos not everyone would do that. Most people would be nice to me. Even though you've got all the power and you're bigger and stronger and cleverer, and whatever else. You don't have to treat me like this. But you can't help yourselves. *Steve* can't help exploiting me. And *you* can't help going along with it and being his puppet and doing whatever he wants you to. You're the animals, mate. You're the dirty ones. I'm just trying to survive, cos there's nothing else I can do. You should have a look at yourself, mate, if you wanna see what a dirty animal looks like. And look at what you're doing now,' I'm like. 'Why are you milking those goats, instead of forcing me to do it? Cos you don't want me to learn how, cos then I might milk the goats myself, while I'm locked in the cage, and drink the milk, and you and Steve wouldn't get any.'

'That's not the reason.'

'Yes, it is,' I go. 'And even if it isn't the reason, it might as well be.'

'You just shut your mouth, you filthy pig.'

'There you go again – acting like an animal. When something happens that you don't like, you can't help yourself. You just lash out and attack me. You don't care about me as a person. And when I make you have the tiniest bit of discomfort you do whatever you think it will take to shut me up. What's disgusting is putting another human in the situation where they have to act like an animal, just so you can have an easier life.'

'Just shut your mouth for two seconds, would you?' goes Meena, and her milking's getting faster now, I suppose cos she wants to get away from here, so she doesn't have to listen to me telling her the truth any more, or maybe she's doing it unconsciously cos the anger's firing up her muscles.

'Why do you want me to shut my mouth?' I go. 'What are you gonna do?'

She can't think of anything.

'That's right,' I'm like. 'There's nothing else you can do, is there? You can't take anything away from me, cos I haven't got anything to take. You could rip my shorts and T-shirt off my back. But who gives a shit? Not me. The clothes are rubbish anyway. I live in a cage anyway. Steve rapes me every day anyway. My whole life is gonna be stuck in basically a prison, and I'm never gonna have any friends, or any fun, or anything good happen to me. And you and Steve think you're making me more and more scared, the more you fuck me over. But you're wrong, you pair of absolute *idiots*. You're just making me stronger. Cos it's gonna get to a point where there really is nothing else you can take away from me. And then there'll be nothing you can do, apart from injuring my body or, like, torturing me. And that would stop me from being able to work properly, so really it would be hurting you, cos your slave would be less effective. And I know for a fact that you'd never do that, cos you're too selfish,' I go. 'So what are you gonna do now?'

'Just shut up. You dunno what you're talking about.'

'Oh, I know exactly what I'm talking about,' I'm like. 'And so do you. I could tell this was all true the minute it came out of my mouth.'

And she just shakes her head.

'What's the matter, Meena? Got nothing to say?' I'm like.

'You filthy pig,' she goes under her breath. And for some reason I know that I've won.

'I haven't eaten a proper meal for days,' I go. 'Not since you were giving me those bowls of soup when I was getting well. But you and Steve are still eating all right.'

'None of us have got any food,' she's like. 'We're all waiting till the crops come up.'

'How come I'm like a skeleton, then, and you and Steve haven't lost any weight at all?'

'You're just burning more calories, cos you're working more.'

'That's not true, and you know it,' I go. 'Now I'm gonna have a massive drink of that milk. And you're gonna not tell Steve about it.'

And I walk over and pick up the bucket from where she's gripping it between her bare feet. And I lift it away from her feet and bring it up to my mouth. And I'm careful to only tip it up really slowly, cos I know that with big containers like that, the liquid all rushes into your face and drips down your chin. So I tilt it really slowly, until the creamy white milk creeps down the inside wall in a soft, cream-coloured, pointy curve, till it gets to my lips. And I gulp it down, mouthful after mouthful, and I can feel it going down my food pipe into my tummy and filling it up. And I keep glugging down more and more, till my stomach feels like it's gonna burst. And then I rest the bucket upright on the floor and wipe my mouth with the back of my hand. And Meena's just sitting there on the little wooden milking stool, watching me.

And I hand the bucket back to her, and she grips it between her bare feet again, under the goat's udders.

'I'm going to the loo,' I tell her. 'And then I'm gonna wash myself off at those rock pools.' And I don't wait for her permission. I leave her sitting there, muttering, *Whatever, you skank,* under her breath. And I just walk off down the path, feeling pretty good about myself, for telling Meena off like that. And I go to the loo and then have a wash, and then I come back to the goat cage, and Steve's there now.

And all this dread drenches through my veins. Cos if Meena told him how I just shouted at her, he's gonna do something terrible to me. And I instantly realise that there is actually a lot more they could do to me, to make my life worse.

'Right,' goes Steve. 'The seeds you wrapped in manure have started springing up. So first, you're going to clean and store the plough, to stop it rusting. And then you're going to water every seedling, using a bucket and the rainwater we've collected, and I'm also sinking a new well you can use.'

And I'm so relieved that Meena didn't grass me up. And I wish I could tell Steve off, like I did with Meena. But I don't have the guts, cos there's no way that he'd just sit there and take it like Meena did. He'd definitely do something evil to me straight away to punish me.

So I drag the plough off to the side of the field and clean it and Steve ties a tarpaulin over it, to keep it dry. And then I spend the entire day carrying water in a bucket from these huge stainless steel rainwater tanks that I'd never seen before and pouring it first over the little green seedlings, and then Steve makes me water the whole field, twice, which takes two whole days.

And then as more shoots come up, I have to inspect every single one of them, every day, and pick off the insects, as well as water the whole field by hand using a bucket. And then I'm sleeping in the cage every night, with Steve coming and attacking me every evening. And after about a month of trying, I'm able to pretend to be made out of wood and give no reaction to him at all – not happy and not scared and not crying. And when he forces me to say things, I just talk in this empty wooden voice. And when he makes me say them again, I say them a bit different but still as fake and wooden as I can. And I do think he enjoys it less and less. But he keeps doing it.

And after about another few weeks of me being wooden when Steve's attacking me, he stops bothering to lock me in the cage. And instead of attacking me there, he attacks me while I'm working in the field, and I act like I can't feel anything, which gets easier and easier, cos my feelings have started, like, shutting down, which I'm glad about, cos it's much easier to live that way, instead of crying and feeling this desperate fear and despair all the time. And at night I start sleeping in the forest. And the wheat gets taller and thicker, till the field's filled with lush, fresh green shoots, with ears of wheat lining the top of each stalk.

And Meena's tummy gets fatter and fatter from the baby. And Steve's started catching fish again, plus he's bringing in this seaweed which we all eat, like salty greens. And I keep meaning to explore the island and look for a secret boat or a way to escape, or some fruit trees I could eat from, but I'm so tired all the time I never get round to it. And there's no days off. And the only time they leave me alone is at night, when it's too dark to explore properly and I'm so knackered all I wanna do is sleep. And I make a sort of bed for myself in the trees, where I sleep at night, with ferns to lie on.

And the wheat grows waist high, and starts turning from green to golden yellow. And by this time, Meena's getting well fat, with the baby. And Steve's actually getting a bit of a belly, himself, which he never had before. But not me. I haven't seen a mirror since I got to the island. But when I look down at myself, I can see my ribs sticking out through my chest, and my arms and legs are like skeletons'. So Meena and Steve must be eating secret food while I'm working.

CHAPTER TWENTY-THREE

And one morning I'm going round the field, picking these hard black beetles off the wheat plants and crushing them between two little stones I carry, which is a never-ending job, cos there's thousands of them. Plus I think they're getting stronger as time goes by, and living deeper inside the ears of wheat, probably through a sort of natural selection, or whatever, cos the ones that are clever enough to hide from me are the ones that survive and breed, so the more I hunt them, the better the species gets at hiding from me and surviving. And out of nowhere Steve's walking towards me really quick and excited, which is weird, cos he never normally attacks me until the evening. So I brace myself and try to make my feelings run cold.

'Meena's having her baby,' he goes. 'And she's asked for you to be there. So go to the rock pools and clean yourself off and sterilise your hands. And I'll leave some clean clothes out for you to change into.'

And my heart starts racing, cos this is the first time they've treated me like a person since I dunno when – since I was ill in bed, I suppose. So I have a wash and put on this fresh white

T-shirt and shorts and knickers that Steve's left for me on the table in the garden. And it feels so amazingly nice, having fresh clothes against my skin. And the fabric on the T-shirt's slightly stiff and soapy smelling, like it's been washed in real washing powder, even though Meena told me there wasn't any. So God knows what they've got hidden from me in that store room. And I pick up my filthy, torn old clothes and run back to the rock pools and throw the clothes into the sea, so that Steve won't be able to force me to put them back on after Meena's had her baby.

And then I walk inside the bedroom building for the first time since that 'feast' night when Steve first forced himself on me. And I'm expecting to see Meena lying on her back with her knees up and spread apart, like women on the telly lay when they have babies. But instead she's standing bent over, resting her face on the bed.

'All right, mate,' she's like. 'I'm having a baby.'

'Yeah, I heard,' I go.

And it's this really nice, close moment, where Meena's treating me like a real person again. And maybe this will be the turning point, and we'll bond over this baby. And then her and Steve will see how horrible they were being to me, and start treating me nice again. Maybe they'll make me into their nanny. And maybe it would be best if I did have a baby myself, cos then I could bond even more with Meena, cos we'd have, like, motherhood in common, plus I'd become the mother of one of Steve's children, so hopefully that would make him become kind to me.

'How you feeling?' I go.

'I've been better,' she's like.

And Steve butts in:

'Shruti, could you start by cleaning up this mess on the floor?' And he points to a puddle of clear liquid, near where he's sitting on his stupid throne chair carved out of the tree trunk. 'That's where Meena's waters broke. We want to get it all cleaned up before the insects find it. I'll bring some disinfectant.'

And as soon as he goes out of the room, Meena goes to me:

'I'm dying, mate.'

'Yeah, I heard it hurts like mental, having a baby.'

'No, listen to what I'm saying. I'm actually dying,' she goes. 'I can feel it.'

'Yeah, it probably *feels* like you're dying,' I go. 'But it's just the contractions, or whatever.'

'The baby's already dead inside me,' goes Meena. 'He stopped kicking about two weeks ago, and his body's rotting away and killing me,' she's like. 'I'm not gonna last till tonight. So there's some stuff I've gotta tell you before Steve gets back.'

'All right, then,' I go. Cos I wanna hear what she's got to say, even though I don't believe for a second she's gonna die. She just wants to make this even more of a drama than it already is.

'First of all,' she's like— but then bloody Steve comes back with a little bottle of disinfectant and a metal bucket and a scrubbing brush.

'Right then,' he goes. 'Go and get some water – seawater's fine for this kind of job – and clean up this mess.' And he hands the bucket to me. 'Chop-chop,' he goes.

So I run all the way to the rock pools and fill the bucket, as quick as I can, cos I don't wanna miss the birth, and I don't want

Meena to have the baby before she's had a chance to tell me whatever it was she wanted to say.

And when I get back, there's candles burning all around the room, and Steve's rocking back on the bottom edge of his tree-trunk chair, which I dunno how he managed to squeeze past the tall woven wooden fence in front of the doorway. And I pour a bit of disinfectant into the bucket of seawater and scrub the floor with it. And Steve makes me fetch a second bucket of water and rinse the floor.

And now Steve's lounging back in his tree-trunk chair, with his feet on the bed, going, 'I'm staying right here until this whole thing's over, darling. And Shruti's here as well, to bring us food and drink, and she'll operate a kind of bed-pan system, so I won't even have to leave to use the toilet. I'll be here, right the way through.'

And Meena grabs her sides. 'Arrrh,' she goes, and she curls into a ball, on the bed. 'Get me the knife,' she goes. 'I'm doing a caesarean on myself.'

'You'll get through this,' goes Steve. 'You'll be fine, and it'll all be over soon.'

And Meena curls up like a prawn. Then she turns to face the ceiling, trying to get comfortable, and arches her back with her tummy in the air. Then she tries lying on her front. 'All right,' she goes. 'Gimme the drugs.'

'We've only got paracetamol,' goes Steve. 'And there's only twelve of them.'

'Fine,' Meena's like. 'Give me all twelve.'

'Ha. Well, we'll save some for later,' goes Steve. 'We don't

304

know how long this might take. And what if you have another baby?'

'Or me,' I go.

'That's right, or Shruti,' goes Steve, getting a white plastic aspirin bottle out of his pocket and rattling out two pills. And he's like, 'Start with these, and we'll see how we go.'

And Meena picks them out of his palm and eats them both with no water. And Steve's like:

'And remember your tolerance will be low, so they'll probably have a strong effect.'

'Oh, my fucking tolerance is low, all right,' goes Meena. And she lies there for a while, shifting from one position to the next. And suddenly she clutches her sides. '*Ahh*, Jesus Christ this hurts,' she's like. 'I'm just gonna top myself,' she goes. 'This isn't worth it.'

'No you're not, mate. You're gonna get through this,' I go, cos if she keeps talking about suicide like that, Steve's never gonna leave us alone again, cos he'll wanna keep watch over her.

'If I had a gun in my hand, I'd put it in my mouth right now and pull the trigger,' she goes. 'And you can take that to the bank.'

So I leave her alone. Cos with this suicide stuff, the more I try to calm her down, the more she's gonna talk about it, for attention. And I'm trying to think up a way to get Steve out of the room.

'Meena,' I'm like. 'Do you think that having a walk around a bit might help?'

'Yes,' she goes. 'That's just what I need. A lovely stroll through

305

the forest. Let's go hunting elephants with the blunderbuss while we're at it, you stupid muppet.'

So I let that idea go. And I lean on the wall, cos there's nowhere to sit. And Steve's sitting there in his tree-trunk chair, and staring up at the rows of spiky-leaved branches that the ceiling's made of. And neither of us know what to do. And he looks at Meena, squirming around on the bed, trying to find a comfortable position, and he looks at me, and shrugs his shoulders. And that's another thing he's done to acknowledge I'm a real person. And I really hope this baby will finally bring all three of us together.

And eventually Meena seems to find a comfortable position, kneeling up on the bed, with her hands on the wall, like she's holding it up in case it falls on her. 'Someone say something,' she goes. 'I'm bored out of my mind, here. Someone sing,' she goes. 'I haven't heard any music for ages. Sing something. Like pop songs, or whatever.'

'What, me?' I go.

'Yes, you,' she's like.

So I start singing this old Kylie Minogue song, *Especially for You*. And Meena joins in, doing the Jason Donovan bit. And Steve's tapping his foot to the music. And if I can just think of some more enjoyable stuff we can do, then they'll see how much fun they could be having with me, and they'll definitely wanna be friends with me again.

So I sing *Wannabe* by the Spice Girls, cos everyone knows that. And Meena joins in, but before we've even finished the first chorus, she goes, '*Aaarrrragghh!*' and clenches up her body. So I stop singing.

'Keep going,' she's like, with pain stretching her voice tight. 'Keep singing.'

So I keep singing, while she groans with agony, in the background. And I have to keep weaving bits of the first verse into the rest of the song, to patch over the gaps where I can't remember what the real words should be.

'That's enough music,' goes Meena, panting, when I've finished. 'I need everyone to be quiet now.'

So while we're sitting there in silence, I try to think up a plan to get rid of Steve. And I'm pretty sure that him and Meena have got a store of nice food they keep secret from me. Cos how else are they getting fatter, while I look like someone in a prisoner-of-war camp?

'I heard that eating nice food helps you feel better if you're giving birth,' I'm like. 'Is there anything I could get you?'

'Chocolate,' goes Meena. 'Like a Snickers or a Dairy Milk, or anything like that.'

And Steve's shoots me a quick guilty glance, cos this proves they've been lying about what kind of food they've got. And he pauses while he has to decide whether he wants to make me go and get the chocolate – and see the secret food stores for myself – or whether *he* wants to get it and leave me alone with Meena. And whichever thing he decides to do will help me.

'I'm pretty sure we haven't got any chocolate,' Steve goes. 'But I'll check all the pockets of my old coats and whatnot, and see what I can find.' And he stands up. 'Shruti, sit on the bed with Meena and don't move until I get back,' he's like.

So I sit next to Meena, who's curled up on the bed. And Steve walks off.

'Mate,' she's like, and she pats the duvet next to her, 'just lie down here next to me for a minute.' So I do. And we're facing each other, with our heads resting on the same pillow. And she picks a piece of leaf out of my hair. 'Shruti, mate,' she goes. 'I just wanted to say that I'm sorry for bringing you here. I honestly didn't know it would turn out like this, with Steve treating you so badly,' she's like. 'He said we'd all be equal, when he was explaining the whole idea to me. And then when he started making you work so much, there was nothing I could do to stop him. You know what he's like.'

'Yeah,' I go, just to keep her talking, to try and make her say whatever secret she was planning to tell me.

'And if there's anything I can do for you in my last few hours, then I will.'

'All right,' I go. 'Well, first of all, tell me is there any way to escape from this island?'

'No,' goes Meena.

'What about a secret boat? Or a phone?' I'm like.

'No,' goes Meena. 'There's nothing.'

'Is there someone who comes to visit, to bring extra food, or whatever?'

'No,' she's like. 'Those Filipino sailors were supposed to do that. But then Steve shot them all.'

'The old one didn't die, though. He might come back.'

'I doubt it, with a massive gunshot wound to his neck,' goes Meena. 'I honestly think he bled to death while he was trying to sail home.'

'All right,' I'm like, trying to think of something else it would be useful to know. 'What happened to that Amanda girl?'

And Meena suddenly looks at me. 'How do you know about Amanda?'

'You told me months ago that Steve locked her in the goat cage.'

'You don't wanna know about her, mate,' Meena goes. 'Trust me.'

'Well, she's not here now, so she must have either escaped or—'

'Look, Steve's come back with the chocolate!' Meena goes, interrupting me.

'I managed to find one of these Indian chocolate bars,' Steve's like, handing this Five Star to Meena, who unwraps it and immediately starts scoffing it down. And my mouth's watering so badly, cos I haven't had chocolate since I got here. And she eats the entire thing herself and drops the wrapper onto the bed. So I secretly sneak it into my pocket, cos I'm gonna lick the crumbs out of it later, when I'm on my own.

'What I need now,' she goes, 'is a lovely fresh piece of fish. Like a butterfish. But anything would do.'

And Steve's looking pissed off now. 'I'm not leaving you for that long, to go fishing,' he's like. 'I need to be here in case of emergencies, and I'm not going to miss the birth of my own child.'

'Well, I've gotta eat some kind of meat or fish or something. I haven't eaten a proper meal since the day before yesterday.'

'Okay,' goes Steve. 'I'll bring a selection of food. And that can last you through the night.' And he hesitates in the doorway, and we're both staring at him from the bed. And then he leaves again. And Meena waits till we can't hear his footsteps any more.

'Just tell me what happened to Amanda,' I'm like. 'Did she escape or did she die?'

'She died,' goes Meena.

'How?' I'm like.

'In the cage,' Meena goes. 'But it was horrible. I don't even wanna think about it.'

'What happened?'

'Look, this is a waste of time,' goes Meena. 'I've got important stuff I've gotta tell you. So shut up about Amanda for a minute, and listen, all right. Steve changed all his money into these little one ounce tablets of gold, cos he reckons gold won't lose its value like normal money will,' she's like. 'They used to be hidden under the floorboards of the chicken house. But then Steve moved them – after he shot the sailors – and I dunno where they are now. But if he dies you should search everywhere, cos there's at least half a million pounds' worth there.'

'All right,' I'm like, but in my head I'm thinking, That's no help at all, cos even if it's true there's gold buried somewhere, it would take me, like, a thousand years to dig up this whole massive island and find it. 'What else did you wanna tell me?' I ask her.

'Just that I hope everything works out all right for you,' goes Meena. 'And that I know you don't believe that I'm gonna die. You just thought you'd get some information out of me while I was vulnerable. Cos you're just an animal, just like the rest of us, ain't you?' she goes, with a little grin. 'You don't have the

310

strength to bully or manipulate people. But now that you've got the chance, you're being fake to your best friend on her deathbed to weasel a bit of information for yourself.'

And that makes me feel scummy, cos that is sort of the truth.

'It's all right, though,' Meena's like. 'Anyone would have done the same thing. And I don't think you— *Ahhhh*,' she's like. 'Oh, Jesus Christ, I think the body's coming out. Go and get Steve. Go and shout for him. And tell him to bring a knife.'

'A knife?'

'Just fucking do it,' she goes. 'Go!'

So I run to the door and step around the woven wooden fence that's in front of it. 'Steve!' I shout out. 'Meena thinks she's having the baby!'

'I'm coming!' comes his voice from in the woods. 'Hold on!'

So I shout:

'And she says bring a sharp knife, but I dunno why!' And I go back inside, cos Steve doesn't want me to see what direction he's coming from, cos that's where the secret food must be. So I sit back down on the bed, where Steve told me to wait. And Meena's lying on her back now, and she's wriggling out of her shorts and knickers, so I help her take them off. And she's scrunching up her face in pain, and straining to push the baby out.

And Steve walks in, carrying a cloth bag filled with food in one hand and a kitchen knife in the other.

'This is it, then,' he goes. And he puts down the bag and knife and stands at the bottom of the bed, between Meena's feet. 'All right, Meena. I think the best thing here would be to follow your instincts. So push whenever you feel like pushing. And we'll be here to support you however we can. Okay?'

'Just tell me when you can see his head,' goes Meena, panting really hard, and her T-shirt's soaked in sweat.

'Of course,' goes Steve. 'We'll tell you everything we can see.'

'And make sure Shruti stays here the whole time,' goes Meena.

'Naturally,' Steve's like.

And I hold Meena's hand while I sit on the side of the bed. And she screams and tenses up her body and pushes.

And Steve goes:

'Okay, let's try this. Why don't you have a rest from pushing for a few minutes. And build up your energy for one really hard push. And then maybe we can get the baby's head out. And after that it should be easier.'

'Do you think that'll work?' goes Meena.

'I think so,' goes Steve, although blatantly he hasn't got a clue, cos a minute ago he was telling her to push whenever she wanted to. And Meena's face is sweaty in the blacky-orange light from the candles, cos there's no windows, and the wooden fence is blocking out most of the daylight from the doorway.

'Right,' goes Steve. 'I'm going to count down from five and when I get to zero, I want you to give the push of your life, and let's get this little fellow's head out.' And Steve slides his fingers inside her, I suppose to open up the way for the baby to come out.

So Steve counts down, 'Five – four – three – two – one – zero. And *push*!'

And Meena's like 'Aaaarrrrgghhhh!' with all these strings of muscle standing out in her neck. And as she pushes, a jet of wee squirts out of her and into Steve's face and makes him blink and pull his head away. And then he wipes his face, laughing. And then the room smells like poo. And I look down at the bottom of the bed, and Meena's pooed herself as well, with that massive push.

'Well, at least that's out of the way, now,' goes Steve, making a joke of it. 'Shruti, go and get some leaves and another bucket of seawater and clean all this up, would you?'

So I go and get leaves and more water, and I clean up this long poo that dropped onto the floor and the wee that sprayed all over the place. And I wipe Meena's bum clean with a few of those furry leaves. And I throw away all the dirty water and the leaves by the rocks at the edge of the sea where we go to the toilet. And while I'm there, I clean my hands with the disinfectant leaves, cos I don't wanna get the baby ill.

And I rush back to the sleeping room. And I sit down on the bed again next to Meena, who's panting and has a soft painful expression on her face, but she's limp and weak now, like she's not really even trying any more, which is weird, cos she was acting fine when I left, just like twenty minutes ago.

'I ain't got long, mate,' she whispers to me, as I take her hand. And I wipe away the hair that's sticking to the sweat on her forehead. 'Just tell me when you see the head,' she goes, 'and say if he's alive or not.'

'Course he's alive,' I'm like. 'You're gonna be fine, and so's the baby.'

And then me and Steve persuade her to keep pushing every so

313

often for the next half an hour. And little by little, the baby's head comes out, and I stay up at the top of the bed, holding Meena's hand, while Steve's down the bottom, where the baby's coming.

'The head's completely through, now,' Steve goes. 'I can see his whole face.'

'Is he alive?' goes Meena.

'I think so,' goes Steve. 'His face is very white, but he's warm.'

'Is the face moving, though?' Meena asks. 'Are his eyes moving, or his mouth, or anything?'

And this wind blows in through the door and snuffs out a couple of the candles and bends the flames on the other ones. 'No,' goes Steve. 'They're not. But he is alive, I think.'

'Ah,' goes Meena. And she closes her eyes. And it's stupid, the way she talks like she's acting in a film. And I lean over and give her a kiss on the forehead. And the candles are giving off this yellow soft light that makes her face look really smooth and calm. And she takes one deep breath. And then there's a long, long gap. And then she takes another breath. And then I'm waiting and waiting for her to breathe again, but she doesn't.

'Steve,' I go. 'I think there's something wrong with Meena.'

And he rushes up to the top of the bed, opposite where I am. And he puts two fingers on her neck to feel for her heartbeat there.

'Jesus Christ,' he goes. And he leans over and pinches her nose shut and starts breathing into her mouth, so that her chest goes up and down with Steve's breath in her lungs. And he does about

314

ten of those breaths, and then he pushes down in the middle of Meena's chest about ten times. And then he stands up straight, with a look of total panic. And he runs his fingers through his hair. 'Okay,' he's like. 'We're still okay.'

And he does the breathing and the chest pump again, five times each. And he's shaking his head and muttering to himself in this angry, sweary little voice, 'Oh, for fuck's sake, this isn't happening. This is not happening.'

But it blatantly is happening. And I'm just getting in Steve's way, sitting on the edge of the bed while he's doing the mouth-to-mouth on Meena and the heart-pump thing. But I don't want to let go of Meena's hand, cos that'll tell Steve that I think she's dead, when he doesn't want to believe that. So first of all I'm like, 'I'm just gonna check on the baby,' to let Steve know that I'm not letting go of Meena's hand cos I think she's dead but just so I can move.

And then I quietly rest Meena's hand on her thigh, so she looks more alive. And I walk down to the bottom of the bed to look at the baby. And it looks like something from a horror film: cos I can just about see the baby's head, and the skin on its little face is almost completely white, like it's made out of wax, and there's purpley-red bruises around its eyes and in the middle of its forehead. And on one of its eyelids, there's a purple blister, like a bubble of purple skin. And I have to look away, cos it's so horrific, I keep expecting it to open its little eyes and scream at me.

'I'm afraid, I think,' goes Steve, with his voice quavering, 'I think Meena has passed on.' And Steve starts sobbing, and he bows his head over and his mouth turns down, and tears are running down his cheeks. So I have to go over there and put my arm round his shoulders, even though I hate him, cos it's hard not to be kind to someone who's so upset.

CHAPTER TWENTY-FOUR

And we're both sitting on the edge of the bed, and Steve's crying, and I've got my arm round his shoulders. And I just feel this cold shock all around me, like a white force field in a superhero comic strip, stopping any feelings touching me. And I can't stop thinking about the baby. And what are we gonna do about it? Cos what if Meena's body goes totally stiff, with, like, rigor mortis, or whatever? How are we ever gonna pull the baby out, then? So I'm like:

'Steve, I think we should do something about the baby, before Meena's body gets stiff.'

And he just nods through his crying, and he picks up Meena's hand and strokes it. So I go back down to the bottom of the bed. And I gently put Meena's legs down so her feet are dangling over the edge of the bed, and that rests the baby's head down onto the mattress. And I move Meena's knees apart and put my hands on the poor little baby's tiny head, and I try to pull it gently out of Meena, but it won't budge an inch, and I don't wanna pull too hard, cos I don't want to break his poor little neck.

'Steve, do we need to pull the baby out, or could we just leave him in there?'

'No, we should take him out,' he goes. 'It would be,' and he takes a sobby breath, 'disrespectful to leave them like that.' And he takes a few minutes to pull himself together, and carefully drinks in a few deep breaths, to calm himself down. Then he picks up the kitchen knife from the floor. And he stands next to me, next to the baby's head. And he hovers the knife over Meena at different angles, but nothing seems right.

'What are we doing?' he goes, making a fist of his other hand and rubbing it against his eyes. 'I can't do this,' he goes. 'I don't know what I'm doing. I can't just start slicing Meena up.' And when he says 'Meena' he starts full-on crying again. So I'm like:

'It could be better to leave them together, like they are.'

'Yes, we'll do that,' he goes.

'Let's straighten out her body, though, before it gets stiff.'

'Right,' goes Steve, coming out of his crying a bit, but still dazed, like he wants me to take the lead.

So I walk to one side of the bed, and he sees what I'm doing and walks to the other side. And we lift Meena, under her arms, and gently slide her up the bed until her head's on the pillow, and her legs and feet slide up onto the bed. And we fold her arms crossed onto her chest, like they do on films. But that just looks freaky, like a vampire. So I have this idea, and I put one of her hands on the bottom of her baby bump in her tummy and the other hand on the top, which is how she used to walk around when she was pregnant, and Steve nods, so I know it's the right

318

thing to do. And the baby is still mostly inside her, so the bump is still quite big.

And we lay her legs straight, but slightly apart, so we don't squash the baby's poor little head. And then Steve untucks the sheet from his side of the bed, so I do the same thing on my side, and we wrap the bed sheet over Meena and the baby.

'Let's bury her tonight,' I go. 'Cos we can't leave her in here while you're sleeping. And it wouldn't be right to leave her outside, in case animals find her.'

'You're right,' he goes. 'And let's cremate the body. That would make more sense than digging a hole in the middle of the night.'

'That's a really good idea,' I go, cos I'm looking for any opportunity to say something kind to Steve, to take away any tiny bit of his sadness.

And outside it's twilight now and getting dark. And Steve starts building a massive fire in the middle of the courtyard of the garden, and I help him pile up all different sizes of logs and then branches with dried leaves growing off them, from these huge piles he keeps behind the empty chicken cages. And I'm glad I can help with this, cos I just need to be doing something, I need to feel like I'm doing something to help with this absolute disaster of a situation, even if it is just in this tiny way. And pretty soon, we've made this massive great pile for the bonfire. And Steve crams strips of tree bark around the bottom.

'Come on, then,' goes Steve, giving me a little half-hug around my shoulders. And we go back into the bedroom, and we pick up Meena's body with the sheet still around it. And we carry her under our arms, past Steve's tree-trunk chair, and out of the doorway, and we guide her around that wooden fence in front of the door. And we rest her body on top of the mound of sticks and logs, and we re-wrap the sheet tight around her.

'Here's goes, then,' Steve's like, lighting a disposable cigarette lighter and touching the flame to the bark he stuffed round the bottom of the pile, so yellow and orange flames start spreading to the other strips of bark and catching fire to the dried leaves attached to the branches.

And then Steve gives a little speech about how much he loved Meena and he'll miss her, and how her death has made him see how cruel he was and now he's gonna be kind to me. Then I make a speech about how Meena did so many nice things for me when we were at school, and I don't mention what happened after we left school. I just stick to the good stuff she did. And now the flames are getting higher, about as high as my shoulders, and it starts burning away the sheet, and we can see Meena's skin burning and bubbling, and it smells like cooking meat, and her hair's on fire, and it's absolutely horrific. And, I hate myself for reacting like this, but my mouth starts watering and getting hungry – cos it smells like roast pork – and I can't control it, cos my brain wants stuff without asking me, stuff that's already programmed into my head.

'Come on,' goes Steve. 'We don't need to watch this. Let's walk to the beach.'

'There's a beach here?' I'm like.

'You've no idea how different your life is about to become,' goes Steve, and he takes my hand and leads me out of the garden and right into the jungle and we walk through the dark for a long time, until it's proper black nighttime. And eventually we come out on this beautiful wide beach with a long stretch of sand, and the sea looks like black silver, with the big moon rippling flakes of white onto it.

And we sit down next to each other on the sand. And I can smell the smoke of the bonfire on our clothes. And that was the first time I've ever seen Steve cry or be upset or act like a normal person as opposed to just a cold, vicious manipulator.

And now it's just me and Steve on the island. And this weird part of me's thinking, This is my big opportunity to be in a real family again. Cos Steve's gonna keep having sex with me, whether I want it or not, and then I'll probably get pregnant eventually and have a baby. And then we'll be a sort of family. And this weird part of me wants that, even though Steve's been such an absolute bastard to me, ever since the first minute I met him. And on a logical level, I know that I hate him and I should just murder him in his sleep. But my, like, heart just wants to be in a family again, any kind of family.

And Steve puts his arms round my shoulders, and I can feel my body turning to stone, and going completely cold inside. And it would be so much easier if I could just forget the past and be attracted to him. Or even just tolerate him. But I can't. My blood's running cold, with him just touching me. And then he sits behind me with his legs either side of mine, hugging me from behind, and I get filled with this cold, detached hatred, like I'm standing somewhere else watching this dead statue of myself getting hugged by Steve. But I let him keep doing it, cos maybe this'll help me warm up to him over time. Cos it really would make things so much easier if I could just get into this, which is sick to say, but it's true. But after maybe an hour like that, I still feel just as cold and stale. And I suppose the second best thing after being attracted to Steve would be to never have any feelings at all, cos that'll make things simpler too, even though that would be a horrible way for me to live.

And finally Steve goes:

'Let's go back to the house.'

Which is a relief cos it distracts me from that horrible shadowy chain of thoughts about how I'm gonna get through life now that it's just me and Steve on the island.

So we walk through the pitch-black jungle. And as we get near the garden, there's something shining through the trees, and it smells really strongly of burning. And we get closer, and we can see a wall of orange blazing in the background. And finally we get to the garden, and the whole place is on fire – with flames covering the chicken cage and the store room roof and the wooden fence in front of the sleeping room and some of the trees nearby. It's like a horror film version of what the garden used to be, with everything built out of fire, instead of bricks and wood.

And Steve's standing there, gripping a handful of hair at the back of his head, almost like he's trying to stop his head from falling off his shoulders. And the bonfire's still blazing in the middle of the square, and Meena's body's covered in flames, and the flesh is almost completely burnt off her face so her teeth are showing through, in this sad painful grin.

And a gust of wind blows through, which makes all the fires flare up and orange flakes swarm out of the bonfire and up into the darkness, like evil wasps. I think they're dried leaves, which is probably what spread the flames to the buildings in the first place.

'Should we get some water?' I'm like.

'We've got nothing bigger than a bucket,' goes Steve. 'Let's just carry as many supplies as we can away from here, before the petrol tanks explode. I'll take the storage room, and you go to the sleeping room and drag out the mattress.'

So I run over to the sleeping room, and the fence in front of it is just a wall of flames. But I'm able to squeeze behind it and in through the doorway, with sparks burning me from the blazing fence. And inside, nothing's on fire, but I've gotta move quickly, cos the roof's made of a thick layer of branches, so if that catches on fire, this whole room will start burning. So I walk past Steve's tree-trunk chair and pick up the corner of the mattress to see how heavy it is. But just then, there's a snapping cracking noise, and I look over, and the fence has collapsed against the doorway, blocking the way out. And now smoke's flooding into the room, and there's no windows and no other doors, so it's gonna fill up and suffocate me.

'Steve!' I shout through the burning fence. 'Help me! I'm trapped!' But I don't think he can hear, cos he's far off on the other side of the garden, at the store room. And I can feel the thick, dry smoke in my lungs. And I look up at the ceiling – which is packed with branches of long spiky leaves – and it's starting to burn in the corner above the doorway, but it's quickly spreading across the room. So I think the fence falling against the side of the building must have set them on fire. And all I can see now is

323

thick smoke coloured orange by the fire. And each time I breathe, I get a lung full of it, so I crouch down low where there's still some fresh air.

And I can't push the fence away with my hands, cos it's heavy and covered in flames. And I'm not wearing any shoes, so I can't kick it away. So I need to find anything heavy I could smash it out of the way with. And I try to pick up the bed, but the bed frame's so heavy, I can only lift one corner off the ground a few inches. It must be solid steel, or something, plus it's a king-size. And the ceiling fire's spread about halfway across the ceiling now, and it's raining down burning leaves and twigs, and some of them fall onto the bed and catch the mattress on fire. So I quickly grab the pillows and rush over to the side of the room that the ceiling fire hasn't reached yet.

And I grip the corners of one of the pillows in my fist so it's wrapped over my knuckles like a gigantic boxing glove, and I hold the other pillow over my head to protect me from the ceiling fire dripping flames onto me. And I run to the doorway, keeping my face turned away from the blazing heat of the flames, and I punch the fence with my pillow boxing glove, hoping to smash the fence clear of the doorway. But it's so heavy it won't budge. The punch just leaves my wrist bones condensed into this throbbing pain. But I try punching it again, cos I've got no other ideas to escape from here. And this time the pillow comes back covered in flames, so I throw it away into the corner of the room. And burning bits of leaf are dripping down onto my arms and back, which aren't protected very well by the second pillow I'm holding over my head, so I rush back to the last corner of the

324

room that the ceiling fire hasn't reached. And I need to find something else that I can bash the fence away with. But it's impossible to see anything now, cos the room's filled with orange-tinted smoke.

And I remember Steve brought in that bag of food when Meena was in labour. And I'm not sure if it's still in here, but if it is, maybe it'll have a bottle of water inside that I could throw at the fence, to put out enough of the fire to let me lean all my weight against it and push it over, or maybe I could find the knife that Steve brought in and try to hack the fence a bit so that it collapses completely and falls to the ground so I'd be able to jump over it and get out of here. So I keep holding the second pillow over my head to protect me from the fire dripping down, and I pat around the edge of the floor, searching for that bag. And I steer clear of the bed frame, cos the mattress is covered in fire now. And I'm feeling along where the floor meets the walls, and then the corner of the room, and then I feel a tall rough heavy cylinder, and it's Steve's stupid tree-trunk chair. But then I realise this is my chance. Cos I can try to use that as a sort of battering ram.

And it's so heavy I'm going to need both hands to move it. So I pull off the pillowcase and put it over my head, like a hood for a bit of protection, so now fire spots are falling all over my shoulders and back, and they burn like a bastard before I can brush them off. And I'm gonna look like a leopard with all these burn marks all over me. But I've got no choice. It's either get burnt trying to escape, or do nothing and suffocate to death. So I grab the chair, but it's much too heavy to lift up. So I tilt it onto its bottom edge – which is the circle of the tree trunk – and start rolling it towards the door on that edge. But I'm choking cos the smoke's so thick, so I have to crouch right down next to the floor to breathe for a minute to recover. And I drink in a massive deep breath and I stand up again and tilt the tree-trunk chair onto its bottom edge again and roll it towards the doorway.

And the pillowcase protecting my head catches on fire – near my shoulder – so I quickly rip it off my head and throw it onto the floor. So there's nothing protecting me at all now, and bits of fire are landing on my hair and shoulders, and I brush them off as quick as I can. But each time I do, I have to stop rolling the chair. And I can't breathe any more. So I put the chair down and crouch so low that my face is touching the floor, but I still can't get any real clean air. It's all smoky and thick, even right next to the lino floor tiles. So I have to just take a deep breath of that, cos it's better than the ashy smoke up at standing level. And I stand up again, and my head's dizzy and my muscles are feeling dried out and weak, probably from not having any proper air going round my blood. And I keep rolling the tree-trunk chair towards the doorway, which is a burning rectangle through the smoke. And I hear an explosion from outside, which must be one of the petrol tanks Steve mentioned. And maybe that's killed him, for all I know.

And the doorway's giving off such fierce heat that I have to keep about a metre back. And I line up the chair and push it against the burning fence. But it just leans against the fence which keeps burning and standing upright, blocking the way out. So I push on the tree-trunk chair with both my hands, and I can feel the fence moving a little bit. So then I lean all of my weight onto it, and gradually I feel the fence going more and more upright and eventually it topples over, leaving the doorway open, and the tree trunk falls on top of it. And first of all I drink a few massive breaths of slightly cleaner air from outside the room.

And now the doorway's open, but there's a massive burning carpet of fire all the way round it, and I've got no shoes on, so I still can't get out. But there's the tree-trunk chair lying on top of it, stretching about a quarter of the way across like part of a bridge or a diving board. So I balance on that tree trunk with both feet, and I start edging along it with the fire all round me. And I'm out of the sleeping room now, and I can breathe normal air again. And I'm balancing on this big fat log carved into a chair. And if I walk any further forward, it's gonna see-saw me down into the flames, cos now I'm on the 'legs' bit of the chair, which is a solid log, but the bit up ahead is the 'back' of the chair, so that's gonna tip down and dunk me into the flames. And I look down at the log, and the bark's starting to smoulder and get hot. And I think it must be like Steve said that the bark burns easiest, cos it's got sap in it, plus it's got more surface area, and it's drier than a solid chunk of wood. So the log I'm standing on is gonna be on fire as well soon, and there are already a few flames burning off the sides of the log. So I just think, Sod it. And I put one foot on the end of the log – right where someone's head would be if they were sitting in the chair – without putting any weight on that foot. And then as gradually as I can, I shift my weight from my back foot onto that foot, and the log see-saws down so my front foot's right down in the fire. And when the head of the chair touches right down into the flames, I spring off my front foot and leap as far as I can towards the ground beyond the carpet of fire. But my foot touches down right on the burning flattened fence. So I spring off it, as soon as it touches down. And my next step is on the cold normal ground. And then I keep running for a bit so I'm far away from the burning carpet of fire. And I look back and the whole roof of the bedroom building is burning. And half of it collapses and falls burning into the room, and that drags the other half down. And the bonfire's still burning, in the middle of the square, with Meena on it, and she's down to just the skeleton now.

And then, *boom!* There's a blast of heat and another massive explosion from the store room building. And it must be another tank of petrol blowing up. And there's gonna be nothing we can save from the store room now. And who knows how many more tanks might be in there. Or maybe there's bullets or dynamite or God knows what Steve might have that could kill me if it catches on fire and blows up. So I'm getting away from here till the fire burns itself out. I have a quick look around for Steve. But I can't see him anywhere. And I'd really like to look inside the store room, to see if I can find any chocolate or anything else that they were keeping hidden from me. But it's not worth the risk. So I limp off into the woods, on my burnt-up feet, planning to keep walking till I can curl up and go to sleep next to the sea, cos that'll be the safest place away from the fire. But then I have another idea, and I walk to the middle of the wheat field, where I feel safer, even though there's trees all around it that could catch on fire, and the wheat's pretty dry now, and it would probably burn like paper. But for some reason I just feel safer here in the middle of the field of wheat, which I planted and raised, and also I can try to guard it, if I'm right here, and if the fire starts getting close. I dunno how I'd guard it exactly, but at least I could try. So I walk to the middle of the field, and I curl up and go to sleep.

CHAPTER TWENTY-FIVE

And I wake up to two loud bangs in the distance. And I sit up, and it's early morning daylight, with a bit of damp haze still hanging in the air, which the sun hasn't dried up yet. And the field's safe. It doesn't look like the fire reached any of the jungle surrounding it. And while I'm looking around, I hear another echoey bang, which sounds like a gunshot. And then in the direction of the goat cage, there's the distant sound of someone shouting angrily, and it's a man, but with a higher voice than Steve's, and it sounds like another language. So I lie back down in the tall wheat to stay hidden, cos whatever's going on, it could be dangerous, and I wanna know the situation before I let anyone see me. And I crawl out of the field, keeping below the wheat, and then I sneak through the woods, till I get near the clearing where the goat cage is. And before I'm properly in view of it I crouch down low and creep along like that.

And as I get nearer and nearer, the layers of trees gradually thin out, and I see Steve walking up the path towards the clearing, but really slow, and sort of staggering. And there's a Chinese bloke behind him, poking a gun into Steve's back. And there's a pair of handcuffs around Steve's ankles with a chain between them, so he has to take little steps. And the Chinese bloke marches Steve right up to the cage and shouts at him, 'Open! Open!' So Steve opens up the cage door and the two goats walk casually out past him. And the Chinese bloke shouts, 'You get in!' So Steve walks into the cage. And the Chinese bloke keeps the gun pointed at Steve and walks round, outside the cage to its back corner and taps the thick corner bar, which is about as thick as my arm. And he waves Steve over to that corner, pointing the gun at him all the time, and he puts out his two hands to show that he wants Steve to put his hands through the bars of the cage either side of that thick corner bar, so Steve does that, all the time looking really calm but keeping his eyes fixed on the Chinese bloke's face, probably looking for any opportunity to get away or grab the gun or whatever.

And the Chinese bloke takes three pairs of handcuffs out of his pocket and picks one pair and puts the other two pairs back into his pocket. And the Chinese bloke snaps one ring of the handcuffs round Steve's left wrist and goes to snap the other side around Steve's other wrist, but the little chain between them isn't long enough. So the Chinese bloke goes, 'In! In!' to Steve and motions with his hands to show Steve to put his wrists closer together. But Steve pretends he doesn't understand, and he moves his face closer to the bars and then his feet closer to the bars. And the Chinese bloke's getting annoyed and shouting at Steve in Chinese. And pointing the gun at him and motioning Steve to put his wrists closer together, and Steve pretends that the angle of the bars won't let him put his wrists closer than they already are. And the Chinese bloke's getting pissed off. And he tucks the gun into the waistband of the back of his shorts and grabs the open second ring of the handcuffs in one hand and Steve's free wrist in the other hand and forces Steve's wrists nearer and nearer to each other. And Steve's resisting. And the bloke looks pretty old, probably at least sixty, but wiry and strong, and he's straining and bending his elbows to get more leverage, and he gets the open ring of the handcuffs around Steve's free wrist and he snaps it closed and squeezes the ratchet tight. And quick as a flash Steve's hands fly up and loop the handcuffs chain around the back of the Chinese bloke's neck and pull it inward, smashing the Chinese bloke's face into the thick metal corner bar of the cage, smashing his nose and mouth and spattering blood into Steve's shirt and face. And Steve slams the Chinese bloke's face into that bar again, and there's a succulent, crunching sound of the bloke's face bones slamming hard into the thick metal bar. And the bloke's face is a mess of blood now, smearing out from his nose and mouth, and there's a jagged little white bone sticking out through the flesh of his nose. And his face is all woozy, like he's dazed. But then he blinks a couple of times, remembers the gun and pats his front pockets first, cos he must have forgotten where he put it. And Steve sees what he's doing, and Steve's still got the chain of the handcuffs round the back of the bloke's neck, and he yanks the Chinese bloke's face into the bar one more time. And there's a *clong* sound like the bloke's skull connected with the metal pole this time. And the bloke's head's flopping around, now, like a boxer who's about to fall over. And Steve brings his thumbs round to the front of the bloke's neck and starts pushing them into the bloke's throat. But as soon as Steve does that, the Chinese bloke's legs collapse from under him and he slips through Steve's grip and he falls to the floor, with his feet near Steve's corner of the cage and his body stretched away from it.

And Steve pokes one of his own feet through the bars of the cage, but he can't reach his foot out very far, cos his feet are still chained together inside the cage. And his foot will only reach as far as the Chinese bloke's shin. And Steve reaches his arms out of the cage as far as he possibly can, reaching down for the old Chinese bloke, lying on the floor, but Steve can only reach down as far as his own knees, cos there's a rail that runs sideways around the cage about waist height, so he can't reach much lower than that.

'Shruti!' Steve shouts out. 'Shruti! Come here quickly! There's an emergency!' And he uses his heel to smash down on the Chinese bloke's feet, which is all he can reach. And he's bringing his heel down on the bloke's feet, again and again, trying to smash the Chinese bloke's toes. But blatantly the Chinese bloke's gonna wake up eventually, get the gun out of his waistband and shoot Steve in the fucking head. That's what I'd do, anyway.

'Shruti!' Steve's shouting, and his voice is desperate, almost breaking. 'Shruti! Come here! I need you, immediately!'

So I come running out of the trees where I was hiding, to pretend that I've only just heard him and haven't been spying on him this whole time, cos if he knows that, he'll be angry at me for not helping him earlier.

'Oh, my God. I'm so happy to see you,' Steve goes. 'You've got to go into this little fucker's pockets and get me the keys for these

333

handcuffs. But first get me his gun. It's tucked into the back of his waistband.'

And I'm thinking, All right, this is an opportunity for me to change my entire life now. Cos this Chinese bloke must have arrived in a boat. So if I can steal his boat, this is my one chance to escape off the island.

'Shruti,' goes Steve, with his voice angry and ordering. 'Get his gun, right now.'

'Just a minute,' I'm like.

'There are two other Filipino sailors up at the garden, and they'll be here any minute, and then we'll both be tortured to death,' Steve's like. 'Is that what you want?'

And I dunno if Steve's telling the truth. But I just need a minute to think.

'Shruti,' goes Steve, 'we're got three minutes, at most, before his two friends get here. And then we'll both be tortured. They've all got guns, and you saw what this guy was about to do to me.'

And I look down, and I recognise the old Chinese bloke – he's the granddad off the boat that brought us here. I can see that it's him, even through the blood and messed-up bones and gore on his face. And I think I can even see a tiny brown circle on his arm, where Meena burnt him with the cigarette. And he starts moving his head groggily around, just gentle weak movements, like an old tortoise on its back.

And I reach into his pockets and pull out the two extra pairs of handcuffs. I don't want to touch the gun, cos once I've got it in my hand, Steve will force me to pass it to him.

'What are you doing?' goes Steve. 'Give me the fucking gun, *now*, you stupid little girl. We're both going to get killed.'

But I avoid looking at him, and instead I grab the Chinese bloke by his wrists and drag him, near the door of the cage, which is still wide open, and it's the opposite end of the cage to where Steve is. And I poke the bloke's wrists through the bars and handcuff him to the cage with one of the pairs of handcuffs, so he's locked to the thick corner bar of the cage, completely out of reach of Steve. And Steve's watching me do all this.

'All right,' he goes. 'That was good thinking. We don't need to worry about him any more. But the other two will be here any minute. So just roll him over and grab his gun before he regains con— before he wakes up.'

That patronising twat. He doesn't think I even know what *regains consciousness* means.

And the Chinese bloke's lips are moving like he's talking to someone in a dream. And so no matter what I wanna do next, I've gotta get his gun before he wakes up. And I still remember the recovery position from swimming lessons at school. So I lift one of his knees up so it's bent, and then I push that knee which rolls him onto his side, and I pull the gun out of the waistband of his shorts and I tuck it into the back of my own waistband. And then I think: What if he's got other weapons in there? So I pull everything out of all his pockets. And there's just a plastic comb with hair in it, a wad of folded up papers with Chinese handwriting on them, and a bunch of keys.

'Give those keys to me,' goes Steve.

'Hang on a minute,' I'm like. I'm putting all this stuff into my

335

own pockets, except for the comb, which I throw away into the woods, cos I don't want anyone using that to pick the lock of their handcuffs.

'Right,' goes Steve. 'Give me those keys immediately.'

'I'm just gonna go and see if I can find the boat,' I'm like.

'No, you're bloody not, you little idiot. You're going to unlock me, or we'll both spend the rest of our lives being tortured by this man's two friends.'

'If we can find the boat, though, we can escape.'

'If you unlock me, we won't have to escape,' Steve goes.

'I want to escape, though,' I'm like.

'All right, well, unlock me,' goes Steve, 'and then I can pilot the boat to anywhere in the world that you want to escape to. It's extremely difficult to navigate a boat on open waters, and they only carry a limited amount of fuel. You'd need to know the type of port you could go into and refuel without getting arrested for having no transport papers and visas and the like. And I've got twenty years of experience in—'

'I'm gonna look for the boat first,' I go, interrupting him. And I stick my fingers into my ears to stop myself hearing what Steve's gonna say to me next, cos I don't want him to persuade me to unlock him. And I avoid looking back at him, and I walk into the jungle as quick as I can, not down the path, in case Steve was telling the truth that there are two other Chinese blokes out looking for us.

And I go to the rock pools and look up and down the coastline but I can't see a boat anywhere. And I pull the gun out and hold it in my hand, just in case. And for a weird few seconds, I think to myself whether I would actually be better off staying on this island than going back to England, where I've got absolutely no one, now that Meena's dead and my family's gone forever. But that's a stupid idea – I've gotta get back, if I possibly can. And I walk along the coastline, staying hidden in the woods as much as I can. But every so often, I go out to the sea and look up and down the waterline, to look for a boat. But it's always just empty water and beaches, or rocks, or jungle bulging over the edge. Then I get to a long beach, which I suppose is the one Steve took me to last night. And there's one of those beds made out of ropes tied to two palm trees on the edge of the beach, in the shade of the trees. And I bet that's what Steve used to do all day, when he said he was out fishing – sleep in there. But I'm too excited and scared to be angry about that now. And I keep walking, staying in the trees next to the beach, to stay hidden.

And then I suddenly think: I never checked Steve's pockets. He could have anything in there – his own gun, or tools for sawing through the handcuffs or picking the locks. And the longer I leave him alone, the more time I'm giving him to escape. And I'm petrified now. Cos if he escapes, that's my life over. If I thought he was horrible to me before, God only knows what he'd do to me now that I left him deliberately locked up in the goat cage.

CHAPTER TWENTY-SIX

So I speed up and start jogging through the trees, instead of just walking. And I realise that I don't even know how big this island is. And it's mental, really, but this is literally the first time I've properly explored – cos it doesn't count when I was blind or when I ran away in the middle of the night, when Steve came and found me, cos it was dark then, and he put a bag over my head when he brought me back, so I couldn't see anything.

And I get to the end of the beach, and then I break into a full-speed run. And the jungle starts getting really rocky. And I climb up on this big rocky mound and look along the coastline. And way off in the distance, there's a fishing boat! It looks like the one that brought us here, and it's roped up to three trees, by the stone ledge thing where it first pulled in when me and Meena first got here. So I keep running. And eventually, after a lot more slogging through the trees, I get near to it. And I stay hidden in the jungle. And I can't see any people on the boat. And I've still got the gun in my hand, not that I could probably hit anything, cos I've never shot a gun in my life. And I quietly find a stone about the size of a tennis ball, and I throw it high in the air so that it lands on the deck of the boat with a loud smack. And I wait for about five minutes, keeping hidden. And if there was anyone on that boat, they'd definitely come out and see what was going on. But no one comes.

And the boat's not gonna float off anywhere, cos it's tied up with big fat knots to those trees. So I walk across the stone ledge, keeping the gun in my hand, and I jump onto the boat. And this is the exact same boat that brought us here, I'm sure. And next to the steering wheel there's a keyhole, like in a car. So I look through the Chinese bloke's bunch of keys that I grabbed out of his pocket, and there's one really big fat key. And I slide it into the keyhole and turn it, but nothing happens. And I turn it again. And still nothing. So I look around a bit more, and I notice there's a round black button on the other side of the steering wheel, about the size of a pound coin. So I turn the key one more time and press the button, and the motors start chugging and vibrating the wooden deck under my feet. And it releases this surge of hope sparkling through my blood. Cos I'm sure I can drive this boat: I'll steer it with the steering wheel and control the speed with the handle on the side, which I remember the other Chinese bloke pushing forward to go faster and pulling back to go slower.

But then this black disappointment clouds through me. Cos I've got no money for petrol. So I'll probably, like, run out of petrol in the middle of the ocean and starve to death. So I've gotta force Steve to give me some money or those gold coins Meena told me about, so I can refuel, or I'll just die in the middle of the sea. But I'm not going to let Steve out of the cage. I'll just threaten him with the gun and force him to tell me where I can find the money, and then I'm gone.

So I stop the motor and put the keys back in my pocket. And I jog back along the waterline till I get back to the rock pools. And I creep up near the clearing where the goat cage is. And the Chinese bloke's woken up now, and he's wiping some dried blood off his face with his shoulder. And Steve's picking at the lock of his own handcuffs with some kind of little stick – which is good, cos it means he wasn't able to get away in, like, three hours of trying, while I was away. But, I'm thinking, he has had a long time to think up plans, so I can't relax too much.

And then I creep away and walk up to them from the main path, so Steve won't know I was spying on him. And Steve quickly stops fiddling with his handcuffs.

'Right,' I go. 'I'm leaving on the boat. And if you wanna come with me, you've gotta tell me where the gold is.'

'It's impossible to explain,' goes Steve. 'I'd have to show you.'

'Is it really impossible to explain?' I go.

'I'm afraid so,' goes Steve. 'But I'd be happy to show you.'

'That's too bad you can't just tell me where it is,' I'm like. 'Cos I'm leaving now, so you'll have to stay here and starve to death.' And I turn around and begin walking off down the path. And I'm waiting for Steve to call after me, to try to make a deal. But he doesn't say anything. And I slow down my walking to as slow as I can without making it obvious. But he still doesn't call me back. And this isn't working at all. Cos I was supposed to have all the power over him, and he was supposed to do whatever I wanted, cos he'd be scared to die. But it blatantly isn't working out like that. And I walk off down the path, so I'm out of sight of the goat cage. And I wait a while for him to call after me. But he still doesn't. So I have to walk back to the clearing, looking and feeling like a total muppet.

And Steve laughs when he sees me back again. 'I thought you were leaving on a jet plane,' he goes.

'Yeah, well, I decided to give you a second chance.'

'Nah, that's all right,' goes Steve. 'You just leave. I'll be fine.'

'You'll die if I leave you here,' I'm like. 'You're gonna starve to death.'

'I shouldn't think so,' he goes. 'I'm sure I'll think of something. I'm a pretty resourceful person. If anyone's going to die . . .' he's like.

'I ain't gonna die,' I'm like.

'That's all right, then. See you later,' he goes. 'Good luck in the boat.'

And why won't that fucker be scared?

'I'll set you free if you tell me where the gold is,' I tell him.

'No, I appreciate the offer, I really do. But I'm going to pass.'

And I just stand there, cos I wasn't expecting this. He's fucking got me.

'Was there anything else?' goes Steve.

'Yes,' I'm like.

'Well?' he goes.

And I've got nothing to say. And he's making me look like a total fucking idiot. And I dunno how on earth he's doing this. Cos even though he's locked up and he's gonna starve to death if I leave him here, and I'm holding a gun in my hand, and I've

341

got the keys to the boat and his handcuffs – I still feel like he's got more power than me. He's a genius, really, in an evil sort of way. And I honestly dunno how he does it.

'Why don't you want me to unlock you?' I go.

'Oh, you know. I like a challenge,' he's like. 'Houdini was always a hero of mine. And . . . and I'm looking forward to making friends with this gentleman,' he goes, nodding at the Chinese bloke on the floor.

And I've gotta make Steve take me seriously. So I'm like:

'I'll kill you with this gun if you don't tell me where the gold is. And if you tell me the wrong place, I'll kill you as well.'

'Oh, my!' he goes. 'Well, if that's the way it's got to be.'

And he knows that I don't wanna shoot him. And to be honest, I don't think I could do it.

'All right,' I go. 'I'll make a deal with you.' And I pause, cos I dunno what I'm gonna say next. 'You've just gotta tell me where my New Zealand dollars are – the ones I had in my pocket when you found me in that desert on the other side of the island. And then I'll let you go.'

'It's a very generous offer,' he goes. 'But I think I'll pass.'

'Don't you wanna get out?' I'm like.

'No, that's okay,' he goes.

'Oh, for fuck's sake, what's the matter with you?'

'I'm fine actually. But thanks for asking. How about yourself?'

'Shut up! Shut your fucking mouth!' I go.

'Oh, dear,' Steve's like. 'Have I said something to offend you?'

'No, you're just a fucking idiot, cos you're gonna die, but you could save your life if you just told me where my New Zealand

342

dollars are. And you can't even spend them. You're an idiot.'

'Well, brains never was my strong suit,' he goes.

And he's doing my head in. How can he have power over me, even now? And all I need is just some money, in case of emergencies on the boat. Cos England's thousands of miles away from wherever this island is. And I'm sure I'll need to buy more petrol along the way, especially as I don't even know what direction to drive.

'I'm gonna leave you to think about it,' I go. 'And when I come back you'd better have a decision. Cos if you haven't, I'm gonna just drive off and leave you here to die.'

'No, that's okay,' goes Steve. 'Don't worry about little old me. I'll take my chances. So you're free to go. I give you full permission to leave immediately. In fact, I order you to go. I command you to leave.'

'No, I'm not gonna leave just yet, actually.'

'That's okay,' goes Steve. 'Suit yourself.'

And he starts casually looking around, like he's perfectly happy being where he is, and he's interested in everything, and he spends a long time looking at one of the goats, who's chewing some leaves a little way off in the forest.

And I'm just standing there like an idiot, trying to think what to do, or hoping Steve'll just cave in and tell me where the money is. And I've gotta think up an excuse to stay standing here without looking stupid. So I pull the Chinese bloke's papers out of my pocket and start looking through them. And after a while Steve calls over to me:

'How about this?' he goes. 'If you give me ten deals that you'd be happy with – things you'd like in return for unlocking me – then I promise that I'll pick one of them, as long as there's at least one reasonable option. How about that?'

'Ten?' I'm like. And I know this has gotta be some kind of trick.

'I can't say fairer than that,' goes Steve. 'You get to choose the terms of the agreement.'

'All right, then,' I go. Cos as long as I make sure that all ten deals give me what I want, then I can't lose. And even if this is a total lie, it's not like I've lost anything. And I do sort of wanna stay standing here for now. Cos I wanna get to a point where Steve's squirming and begging for mercy and he'll apologise for everything he's ever done to me, and he'll do absolutely anything if I'll only spare his life. And the more time goes past, the nearer he'll get to starvation, so the more power I'll have.

'Right,' I'm like. 'Number one: you tell me where the gold is, and then I'll dig it up, and then I'll let you out.

'Number two: you tell me where my New Zealand dollars are, and then when I get my hands on them, I'll let you out.

'Number three: you tell me where some other kind of money is – but a decent amount of it – and once I get my hands on that, then I'll let you out.'

'Okay, that's three,' goes Steve.

'Number four,' I go. But I can't think of a number four. 'Can we just go up to, like, five?'

'No, it's got to be ten, or I'm going to bow out. No pressure, obviously, if you'd rather not do ten – I wouldn't want to force you. But I won't be involved.'

344

'No, I'll do ten,' I go, cos this is my only real option, at the moment. And I do need some money before I can go sailing off on that boat. 'Number four . . .' I'm like, and I'm thinking about it. 'Number four,' I go, 'you give me something else that can blatantly be used as money, like diamonds or something, and once I get it, I'll let you out.'

'Okay, that's four.'

'Number five . . .' I'm like. And I've gotta finish this list quickly, cos the longer I wait here the more chance I've got that Steve's gonna think of a way to escape on his own, or maybe he knows something that I don't and he's just stalling me here and leading me into a trap.

'This is your last chance, by the way,' I go. 'If you don't do any of these options, I'm just gonna go off in that boat and leave you.'

'You can leave now, if you like,' goes Steve. 'I wouldn't be offended.'

'No, I'm gonna do that ten deals thing. But I'm just saying that if you try to mess me around, then I'm leaving. And I'm not giving you any more chances.'

'Seriously,' goes Steve, 'you should just leave right now. I think I've offended you by suggesting this arrangement. I apologise and I humbly retract my offer. I'm sorry that I offended you.'

'No, you didn't offend me. I'm just saying—'

'I hear what you're saying, Shruti. And *I'm* just saying that you should leave now, if you don't like the terms of the agreement. I would only want to do this if it's on mutual terms. And if it doesn't work for you, you should just walk away from the deal.'

'Well, can you tell me if any of those first four reasons are okay? Cos I can't think of any others, at the minute.'

'I'm afraid I'll need to hear all ten deals before I give you my answer. I wouldn't want to miss out on a deal later in the list that might be more favourable to me.'

And that does make sense, I suppose. Cos if it was me, I'd wanna know all ten, cos the tenth one might be amazing. So I keep going.

'Number five . . .' I'm like. And I'm trying to think of some other thing that I want instead of money. But there's nothing else I need.

'I've just had an idea,' goes Steve. 'How about this for a little side deal, while you're in the process of thinking up the final options—'

'What do you mean by a side deal?' I'm like.

'Well, Meena's skeleton and my son's skeleton are laying on the ashes of the fire in the middle of the garden square. And it's breaking my heart to know they're lying there like so much litter,' goes Steve. 'So if you'd do them the dignity of digging a grave here and then burying them, I'd be deeply grateful. And as a token of my gratitude, I'd be happy to give you some advice on navigating the boat on the open seas. What do you say? A little side deal.'

'I suppose that would be all right,' I go. Cos he has got a point about it being disrespectful to leave Meena's skeleton out to rot. And if I did sail away now, that's what would happen.

'And also, this will let us do three things at once – with me giving you some advice about navigation, which is one, while

346

you're digging the grave, which is two. Plus you can think up your remaining few deal options to present to me, while we're talking, which is three. It will probably save some time.'

'Okay, then,' I'm like. 'I suppose that does sound like a good idea.'

And I'm pretty sure this is a trick of some kind. But I honestly can't see how. And maybe I am just being paranoid.

So I walk back to the garden. And my knees almost collapse when I see the two skeletons of Meena and her poor little baby, cos they're charred this dirty black colour, and their bones are this flaky crispy texture like charcoal. And one of Meena's leg bones has completely burnt through and snapped in half. And they do look like rubbish that someone's just chucked away onto a pile of burnt-up logs. And there's the tiny little skeleton of the baby, all burnt black with a pockmarked texture almost like burnt toast – I suppose cos his bones were, like, softer than Meena's, so the fire damaged them more. And it's so shocking and horrific, on top of everything else that's happened. And she only died yesterday. Just yesterday I was talking to her and singing with her. And she was giving birth. And so much has happened since then. And this uncontrollable violent crying seizes my whole body.

Cos now that Meena's gone I've got nothing. I've got no one. Cos at least when she was alive, even if she was being so horrible to me, at least there was a chance we could still get back to being friends like we used to be. And it really looked like that was gonna happen. And I'm sure the baby would have really helped. But now I've lost everything. And I'm crying and crying. And it feels like the tears are coming straight out of my heart, and my heart is so soaked in sadness. I've lost so much, I feel like. I've lost so much. And Meena was the last possible good thing in my life. Even living on this horrible prison island, if only I could have got my friendship back with Meena, I could have put up with Steve. But now that can never happen. And I'm crying and crying. But I've gotta get through this and bury Meena and leave, cos of what Steve might be planning.

So while I'm sobbing, I force myself to walk over to the burnt-out fire and slide my arms under Meena's skeleton, which only makes me cry even harder, cos it feels as if I'm caring for her. And her skull's got this massive grin on its face, like she's happy that I'm gonna lay her to rest, like she's telling me thank you and that she's sorry. And it's getting a black sort of charcoal all over my arms and my new white T-shirt, and pieces of bone are falling off, so I put it down again and quickly search inside the store room, and find a half-burnt tarpaulin, which I wrap both the skeletons in, to keep them together.

And I carry them along the path to the goat cage, and Steve and the Chinese bloke are both still handcuffed to it. And the Chinese bloke's lying on his side, facing away from me. But when he hears me, he rolls over so he's on his other side and watches me carrying the skeletons. And his face is a mess of dried blackish blood around his nose and he's missing a couple of teeth, and there's blood all over his vest. And one flap of the tarpaulin falls open, showing the skeletons inside. And the Chinese bloke gives me this sorrowful little nod of respect with his head, cos he can see I'm still sobbing, and he can see how

348

horrific this situation is, even if he doesn't understand exactly how this all happened.

And I lay the skeletons down on the ground, far away from the cage, where Steve and the Chinese bloke could never reach them, or reach me while I'm digging. And Steve's face has dropped into this horrified despairing expression, cos Meena was basically his wife and the baby was his own child. And I just feel like I can't be angry at him any more, like I can't give him any more pain than he's already in. And after I've laid the skeletons on the ground, I walk out to the wheat field and unhook the little trowel that I keep hanging off the handle of the plough, under the tarpaulin. And I come back to the clearing and start trying to dig a hole to bury the skeletons in. But the ground's so hard here, I can't dig the blade of the trowel into the soil at all the first time I stab it in there, cos this ground has never been ploughed or watered, and it's been walked over millions of times, so it's hard and compacted down. But my arm muscles are pretty strong now from working in the fields. So I stab the trowel into the ground a few times, to open up a little crack in the surface, and then I go along a line like that, making a row of stab marks, and then once the earth's opened up with cracks, I dig out a little trough, just deep enough to bury the skeletons in. And when I've finished the hole, I stand up, so I can place them inside it.

'Shruti,' goes Steve, and he's got tears in his eyes now, and he's talking through his tears, and the crying's making his lips curl down. 'Shruti, please, can I just have – can I just say goodbye to my child? And to Meena.'

'Yes, of course,' I'm like, and I stand back.

'I just need to hold them, one last time,' he goes, still crying. 'Just unlock my hands, just for a minute, and then I swear I'll go back into the handcuffs. You can train the gun on me the whole time, if it makes you feel safer.'

'No,' I go. 'I can't do that.'

'Please,' he goes, crying even harder. 'Please, I beg you just one last time. That was my only child. I loved him so much. I loved Meena so much.'

And I'm feeling terrible about this. And I suppose if I'm pointing the gun at him, then he's not gonna try anything. And he's crying so hard, now, it makes me feel terrible.

'I loved her so much,' he's going.

'I can't let you out of the handcuffs,' I go. 'But is there anything else I can do?'

'Please, Shruti,' he's like. 'I promise you I'm not going to try anything. Just let me hold them one last time. You have no idea what it's like to have a child and never even get a chance to hold him.'

And I feel terrible. And I wish there was something else I could do. But I just can't risk unlocking his hands. So I have to just ignore him. And I carefully slide the tarpaulin with the skeletons on it into the grave, and I wrap the tarpaulin over them again, as a sort of shroud. And I start covering them with the mud from the long mound of earth I made next to when I was digging the grave out. And the whole time, Steve's weeping and trying to persuade me to just bring the skeletons over so he can hold them. But I can't do that, in case he grabs me and strangles me.

And after I've placed a few trowels of earth over Meena and

her baby, I realise that I want to say goodbye to Meena myself. So I stop, and quietly I go, 'Meena, I know that you weren't always nice to me. But when we were at school, you always—'

'Okay,' interrupts Steve, who's still got tears on his cheeks, but his voice is cold now. 'I'm going to keep my promise. And I'm going to give you some advice on how to navigate the boat.'

'Not right now, though,' I'm like. 'Can we do it later?'

'No, I have to do it now,' he goes, with his voice completely businesslike and calm. 'The pain's too much. I need to do something to just take my mind off it for a few moments. So here's some advice on how to navigate the boat,' he goes. 'First, make sure you know where to refuel, because if you run out of fuel while you're in the open water, no one will come to your aid, because that's a fishing boat, so they'll just assume you're waiting for fish to bite on your lines or catch in your nets. So that's the number one most important thing.'

And I'm trying to ignore him, so I can just have a quiet moment to say goodbye to Meena saying the words in my head, but it's impossible to not listen to what Steve's saying, cos it's so relevant to what I'm gonna do next.

'When you stop in a port to buy fuel,' Steve's like, 'always, always leave one person in the boat, at all times, because it's very easy to steal a boat, even without the keys. And once your boat's gone, you're lost. You'll never get that back. Especially seeing as it's a stolen boat that you'll be piloting. So actually you should steer clear of any legitimate port of any size, because you'll be immediately arrested, when they check the boat's registration details.'

And I can't make any words form in my head to say goodbye to Meena, cos I can't concentrate with Steve saying all this stuff.

'That little fishing boat can handle a mild rainstorm,' he's going. 'But anything stronger than that you should definitely avoid, even though it's cyclone season, because you'll capsize in anything heavier than a gale. And once that happens you'll either be trapped inside the boat as it sinks or if you're lucky you'll be thrown into the sea. And that would be another crucial piece of advice,' Steve's like. 'Stay out of the water, because you'll get hypothermia within seven minutes, after which time you'll be paralysed and you're basically dead, although you might have another ninety seconds before you die, if you can keep your lungs full of air and you can avoid the currents pulling you under. And even if you could get out of the water there'd be permanent nerve damage, so you'll probably never walk again. Oh, when you're anywhere near Asia or the coast of Somalia don't try to outrun pirates or put up a fight against them, because they've got machine guns and speedboats,' goes Steve. 'So your best bet is to give them whatever you've got and hope that they'll hold you hostage for a ransom, rather than kill you, and then you'd better hope you have a rich family, because they don't give very long deadlines to hand over the money. But the more likely scenario for a young girl like you is that you'd be sold into the sex trade, in which case you'd be kept in what's basically a prison cell, where you'd be forced to have sex with different men all day long, without protection, so your likelihood of contracting AIDS and other STDs is very high. And you should also watch out if you pull into the wrong type of port to refuel, because you'll probably be kidnapped. That's incredibly common, because from a port they can transport you anywhere in the world almost instantly, and that will lead to you being sold into the sex trade, too, probably somewhere like a truck stop brothel in Nigeria. And if your boat runs aground or into submerged rocks—'

'All right, you can stop now,' I'm like.

'Of course,' goes Steve. 'I'll give you all the advice you need, and then I'll stop.' And he keeps on telling me about the different ways I can drown or sink or become a slave if I sail on my own, and how quickly I'll run out of fuel.

And I'm scooping the earth onto the skeletons as fast as I can with that little trowel, so I can walk away from Steve's voice. And Meena's hip bones and skull are the only things still poking through now, so I pile up more and more earth till they're totally hidden. And then I pat the earth down.

'All right,' I'm like, interrupting Steve, hoping this will shut him up. 'Deal number five: You tell me where the gold is, I'll only take *three quarters* of it, but you've gotta tell me where the rest of the food is.

'Number six: I'll only take *half* the gold, but you have to apologise on your knees for all the horrible stuff you've ever done to me.

'Number seven: I'll take *quarter* of the gold, but I let the Chinese bloke torture you for an hour.'

'It's getting spicy, now,' goes Steve. 'I like it. And number eight?'

'Number eight . . .' I'm like. And it's all taken much longer than it was supposed to. And it's already the afternoon, and

Steve's probably just trying to drag this out for as long as he can, so it'll get dark and I won't be able to find the gold or sail off. So I've gotta get this over with.

'Number eight,' I'm like, 'tell me where the gold is plus you eat a mouthful of mud.'

'Oh, come on,' goes Steve. 'That doesn't count as a real suggestion. You're just padding the list,' he's like. 'Think what you might want – things that I might realistically be able to give you – and that should give you some ideas. For instance, you might want Meena's diaries, where she writes exactly what she thought of you from her childhood until last week.'

'Okay, number eight: the diaries plus half the gold.

'Number nine: you let me shoot you in both legs, so you can't run after me, plus ten per cent of the gold, and then I'll let you go.'

'That's a tempting option,' goes Steve, sarcastically.

'And number ten: you tell me where my suitcase is, plus you give me half the gold. And that's the tenth deal. So now you've gotta pick one. And if you don't, then I'm leaving you to die.'

'Oh, I won't die,' goes Steve. 'No need to worry about that. But I appreciate your concern. So just summarise the ten options for me, and then I'll give you my response.'

And this is probably a trick, but I might as well hear what Steve says, cos I've come this far. So I go through all ten deals for him, stopping to think quite a lot, and going:

'*One*: all the gold. *Two*: the New Zealand dollars. *Three*: some other kind of money. *Four*: something like diamonds, or whatever, that I can use as money. *Five*: all the food and clothes plus three

354

quarters of the gold. *Six*: Meena's diaries plus half the gold. *Seven*: the suitcase plus half the gold. *Eight*: you apologise on your knees plus half the gold. *Nine*: the Chinese bloke tortures you for an hour plus quarter of the gold. *Ten*: I shoot you in both legs plus ten per cent of the gold.'

And some of those deals are blatantly better than others, which is good, cos that'll make it easier for Steve to make a decision, and really any one of them will help me get home.

'Upon careful consideration,' Steve goes, 'I've decided to give you every single thing you asked for – apart from the physical violence towards me. And that's about two million dollars' worth of gold. So just unlock these handcuffs, and I'll show you where it is.'

'No, I've already said I'm not unlocking you till *after* you give me the stuff.'

'But let's be honest, here,' Steve's like. 'You're not going to unlock me, after you get your hands on it, are you. Why would you? You'll just take off and leave me locked up, because you believe I'll stop you escaping on the boat if I'm freed,' he goes. 'That's true, isn't it?'

'No,' I'm like.

'Oh, come on,' goes Steve. 'Don't talk to me as if I'm stupid. Let's communicate like adults, here. That is true, isn't it, that you're planning to leave me locked up? That's patently true, and we both know it is, don't we?'

'Yes,' I'm like.

'Okay,' goes Steve. 'Well, at least we're talking at a basic level of truth now. So the question now is how much do you value your life? Because if you leave without any money, you're going to die. That's the fact of the matter, and you're fully aware of that, aren't you?'

'I suppose so,' I go, cos it is true, so I might as well admit it.

'So you've got two options,' goes Steve. 'Either you can drive off in the boat, with no money and no sailing experience and try your luck on some of the most dangerous waters in the world, and sail into your certain death. We'll call that option: Shruti Kills Herself. And then there's option two, which is you release me, and I'll show you where a significant portion of the gold is. Not all of it, mind you. I'm reducing my offer by ninety-five per cent every five minutes. Because the more time goes by, the closer I'll be to getting free on my own, so the less I'll need you. So we're now at five per cent of the gold, which is one hundred thousand dollars' worth. And in five minutes it'll be five thousand, then two hundred and fifty dollars, and then nothing. And then all bets will be off,' Steve's like. 'So those are your two options: die at sea or become rich and return to England. And obviously when you unlock me to show you where the gold is, you'll keep the gun trained on my head the entire time, including while I'm digging up the gold.'

And whatever I do, I'm screwed. If I let Steve free, he'll grab the gun off me. And if I leave him locked up, I'll die at sea.

'Okay, that's five minutes,' goes Steve, 'so we're down to five thousand dollars.'

'That was only, like, two minutes.'

'I said five minutes *by my reckoning*, and that was five minutes by my reckoning. So you're down to five thousand dollars' worth

356

of gold now, which is the bare minimum you'd need to pay for fuel, food and supplies to get you back to England. But you should do whatever feels right. It doesn't really make much difference to me, one way or the other.'

And I wish I just had a bit more time, cos all the pressure makes it impossible to think. And I've never even driven a car, let alone navigated a boat across half the world. Plus I don't even know which direction England is from here. And I'm paralysed, just waiting for Steve to say the time's up. But now he's pretending not to be interested in me any more, and he's trying to start up a conversation with the Chinese bloke lying on the floor:

'You all right down there, mate?' he goes. 'I said are you all right? Understand?'

And I feel like I sort of *want* the time to run out, to release the pressure off me. Even if that will mean I've missed my chance to get the gold. But Steve doesn't say anything. And I just keep waiting. And after ages, at least twenty minutes, he goes, 'Two minutes left,' cos he makes up the time, so he can say what he wants.

And I wanna just set him free, to be honest, cos even though he'll capture me, it's better the devil that you know, which is Steve, than the devil you don't know, which is the sea and living back in England completely on my own.

'I've made my choice,' I go, but my mouth sort of makes a decision for me as I'm talking, 'I'm gonna leave you here and take my chances in the boat.'

'Ha!' he goes. 'That a girl. Well, now you need to make the decision whether to set sail now it's nearly evening and you'll have to navigate the submerged rocks and outcrops surrounding this island for a hundred miles or so in the semi-darkness, or whether you'd prefer to sail early in the morning, when you'll be able to drive slowly and see them all clearly.'

'Morning, I suppose,' I go. Cos he is right about those rocks, cos I remember them from when I first arrived here, and I was trying to swim to the island. And it isn't really evening yet, but it will be soon.

'Probably a good idea,' goes Steve. 'Now, there's a system to avoid the submerged outcrops when you're sailing off this island, by lining up a few of the landmarks on the shore, like in *Swallows and Amazons*.' And then Steve spends, like, a solid hour telling these stories about how he used to sail in and out of the island before he moved here, and it always sounds like he's about to tell me the trick for avoiding the rocks, but it always ends up turning into a story about how he wrecked another boat on them and it sank.

And I know that he's deliberately trying to hold me up by telling me all these stories and that he keeps mentioning the hidden rocks on purpose to scare me, and he keeps telling me that I should just leave. But I'm scared of doing it. And it's nice to have Steve's stories to distract me from having to worry about the fact I should get out of here, cos it's an excuse for me to avoid having to think.

And it's twilight now. And Steve's started telling stories about going out with Meena in England, and footballers and actors they met at clubs in London. And it's basically this secret history of what Meena was up to during our first term at university. So

I sit down on the floor, and we talk for ages and ages about Meena, which does feel good, to just talk about how much we both miss her. And it's totally dark now. And we talk right through the night, till the sun starts coming up again.

'I've gotta go to sleep,' I'm like, cos I'm exhausted now.

'Of course,' Steve's like. 'I should try to get a bit of sleep myself.' And his handcuffs are looped above the horizontal middle rail of the cage. So he crosses his wrists and sits down leaning back against the bars, with his hands hanging crossed above his head.

'Night,' he goes. 'Come and say goodbye before you leave, and I'm sure I'll have remembered the trick for navigating out of here. Things like that have a habit of coming to me during the night.'

And I go off to sleep in my old sleeping place at the edge of the field. And maybe I'll just stay on the island until my wheat's fully grown, I'm thinking, which would be satisfying to see after I put so much hard work into it, plus I could take a load of wheat on the boat to eat while I'm sailing back to England, and maybe I could even sell some of it at ports that I stop in, to get money for fuel.

CHAPTER TWENTY-SEVEN

And when I wake up, the sun's already high, but clouds are dulling the heat. And wind's blowing the top surface of the browny-yellow wheat field next to me like waves on the sea, showing up patches of pale green underneath, where the sun hasn't reached the ears of wheat on the shorter stalks yet.

And nothing feels like a stressed out rush any more, like it did yesterday when I was desperately searching for the boat, or like a tense horrible distraction, like when Steve was telling me stories about Meena. Now, it just feels like this slow heavy doom I'm carrying around on my shoulders and inside my chest, weighing me down. Cos I've either gotta deal with Steve again and try to force him to give me the gold, or I've gotta drive off alone into the middle of the sea with no money.

And I sneak up and spy on the goat cage. And the Chinese bloke's sleeping on the floor. And Steve's standing inside the cage, with his arms handcuffed through the bars still, and he's squeezing his fingers into a tight thin bunch and then forcing one of the handcuffs loops as far as it'll go, down his hand towards his fingertips. But luckily it gets stuck at his knuckles and won't come off. And one of the goats has come back right into the cage, through the open door! It's just standing there next to Steve, chewing, with a few thin green vines clinging to its fur around its ribs. Which is mental, cos why would it come back to live in a cage, when there's the whole island full of different kinds of leaves to eat, and jungle to roam around in? But I suppose it's lived in the cage so long that's all it knows.

And Steve reaches up and feels around on the cage's roof till he finds this little metal stick, which he pokes around in the lock of his handcuffs. And I should point the gun in his face and make him hand it over, but I can't handle talking to him just yet, cos I know he'll start manipulating me, as soon as I do. So instead I head to the garden to look for food.

And inside the store room, the floor's knee-deep with charred, burnt-up shoes, and bottles, and magazine pages, and a toilet brush (did Steve plan to put plumbing in?), and cloth sacks of rice – all burnt black – which is heartbreaking cos I've spent months starving on seaweed and goats' milk. There's nothing usable in here. So I walk around the woods behind the store room, looking for stuff Steve might have hidden there during the fire. But it's just ferns, like a green force field about as high as my waist. And I walk in wider and wider circles, away from the store room. And eventually in the ferns I find two bottles of washing-up liquid, which I keep, cos they might come in handy on the boat. And then there's something black on the ground. And it's my suitcase! And it's in pretty good nick, actually. Not burnt at all. And I'm hoping it'll be filled with gold, or at least Meena's clothes. But it's empty except for one lacy, white, child's sock. And just then I hear the goat bleating like mental, which is weird.

So I sneak back to the goat area, keeping hidden in the jungle. And I see Steve's got the goat's neck trapped between his legs, and he's trying to grab the goat's head. And after a few tries, Steve manages to grab its horns and force its head out through the bars of the cage, and that lets Steve get a firmer grip on the goat's horns. And he twists the goat's head till there's a snapping sound, which must be its neck breaking. And the goat's little legs are staggering around. But Steve's gripping it so tightly between his legs the goat can't move anywhere, so its little hoofs just skid over the metal floor of the cage. And Steve picks the little metal stick off the cage roof and stabs it into the goat's shoulder a few times, and the goat shudders, and its hoofs skid around on the metal floor a bit more, and it's half falling over now, but Steve's holding it up between his legs. And Steve stabs the metal stick into the goat's shoulder again and stirs it around, to open up a round wound. And then Steve places the bit of metal carefully back on top of the roof of the cage. And something really dodgy's going on here, so I come out and show myself, hoping that'll make Steve stop.

'Shruti,' he goes. 'I've slaughtered one of the goats for you to cook and take on your journey. So start gathering up some sticks for a fire, and I'll show you how to cure the meat.' And while he's saying this he's digging his two main fingers inside that hole in the goat's shoulder. 'You should be able to find plenty of firewood around here,' he goes. 'Look, there's a couple of logs, right behind where you're standing.'

'What are you doing to that goat?' I'm like.

'Just making an incision to help bleed it out,' he goes. 'You have to drain the blood before you cook it, otherwise it ruins the meat.' And with his two fingers he gouges out a fingerful of cloudy-clear jelly-like stuff, which must be the goat's fat. And he smears the fat around one of his wrists. 'Just need to soothe my skin a little bit, from the handcuffs.'

And the fat's slippery like Vaseline, except with streaks of blood. 'That's better,' Steve goes, while he's smearing the fat around one wrist and wriggling the loop of the handcuff down his hand. And shit. I see what he's doing. He's gonna make his wrist slippery so he can slip out of the cuffs. So I run over there to lock the cage door, before he gets free.

And Steve's wriggling his hand like crazy. And I run over there and slam the cage door shut and slide the bolt across. And the handcuff loop is right on Steve's knuckles, and he takes a little glob of fat from the back of his hand and smears it under the metal handcuff ring. And I can't find the padlock that used to be on the cage. But then I have the idea that I can use the spare pair of handcuffs from my pocket to lock the cage door to the frame, and keep it locked shut. So I'm fumbling in my button-up back pocket of my shorts to get out the handcuffs. And Steve's slipped one wrist out of his handcuffs. So his hands aren't locked to the bars of the cage any more. But he's still got the goat trapped between his knees and the chain around his ankles. And while he's wrestling the goat away from his legs, I'm opening up one ring of the spare handcuffs. And Steve's shuffling towards me.

But already he's over here, before I can get the handcuffs onto the cage. And I pull my body right back as he throws one of his hands through the bars of the cage to try and grab me. And he misses. But that's it. I can't go near the cage any more, to lock him in. Cos I saw how Steve battered the Chinese bloke's face into the cage when he grabbed hold of him through the bars.

So while Steve's drawing the bolt open, I reach around to the back of my waistband for the gun, but it's not there. And actually, I can't remember having had it with me all day. So it probably fell on the ground while I was sleeping. So I begin running towards the edge of the field, where I slept. And Steve's opening the cage door, and as I'm running, the Chinese bloke sticks his legs out and trips me over, that little fucker, and I smash my knee on a tree root. So I'm scrambling to get to my feet, but that fucking little bastard's trapping one of my feet between his legs, so I reach over and elbow him on his broken nose. And he yelps in pain and lets go of me.

And I scramble to my feet, just as Steve's hobbling round the open door of the cage. And he dives at me and manages to grab hold of one of my feet, but only the bottom half, so I'm able to yank my foot free. And I get up and start running. And Steve's back on his feet. And I've killed my knee from where I smashed it on that root, so I'm limping towards the field, but Steve's running much slower than me cos of the chain between his ankles.

And I run straight to my sleeping place, at the edge of the field. And I look through the heap of ferns I was sleeping on, but the gun isn't there. And I can hear the metal chinging sound of Steve's chains, as he's running towards me, up the edge of the field. And I start looking in a wider circle now, and I see the gun, bright silver, by the side of the path about halfway between me and Steve. And Steve sees it too, so we're both running towards it. But I get there faster, and I fumble it into my hands and point it at him. And he slows to a walk, but he keeps coming.

'Now I'm just going to walk slowly towards you, Shruti,' he goes, 'and I'm going to come over and take the gun out of your hands, because you know that you don't want to shoot anyone, and everything's going to be fine once you give it to me, because I'm going to help you get on the boat, if that's what you want to do, and if you want to leave right now, that's absolutely fine with me, but I just need to get my gun back, because after you leave, that Filipino gentleman is going to be taking over your duties in the field, and I'll need some incentives to keep him working, or if you prefer, you can stay here for a few days or a week or however long you want, and I can help you plan out your journey, and then you can leave whenever you want, but in the meantime, you'll be living like a queen, because there'll be no work for you to do, and we'll have the use of a boat, so we can sail out and buy whatever you like, in terms of food and clothes, and we can buy fruit trees and real livestock that are suited to this type of climate—'

And he keeps talking and talking without giving me anywhere to cut in. And he's so close now he could probably dive on me and it would all be over, so I'm backing away. And he never stops talking for one second. So I have to just talk over the top of him:

'Stop walking or I'm gonna have to, like, shoot you,' I'm like. But he won't stop:

'—and you can spend all day on the beach, and I'll give you Meena's bikinis to wear and her Chanel beach towel, so I'm just going to walk slowly up to you—'

And he's shuffling faster and faster, as I back away pointing the gun at his face.

'Stop!' I go. 'Just stop walking!'

'—and we've got the boat and two million dollars. So we can buy anything you—'

And he's reaching his hands out now, right towards me.

'Stop!' I'm like. 'Please, just stop coming towards me.' But he won't stop talking or walking closer. And his hands are right near the gun now. And if he just gets one hand on me it's all over. And he won't let me say one single word to him. Cos he just keeps talking and talking. So I point the gun down and I squeeze the trigger, cos I just wanna scare him and make it look like I'm gonna shoot him, so he'll back off. But he doesn't even notice. So I squeeze the trigger a bit further, and it *bangs* and my hand flies up, and it smells a tiny bit of fireworks. And I look down and there's a wound on Steve's thigh, and it's bleeding slightly, and I've shot him. And he finally stops walking. And he winces in pain. And he looks down at the wound.

And I dunno if he can tell that it was an accident I shot him, which it was. But I hope not. Cos this is my big chance to bluff that I would kill him. And he's looking at me now like he doesn't know me. And it's the first time I've seen him a tiny bit scared of me, with his face all tense, and his mouth doesn't quite know what to do, instead of his normal relaxed arrogant, cocky expression.

366

'If you don't tell me where the gold is, right now,' I go, 'I'm gonna shoot you in the other leg, till you can't walk, and then I'm gonna shoot you in both arms, and then I'm gonna handcuff you and drag you over to the Chinese bloke and let him torture you to death with a hammer and a screwdriver that I found in the store room. And you've only got one chance,' I'm like. 'I want you to show me exactly where the gold is and then dig it up for me. And if it's not there, I'm gonna leave you to get tortured to death. But if it *is* there, I'll leave you with the keys to his handcuffs, and you can make him into your slave,' I go. 'Is that a deal?'

'Come on now, Shruti,' goes Steve. 'Think about what you're giving up here. Because when—'

Bang and I just shoot him in the other leg. I didn't even know I was going to do it. And I'm shaking now, I'm so scared and guilty.

'I'm gonna keep shooting, till you shut up and just answer the question,' I'm like. 'Where's the gold? Or do you wanna get tortured to death?'

'Okay,' he's like, drawing in this slow painful breath through his teeth. 'I'll show you where the gold is.'

And I can't believe that he's finally doing what I asked him to. And it's taken so much to make him take me seriously. And it's weird that the gun shots aren't hurting him more, cos on the telly, if you get shot, you fall over and start dying right away. But Steve's still able to walk pretty much okay. So I've gotta get this over with quickly, before he can think of another plan to screw me over.

'All right,' I'm like. 'Where's the gold?'

'Well, it's impossible to—'

And I point the gun at his chest this time, which shuts him up. And then he swallows. And he's like:

'It's in small nylon sacks buried in the jungle behind the sleeping house.'

'Right,' I go. 'Walk over there, and I'll follow. And don't say anything to me. Cos if you talk, I'm gonna shoot you again.' And I have to say that, cos he's such a good talker that if he starts talking, he'll start manipulating me again.

And he turns and walks back down the path to the goat area. And it's still not like on films where people have massive bleeding holes with blood gushing out. Steve's wounds are small and not bleeding much. And we get to the goat enclosure, and the Chinese bloke looks like he's trying to kick the dead goat – which is lying inside the cage – by sticking his feet through the bars. And I dunno what on earth he's doing. But I can't get distracted. I've gotta keep my eyes on Steve, in case he tries anything. So I march Steve back to the garden, with all its burnt-out buildings. And I tell him to walk slowly to where my old suitcase is in the woods, and I grab that so I'll have something to put the gold in. And this is absolutely stupid. Cos I know for a fact that I should just shoot Steve dead and leg it to the boat as fast as I can and start sailing away. Cos even if I do run out of petrol or food, at least there's some kind of chance that another boat might find me and save me. But if Steve overpowers me now and I end up getting stuck here, there's no chance whatsoever that I'll ever escape.

But at the same time it would be so dangerous to go out to sea with no money – not even ten quid in my pocket. Plus, if I can pull this off, I'll be set for life, cos two million dollars is like one million quid, I think. And that would be a pretty decent compensation for all the horrible stuff that Steve's put me through, instead of crawling back to England with nothing.

So I tell Steve to lead us to the gold. And he's walking slowly back to the square in the middle of the burnt-out buildings. But I've got a bad feeling about this. Cos Steve isn't even trying to talk me out of this, so he's probably leading me into a trap. But maybe he really is scared of me now, cos I showed him that I'm not afraid to shoot him.

CHAPTER TWENTY-EIGHT

So I follow Steve behind the sleeping house, where a spade and a big garden fork are leaning against the back wall. And Steve picks up the spade. So I drop back and walk further behind him, cos that spade is basically a big weapon, which he could smash me round the head with. But the further away I am, the harder it'll be for me to get the bullet into him, if I have to shoot him. Plus I've got this dodgy feeling, cos he's too well behaved. He's just doing whatever I ask him to, and it doesn't make sense. So I'm keeping the gun pointed right at his back.

And I follow him through the jungle, where there's old bricks and planks of wood scattered around the floor. And Steve stops walking and jams the spade into the ground. And he digs a hole for about ten minutes. And then he bends over and pulls out a plastic woven little rice sack and jingles it. And I look into the hole he's dug, and it's filled with those little rice sacks.

'There's about two hundred thousand dollars' worth of gold bullion in each bag,' he's like, 'and eleven bags in total. So that's about two point two million.' And he opens one of them up and shows me the little gold tablets inside. 'I assume you want to load these into the suitcase yourself.'

'No,' I'm like. 'Could you do that, please?'

So he unzips the suitcase and slowly starts loading the bags into it, going, 'Now, the reason your gun only gave me minor flesh wounds is that it's very low calibre.' And then he stops. 'Looks like this is going to take a bit of extra digging to get these last few bags out.' And he digs away earth from the sides of the hole with his hands. 'Now what you really want, if you're going to hold someone at gunpoint,' he goes, while he's digging, 'is a high-calibre handgun that will cripple you for life with a single shot. You can just tell by looking at a gun when it can do that.' And he's digging and digging. 'Nearly there,' he goes. 'Right.' And when he stands up, he's holding a fat black handgun, with a barrel about twice as long and thick as my one, and pointing it at my face. 'This is the kind of gun you want,' he goes. 'This is a Smith and Wesson nine millimetre, loaded with hollow-tip bullets. One of these bullets will tear right through your vital organs and splinter through your bones. Whereas that piece of cheap Chinese junk you're holding barely even gets past the muscle tissue.'

And I'm fucked again.

'So why don't you be a good little girl,' goes Steve, 'and just throw that little cap-gun into the suitcase.'

So I throw my little silver gun in there, next to the sacks of gold, cos I have to.

'That, my friend,' goes Steve, 'is what they call a plot twist.' And Steve zips up the suitcase. 'You know what I'm feeling like?'

he goes. 'You know what I haven't had in a long time? I'm feeling like I haven't had any love, in quite a while. Do you ever feel that way? I'm usually—'

Thwack goes this black shadow, behind Steve's head. And he falls onto his face on the ground and I quickly grab the gun out of Steve's hand, and he's passed out. And I look up and standing behind him it's the Chinese bloke! He's holding a thick beam of wood that's burnt black at one end. And he's got grease, streaked with blood, all over his wrists. And his handcuffs are only attached to his right wrist. So I suppose he watched what Steve did with the goat fat to slip out of his handcuffs, and did the same thing to free himself.

And Steve's lying groggily on the ground. And the Chinese bloke smashes the beam down onto the back of Steve's head one more time. And Steve's out cold. And the Chinese bloke rolls him over and grabs the handcuff that's still attached to one of Steve's wrists, threads the empty loop through itself, to open it. And he clips it onto the chain between Steve's ankles, so Steve's hand is basically tied to his feet.

Then the Chinese bloke ratchets the other loop of Steve's handcuff tighter around Steve's wrist, till it's digging into his flesh – I suppose cos he knows how easy it is to slip out of these handcuffs, if they're not tight enough. But as he's crushing the metal loop into Steve's wrist, Steve wakes up and suddenly grabs the Chinese guy around the throat with his free hand. And they start fighting. And Steve's younger and bigger and stronger, but he's also got one hand chained to his ankles, so it's hard to know who's gonna win.

And I shoot Steve's gun twice into the ground, to scare them. And they stop fighting and look at me. 'Steve,' I go, pointing the big black gun at his chest. 'Clip the open loop of that bloke's handcuffs onto your ankle chain.'

And Steve does it. So now neither of them will be able to walk properly, cos they're so tangled up with each other. And they're both stooped over, like a weird game of Twister, looking at me, waiting to see what I'll do next.

'All right, then. Just stay there and don't try to follow me or I'll kill you,' I'm like. And I feel like I'm supposed to make some big speech, putting Steve in his place. But sod that. I just grab the handle of the suitcase – which has got eight bags of gold plus the little silver gun packed into it – and I start wheeling it away looking over my shoulder every two seconds to make sure they're not coming after me. And Steve starts to call out, persuading me to stay. But then the Chinese bloke starts attacking him, so he has to stop talking so he can fight back. And the suitcase is bloody heavy, and it's difficult to pull it over the bumpy rough undergrowth. But I make it to the flat ground of the garden square. And I stop to pat my pockets, and I feel the big black gun in my left pocket and the bunch of keys in my right.

CHAPTER TWENTY-NINE

And I look behind me, and Steve and the Chinese bloke are still fighting each other, which is good, cos the longer they fight, the weaker they'll get, and the less likely they are to come after me.

So I drag the suitcase through the jungle, heading for the boat, which is bloody hard work, cos I have to drag the suitcase over roots and branches and mounds of stone, cos it's too heavy to lift off the ground. And it's killing my arms and shoulders. And after a few minutes, I notice this metal *Ching! Ching! Ching!* sound echoing out from the direction of the garden, so I suppose they're trying to smash off the handcuffs. But as long as they're still hammering, that means they're trapped with each other, so I'm safe.

But just then the hammering sound stops. So maybe they've got free, and maybe Steve's on his way to trap me or the Chinese bloke's coming to save his boat. So I try to wheel the suitcase faster, but it's hard, cos the suitcase is so heavy, and the jungle floor's so rough that I have to keep lifting it over rocks and dragging it over big roots and whatever. And eventually I get to the beach, where I have a little rest. And then I force myself to keep slogging through the jungle, keeping close to the sea. And finally after, like, two hours I get to the boat, which is bobbing gently in the water. And it's still got tyres chained round it to protect the wooden sides from smashing against the stone ledge, where it's tied up with those three fat ropes tied in complicated knots around three trees.

And I look back down the island, and I can see two beaches curving round, a way down. And on the closer one, it's Steve hobbling towards me. And his hands are free, but he's still got the chain round his ankles, I suppose because the ankle chain is much thicker than the handcuffs. And he's hobbling with short little steps as quick as he can. And he'll probably be here in, like, thirty minutes. So I keep the large black gun in my hand.

And I wheel the suitcase to the edge of the stone dock. And there's about a metre gap between the boat and the dock, where the suitcase could fall into the sea. And it's too heavy to lift onto the boat. So I unzip the case and throw the bags of gold into the back of the boat, one by one, keeping the gun in my hand. And then I zip up the suitcase and throw that in, as well, but it catches on the handle of the gun, which clatters off the stone ledge and plops into the deep water of the sea. And there's no time to try and fish it out, cos Steve's gonna be here soon, and I've gotta make a start on the three ropes tied to the trees.

So I go to the first tree, and the rope's about as fat as my wrist and fastened in a tight knot, which I start trying to undo. But each time the boat bobs on the water, it pulls the rope and tightens whatever loop of the knot I was easing undone. So it takes me, like, twenty minutes to untie just this first knot. And at this rate Steve will get here before I've even got the second knot open. So I follow the ropes onto the boat, to see if the knots at *that* end of the ropes would be easier to untie. But on the boat they're looped at the end like the eyes of needles – with their loops lined with metal – circled round these metal rings bolted to the deck. So there's no way I can undo them.

So I look around for one of those sword things that the Chinese blokes attacked Steve with, when we first got to the island. But there's nothing on the deck, nothing in the cabin, and nothing in the underground room. Although while I'm down there, I find a set of tools mounted on the wall, plus ropes and strings and fat rolls of gaffer tape. And I grab the only saw I can find, which is a metal arc with a thin blade strung between its two ends.

And I rush back to the stone ledge and start sawing through the second rope. And in the distance I can hear this quiet *chang-chang* of Steve's ankle chains. So I speed up and saw like mental. And I'm halfway through this second rope, and then all the way through. And it drops, slack, to the floor. So I move on to the last rope. But when I'm about quarter of the way through, the saw blade snaps in half. So I try sawing with the broken blade, holding it in my hands, but that doesn't work.

So I run back down to the cabin under the boat and look for any possible thing I can cut the rope with. And I find a Stanley knife in a drawer. So I rush back to the last tree and start slashing at the fibres of the rope, over and over again in the same place, with the little triangle-shaped blade of the knife.

And I'm about halfway through when I see Steve hobbling towards me in the distance through the trees. And I have an idea that if I start up the boat, the pull of the engine might just snap the last rope, cos I'm already halfway through it. So I jump back on board and start the motor, and I push that big lever forward and the boat's nose tilts up, as the engines dig into the water. But the rope's not snapping, and the boat's still tied to the island, and it starts curving round to the left-hand side, like the minute hand of a clock slipping backwards from twelve to eleven to ten. So I turn the motor down slow, to keep it pulling at the rope, but to hopefully stop the boat curving round and smashing into the island. And I stay on the boat, to keep away from Steve, and I start a new cut on the rope, next to the low back wall of the boat, hacking at the rope with the Stanley knife. And the boat pulls the rope nice and tight, snapping some of the strands, while I'm hacking at it.

'Shruti!' shouts Steve, hobbling towards me through the trees. 'Shruti, don't leave just yet. There's something I have to tell you about your mother.' And he comes out of the trees, onto the stone dock, hobbling towards me. And he quickly sizes up the situation and picks up one of the slack ropes that's attached to the boat, and he keeps walking towards me.

And I'm on the back of the deck, chopping like mental at the last rope. And over by the tree, the rope makes a snapping sound, and the boat starts curving slowly sideways again. But there's no time to adjust the engine or the steering wheel, cos now I've gotta guard the back of the boat to stop Steve jumping on. I'll just have to hope the boat won't curve all the way round to smash into the island.

'Don't come near me or I'll stab you with this knife,' I'm like, holding out the knife towards him. 'And I've got the gun in my pocket, and I'll shoot you in the head.'

And Steve holds his hands up. 'I just want to talk,' he goes. 'You're free to go, if you like. But there's something I need to tell you about your mother.'

And as I'm holding out the knife, I notice there's a little button on the side of the handle. And when I press it, it lets me slide the blade further out, revealing this new fresh bit of blade. So I use that to hack at the rope, and it's much sharper. And I'm slicing and slicing and the strands are snapping from the pull of the boat and suddenly the rope snaps and the boat starts moving slowly forward. So I stay on the back of the boat, holding the knife towards Steve, to stop him from trying to jump on. And after the boat's about five metres away from the dock, I run to the steering wheel and shove that lever all the way forward. So the boat speeds ahead. And I look back and Steve's disappeared from the dock. So I slow the boat down and walk to the back of the boat, holding the knife in front of me.

And when I look into the sea behind the boat I see Steve holding onto one of the ropes and steadily pulling himself up, hand over hand. And I can tell by the way the island's moving to the side that the boat's curving round. So I look at the front of the boat, and I see we're heading for a rock pile sticking out of the water, like the ones I was clinging to when I had to swim on shore all those months ago.

So I run to the front of the boat and pull the steering wheel round, to steer clear of the rocks. And then I stop the engine, to stop us from crashing. And then I rush to the back again, so I can fend off Steve, who's still pulling himself hand over hand up the rope and is almost at the boat now. And I look around for a weapon to attack him with to make him let go. And I've lost my little knife somewhere. And here on the back of the boat, there's just the suitcase – which is too bulky to swing properly – and the little rice sacks filled with gold. And I remember this thing in *Cosmo* about women prisoners who make their own weapons by putting a snooker ball or a few batteries in a sock and using it to smash someone's skull in. So I open up one of the little sacks of gold and tip out most of the gold onto the deck, so there's about a cricket ball's worth of gold in there, and I grasp the opening of the sack.

And Steve pulls himself up and gets his elbows onto the wooden wall that goes round the edge of the boat. And I swing the little sack down onto his head. But it doesn't crack his skull, like a snooker ball would. It just feels like the gold tablets spread out, as they hit him, like beans in a beanbag. And Steve closes his eyelids for a second and then shimmies himself up so he's gripping the boat wall under his armpits. And he's wiping the seawater out of his eyes. So I crack the bag of gold down on his skull two more times, but it's not even hurting him. And I can't get too close, cos if he grabs my leg he'll never let go.

'Shruti, this is important,' goes Steve. 'Just before your mother died, she wrote a long letter and gave it to Meena.'

'My mum isn't dead,' I'm like.

'Yes, she is,' goes Steve. 'She died of aggressive pancreatic cancer about a week before you came out here. She specifically requested that you not be contacted because she didn't want to ruin your holiday in New Zealand, but she gave Meena a six-page letter for you. A handwritten letter. I've got it back at the island, in a strong box I keep buried with all our passports and paperwork inside.'

And this is blatantly another trick. I'm almost sure it is. But there's a one per cent chance that he's telling the truth. So I just wanna hear what he's gonna say next, so I can know for certain that he's lying.

'I'm so sorry to have to break it to you this way,' he's like. 'I haven't read the letter myself, because Meena made me promise never to tell you. She thought it would be too devastating – and that you'd never have to find out, if you stayed on the island. That was another reason why she wanted you to join us, that it would stop you from ever having to find out about your mother. But now that you're leaving, you probably should read it. You won't have another chance.'

And I'm trying to think what I can smash his skull in with, but now I can't stop worrying about my mum being dead and what might be in this letter, even though I know Steve's lying. And I'm looking around the floor of the boat, cos that Stanley knife must be around here somewhere. And my brain's thinking: What if my mum wrote that she's sorry for everything, and then what if I leave and I'd never ever get to read that? And then I'll always be wondering what she wanted to tell me. But I'm sure Steve's lying. I'm, like, ninety per cent sure.

But even if he is telling the truth, I'm thinking, it's still better that I escape – even if I miss out on the letter – than it is to live the rest of my life as a prisoner. And I look around one last time for the knife, but it's just not here. There's only the bags of gold and the suitcase. But inside the suitcase is the other gun! The little silver gun! So I unzip the suitcase, as Steve's trying to swing his feet up onto the sidewall of the boat, which is difficult, cos his ankles are still chained together. And I get the little silver gun out of the suitcase and point it right at his face.

'Okay, okay,' he goes. 'You win.' And he puts his feet back down into the water. 'Now, you don't want to have two murders on your conscience for the rest of your life. And that's what you will have if you shoot me now, because I left the Filipino man padlocked inside the goat cage, and he'll starve to death if I don't get back. So I'm just going to hold onto the very end of this rope, so I'm nowhere near the boat, and you're going to tow me back to the island, or one of the rocks near to it. And when we get there you're also going to give me all of the keys except the one you need to drive this boat, so I can unlock myself,' he's like. 'Okay, so now I'm holding onto the rope, and I'm slowly working my way to the end of it.' And he lets himself further and further down the rope. And he has to shout now. 'So just turn the boat around. You can keep hold of the gun and keep looking back here to make sure I'm not trying any funny business.'

So I keep hold of the gun and start the boat up and drive it towards the island. And while I'm driving, I take the boat key off the key ring, to free up all the other keys. And I keep looking out the back, but I can't see Steve, cos the back of the boat's blocking my view. And the closer I get to the island, the more piles of rock there are sticking out of the water, and I remember all the hidden rocks under the sea, and I'm afraid I'm gonna crash the boat. So I stop near enough for Steve to swim back to the island. And I turn off the boat's engines and run to the back of the boat. And I'm dreading Steve not being in the water, cos if he isn't, he'll be on the boat somewhere. But there he is, treading water with the rope wrapped around his wrist.

'Get on that rock,' I go, 'and I'll tape the keys inside a lifejacket and throw them to you.'

And he gives me a thumbs-up and lets go of the rope and swims to the rock I pointed out. And I pull a lifejacket out of this little cubbyhole below the steering wheel, and then I go downstairs and get some of that black tape, which there's about twenty rolls of, in a big box, and I tape the keys to the lifejacket and drive the boat near to the pile of rock, where Steve's sitting like a chained-up mermaid. And I throw the lifejacket, which lands near him in the water.

'I taped the keys to it!' I go.

'Thanks!' he's like. And I stay there and watch him while he swims over and brings it back to the rock. And then he untapes the keys and unlocks the chains off his ankles. And he puts the lifejacket on and carefully buttons the keys into his shorts pocket and wraps the chain round and round his wrist so that he can keep hold of it.

'What do you need that for?' I'm like. 'Just chuck it away.'

'Got to keep the Filipino gentleman doing his job properly,' Steve's like.

And I realise what a horrible thing it is that I've just done – what a horrible, terrible thing. Cos I've left that poor Chinese bloke to be Steve's slave forever. And for a second I think about going back there and trying to save the Chinese bloke. But I just can't risk it. And it's better that he's Steve's slave than I am. And I know that's an evil thing to think. So I just try not to think about it.

And I feel like there should be some kind of momentous goodbye where I force Steve to apologise, or he threatens to kill me if he ever sees me again, or I threaten to kill him, or something, like always happens on films. But weirdly it's totally casual, cos Steve's so good at telling people how the situation's gonna be, without saying anything. He just makes it happen, like he hypnotises you into hearing this script that you find yourself reading from.

'No use trying to tell anyone about this,' he goes, 'because whatever happens you'd be put away for assault with a deadly weapon and criminal imprisonment, for what you did to me, plus there's that old arson charge – or arson with murderous intent – from when you tried to murder your uncle. Plus, of course, I know people who can kill you without the police finding out about it. So that might happen, too, of course. But I know that you won't say anything, so there's no problem, is there?'

And he wants me to say, *No, I'll never tell anyone.* Even if it's not true, he wants me to feel like I have to say whatever he wants me to. And everything in me is trained to say that. And I know it would be easier to just say it.

'I'll do whatever the fuck I want,' I go. 'So fuck you!'

'Ha ha! That's the spirit!' he's like. 'See you around!' And he waves to me, like it's all just a joke to him. And he dives off the rock, into the water, and starts a strong front crawl towards the

383

island. And I think he sort of enjoys all this. He didn't really even seem to mind that much that he couldn't get me to come back to the island. He just said to himself, *Whatever: I'm gonna move on.* And he knows that whatever he does, he's gonna be all right. And he probably has got a secret boat on his island or some other way to escape. And although I absolutely despise him for everything that he's done, part of me is sort of jealous, cos he will be all right, no matter what happens. He's that kind of person. But me, on the other hand. I dunno.

CHAPTER THIRTY

And I watch Steve swim back to the island and disappear into the jungle. And I dunno what the hell I'm doing with driving this boat. But so what? I drove it this far. So I pick a random direction and put the boat on full speed and just start driving. And I lock the steering wheel in place with this plastic clip, next to it, to make sure I'm going straight. And I have a proper look around the dashboard. And there's three unlabelled dials. And the needles on all of them are dead and lying on the left-hand side. So I hope they're broken, or I'm about to run out of absolutely everything. Or perhaps I'm completely full of everything, but I doubt it.

And there's a little cupboard on the right-hand side of the dashboard, with this little telly inside it. So I turn it on, and the screen lights up in black, with a green circle in the middle, and green writing going, USE SCROLL KEYS TO SELECT DESTINATION OR ENTER GPS COORDINATES. So this must be a navigation thing. So I scroll through this whole long list of about two hundred place names, with the arrow keys. And the only ones in England are LONDON, UK, and SOUTHAMPTON, UK. So I go back to

SOUTHAMPTON, UK – which is a smaller town so it'll be easier for me to sneak into – and I press ENTER. And it's like, SOUTHAMPTON, UK: DISTANCE: 7,387 MILES. So I'm never gonna make it there without stopping for petrol, which I knew already. And I press all the different buttons, trying to find out where I am now, so I can find somewhere nearby to refuel and ask how far this boat can drive on a full tank. But there's no screen that just says, *You are here,* or *Current location,* or anything like that. So instead I go through each place name and click SELECT to see how many miles away it is, looking for the closest one, which turns out to be Colombo, Sri Lanka, which is 754 miles away. So I click SELECT. And after a bit of playing around with driving the boat in different directions, I work out that the circle on the screen tells you which direction to go. And it's sort of like a clock, where the little hand shows my direction, and the big hand stays at twelve o'clock, and that's where I'm supposed to drive. So I keep turning the steering wheel till I'm heading that way, and the two hands are on top of each other. And I cruise along like that for a while, and there's a real digital clock on the screen as well, so I can see the distance is going down by about twenty miles each hour, and I work out that I should get to Colombo, Sri Lanka, in, like, thirty-seven hours at this rate, which is a day and a half. And I've gotta keep focusing on practical things at the moment.

Like is there even any food here, or any warm clothes in case it gets cold at night? Cos I'm still just wearing shorts and a T-shirt. And I've gotta hide the gold tablets, for when I arrive at the port, to stop people trying to steal them. So I put the plastic clip back on the steering wheel so I won't veer off in the wrong direction. And I start searching the downstairs cabin to see if there's any food I can eat, or cash I can buy petrol with, or a hiding place for the gold. And I walk down the stairs and search all the drawers and cupboards. But they're nearly all empty. There's just those tools mounted to the wall, and that box of gaffer tape, and lots of empty white plastic crates. And there's a box of food with, like, a hundred packets of instant noodles, and a sack of tiny little dried fish, as short as matchsticks, and another sack of dried green shredded cabbage, or something, which stinks like rotting seaweed. And there are five huge plastic barrels of water. But there's no cash, so I'll have to pay for everything with the gold tablets. And I remember that Steve said each bag had two hundred thousand dollars' worth of gold in it. So I go back up on deck and gather up the loose gold tablets that I emptied out earlier, when I made that stupid weapon to hit Steve with. And each tablet is about the size of a credit card but, like, three times as thick, and each one's printed with the words CREDIT SUISSE 99.9% PURE and a serial number. And then I count out the tablets in one of the unopened bags, and there's exactly one hundred tablets in there. So each tablet must cost two thousand American dollars, if Steve was telling the truth, which he probably wasn't.

So I put five of the tablets in my pocket, to pay for petrol and food and clothes. And then I take all the bags of gold downstairs, empty out all the tablets on the floor and wrap them up into little bundles of ten tablets each with the black gaffer tape, and I wrap the tape round and round, so no gold's showing. The bundles just look like small black bricks. And I stack them neatly at the bottom of this wooden box, and I pile the packets of noodles over them, and then I pile up empty plastic crates around and over the top of the box.

And I go upstairs and find I'm totally off course, even though I had the steering wheel locked straight with that plastic clip. So there must be, like, currents dragging the boat around. So I keep adjusting the wheel till I'm back on course. And I keep looking around the boat, but coming back every few minutes to keep the boat heading in the right direction. And I find some bags of spices in the cabin, and a little camping cooker thing with a bottle of gas attached to it, and a saucepan. So I cook two packets of noodles – while I'm sitting at the steering wheel – with a handful of those tiny fish, some of that seaweed stuff and a pinch of this golden-red-coloured spice powder. And after dinner, I'm looking around the side of the deck, and I find this double-handle on a cog – like the pedals on a bicycle – that turns a chain that disappears down into a hole in the deck and out through the side of the boat, where it's holding up a big anchor.

So when it gets dark and I get too tired to carry on, I stop the engines and turn off the navigation thing, and I let down the anchor, and I go to sleep on the bunk beds. And it's absolutely freezing, cos I can't find any clothes or clean blankets, just the filthy old grey ones that smell like mud and layers of old sweat. So I'll buy some blankets too when I stop in Sri Lanka.

And I wake up and sail all day for the next two days, following the direction that the navigation screen tells me. And when there's eighteen miles left until Colombo, Sri Lanka, I can see land, and then a huge port with hundreds of boats. So I cruise along the coastline for about forty miles, till I see a smaller port with about fifteen little fishing boats that look like mine. And I'm hoping this will be safer and have fewer police than a big city for me to buy petrol, seeing as I've got no passport and I'm driving a stolen boat. And I pull in to an empty parking space next to another boat, and I get the two long ropes still attached to the boat, and I tie them to this metal tree stump thing built into the dock. And I don't wanna leave the boat here on its own in case someone steals it or steals the gold tablets. So I stand on the concrete dock till eventually this old bloke comes up to me, with scraggly grey stubble all over his face and neck, and wearing a sort of wrap-around skirt, with the hem tucked into the front. And he starts talking to me in another language.

'English?' I go to him. 'Do you speak English?'

And he brings over this young bloke who speaks English.

'Yeah,' I go to him. 'I need to buy petrol for the boat.'

'Petrol?' he goes. 'What is this?'

'Petrol. To make the engine go. You know, like you put in a car? Like oil, diesel . . .'

'Oh, diesel fuel, diesel fuel,' he goes. 'Yes, okay, I come with you and we buy.' And he drives my boat, with me inside it, down the coast to this big rusty metal tank where they fill up my boat. And I ask the young bloke if that's enough to get me back to England.

And he laughs. 'No, no. You must refuel many times.' And he asks me if I'm going round the Cape or through the Suez Canal.

And I ask him which is the best way. 'Suez Canal is quickest but you'll have to pay bribes if you don't have paperwork.' So I tell him I'm going round the Cape. And I show him my navigation thing and he sets it for CAPE TOWN, SOUTH AFRICA, for me. And I tell him I wanna buy food and blankets and a wristwatch and a map of the world. And I want someone to screw a padlock onto the cabin door of the boat. And he calls a boy over and talks to him in their language, and the boy runs off to get the stuff for me from his village, or whatever.

And I ask the bloke, 'How much will all this cost?'

'One thousand dollars, US,' he's like, which might be a rip-off, but whatever. I can afford it. So I give him one gold tablet.

'No, no,' he's like. 'You must pay with US dollars.'

'I haven't got any,' I'm like. 'I've only got these gold things.'

'Okay, please wait here,' he goes. And takes the gold tablet and the key to my boat and disappears. And I wait. And finally after about an hour he comes back with three boys, each carrying a box of food and bottles of Coke, and blankets, and an old map of the world in a picture frame.

And the bloke goes to me, 'Three more of these coins is okay.'

So I give him three more out of my pocket.

'Okay. Now you will stay with me tonight, in my house,' he goes. 'I'll give you traditional five-course Sri Lankan dinner in my home. It is very beautiful.'

'No, that's all right,' I go, 'I wanna start sailing right away,' cos I don't wanna spend the night in some strange bloke's house, plus I can't just leave all that gold in my boat.

And he keeps trying to persuade me to come with him, and

he won't take no for an answer, and I keep asking for my key back, but he keeps telling me I have to come to his house to get it. And after a while I can't be bothered to argue any more, so I just pull the little silver gun out of my pocket and point it at his face. 'Okay, okay, okay,' he's like, and he hands over my key and backs away from me and climbs off the boat.

'I'm sorry,' I'm like. 'I don't wanna be horrible, but I've just gotta leave now.'

'No, it's okay, it's okay,' he's like, fixing his eyes on me, looking scared. And he quickly tells the little boys to run away. And he walks off after them.

So I untie the boat and turn on the motor and the navigation thing. And that bloke already set the destination to CAPE TOWN, SOUTH AFRICA. And it says 5,322 miles. And I'm guessing that will take about twenty days, and then maybe another fifteen after that to get up to England. (And I suppose that shorter distance to Southampton it showed before was taking the short cut through the Suez Canal.) And I'm well stocked up now. So I set off, sailing all day and putting down the anchor at night, which I don't think is actually reaching the bottom of the sea, but I like the feeling of lowering it down there anyway, for the sort of security of it. And this is a fishing boat, so it's designed to go for long distances and to be all right in storms, and whatever. And in a cupboard downstairs I find a fishing rod and hooks. I teach myself how to fish, and I catch all kinds of different fish, which I cook on the little gas cooker.

And while I'm heading towards Cape Town, I see on the map that I'll be going past these islands call Mauritius. So I reset the navigation thing and stop there and buy more food and fuel and water, at another little fishing port, where no one asks any questions. And I do the same thing at a little fishing port near Cape Town, plus I change up a load of the gold tablets there, for ten thousand American dollars in cash.

And next I stop on the west side of Africa at this country called Ivory Coast, which I picked cos it's right on the way home and it's got a nice name. And when I tie up there, this bloke comes on board my boat with a machine gun and demands cash. So I give him three hundred dollars and then he stays there guarding me and stopping anyone else coming on the boat. And he gets his friend to have my boat refuelled and stocked up with water and food for six hundred dollars. And I give the bloke with the machine gun another three hundred, when I want him to go. And he leaves.

And then I stop in Portugal, and I buy five large plastic tanks of petrol, to keep with me on the boat, in addition to the usual fuel and food. And finally I set the navigation for SOUTHAMPTON, UK. And when I get near, I wait till the middle of the night and drive up the English Channel past Southampton, past Brighton, and up to the town where my university was, where I know the coastline really well. And there's a little promenade thing, which I can easily throw the gold and the suitcase onto and then jump on there myself, cos the rest of the coast round here's all wide pebble beaches or high cliffs that I couldn't get the suitcase full of gold over.

And it's four a.m. on a Tuesday, so there's no one around. And I pull up to the promenade and tie up to the railings. And I put the suitcase onshore and load the gold into it. And I tie a long rope to the throttle-handle that makes the boat go faster or slower, and I pour the cans of petrol I bought all over the boat, till the floors are all wet with it and it stinks like a petrol station. And I start the boat's engine, and I untie the ropes holding it to the railings. And finally I jump onto the promenade, set fire to a rag, throw it onto the boat and let the fire blaze up a bit. And then I yank the rope attached to the throttle and send the boat onto full speed away from me, and the whole boat's on fire and blazing into the middle of the night, flying away from me through the water, like it's crashed out of the sun.

CHAPTER THIRTY-ONE

And I wheel the suitcase towards Brighton, which is a hard three-hour walk, cos the suitcase is basically full of metal, plus my walking muscles are weak cos I've spent the past four weeks cooped up on a little boat. And I can't catch a bus or a taxi, cos I've got no English money to pay the fare. And obviously I should've changed some dollars into pounds in Portugal, but I didn't think of that at the time.

And eventually I reach Brighton town centre, and I wait till the banks open, and then I change my last four thousand-odd US dollars into English pounds, doing five hundred dollars at each bank and building society in the High Street, so no one gets suspicious about why I've got so much money. And then I catch a train to London Victoria, where I find an estate agent, and I rent a little bedsitter flat near Victoria for six hundred pounds a month. And I put down the first month's rent and the security deposit in cash on the spot, and I move right in that afternoon. And first, I get a locksmith to install three new locks on my front door, to stop anyone breaking in and stealing the gold tablets. And then I buy a sleeping bag and a bed-roll and a pillow to sleep on from a Millets. And then I go to a Barclays, which is my bank, and I tell them my new address and ask them to post me a new bank card and chequebook.

And I wanna sell the gold and keep the money in a bank account, so I won't have it hanging around the flat where it could get stolen. But I'll have to do it slowly, cos there's more than a million pounds' worth, and I don't want anyone calling the police on me. So I go to an internet café, and I look up 'money laundering'. And it says you're supposed to start a business where your customers pay you in cash, like owning a pub, and you just mix your 'dirty' money in with the 'clean' money you really earned, and you deposit it all in the bank mixed together, so people think you earned the whole lot honestly, and that 'washes' it. And I walk around London for a few days, trying to think of a cash business I could start, cos I blatantly can't open my own pub. And eventually I come across Camden Market, where people are selling homemade T-shirts and handbags and jewellery and everything. So I ask around till I find the manager, and I reserve a stall from him for the next month, which is three hundred quid a week.

And I buy a load of silver pendants and ceramic beads and earring hooks and silver chains and clasps from this cool handmade bead shop I remember in Brighton. And I make earrings and bracelets and necklaces, which I sell on my stall for five pounds each, cos I don't care about making a profit. I've gotta just have a cash business, so I can launder the money from my gold. But cos I'm selling the jewellery so cheap, it sells like crazy, mostly to teenagers and especially teenage kids from

Europe and Japan on bus tours, who want stuff that looks nice but costs nothing. And each night I make more of the stuff that sells well (like these silver miniature casts of skulls of animals, like hummingbirds and foxes) and I stop making the stuff that no one buys. And after three days, I'm virtually sold out, so I go back to Brighton with my suitcase this time, and I buy a ton more beads and pendants and chains – but only the stuff I know will definitely sell. And I'm sold out again by the weekend, so I have to go back to Brighton again. And I pay for another four weeks on the stall, and I experiment with different prices, till I find that I can still pretty much make six hundred quid a day, by charging between five pounds and forty pounds per item, and I'm making a real profit on each thing I sell.

And Tuesdays are my day off from the market, when I visit shops around London that buy gold. And I sell one gold tablet at each place, for about twelve hundred quid each. And I make a note of which places ask where I got the gold (my granddad left it to me, I tell them) and which places don't care, and I only go back to the places that don't care.

And I get Barclays to give me a small business account, where I put all the cash from my jewellery stall, which is like eight grand a month – after I've paid for supplies and the market fees and the rent on my flat – plus I add in an extra dirty five thousand each month from the gold tablets I'm selling. And I start buying my jewellery supplies mail order from artists in Denmark and San Francisco, which saves me from having to keep going down to the bead shop in Brighton, plus it means I have beads no one else has ever seen before, and I constantly have different necklaces and bracelets and earrings, so a lot of my customers come back to the stall every week, cos I've always got something new. And after six months, I get this massive surge of French and Belgian teenagers, and I dunno why, until one of them tells me my stall was written up in a French language guidebook to London.

And I get a bigger stall, triple the size of my old one, and I hire a few girls to help me, and I start selling jewellery with seed pearls and small emeralds and sapphires – which I keep in a glass case – as well as the cheap stuff, and I'm bringing in twelve grand a month, and I'm adding an extra dirty seven grand from selling the gold tablets. And the value of gold tablets keeps going up and up, so I get more per tablet, pretty much every time I sell some.

And after a year I open up a little shop in Camden, and I call the shop Island. And I leave two of my assistant girls tending the stall, and I hire a few more girls to work in the shop, plus two more girls to make the jewellery from my designs, in the back room. And then I open up another branch in Covent Garden. And that does well. And I get good at people management. And I open up more shops – on Carnaby Street, and just off Leicester Square, and one in Brighton. And I hire a bookkeeper. And I hire someone to make me a website and update it and take care of online sales. And then I start having custom beads and pendants made in Malaysia, from my own designs, because I know pretty well what sells.

And to be honest, I much prefer managing the staff at the jewellery business than doing the whole dating or friendship thing, cos I get total control over the people who work for me, and there's nothing they can do to screw me over. And I only ever hire girls, cos they're less likely to play up, and if they do, I give them a verbal warning, then a written warning, then I set them an action plan, and then I fire them. But with friendships and boyfriends, it's impossible to keep control like that, plus there's always the risk that friends or boys would find out about my money laundering or I might accidentally let something slip about the island, which I want to keep secret so I can completely put it behind me, plus I could get put in prison for when I shot Steve, plus they might find out how much money I've got and try to exploit me or steal it or sue me, because I've got about four million in the bank now, and my income's about six hundred thousand a year, after taxes.

But even so, I have a desperate urge to tell my story, and I desperately want someone I can talk with about what a bastard Steve was, cos that's what it all boils down to: I was good, and Steve was bad, and Meena was bad. And I need to hear some other people say that. But I can't tell anyone I know, obviously, cos that would give them too much power over me. And I can't see a counsellor, because she might tell the police, who'd arrest me for shooting Steve and money laundering. And then it would be in the newspapers, and everyone in the country would know about what happened to me, and that story would stick to me forever, because people could always google it, and I'd never be able to leave it behind and move on. And on top of that, I'm not sure a counsellor would even believe me, it's such a bizarre story. And I can't stand the idea of her nodding her head and humouring me or diagnosing me as delusional.

And I think I'm developing post-traumatic stress disorder,

because I have regular panic attacks and flashbacks. And I lie to my GP and tell her that I was traumatised by a car crash when I was a child, and she gives me tranquillizers. But they just make me want to sleep all the time and stop me from being able to concentrate properly at work. So I stop taking them. And when I come out of the haze, I'm still dying to hear people talk about how evil Steve is.

So I type up a summary of everything that happened to me growing up and on the island, and I change everyone's names and pretend it's a fiction short story, and I take it to a continuing education class in fiction writing at Queen Mary and Westfield College. But when I 'workshop' it, the teacher keeps talking about how my story is an allegory of colonialism and Steve represents the British colonial power conquering India, which is me, or it's an allegory of slavery, and I represent the enslaved people transported from their homeland. And then eventually India gets its independence, which is represented by me leaving the island. And then most of the other students go along with that, and then a few of them criticise 'the Shruti character' for abandoning the 'Chinese bloke', and leaving him to become Steve's slave, and they say that's evidence that 'the Shruti character' is just as morally corrupt as Steve, when she's blatantly not as fucking bad as that bastard Steve. Plus they say the 'Chinese bloke' is an offensive stereotype of an Asian man, and he fits into one of the four main Asian racial stereotypes, which is the inscrutable and cold older Asian male – when blatantly he *was* inscrutable and cold to 'the Shruti character', because she bloody well couldn't speak his language and he tried to attack and probably kill her. And I try to tell the class my whole short story was supposed to be from 'the Shruti character's' point of view, and the depiction of the 'Chinese bloke' was supposed to be how a scared, naïve teenage girl would view him. But my classmates have got these ready-made answers they've been taught at their universities, that my response doesn't redeem my act, and that to make the 'Chinese bloke', who was really from the Philippines, a non-stereotypical character I would need to give him more interiority, which is probably a fair point. And I remember that I still have his handwritten letters, which I stole from his pocket. So I pay someone to translate them. And they turn out to be a long letter to his elderly sister, explaining how he sold his family's orchid farm to pay for a GPS navigation system, so he could find the island again and kill Steve, in revenge for killing his nephew (who must have been the middle-aged bloke on the boat) and his nephew's son (who must have been the boy). So I type up the translation, word for word, and bring it into the class as another 'short story', and this time the class is ecstatic with praise for 'my' writing, and they tell me how much more of a sympathetic character the Filipino man is than 'the Shruti character' (even though he's out to commit murder, I'm thinking!) and how his story was more believable and compelling than 'the Shruti story', and that's exactly what 'the Shruti story' was lacking. So at least they don't think I'm racist any more. But I can never go back to that workshop, because my own story's been, like, taken away from me again by a bunch of white people and turned into something that I don't want it to be, and I don't think I've got the power to wrestle it back under my own control, or actually, I don't want to have to fight to make people understand my own story of my own life. People should just accept it, because I said it and it's true.

And all I really want is for people to read my story, and to see what these characters did and maybe get involved in the plot, and then talk about how evil Steve was and how much they hate him, and how they feel sorry for 'the Shruti character'. And you'd think it'd be fairly easy to make people read your own story the way you want them to, but apparently it isn't.

So then I have another idea, and I pay one of my shop girls to come to a different fiction writing class with me and to pretend that *she* wrote my story and pretend that she doesn't even know me, so then I'll be allowed to talk about the story during the workshop, and then I can steer the conversation and make everyone see what a bastard Steve is, and then they'll all talk about how much they hate him and how it's *not* a stupid allegory about colonialism.

But this time, the new workshop leader starts off by saying he just wants to raise the question of whether my shop assistant, as a white person, has the right to occupy a character of South Asian ethnicity, and whether there might be questions of cultural arrogance in making such a choice. The workshop leader just wants to put that question out there, without commenting one way or the other, he says. But once that 'question' is out, people feel free to talk about how my shop assistant 'isn't racist, but maybe lacks racial sensitivity', and my uncle 'might be read as a crude stereotype of Asian men', and when he was cruel to me in the story whether that negatively stereotypes the Asian community, and how 'the voice of the Shruti character might be an inauthentic representation of an Asian woman' – which is bizarre, seeing as it's *my* voice, and I'm definitely Asian myself. And strangely no one ever made any of those criticisms in the workshop where I said I'd written the story myself. And then it gets to my turn to comment on the story, and I say that I thought the protagonist's voice *was* realistic, and then a few of the workshop group chime in with little sections of the story that *they* thought were authentic too, even though just ten minutes ago they'd suggested the whole story was inauthentic. And after that, I just give up, cos I see what a stupid idea it was, trying to pass off my real life story as fiction, and then hoping people would take it seriously.

And quite a while after that, I let one of the shop girls move in with me, in the little flat in Victoria, where I still live. And she sleeps on the sofa, and she tells me all about the terrible things that her mum's boyfriend did to her from when she was eleven until she turned seventeen, when she ran away to London and met me in one of my shops. And I tell myself that this is how I can create something positive from what happened to me, and I can help her and then help other victimised young girls. So I let her stay with me. And when she steals twenty-pound notes from my purse, I turn a blind eye.

And I win a British Business Woman of the Year Award, from the Department of Trade and Industry. And Princess Beatrix presents the award to me. And the following week, poor Meena's parents phone me and say that they saw me in the papers and remembered I used to be friends with Meena, and they thought

I might know something about what happened to her. And I say I've no idea and that I'll call them back, but I never do, and then I refuse to take their calls. And I look up the old newspaper stories online from the time when I was on the island. And there are stories about eighteen-year-old student Meena Saigal, thought to be missing in connection with financier Steven Butler. But the clips faded out after a few weeks. And then she was forgotten about. There were no clips about me.

And I pay a private detective agency to find out whether my mother really did die like Steve said she did, and they track her down to a village in Uttar Pradesh, so Steve was completely lying. And I write her a letter with my contact details and have it translated into Punjabi, and we write back and forth for a few months, and I get a translator to sign a non-disclosure agreement and translate the letters. But then my mum stops writing back to me. And then a year later, her husband writes to me and says she was struggling with lymphatic cancer and she didn't want to worry me, but now sadly she's passed away. And I didn't get a chance to see her before she died. And I bitterly, bitterly regret that. Because there was no reason I couldn't have flown to India and paid her a visit, after the letters stopped, or even while we were still writing. I just kept putting it off, because I was scared that she wouldn't want to see me and that she'd refuse to speak to me. And the funeral's already happened by the time I find out that she's died, but I fly over there to just talk with her family. And her husband's a nice bloke actually and misguidedly offers to help me get married, which I politely decline. And my uncle Aadesh is living with him, and my uncle smirks at me about my not being married. And then

403

he takes me aside and tells me that it's my duty to support him financially, now that my mother is dead. 'I don't think that's going to happen,' I tell him, with my blood boiling. And I do a little bus tour around northern India and see the Taj Mahal and the Red Fort. And then I fly home. But afterwards I wish I'd told my uncle what an evil piece of shit he is. And the real reason I didn't say anything at the time was because I didn't want to make a scene. I was actually protecting him, I realise. And that's exactly how abusive men want you to think: *You're causing a scene. You're making trouble. You're embarrassing yourself. Keep quiet.* That's how they protect themselves.

And I fantasise thousands of times about killing my uncle, who's still going in his late eighties. And I wish that instead of the Filipino man it was my uncle who somehow became Steve's slave and lived a life of slavery and misery. But needless to say, I never do anything to my uncle. I just throw myself into the business, opening up more branches, poaching jewellery designers, branding, getting social media traction, that kind of thing. And I fool myself into believing that if I can ignore my past effectively enough, it will dry up and I'll be able to slough it off, like a snake sheds its old skin and crawls out of it. But really, events like that aren't a skin, they're your skeleton, and you can't shed your skeleton. You can only shed yourself, and the skeleton will still remain. Like poor Meena's skeleton and her poor little baby's. (Just rambling now. Random thoughts.)

And that shop assistant girl who I let live with me begins stealing my things to sell, when she can't find cash – my iron, my television, my computer. And one day she disappears forever with my old suitcase and as many sellable items as she can stuff in there – that suitcase that I went through so much with, that suitcase that I got for the New Zealand trip for what was going to be the best holiday in the world, back when I was just a child who had everything ahead of her and so much innocence and so much love and just wanted to be good enough for her best friend to like her, back before she became this dried-up, closed-off old woman, who could never move forwards and never move backwards, someone who was able to sail around the world alone in a stolen fishing boat, at the age of nineteen, and hasn't been able to *get* anywhere in all the years since then. And I think back to that girl I was, as remote as the island, and I think across to Steve growing old on the island and tormenting the Filipino man and God knows what else – mainly enjoying the thrill and the challenge of tormenting people and manipulating them into obeying his every word.

And one day, years later, I try to work out where that island must have been. So I draw a circle 754 miles from Sri Lanka, on a map. And the island must be somewhere on that curve. And it makes me want to *do* something. To *go* somewhere and *take action*. But what can I do? Steve's probably dead. Meena's dead. The Filipino man's probably dead. What can I do? Get into a boat and sail in a big circle, at an exact 754-mile radius from Colombo, Sri Lanka, and stop at every island on that imaginary archipelago, and free every captive, and kill every tyrant, and save every young mother in childbirth, and set everyone free? No, because even if I hired my own army and literally did just that, it wouldn't change a thing.

And I think back to the girl that I was back then. And I know how bizarre and cruel and perverted this sounds, but I don't regret being so dried-up and isolated now – no, what I regret is that I was ever so innocent and pure and filled with hope when I was young, because it would be so much easier now to have never known any good times, so much easier to have always been like this, the way I am now: not wanting to live, not wanting to die, just wanting things to stop, to just stop so I can get away from them, to climb into bed in the middle of the night with someone who loves me in secret and with the enemy safely asleep in the next room, and live in a non-existent little make-believe world that only we know exists.

ACKNOWLEDGEMENTS

Thanks first and foremost to my editor James Gurbutt, to Shruti Uppal whose notes, insights and suggestions helped immeasurably and to Sruthi Atmakur Javdekar for so diligently checking the cultural references herein, sentence by sentence, in multiple drafts and for providing innumerable useful suggestions of all kinds. Any shortcomings that remain after the generous help of the people listed in these acknowledgements are of course entirely my own. Thank you to Peter Carey and Colum McCann for their invaluable advice and support, to the K. Blundell Trust for such a generous award and to the following people: Caroline Michel, Laura Williams, Rachel Mills and everyone at PFD; Olivia Hutchings, Kate Doran and everyone at Corsair and at Little, Brown; Sarah Chinn, Jennifer Raab and everyone at Hunter; Aditya Mishra for kindly showing me around Punjab and for opening many doors to me in Delhi; Dr Raju Voleti; Varma Rameswar; Bettina Mangiaracina; Hannah Bailey; Atul Singh; Sunil Param; Roberto Foa; Sinha Jayant; Roger Van Heaften; Anesh Roy; Sasha Weigel; Shubh Sharma; Ashley Tellis; Upendra Singh; Rhona Royale; Ram Kumar; Avimukt Dar;

Sukhjinder Singh Mulitani; Rajesh Malik; Vidya Parkash; Barat Gupta; Sunny Rocky; I. B. Rani; Swati Dab; Amit Jha; Suparna Bhasin; Laksmi Reddy; Kimi Kumar; Avery Cardoza; Loveleen Mann; Cynthia; Aaron; Bill; Lauren; Jeff; Aricia; Julie; Jennifer; Richard L; Richard B; Deirdre; Neil; John; Louise; Adrian; Rebecca; Ron; Dave H; Russell; David B and Susan.